web
of angels

web
of angels

a Novel

LILIAN
NATTEL

Alfred A. Knopf Canada

PUBLISHED BY ALFRED A. KNOPF CANADA

Copyright © 2012 Moonlily Manuscripts Inc.

Published in Canada by Alfred A. Knopf Canada, a division of Random House of Canada Limited, Toronto, in 2012. Distributed by Random House of Canada Limited.

Knopf Canada and colophon are registered trademarks.

www.randomhouse.ca

This book is a work of fiction. Names, characters, places and incidents either are the product of the author's imagination or are used fictitiously. Any resemblance to actual persons, living or dead, events, or locales is entirely coincidental.

Library and Archives Canada Cataloguing in Publication

Nattel, Lilian, 1956–
Web of angels / Lilian Nattel.

Also issued in electronic format.

ISBN 978-0-307-40209-7

I. Title.

PS8577.A757W42 2012   C813.'54   C2011-904073-5

Book design by Kelly Hill
Cover photograph: John-Francis Bourke/Getty Images

Printed and bound in the United States of America

2 4 6 8 9 7 5 3

For Hadara and Meira.

And in honour of everyone who breaks the cycle—heroes all.

Do you take it I would astonish?
Does the daylight astonish? does the early redstart
    twittering through the woods?
Do I astonish more than they?

This hour I tell things in confidence,
I might not tell everybody, but I will tell you.

(I am large, I contain multitudes)

WALT WHITMAN, *Song of Myself,*
VERSES 19 AND 51

CHAPTER
ONE

*O*n a narrow street in the grey of dawn, in a row house with stained glass, a sixteen-year-old girl lay motionless. Her hair was blonde, short, gelled in spikes, her legs unshaven, her pink nightgown straining over a nine-month belly. Her sister leaned against her, whispering her name, while far away in a watery world, the baby opened her eyes. She tried to turn the other way, her heart beating quicker as she searched for the sound of her mother's heart. She kicked hard, but she was wedged downward, stuck. All she could do was wait, watching shadows darkly drifting. Watching light shine crimson through a membrane. And while she waited, the sun rose through a veil of sleet, rainwater licked the gutters in front of her house, alarm clocks rang up and down the nearby streets.

The house was in Seaton Grove, a city neighbourhood south of the railroad tracks, a refuge for academics and artists with kids. They'd given up protests and all-night cafés and wearing black to renovate tall, gaunt houses with peculiar wiring and gasping plumbing. They sank into Seaton

Grove, they nestled into it, a village annexed in 1888 by the growing city on the shore of Lake Ontario, a bubble of the golden age where cultures and races mixed and met, married and celebrated every tradition. As their houses rose in value and people who were better off bought into the neighbour-hood, they felt confirmed in all their virtues. This was not the suburbs where trees were spindly and neighbours too far from each other to hear what went on behind closed doors. Here the streets were lined with old silver maples, lindens, cherry and mulberry. And though the trees were bare, sap was rising with a promise of shade and fruit for anyone who happened to look up.

A block and a half from the railway tracks, in a house on Ontario Street, Sharon Lewis was lying in bed that Friday morning, listening to her husband, Dan, sing in the shower. Their bedroom was under the slanting roof, facing east, and as clouds broke up, the sun touched the curtains and the wall hanging and the cushions kicked onto the floor, colour springing back from the neutrality of night, gold and russet, earth colours in the velvety fabrics Sharon loved to touch. She sewed, she baked, both of which she enjoyed, and she kept the accounts for Dan's company, which she did not. There were three children asleep on the second floor, a teenage son in his room at the back and little sisters in the front bedroom, a seven-year-old in the top bunk and a five-year-old in the bottom. There would have been more children if Dan hadn't said enough is enough.

He showered for exactly fifteen minutes, and at 7:15, when the second alarm rang, he turned the water off, dried himself and walked into the bedroom. He bent to kiss Sharon, whose eyes were still closed. He made her beautiful with his kiss, even though she believed she was too skinny, too flat, too red-haired, too freckled, and now, at forty, too old to have another baby without the assistance of modern medicine.

He'd just turned forty-two, his birthday on Groundhog Day. His father was Jewish, his mother Chinese, joining the planet's least and most populous peoples who, in a symbiotic miracle, share the same taste in food. In Dan they'd produced a man of average height with brown hair, black eyes, a smooth chest and a mole on his shoulder, which Sharon regularly checked for changes. His teeth were perfect due to his own diligence, wearing out a toothbrush a month. He owned a company that ran fundraising campaigns for causes that were both good and respectable.

"Did you call the plasterer?" he asked, getting cotton briefs and wool socks from the dresser.

"I forgot."

"How could you forget?" From the wardrobe he extracted a freshly pressed shirt, polished shoes, a good suit and a hideous tie, which was a birthday present from the girls. They'd picked it out and paid for it on their own, making Sharon wait near the entrance of the dollar store. "It's on the list," he said as if she ought to notice a list on the fridge just because she knew exactly where everything was in the dining room, where she kept a mess of cloth and yarn in various stages of completion. A finished sweater was in a bag on the table. The quilting squares were on the third shelf of the cabinet. On the bottom shelf, in the back, was her money jar, with cash and cheques that she was always forgetting to deposit because her head was filled with too many thoughts, too many opinions, too many silent arguments.

"Daddy, you're wearing the tie!" Nina shouted as she ran into the bedroom, jumping on the bed, Emmie right behind her.

"Of course," he said. "It's my birthday tie."

Her older daughter and her son both looked like Dan, and Sharon was glad of that. Only Emmie took after her, with curly red hair, green eyes, and chipmunk cheeks, pinchable cheeks that she would probably outgrow as Sharon had. She closed her eyes. Maybe she could sleep for another five minutes while they jumped on the bed. She'd been up late again, chatting online; morning always seemed so far away at midnight.

"Mom! I can't find my calculator," Josh shouted up the stairs. Sharon kept her eyes closed.

"You'd better get up," Dan said.

"You look," Sharon said.

"I'd just be wasting time. You're the finder in the family." He glanced at the mirror on the dressing table, giving his tie a twitch to straighten it.

They'd celebrated Dan's birthday at the rink in Christie Pits, yesterday. She was someone else skating, lithe and free and not shy at all. That was how she'd met Dan, by skating backward right into him, laughing as they both fell. They always celebrated Dan's birthday by going skating with their children and his sister and her family, who lived around the corner. Yesterday Josh's girlfriend, Cathy, had come, too, and afterward they'd all had cocoa at Magee's. Cathy was his first girlfriend, and Sharon was glad she was a nice girl—her mother a doctor and her father a professor. The family lived near the public school.

A thaw hinted at spring, mud under the sprinkling of snow. They'd gone home along Seaton Street, stopping to look at the funny house painted candy colours, the yard a display of plastic frogs and superheroes arranged around the fountain of the naked boy, turned off for the winter. A knife grinder had come along in his truck, his bell ringing, and stopped when the owner of the house flagged him down. Josh and Cathy had walked ahead of them, two gangly kids with skates slung over narrow shoulders, ignoring his sisters who'd followed making kissy noises. Cathy had a white jacket. How she kept it white was a mystery. She had straight blonde hair, too, and a perfectly straight part. Perhaps people with that kind of hair simply repel stains.

"Mom!"

"All right." Sharon opened her eyes and sat up. "You can stop shouting, Josh!"

Halfway down the stairs, she heard his cell ring, and she was certain that it was Cathy calling because the girl was on her mind. Dan would say, *Don't be silly, even if you're right, it's only a coincidence. A statistical inevitability. How many people do you need in a room to have better than a fifty percent chance that two of them share the same birthday? Only twenty-three. Don't treat it as a miracle.* That was the kind of thing he'd say at Sunday dinner.

His father would nod and say, *Of course not a miracle. Very natural. God makes it happen.*

She found Josh at his desk, computer on, browser minimized so she couldn't see his Facebook page or perhaps it was Twitter or something newer whose name she hadn't yet picked up. His room was spare and neat, his bed made, hockey posters in a straight line on the blue wall. The sun shining through the window made squares of light on the floor. Outside the cardinals were singing, celebrating the February thaw as if snow wouldn't return.

Her son played hockey, he played the guitar, and if he was in a good mood, he'd do magic tricks for his sisters. His ears stood out from his head. At night he taped them back with masking tape and Sharon pretended not to notice. He was fourteen.

"Who is it?" she asked.

"Cathy," he mouthed. Why had she called instead of texting?

"Right." She turned to his bookcase, thinking of Cathy and her sister, Heather. Last week they'd been looking at the high chair in Sharon's basement, standing with their arms around each other's shoulders. Cathy, fourteen years old, in pink and white; Heather, just two years older, with heavy boots and a heavily pregnant belly. Two girls golden-haired, one sister's long, the other sister's spiked like rays of the sun. The sweater in the dining room was for Heather, who'd kept her coat on because she was cold.

"Uh huh, uh huh. Seriously. I'm so sorry. Okay. Yeah." Josh pressed the off button.

"What's up?" As her hand ran idly over the top of the bookcase, it fell on the calculator.

"Mom."

She looked over her shoulder. Her son's eyes were wet. His girlfriend must have dumped him. How could anyone dump her kid? But it wasn't that. She knew it wasn't though she pushed away any other thought of what it could be.

"Mom." Her boy was trying to talk and getting no further than, "Mom." She went to him and knelt. "Cathy . . ." Josh flung his arms around his mother.

His heart beat against her chest, her arms tightening as he clung to her. "What did she say?"

"Her sister. She . . ." He stopped, swallowed, began again. "Cathy's sister killed herself."

"No!" What about the high chair in the basement? Sharon had offered her the high chair. How could Heather do this?

Josh leaned against her as she stroked his hair, letting his words crash into her, waves against a rock. Cathy's sister was dead. She'd put a gun to her ear and shot herself. Her mom used a kitchen knife to get the baby out and then called 911. The baby was a girl. Heather was still lying there on the bed with a hole in her when Cathy had called Josh and screamed into the phone, "I hate her!" Josh didn't even know who she hated, her sister or her mother or the little baby.

This was Sharon's first-born, the child who'd made her a mother, now shrugging out of her arms, his pained eyes a shade lighter than his father's, a bit of tape still stuck to his right ear. "What am I supposed to do, Mom?" he asked, twisting a rubber band around his fingers.

"You can let her friends know," Sharon said. "Then Cathy doesn't have to tell them."

"Okay." He turned to the computer, tossing the rubber band on his desk and reaching for the mouse.

Dan was calling, *I can't find my keys,* and the girls were calling, *Where are you, Mom,* and before she could get out of her son's room to ward them off, they were here. She had to get them away from Josh and she needed to talk to Dan and she had to figure out what to tell the girls. Her hands went up to herd them out, but there was too much noise in her head, her ears ringing. Nina said, *Josh is crying!* and he said, *Shut up!* and Sharon was thinking of a kitchen knife used for chopping mushrooms and onions in a mother's hand, descending on a daughter.

She looked down for an instant, the room receding, every sound faintly muffled. When she was able to look up again, her face was paler, the freckles across her nose standing out, her eyes the green of bracken and moss. And she was someone else, someone who could carry on the day.

"*M*ama, why is Josh crying?"

"Don't bug him," she said. *Shit shit shit. Fucking hell. Heather had picked out colours for the baby clothes. This didn't make sense. Why'd the kid have to go and off herself?* Those were the thoughts in her head, and, *This is too scary,* and behind that an echo, *Scared scared scared.* She pulled forward, away from the words and the thoughts, the shivers and the panic inside, getting firmly into the outside. "He's busy. You want breakfast?"

Josh was still in his pajamas, plaid bottoms and a T-shirt from last year's Mayfest. He had his back to them, but Nina was walking around the desk to peer at him. "Busy doing what?" she asked as he twisted away.

"Slowpoke!" Her mom grabbed her sleeve. "Who's slower, you or Emmie?"

"Her!" Nina said with that funny little smile she got when her mom's eyes turned dark green.

"You're both turtles."

"No I'm not. First of you," Nina shouted, pushing ahead of her sister, and Emmie, saying "No fair!" ran as fast as she could, both of them pell-mell, down the stairs and into the kitchen. Dan followed, checking his watch as he went to put the trash out. The kitchen, like the inside of his wife's head, managed to expand to hold everything in it, now just the blue Arborite table, but on Sundays also the extra table they set up for dinner guests between the washer and dryer stacked in the corner, the granite countertop and the fridge with magnets holding up kids' pictures and Dan's lists.

He was back by the time she had everything out for breakfast. "Raisins or chocolate chips in your cereal?" she asked the kids, shoving the laundry basket aside with her foot.

"Chocolate chips? No eggs?" He looked surprised.

She shrugged. Sometimes she thought of saying to him, *Hey, my name is Lyssa and I don't cook*. But it never came out. And it was better that way. Like running was better than standing still. Like being mad was better than sad, and wanting nothing better than being laughed at for asking. She put five bowls in a row, sloshed in the cereal and milk, dumped in raisins, threw in some chocolate chips. Five spoons and you had breakfast. The coffee was made; Dan always set the timer before he went to bed. While he poured himself coffee, she put the kids' bowls on the table.

The kitchen was at the back of the house, glass doors opening to the garden where Sharon grew sugar snaps, tomatoes, lettuce. There was no room for flowers in back. Dan's car was parked on the pad behind the garden, his keys on the counter where he'd left them last night.

"Here you go," she said, pushing the keys toward him. She picked up her own bowl with its extra helping of chocolate chips, shifting from foot to foot as if she was going to dash off at any moment. Dan stood beside her at the counter even though he hated to stand while eating. He poured coffee into Sharon's special mug, the gold one, and set it beside her.

"What's up with Josh?" he asked quietly.

"It's so fucked," she whispered. "Cathy's sister killed herself."

"No!"

"I know. It's crazy."

"Sad. She was always different. All the times she ran away. You know?"

"No, I don't." She wanted to smash something. A plate, a cup, anything that would make a satisfying sound. She snapped her fingers instead, right in Dan's face, making him flinch. "I mean not just herself but the baby."

"What baby?" Nina asked, her hearing suddenly acute.

"Are you having a baby, Mommy?" Emmie asked.

"No, Heather's. Her baby was born this morning."

Dan was looking at her as if she'd suddenly grown a tail like one of those fox-women who sucked the life out of men in Chinese stories. Sexy and tricky and a downright liar. "She died," he whispered.

"No, wait." Lyssa pulled him closer, her lips to his ear. The kids were talking, all excited, *When can we go and see the baby, can we bring a toy?* "Emergency C-section. What do I say?"

"They've got to get to school," he said to her. And then to the girls, "We'll talk about it later."

"Awwww," Nina protested. "But . . ."

"Heather is sleeping," he said desperately, looking at his wife for help. He had the wrong one for that.

Sleeping. Okay, whatever. She emptied her coffee into the sink, set the cup on the counter. The only hot drink she liked was cocoa. "You're taking Josh?"

He nodded, putting the mug in the dishwasher. He kissed the girls goodbye, unpeeling them as they hugged him around the waist and the legs. Then he shouted for Josh, who came downstairs and through the kitchen, not looking at anyone, backpack on one shoulder, face shrouded by a hoodie. The glass doors slid open and closed, and they were gone.

Lyssa was cold down to her bones, but she had to get out of her PJs and the girls did, too. She eyed the laundry basket suspiciously. Something they could wear ought to be in there amid the folds of beige. She crouched down, rifling through it. Nina and Emmie crouched beside her, curious to see what the mom who gave them chocolate chips for breakfast would do. "Hey you two. Teeth," she said, without much conviction. Getting kids dressed, cleaned, schooled, that was Sharon's job. Except that she was inside, don't call us we'll call you, and Lyssa was out here in the world, on her own.

INSIDE

Alarm bells were ringing. Lockdown! The sound scattered the inside children through the inside house. They hid in the upstairs rooms, in closets, under beds, those were good hiding places. Behind curtains, no not there, feet stick out.

Here comes a punisher, pulling you out and dragging you down the stairs, bump, bump, bump. Bells clanging. Shut up, shut up, shut up! Something bad happened. Bad means trouble. Trouble means you get it if you can't stop the sound coming out of your mouth. A punisher reaches under the bed, long arms, spider hands. He's got someone by the hair. He's turning to the closet. Someone is in there breathing too loud. Bang, it opens. The punisher's face is big and white. I'll give you something to cry about. I'll give you what for. Down you go. Down to the basement. In the dark. With the monsters. That's where crybabies go.

Ally wasn't a crybaby. She knew what to do. The other lils ran ahead of the punishers, trying to get as high as they could before they were caught, but she crept down the back stairs, Echo holding her hand, making him hurry on his crooked feet. The safest place was in the boot closet, behind the kitchen. It had a little door and a little latch and nobody would notice it. Come on, Echo. She was as cold as if she was sitting naked on the North Pole, but she pushed him inside and snuck in after him.

Echo was sniffling. "Shh," she whispered.

Ally sat quiet as a mouse, holding the tiny teddy bear she kept hidden in her pocket so the punishers wouldn't take it away. She wished she had an outside teddy, a real one with fur and eyes and overalls but nobody was supposed to know there were lils inside. Or else.

If she peeked through the knothole in the boot closet, she could see into the kitchen. It was warm in the kitchen. Sharon was there, under the eye of the Housekeeper, but

Sharon's eyes were closed. She couldn't see how nice it was and bright like there were windows and something outside the windows like a field where you could run or trees that you could climb. Ally couldn't see much, but she could hear the Housekeeper humming and she could smell something like cinnamon and the air that came through the knothole was warm. When the punishers were done with the lils, they'd get Sharon out. They'd call her name and she'd go and then they'd have a nice little talk with her. If Ally knew how to get into the kitchen nobody would ever get her out.

*O*n Seaton Grove the streets were narrow and parking expensive so people walked. From home, it took Nina, Emmie and Josh five minutes to get to the junior school, seven minutes to the subway, three to the boys and girls club, six to the grocery store. Eleven minutes to the fortune cookie factory and twelve to the former typesetting shop, now rented as a film studio. It was eight minutes to the house painted like candy or the luxury condos built where the slaughterhouse had burnt down. Three more minutes from there to Magee's for cocoa or down to the fruit and vegetable store. Add extra time for bouncing a ball. Even more if they decided to go down into the big playground at Christie Pits. If you squinted you could see the shadows of the boys who rioted there in the 1930s when this was a working-class neighbourhood. The first families here had had names like Valiant and Goodchild, and they'd ignored people who called the neighbourhood Satan's Grove because of the smell from the glue factory, conveniently located near the abattoir. But now it smelled of baking, courtesy of the fortune cookie factory, which stood beside the railway tracks.

Mrs. Agostino, the Italian grandma who lived next door to the Lewises, was already sitting on her porch, keeping watch on the street from her plump and pink armchair. While Lyssa turned to lock the door, Mrs. Agostino gestured to the girls to zip up their coats. Stout and grey, she didn't speak any English but every year at Christmas she gave bags of candies to Nina and Emmie, even Josh, the big boy. Sometimes, on summer evenings, she offered them homemade pizza on paper plates. The girls, obedient to a maternal authority that surpassed language, zipped up.

The three of them walked down Ontario Street, pausing to watch the garbage trucks. Nina was slightly in front as she was in most things: hopping into the bath before her little sister, going through the front door two steps ahead, losing her teeth first and learning to read first. Only in one category did Emmie stake her territory. Her backpack was pink and her jacket was pink and when Nina had attempted to sneak the pink elephant into her own bed, Emmie had said, "Stop! That's mine. See," pointing to her own head as if red hair, in its chromatic relationship to pink, entitled her. Nina had bowed to this irrefutable evidence. Her backpack was blue.

"Come on, let's run," their mom said. And they did, running for the joy of it, not because they were late. She grabbed her girls' hands, this mom with the moss green eyes and the pointy chin, freckles standing out across her nose, and the reckless run making a dance of her feet on the pavement. Down Ontario Street and across Seaton they ran, catching their breath at the candy-coloured house, left on Lumley toward the school and the last remaining cottages of the original village. Then they stopped short.

Several police cars blocked the road. An ambulance and the local TV news van were parked on a slant, half on the sidewalk. In front of them on the sidewalk stood a reporter, young and easy on the eyes, wearing a short jacket and short skirt. A few feet behind her, a cameraman was panning the street, taking in the raindrops dripping from eaves, the sunshine pouring through the mist, the boarded-up cottage across the street, once the home of Mrs. Brown, an escaped slave who'd lived to be 111 years old. He turned his camera on the yard signs that said RENOVATIONS BY . . . , the matted lawns, the bare gardens, parents holding kids' hands, toddlers in strollers or riding on shoulders, gawking.

"This is Nicole Antonopoulos, reporting live for Citytv." She pushed her microphone at Lyssa. "Did you know the deceased?"

"What's 'deceased'?" Nina asked.

Lyssa scowled at the cow with the microphone. "I'm getting the kids to school." She wanted to say more, but the hands in hers, Nina's and Emmie's, were soft and small and trusting, and Lyssa wasn't going to do anything to shock them. So she just added, "You mind?" and didn't even flip her the finger. While she led the girls around the reporter, moving toward the schoolyard, Emmie was saying, *Ambulances come in emergencies* and *What is the emergency?* and *Why are there police cars, did a burglar come and will the burglar rob our house?* Nina piped up that the burglar must have fallen out of the window and that was why there was an ambulance and they had reading buddies today and she was luckier than Emmie because their cousin was her reading buddy and not Emmie's and Emmie said, *I want Judy to be my reading buddy. No fair.*

Seaton School was L-shaped, with several big maple trees growing out in front, one of them split by lightning, dead on one side. In spring only half the tree would leaf. On the short side of the L stood a row of saplings surrounded by mesh to keep out squirrels. A wooden sign in front of each young tree announced the class that had planted it. There were three entrances, one for kindergarten, one for primary and one for junior grades. On an ordinary day Emmie would line up with the kindergarten kids, examining the treasures her friend pulled from her pocket—a bead, a stone, a broken bracelet picked up in the park. Nina would stand in a circle of girls playing clapping games near the north entrance, while her cousin, Judy, huddled with her friends in the fifth-grade class at the other end of the schoolyard. But today the schoolyard was uneasy; nobody traded snacks and games stalled. In clusters along the fence, the moms, some with toddlers in strollers or babies in Snuglis, a few dads, a smattering of grandparents and nannies murmured, for this was their village square.

Did you tell your kids? Not yet. Oh God, you can still see the ambulance from here. Heather used to babysit for us sometimes. My boys loved her. She had so much energy. She babysat for me, too. She painted a mural with my kids. It's still on their bedroom wall. You wouldn't know she was the same kid who ran away. I just can't believe this. I heard she shot herself. That's impossible, it had to be pills. Her mother is totally against guns; Debra would never have one in the house. I know, but for sure it was a gun. It's lucky in a way, you know? If it was pills, then the baby would have died, too. Can you imagine finding out that your mother shot herself while she was pregnant with you? The baby will know that she's special. It was a miracle. Thank God Debra's a pediatrician—she saved her granddaughter. I don't know about God but she had nerve. You never know how you'll react in a crisis. Afterward, that's when it hits you. It's so sad. It's scary, that's what. My oldest is turning thirteen—I hope I survive it. Your daughter isn't Heather. She didn't run away when she was twelve. What do you say to the parents? I don't know. I just don't want to say anything dumb. Should we go to the house?

Lyssa shifted from foot to foot, watching the girls, waiting for the bell to ring so she could go. She wanted to run home and keep running. Three blocks wasn't enough, she'd have to go up to the railroad tracks and run on the gravel path above the houses, through Seaton Grove, past the cemetery and up along the trestle bridge. Maybe then, when she was out of breath and had a stitch in her side and sweat dripping down her face, she'd have exhausted the turmoil inside. Nina was looking over at her to see if there was anything to worry about. She waved to show there wasn't.

"Sharon," one of the moms said to her. Her name was Ana Patel. She wore a sari under her coat and her baby, in a stroller, had Down's. "Isn't your son friends with Heather's sister?"

"Josh has some classes with her." When the sisters had come over to look at the high chair, they'd put a doll in it. They'd played at giving the doll a name and she'd played along, naming wildflowers and making them laugh. Swamp rose. Pussy toes. Hairy mint.

"He must have had some hint," Ana insisted.

"Nope." In Chinese you could say *Fuck the eighteen generations of your ancestors*. She wondered if Dan's mom knew that one. Speaking of his family, there was his sister in her purple jacket, making her way through the schoolyard. Eleanor could talk. There was nothing she liked better.

"I heard," Eleanor said, arriving at Lyssa's side. They'd been friends before they'd been sisters-in-law. Eleanor had been the one to introduce her to Dan, arranging for them to meet at the skating rink. She was a plumper version of her brother, a couple of years younger but with the same dark brown hair, straight and thick, cut short. She had dimples but didn't like them because she thought they made her cheeks look fat, yet she wore purple because it was her favourite colour and tough shit if it made her look fat. She had been the one who disappointed her parents, dropping out of college to marry an electrician. Before the neighbourhood was gentrified, she'd bought a house on Lumley, then found one for her brother on Ontario Street. She had one kid, Judy, who was turning eleven and spent as much time at her cousins' house as her own. She was Sharon's best friend. But even so she didn't know that Sharon was one of many alters or that another was standing next to her right now. "How's Josh taking it?"

As Lyssa elbowed her and tilted her head at the moms listening in, Eleanor changed tack without blinking and hardly a breath between words. She said to them all, "We have to bring food. If everyone makes a main dish we could put together a week's worth." *Yes, yes*—the moms eagerly took up the idea, relieved to have something they could do. Ana offered to make a curry and Eleanor to keep a list of who'd bring what. The last bell was ringing, the kids filing through the doors into the school.

"I've got to get out of here," Lyssa said.

In university she and Eleanor had gone skating, they'd gone running. In Hammond House with its heritage plaque and the hundred-year-old sign, LIVE AND LET LIVE, they'd got drunk and on the small dance floor they'd danced. Later Lyssa had danced there with Dan. But after they'd been going out a while, the little stick had turned blue, and, refusing to be pregnant, Lyssa had disappeared inside. By the time she'd come back out, years had passed. There were three kids. And while she was looking at photographs of the life she hadn't lived, Eleanor had walked in, stopped dead in her tracks, and said, "I haven't seen that look on your face for ages. Do you want to go dancing by any chance?" As if time hadn't passed for her either. As if a singleton could know what she was seeing.

Leaving the schoolyard, Eleanor said, "What am I going to tell Judy? It was hard enough talking about Heather being pregnant."

"God I want a cigarette," Lyssa said.

"You aren't going to start smoking again and die on me."

They were walking up Lumley Street as the ambulance pulled away. The house was identical to many others in the neighbourhood, tall and narrow, semi-detached. The front yard was winter brown, but a landscaper had been at it, preparing ground for winning flowers. There was a new cement porch with no railing, a pane of stained glass in the front door. Behind windows they saw a flicker of colour and movement. Someone drew the blinds.

"I don't get it," Lyssa said. "She was talking about having her own place."

"Oh. Like that was going to happen. She was sixteen! Selfish that's what it is. I don't care what anyone says. Rick and Debra did everything for her. Everything! They don't deserve this." Eleanor shook her head. "I wish I'd never convinced . . ."

"What?" Lyssa turned to see Eleanor biting her lip, eyes narrowed against something.

"I'm rambling. Forget it."

"Come on, dudette." Lyssa put her arm through Eleanor's. "Let's go for a run up on the tracks."

"I don't have time."

"Tough. You promised to start running with me. Or I'm going to bum a cigarette from someone."

"I hate when you get like this," Eleanor said, but she was laughing. "Can we at least get fries after?"

"Extra large. With a side of mayonnaise."

On Hammond Street, they climbed the embankment to the overpass where there was a break in the fence. The gravel path was lined with bushes that screened the streets below. Later there would be wildflowers and butterflies. After a rain, sometimes a duck in a puddle. Running at her sister-in-law's side, Lyssa slowed her pace, Eleanor put all she had into keeping up. They teased each other, got hot, unzipped and ran some more with their coats flapping like capes, like the wings of birds picking up the west wind, propelled along the gravel path as if they were flying. While she ran, Lyssa looked up at the blue of the sky, her favourite colour of all, and down at the backs of houses, the messes that people didn't fix up for their neighbours, the old porch with shredding wood, the fallen-in shed, piles of broken stuff, alleys with painted garages, an ancient metal works, a two-storey brick shed with windows, things that weren't on display. She liked seeing what was behind, what was in back of the front. What was like her.

Seaton Grove was older than the neighbourhoods on either side, which had been farmland and estates when the Valiants and the Goodchilds took up residence around the glue factory. Back then the north edge of the village was marked by Hammond Street, and children thought it was the edge of the world, no more streets to be seen, no cottages huddled close, only the wild and the rumour of great houses somewhere on the hill above.

They marked Seaton Grove time by looking up at the sun. Noon was twelve minutes earlier in the next town west, six minutes later in the hamlet to the east. Travellers never quite knew when their trains were arriving or leaving, because time changed every few miles. Some people carried half a dozen watches set to clocks along their journey, to no avail. Time was independent, unruly, untrammelled. Then standard time was invented and clocks became synchronized.

People who were multiple still rode the vagaries of hours that leaped, disappeared, reversed and sped up. But even for them, time moved in the outside world. If Sharon lost it, someone else gained it. Lyssa, who was sixteen in a mom's middle-aged body, was going on seventeen as she ran beside her sister-in-law, her feet pounding the earth, the stones under her feet older than the clock.

*T*he kitchen was an addition to the original house, built large enough to accommodate guests. It was Sharon's favourite room because it smelled good, it smelled of what she was good at, cooking and feeding her family. She could hear herself and yet not herself on the phone talking to Eleanor, saying, *Uh huh, I got your orders Miss Bossy.* In her head were thoughts of running along a narrow trestle bridge, of the thrill when a train whooshed by. Lyssa's thoughts, not Sharon's—she was scared of heights. The girls were upstairs in their room, Josh not yet home from school. Eleanor had already organized the neighbourhood, co-coordinating a week's worth of main courses, bagels and desserts. Tomorrow was Saturday, and her friends would have all day to shop, cook, and drop their contributions at her house. She would arrange delivery. Heather's parents might not eat, but at the end of the day they would have food.

"You should make soup for them," Eleanor was saying. "It's supposed to get colder again." Thoughts of running started to recede. "Carrot or pea." Thoughts of soup were bubbling up. Green pea, yellow pea, lentils, potato and leek. Sharon was moving forward, pulled by the cooking talk, and Lyssa slipping back inside. "Throw in some rice."

Her hand went up toward a cupboard, opening it so that she could check for ingredients. Sharon was forward now all the way, remembering the sound of herself joking around in a voice that was not really hers.

"Are you there?" her sister-in-law asked.

"Hang on." She turned to open the glass doors, the cool breeze coming in from the yard fanning her hot face. Better to think about food and not the uneasiness in the pit of her stomach. "I just want to see what I've got in the freezer," she said. "How about stew and a thick lentil soup? I can bring that over tomorrow evening. Tons of time. No problem. Sure. See you."

When Emmie came into the kitchen, she found her mother chopping, eyes light green with flecks of gold, skin warm from cooking. Céline Dion was singing through the boom box. Sometimes Dan teased her about her old-fashioned tastes and technology, accusing her of being stuck in time.

"I'm Dr. Grizzly and Sister Bear is sick, Mama." Emmie was draped in one of her dad's old white shirts and a stethoscope, wobbling in her mother's shoes. Even as a baby, she'd slept well, woken well. Sitting in a high chair, she'd thrown things to see them fall; Nina had thrown things to see them picked up.

"Is Nina playing, too?" Sharon asked.

"She doesn't want to. She's staring."

"What do you mean, staring?"

"She's mad. Can we have some raisins?"

"Sure." Absently, Sharon took down the big box as she wondered what Nina could be mad about. She'd have to see for herself and while she did, her youngest took the opportunity to sneak the whole box of raisins into the living room, where she turned on the TV.

Nina was sitting on the top bunk, arms crossed, glaring as her mother cleared the dress-up stuff off the futon couch they used for sleepovers. No, she wouldn't come down. No, she didn't want her mom to sit beside her. As Sharon climbed up the ladder to join her, she looked away. Opposite the bunk beds, above the children's table and chairs, there was a sign taped to the wall, ART GALLRY, ADMISHIN $1. Around it were drawings of multicoloured houses under suns and rainbows and puffy clouds. Nina huddled into herself, arms wrapped around her legs, and when Sharon was close to her, she said, "You lied, Mom!"

"What about?" Sharon stroked her daughter's hair, flinching as Nina flinched. Her middle child, quiet, brave.

"You said people die when they're old." She stared straight ahead at the art gallery, at the window that divided her pictures from her sister's, at the rooftop across the street. "Heather wasn't old."

Nina's eyes welled up and she pursed her lips to hold on to any sound that might wish to come out. Sharon's heart groaned. "What did you hear about Heather?"

"She died. Deceased. That's what my teacher said. That's what deceased means. Lots of kids in my class knew that Heather died and the ambulance took her away."

"Most people die when they're old. Do you know how Heather died?" Nina shook her head. "She decided to end her life. That's called suicide."

"How?"

"She shot herself with a gun."

"Did it hurt?"

"I don't know. I hope not."

"But why, Mommy?" Nina let her mother put an arm around her, though she wouldn't rest her head on her mom's shoulder. "Why would she do that?"

"Sometimes people have something wrong with their brain." Heather had tried out all the settings on the high chair. Up and down, forward and back. Touching the thick padding. Asking how old a baby had to be to sit up like that. Her brain had seemed just fine. "It makes them so sad they can't stand it and they forget that lots of people love them and need them. They kill themselves to get away from the sadness."

"But then their people are sad, aren't they, Mommy?" Nina said. And she let herself lean, she let her head fall on her mother's chest. She let the tears soak into her mother's shirt as her mother kissed her head and stroked her hair and made soothing noises with words that didn't signify. Only the sound of her mother's voice mattered, the sound she'd heard before she was born, making the world possible to live in. And when she was done, she went downstairs to watch TV and her sister offered her handfuls of raisins.

Sharon was working at the computer in the dining room while she waited for Josh to get home from school. There was a stack of invoices on her left and a smaller stack face down beside it. Click on pay bills. How was she going to talk to him about Heather? Click on vendor name. She had to do it right. Peerless Printing. What if she said the wrong thing? Click on enter invoice: $2,212.52. What if she made things worse? Account: office expense. Turn it over. Next.

She listened for his arrival. Every door hinge in the house had a different creak, every floor a different rumble depending on whose hand or foot was on it. The compressor in the fridge, the air conditioner on the third floor, the furnace in the basement, each had their thumps and clicks, touching off a flicker in a different set of lights when they went on and off, as distinct and familiar as her own breathing. If there was any change, she would know it as surely as she would know a strange pain in her body. A key turned in the front door. First there was a jiggle, then the smack of the long chain with the whistle on it—Josh was home. Now all her children were safe.

"Mom!" he called. His backpack hit the floor. Those were his footsteps and someone else's, lighter steps, slower, along the hall.

"I'm in the dining room."

"Mom, can you make us something to eat?" He stood in the doorway. "We're starving. Can Cathy stay for supper?" She was hanging back a bit as if uncertain of her welcome today. Josh had hold of her hand.

"Hi Cathy." Sharon's voice was warm.

"Hi Mrs. Lewis." Cathy was a good student and while hanging out with Josh, she had made him a better one. Even today her hair was perfectly parted, falling on either side of her face like a gold frame. She wore a cropped shirt and tight jeans, like any kid, except that she didn't slouch as she looked around at the half-open cabinet with yarns and fabrics poking out, the yard-sale tabletop on end against a wall, the kids' crafts on the oak sideboard, balanced precariously under the bag with the sweater inside that had been intended for her sister.

"Shouldn't you be at home?" Sharon asked.

"Nobody's there." Cathy shrugged. "They didn't want me with them."

"Is that right?" Sharon kept her voice gentle, though her eyebrows shot up in surprise.

"They were staying at the hospital to talk to the doctors about the baby. Then going to the funeral place. They said I should go to school, try to have a normal day." Cathy's eyes were as vague as if she was stoned, which she probably was. Everyone in her family, the ones who were left, had to be stoned on medication strong enough to keep them standing. "How am I supposed to have a normal day?"

"Your parents might be home by now. They'll be missing you."

"No they won't."

"You don't mean that," Sharon said, though Cathy looked as if she did. "Well, you're welcome to stay. Just let your parents know where you are." She listened to the kids' footsteps as they went upstairs and called after them, "Leave the door open."

When she got back to the kitchen, she took out another lamb chop to defrost for supper, and made popcorn for the kids, pouring melted butter over it. Then she blended shakes with frozen strawberries, thinking that even if Cathy couldn't eat she would manage that. She carried the tray up to Josh's room, pushing the door wider, but they were just sitting at his desk, both of them wearing headphones, looking at the monitor. Only a mom would notice that their feet were touching.

Six vinyl chairs had come with the kitchen table. When it was extended, it could accommodate two more chairs, or a single high chair if it was wide and thickly padded like the one that was down in the basement. By six-thirty everyone was at the table, even Dan. His offices were in the old Ford factory on Hammond Street, and in the evening, he'd do some work upstairs in his home office. He had software to keep track of his contacts, his appointments and his Internet pass-words, synchronized with his smartphone and networked to his company's computer system. His desktop wallpaper was a photograph of the kids and Sharon, looking stiff as she always did as soon as a camera was pointed at her.

"Would you like some broccoli, Cathy?" she asked.

Cathy had a lamb chop, cucumber salad and mashed potato on her plate. "Yes please," she said, accepting the broccoli, too. She wasn't really eating any of it, just cutting and poking bits around so that she had something to do at the table.

"What time are your parents expecting you home?"

Cathy poked her food some more. "Maybe eight."

"I'll walk her home, Mom." Josh was sitting next to her, tilting his chair back and balancing on it while Emmie fussed over her lamb chop, having suddenly realized it came from an actual animal like the stuffed lamb she slept with every night.

"Eat it," Josh said. "It's just meat. What difference does it make how old an animal is? It's raised to be eaten."

"Chicken isn't an animal," Emmie said. "It's chicken."

"Sure it is. All of your stuffed animals are meat. In some places, dogs aren't pets and people eat them because they're meat. They've got the same rights as pigs. Or not."

"Pig?" Emmie asked, her face appalled. "Like Miss Piggy?"

"Yeah. Bacon, ham, pork chops. That's all Miss Piggy."

Emmie pushed her plate away. "I don't want any meat," she said, her face screwed up, tears rolling down her chipmunk cheeks.

"Thanks, Josh." Sharon put an arm around Emmie, brushing back the mop of red curls as unruly as her own.

"No problem, Mom." He grinned.

"So make your sister a peanut butter sandwich," Dan said, his tone wiping the grin off his son's face. On Saturdays the two of them liked to play board games, keeping a running score from week to week. Josh looked so much like him, round black eyes, tanned skin, long legs and long arms, and then a touch of his Jewish grandpa, with those sticking-out ears, but nothing of Sharon, as if her genes were just on the inside.

She glanced at Nina, who had Dan's colouring but her pointed chin, struggling to cut her lamb chop, refusing to ask for help. "How was your spelling test?" she asked.

"I didn't know all the words," Nina said.

"That's good," Sharon said decisively, all the more decisive because spelling tests had always scared her to death.

"It is?"

"Of course. You get another test next Friday, right? Well, if you knew all the words today there wouldn't be anything to learn."

Cathy stopped pecking at her food. "If I don't get an A, I get grounded," she said, using a napkin to wipe imaginary smears off her lips. "Because people who do well, do well. And people who don't, don't. Like my sister."

If Sharon had been looking at Cathy, she might have seen something unexpected in her eyes. But Sharon's attention was on her middle daughter's mouth wobbling as she looked down at her plate, knife and fork motionless in her hands. Maybe her mom was lying to her again. Maybe she was in trouble or dumb, dumber than Josh anyway. He knew how to spell everything. All of these thoughts, Sharon could read on her daughter's face just as well as if she'd said them out loud, for she'd been listening to the language of her children's eyes and lips and fingers and toes since their birth. Nina hooked her right index finger over the other when she was upset. She was doing it now.

"Everybody has to start out not knowing ," Sharon said. "I just want my children to learn."

"As long as you try your best," Dan added. "What counts is effort." And he believed it, sincerely. He got up to stand behind Josh at the counter, where he was slicing bread for Emmie's sandwich. *Don't saw at it, cut it,* Dan instructed. *Not like that. Thinner.* But he was still wearing the hideous tie the girls had bought him for his birthday and he always accepted Josh's word, even when the evidence was stacked against him.

This was what Sharon saw reflected in the glass doors of her kitchen that evening: a blue table, the father of her children, her oldest, who looked nothing like her, her middle one with just a bit of her in the chin, her youngest exactly alike, as if child by child, she was becoming visible on the outside, frightening her with what she might be bringing to them. And last she turned her eyes to gaze at a good girl with long blonde hair framing her face, biting her fingernails.

CHAPTER FIVE

*E*leanor's house was on a corner lot at Macklem and Lumley. It was big for this neighbourhood, renovated, with a garage attached, the porch painted in shades of purple, a dream catcher with wind chimes hanging from a hook above the door, the chimes ringing in the wind that brought rain Saturday morning and snow in the evening. Sharon walked over, pulling the children's wagon, in it plastic containers of soup and stew. She carried the food up first, then brought the wagon up the stairs, leaving it on the porch as she tried the door. Unlocked. Not unusual in Seaton Grove. Bending down, Sharon stacked the containers one on top of another, using her chin to balance them as she straightened up and walked in.

Eleanor's husband, Bram, had knocked down all the non-weight-bearing walls to make the most of a long but narrow space. A grouping of two couches and an armchair was at the front end where stairs led to the second floor. Here a bay window faced the street. The dining area was at the far end on the right, the galley kitchen on the left, separated by a counter. Beyond the round dining table, a window over-looked the backyard and a door led outside to it. Knick-knacks were everywhere, on shelves, on the ledge of the bay window, on top of the stereo, all of them dusted. A rubber-tree plant loomed in the front corner, the great green leaves wiped clean every day. Goldfish swam around in a glass bowl on an end table. It was a room that belonged to people who worked with their hands in practical ways, paint-ing porches not pictures, or rewiring houses as Eleanor's husband did. There were a few of these still around in Seaton Grove, a mechanic on Lumley, a couple of retired construc-tion workers in the houses that had been refaced with white stone on Ontario Street.

"Eleanor?" It had taken Sharon a moment to realize that the house was full of women.

"Oh good, you're here." Eleanor bustled toward her. She was wearing one of her plus-sized outfits that came with a plus price tag, a silk scarf and matching earrings. "Do you have any idea where I put the corkscrew? I can't find it any-where and you always know where things are."

Sharon paused, ignoring the sound of chatter in the living room, a picture forming in her head: Eleanor in the kitchen, trying to do too many things at once. "Try the oven," she said.

"The oven?"

"That's what comes to mind."

"Okay, you've got the magic. I'll check. Let me help you with that," she said, taking the containers out of her arms. Sharon clung to her coat, under it a cashmere sweater, ancient, shrunken but warm.

The other moms circulated, voices low and slow, faces serious. They'd come with food and cards, and were dressed in dark clothing as if to make amends for their relief that the tragedy wasn't theirs, for enjoying this unexpected night out, for being nosy, for feeling superior. They stood in groups of three or four, breaking apart and reforming around the couches at one end, the dining room table at the other. On the kitchen counter, wine glasses were lined up.

I like this tulip shape, especially for red wine. And a good size. You don't want to look cheap. My new wine glasses are all ten ounces. It must be so hard on the family. You never get over that kind of loss. Life has to go on. I heard . . . You heard? I heard that Heather's tried this before. Then why would they keep a gun in the house? They didn't. She stole it. You can't stop someone if they really want to. Don't you think there but for the grace of God? To be honest it made me grateful that my son just has Down's. I couldn't deal with mental health issues.

"You didn't tell me that people were coming over," Sharon said. She didn't do well in crowds. She avoided the breakfast club at Magee's and she wouldn't be dragged to Moms' Night Out, which rotated through the neighbourhood.

"It was a last-minute thing," Eleanor said. "Since everyone was coming anyway."

"Where's Bram?" Sharon scanned the living room for Eleanor's husband, who disliked parties too.

"He took Judy to a hockey game. You need to get out more. Be around people. Hang up your coat."

"I shouldn't stay." But she unzipped her coat and hung it in the hall closet while Eleanor took the containers to the kitchen. She couldn't explain to Eleanor what being around so many people did to her. She barely understood it herself though her therapist had explained it, more than once.

When she was pregnant for the third time, the house several doors down was demolished and rebuilt. The construction noise had driven her completely crazy, and she believed it was this noise that had pushed her back into therapy. That and having a child born with red hair.

She was a milk machine with an infant, a toddler who wanted to nurse again, and a son who complained that she was always too tired to do anything with him. Friends advised her to sleep while the little ones napped, but while they napped, Sharon would sit at the kitchen table, comparing photographs of her new baby to pictures of herself at the same age. Just about identical. Like twins. Her mouth would get dry, all the moisture used up by her eyes, which ran, wetting tissue after tissue, which she left crumpled on the table. She'd look at the photographs and feel like she was disappearing until one day Eleanor found her sitting like that, and slapped the Yellow Pages down in front of her. She told Sharon to pick a psychologist, any one of them, and call. Sharon made an appointment with someone who worked out of a basement office on Hope Street, a block from the public school. While her sister-in-law babysat, Sharon spent an hour talking to a total stranger for no reason she could fathom. And for no reason other than it was the only time she'd had to herself in the whole week, she decided to go back.

One Thursday led to another and when Emmie was about a year old, after one of those sessions, Sharon was taking the girls to the library, pushing the baby in a stroller. Nina was walking and whining about it. She scuffed her new shoes on the sidewalk, rubbing them into the blue and slimy mulberries that had fallen unpicked, looking up at Sharon to make sure she knew it was deliberate. "I want to ride," Nina said. "It's no fair." Again and again. Sharon tried distraction, "Do you see the robin going to her nest?" Threats, "Do you want a time out?" And bribery, "I'll get you an ice cream cone but only if you behave."

It was summer, it was hot, and Sharon still nursed at night to get Emmie to sleep. Her right nipple was sore where she'd been bitten. The sky had the smoky look of a heat wave that would never lift. In the playground at Christie Pits, moms and nannies slumped on benches while their children ate sand, threw sand, and stuck twigs into sand birthday cakes. Toddlers chased pigeons, old ladies practised tai chi. Someone, heading into the park with a double stroller, smiled at her sympathetically. Sharon's back was wet, her T-shirt sticking to her. By the time she got to the convenience store on Hope Street, Nina was stamping her feet and wailing. Sharon pushed down the foot brakes on the stroller and sat on the picnic table at the side of the store, staring at baskets of berries, pots of geraniums, and the blue Christmas lights that decorated the store year-round. She didn't dare open her mouth, afraid of what would come out. The words *shut up* came to mind, for starters. The door opened and a couple of big kids came out, sucking on Popsicles.

This was what she heard herself say: "You want a piggyback?"

Nina stopped in mid stamp. "But you got the stroller."

"Yup. You want to try?"

And Nina came onto her mom's back, clinging with arms around her neck and feet around her waist. Her mom ran like that for a whole block, pushing the stroller, both kids laughing uproariously. Then all of a sudden, Sharon couldn't do it. She couldn't run another step. But Nina came down and walked willingly the rest of the way to the library. Later in the day, an obscene caller phoned the house, interrupting a rerun of *The Waltons*. She found herself swearing back. In more than one language. At the next session, after she mentioned these odd things, her therapist didn't seem surprised.

"You've talked about things like this before," she said. Brigitte Felber was a plump, white-haired psychologist from the French part of Switzerland. She never said *zis*, but carefully articulated the *th* sound, tongue touching her front teeth. "For example, you told me you picked me out of the Yellow Pages because you hate driving and you can walk here. Yet your first holiday with Dan was a road trip and you did the night driving."

Sharon nodded, her chest tightening. Sometimes, lately, she didn't hate driving. The radio would be on, the volume deafening, her hands beating time on the steering wheel.

"You've also mentioned that occasionally you forget, for a moment, that Eleanor is your sister-in-law. Especially right after therapy. And sometimes in our sessions your voice sounds very young and I have to explain big words to you.

Do you have any thoughts about what could cause all these kinds of things?"

"Alzheimer's?" Sharon asked, but there was a deeper worry. "Or maybe I'm crazy." There—she'd said it.

Brigitte shook her head. "You show no signs of dementia and you are assuredly not crazy. Your thinking is fine. You have no delusions."

"Then why is this happening? Swearing at people on the phone—it's just not like me."

"I agree. It isn't. But there is an explanation. Have you heard of DID? It used to be called multiple personalities. About one in a hundred people are multiple."

"You mean like Sybil?" Sharon asked.

"No. Not like that. Let me ask you this." Brigitte smiled as if thinking of some delightfully silly joke. "How long can you stand to be in a mall?"

"An hour," Sharon said in a small voice. Her first therapist, in the counselling centre at her university, had never asked questions like this. "How did you know?"

"When you have many people in your head, all looking out, all being attracted to different things, a mall is over-stimulating. Like a loud party. But an hour of therapy isn't long enough for them to talk. I'd like to book you for ninety-minute sessions."

"I don't know what you mean," Sharon said. "I don't like parties because I'm shy. That's all."

Brigitte asked, "Are you always shy?"

Sharon looked around her sister-in-law's living room. A graphic designer, a vet, two or three psychologists, an author, a journalist, a photographer, two scientists, a teacher, a linguist and one stay-at-home mom who homeschooled her four kids and made hand-crafted Christmas ornaments to raise funds for the homeless were waiting for Eleanor to open the wine. She collected people, interesting, talented people, even the odd famous one, proving to herself, if not her mother, that dropping out of school had had no ill effect. None of these people would wear a shrunken, past its best-before-date sweater. If the earth had opened up to swallow her, Sharon would have thanked it on bended knee before diving in. One of the psychologists was sitting on the couch, engrossed in conversation with the homeschooling mom. The psychologist wore pointy boots.

"Hi Sharon." That was Amy Grossman, the vet. She was the mother of a kid in college, her chin-length hair brown with a tasteful touch of red. Once a month Sharon went into her clinic to do the bookkeeping. Amy glanced across the living room to Ingrid, her partner, who was staring out the window. They lived in the other side of Heather's semi-detached, which they rented from her parents. "We've been talking about Heather. You just never know, do you?"

The homeschooling mom, whose name was Sofia Rosales-Oyibo, and Laura Anderson, the psychologist, turned toward Sharon, expectantly. There were things people said when they came together in groups, right things and wrong things, and they knew by instinct which was which, but she'd been born without that instinct and could only stand half-frozen, caught in her awkwardness.

"I guess not," Sharon said finally. And from inside came a barrage of invective: *moron, idiot, useless piece of trash.*

Perfume was wafting from the couch, either Laura or Sofia doused in something flowery and old-fashioned and suffocatingly sweet. From inside voices were hissing, *You can't get anything right, you'll never amount to anything.* Sharon could see it was true. Hadn't she once tried to fix Amy up with a man, too stupid to know that Amy liked girls? And there were worse mistakes, darker ones, hidden ones.

"It's amazing that the baby survived." Sofia was reaching for the chips.

"Don't you think it's . . ." Sharon crossed her arms, trying to stay present. "I mean cutting out . . ."

"Don't get so grossed out. The baby lived." Amy dipped her chips in salsa. "The truth is that we're all animals."

Meat, just meat. Like the lamb or Miss Piggy or the child of your heart lying blasted on a bed. She couldn't hold on anymore. The room wavered and she was falling inside, someone catching her as someone else moved into her place, switching quickly. Eyes momentarily on the floor, then sideways, making note of all the exits, she looked up, not precisely a she, though that is what the neighbours still saw: a mom like themselves, red haired and skinny, cheeks red with an embarrassment that was starting to fade, walking loose-limbed toward the kitchen.

One minute you were inside, keeping things under control, and then all of a sudden you shot out. Boom. Like that. Crashing through the eyes. So you just had to deal, even though you might be thinking, what the hell am I doing here, I'm not a mom, I'm not even a girl. You'd answer to "Sharon," put up with the boobs, and piss sitting down as long as you had to be out in the body. He—for Alec was a guy whatever the body was—looked over at the table set with a stack of plates, cream cheese, smoked salmon, guacamole, brie, bagels. His sister-in-law always put on a good spread. At least he'd have something to eat. He was hungrier than the others inside, and taller, and the body had to stretch to accommodate him. On nights when the girls called from their bunk beds, scared of monsters, he'd fold himself in one of their little chairs, keeping guard until they'd fallen asleep again.

Eleanor was in the kitchen, reaching inside the oven. "You were right. I don't know how the corkscrew got in there. Do you want a glass of wine?"

"Beer. If you got any." His head hurt from switching hard and fast.

Opening the fridge door, Eleanor took out a bottle. "I want you to do something for me. Go and talk to Ingrid. She heard the shot."

"No shit."

"They've only been there a few months." Eleanor had told Ingrid when the house was available for rent. It was perfect, close enough to the university and just a couple of blocks from Amy's clinic. That was what Eleanor did. She collected people and then she matched them up: you marry her; you work with him; you move into that house. "Now this."

44

"Got it." And he did.

"Wait. There's more. It was her gun." Eleanor looked up, daring her sister-in-law to blame her for bringing Ingrid, with her rifle and her handgun, next door to the house of a depressed child. She put the bottle down on the counter, hands on her hips.

"So you ask her to come here where everyone can bug her?"

"She should be with friends. Nobody else knows. Oh, and I'll want you to take the food over later. You can use the minivan. Go talk to her, okay?" Eleanor pushed her sister-in-law in the general direction of Ingrid as if she had no idea that Sharon was shy. But then he wasn't Sharon. He just thought most people were assholes. Picking up the beer, he moved toward the food. The salmon smelled good.

"What do you do?" Bonnie was asking, pushing the conversation along while Ingrid stood with her arms crossed.

"I teach at the university." Trapped between a table crammed with finger food and Bonnie Yoon, the famous author, Ingrid gazed out the window at the small patch of yard, the alley, the backs of other houses pressed together.

"Oh? What do you teach?"

"Astronomy."

"That must be interesting."

"Yes."

Bonnie waited for a question in turn. When none was forthcoming, she fiddled with the gold chain she wore. Her fingernails were painted dark blue. Alec was helping himself to bagel, cream cheese and lox while Ingrid stood quietly, saying nothing until Bonnie moved away, escaping to the hum of conversation at the other end of the room. The lox was good. Alec swallowed it down and slathered guacamole on pita. He didn't say anything either. Silence never bothered him.

"I should be going," Ingrid said. With her black hair, her white shirt and her grey eyes, she looked like she'd stepped out of a black and white photograph, not sepia, not old-fashioned, but angled and sharp. She'd moved here from the west to take a tenure-track position. She smelled of cigarettes.

"Lucky you," he said.

She half-smiled. "I need to drive out to the observatory. I'll be up all night and I want to air the dogs first."

"What kind?" He hadn't thought that the moms would be talking about dogs. He liked dogs.

"Two greyhounds. They're beautiful but hilarious. They go swift as the wind and then poop right out. Forty-five-mile-per-hour couch potatoes. The rescue foundation got them before they were destroyed." In her eyes was a hard and steady anger. "That's what people do when they're finished with racing greyhounds." She was quiet another moment then said, "I'm not much of a people person."

"Me neither. Too many questions."

Ingrid nodded. "Everyone's been asking if I noticed anything."

"Like you want to think about it over and over." He moved away from the table to make room for Laura and Ana, in a black and gold sari. Right behind them came Sofia, the homeschooling mom, who took up space disproportionate to her physical size as if her good works marched before her. Two of her children were adopted, two of them birth children, all of them biracial. The women descended on the food, saying, *I shouldn't, well just for tonight, you only live once.* And before any of them could ask him what he heard or what he saw, he moved further, out the back door, Ingrid following.

Lights went on, triggered by motion detectors. It was cold on the deck and quiet. "I have no idea what I'm doing here." Ingrid pulled a pack of cigarettes from her pocket and lit up.

"It's Eleanor. She does this thing." Alec stepped away from the circle of light, into the shadowy corner of the deck. "You don't even know how she does it. All of a sudden you are somewhere you had no intention to be."

Ingrid was standing right under the lamp, her skin paler, her hair darker. "I detest crowds, even faculty functions. Everyone playing games. I'm no good at it. That's what I like about hunting, it's clean. You know what you're there for."

"And you're doing something useful, not just talking. What do you shoot with?"

"Remington rifle for deer, shotgun for birds." She laughed. "I never imagined that a mother of three, here in granola land, would have any interest in hunting."

"Yeah. Well. You don't know someone till you do."

Ingrid took a deep drag on her cigarette, then flicked it into the yard, lighting another. "It was my gun. The kid appropriated it. But it was mine."

She stood under the porch light, sucking down the nicotine as fast as she could get it into her lungs.

"Feels like you did it?" he asked.

"If we hadn't rented the house . . . But our apartment was too small for the dogs."

He looked over the yard. His eyes were used to making out shapes in the darkness, discriminating between monsters and, say, that ash tree or the tarp thrown over Eleanor's gas barbecue. "She was the one who took it. And the one who used it."

"But I was right next door and didn't give any thought to my gun cabinet except to make sure it met the legal requirements. Anyone could have broken in. I'd just got back from the observatory. I didn't want to wake up Amy, so I went upstairs to my office." She glanced at him. "You live that close to someone's house, you hear things. It can't be avoided." She moved her hand as if to stub out the cigarette and say something else, but instead she took another drag, smoking it down to the filter. The backyard faced the railroad tracks a block north, but the track was hidden by trees. "Whatever. There are too many houses jammed together. I don't know how people can breathe."

"I like it out here. It's quiet. Bet it's a lot quieter when you go hunting."

"Deer and moose season aren't till fall. But turkey's coming up. Can you shoot?"

He was actually a very good shot. But he was here to protect the life, not live it. Everyone inside had to make things look normal. And Sharon hated guns. "I haven't for a long time," he said.

Ingrid was taking a pen from her pocket, writing on a

scrap of paper. "I've really got to go home and let the dogs out. Here's my e-mail address. If you want to come with me to the shooting range, let me know."

Alec shoved the piece of paper in his pocket. What else could he do with it? Someone like him didn't have friends. He did his job. That was all.

*A*lec parked the minivan in front of Rick and Debra's house, wheels on the sidewalk, hazard lights blinking. Then he stacked the cartons and carried them, two at a time, to the porch before ringing the bell.

"Hi Mrs. Lewis," Cathy said as she opened the front door.

"I've got some stuff here for you," Alec said. "Did Eleanor phone about it?"

"Oh. We haven't been answering the phone. Mom!" Cathy called over her shoulder. "Mrs. Lewis is here." Her parents had raised her with an old-fashioned politeness: never call adults by their first names and other rules that she generally obeyed and her sister had not.

"Tell her to come in."

"No thanks," Alec said. "I'd better . . ."

But Cathy's mom was at the door, looking with bewilderment at the cartons on her porch as if she didn't know what to do with them.

"I'll just bring these in then, okay?" he asked. "Kitchen?"

"Yes. Please," Debra said—always Debra, never Debbie or Deb, and in her pediatric office, Dr. Dawson. She looked like her daughters, both of them, the one who'd survived and the one who was gone, slender and blonde, though Heather had countered the resemblance by chopping her hair short, sometimes wearing clothes that swallowed her up, leaving her formless, or at other times showing everything she could legally show. Debra dressed tastefully even in grief. As she often told her daughters, People who do well, do well. She worked here in the neighbourhood, her practice on Hammond Street above Magee's. Parents felt reassured by her assuredness, for she always ordered lots of tests, and they'd heard that in an emergency, someone could even bring a sick kid to her house in the middle of the night.

All of this Alec knew though he drew no conclusions from it. He'd been back out in the life for the last two years, observing how it had changed, watching kids in the neighbourhood play, fight, fall out of trees, get soothed, yammer for ice cream when the ice cream truck drove by the playground with its hypnotically cheerful song. And while he was watching he found things to do.

Last summer Heather had come over one day when he was in the backyard, stripping paint off a table top he'd picked up at a yard sale. She was going door to door, selling raffle tickets for one of her parents' charities. She was practically bald then; her head looked like a grey stone covered with golden fuzz. People said her parents had had her head shaven because of lice. They said she'd shaven her own head out of spite.

"Ten dollars each," she'd said sullenly. He hadn't known she was pregnant. She wasn't showing yet. "Your chances of winning are one in five."

"That sounds like high odds."

"It is." She'd suddenly grinned. One of her eyeteeth was chipped. "I lied."

"Okay, but move. You shouldn't be standing so close to the chemicals. It's bad for you."

She'd put a hand on her belly as she peered at him suspiciously. "Did my sister say something to Josh?"

"It's bad for kids, that's all. I don't let them in the yard when I'm using paint stripper."

He'd gone into the house to get some money for the raffle tickets, figuring that was expected. When he came back, Heather was still outside, sitting in the girls' sandbox, overalls rolled up, drawing with a stick. There were no clues in the drawings, just random shapes, triangles, spirals. When she saw Alec, she scratched a tic-tac-toe board into the sand, putting an *X* in the middle. Obligingly, he made an *O* though he had no chance of winning with the *X* placed there. "I'm going for a draw," he'd said. "Why'd you shave your head?"

"It's the antidepressants," she'd said. "They make me so hot." She'd laughed then.

"I get it," Alec said. "Very funny. But I thought that antidepressants, you know, shut that down."

"I guess I won't make it as a hooker." And then she'd laughed even harder. She'd stayed in the sandbox, making a tower of sand while Alec went back to working on the table. Now and then he glanced over at her. Once she looked back at him, with eyes as lucid as bright moons. "My sister has sold a lot of tickets. She always does, so, like they wouldn't put her on pills. You know what I mean? No matter what, she'll be okay. Thanks for letting me stay here for a while."

"No problem." He'd paused, shaking off bits and pieces of thought from others inside, wanting to see just what was in front of him. It was late afternoon, a half moon rising over the yard, and the wind couldn't make up its mind, coming from the north, then turning south and west, clouds moving in and out. The girl stood there in her rolled-up overalls, ankles bare and mosquito bitten, new sneakers pristine, her chest already starting to swell, not that he would have noticed that then. What he saw was that her overalls had a lot of pockets and that there were things hidden in them, as if she didn't trust them as far away as the bag she carried. There was something he wanted to say to this kid. To tell her he'd run off at her age, too, and had driven up to his uncle's. Only he'd come back because he had a little sister at home. Then he'd ask her where she'd run and why she'd come back. But while he hesitated, unsure of himself in this mom's life, she'd said goodbye, ducking her head as if the sky was too low.

On the porch of Heather's house, Alec bent to pick up two cartons of food, straightened up and walked in. The kitchen was at the back, as in most houses, the front door leading first to what was on display—a living room with pale carpeting and dark furniture built to maximize utility in a small space. Past the living room was the den, more casual, with cushiony pieces, a thick rug, a framed family portrait on the wall and photographs of the sisters in their reindeer costumes, dancing in *The Nutcracker*. Finally the kitchen, efficient and gleaming in brushed aluminum marred only by take-out containers of Chinese food. He put the cartons beside them.

Heather's dad, Rick, was sitting at the table, stirring sugar into his tea. His hobby was digital photography, but he was a professor of business ethics. Nothing important happened in the neighbourhood without his assistance. The arena had been renovated through a corporate sponsorship he'd arranged, the after-school program Learn About the World was his brainchild and had become a model for inter-cultural programs. He sat on the boards of numerous char-ities, some of which raised money through the sale of raffle tickets. He was blond, like his wife, and wiry. They could have been brother and sister. But he wore his grief more obviously, his eyes bloodshot, his clothing rumpled.

Alec returned with two more cartons and Debra was asking, "Couldn't you have some tea?" Without waiting for a reply, she poured it for him and pulled out a chair.

Cathy was leaning against the wall, staring at the blank fridge. There were no photographs or lists on it, the shiny front undisrupted.

"We had a lock on the medicine cabinet," Rick said, putting more sugar in his tea as if he'd forgotten that he'd already sweetened it while Debra sat down in the chair beside his.

"My sister's flying in tomorrow," she said, pouring tea for herself. "Rick's cousin lives in the city, which makes things easier, but his brother couldn't get a flight this morning. He'll be here later tonight. We're going to have her cremated." Alec didn't flinch, though others inside did. "I don't want anyone trying to put her back together and make her look pretty. It wasn't pretty."

Alec sat with his feet planted flat on the floor, knees apart. In his hand the china teacup, rose patterned, held a dainty quantity of tea. It wasn't bad. Milky and sweet. "That took a lot of guts what you did," he said.

"I couldn't be a mother right then. In a crisis one has to focus." As a doctor, she said, she knew there was only one thing left to do: extract the fetus quickly. The body would incubate it for five minutes to eight at most. There was no thought of whose body.

Alec did what he knew how to do, listen rather than speak, taking in whatever strangeness was before him until action was required.

When she fell silent, Alec asked, "How's the baby?"

"She's in the neonatal ICU," Debra replied. "I'll go back to the hospital tomorrow, but there's no reason to think she shouldn't do well."

"I thought Heather would do better at home," Rick said in the same whispery way he'd spoken about the medicine cabinet, as if his daughter's death had left him transparent, his organs barely held in by skin. "There was no reason to make her go away."

"You'd never let her," Cathy said. And then bitterly, "Even though she never did what you wanted."

"She was still our daughter. Regardless." Rick put more sugar in his tea. He hadn't drunk any of it yet. "But if we had sent her away, then maybe she'd be alive. If only we'd left the other side of the house vacant. We were thinking that we would renovate before we rented it out again."

"Without the gun, she'd have done something else," Debra said. "The baby would have died if she'd thrown herself off a bridge. Look, I'm not going to sugar-coat this. Thank God she was close enough to term. Think of the silver lining. We still have our baby and we'll be able to bring her home soon. Heather didn't take her away, too." She turned to Alec. "Thank you for having Cathy over yesterday."

"She can come over anytime she wants. You don't need an invitation, Cathy."

He noticed then that Cathy's feet were bare, her legs were bare, her skirt short even though the house was cold, conserving energy. Her top was thin, you could see the outline of her bra through it. When she felt Alec's glance on her, she moved her shoulders back, making the most of what little she had as if it was automatic, sensing that a guy sat at her parents' table, whatever the outward appearance. "I can help babysit." She flicked her hair, head slightly tilted. "Or whatever."

"There's always place for you at our house, kiddo. No payback."

Cathy didn't answer; she was looking at her dad stir his tea. Forming words had become too hard for both of them.

After a pause, her mother said, "Thank you. As long as she keeps up with her school work."

"I guess the kids can study together," Alec said. "Josh is a good kid. He's doing all right."

"One can't let grades slip. People who do well do well."

Cathy nodded, the familiar phrase a steel rod along her spine, allowing her to shift away from the wall as though she could now stay vertical without it holding her up, moving to stand beside her father's chair.

"Thank God I still have you." Rick looked up at his daughter.

"You always have me, Daddy." She leaned toward him and his arm went around her waist. He put his cup to his lips, took a swallow, then grimaced. "Too sweet."

"I'll be heading out unless there's something else I can do here," Alec said. It had been a long day and even he was tired, the headache getting worse. As soon as he got the car back to Eleanor's, someone else would have to come forward.

"We're fine. Thank you for everything," Debra said.

Cathy was washing the cup in the sink as Alec said goodbye, her hair twisted up and out of the way, held in a knot with a wooden chopstick. Her back was straight, her feet turned out, her elbows oddly bruised.

INSIDE

It was dark and the inside children cried from the cold, but the Overseer was deaf to their whining and indifferent to the chill. The sub-basement was big enough to contain them and the basement just as big, though it felt too small for him as he paced in the darkness. He wasn't afraid. Only someone weak would be afraid of his enemy or his last resort. People averted their eyes from death, believing they knew how it had come when they had barely perceived its outline. How could they appreciate its power, its drive and its cunning? The girl who died had stolen herself from her parents. She could not endure; that showed weakness. She had used a weapon, which took strength. But if she was strong, why did she desert her family? Family is all, it is everything, the one place where you have a place.

He paced and he asked himself these things. It was all he could do because the Housekeeper had blocked his way. He was confined and his nostrils narrowed at the stink of it. This was his: a floor of cold earth and walls of stone, which were wet from the sewage that seeped in. And the darkness, it was his, too. From here he sent out his punishers; he made sure that crying children stayed below. He had his means and ways, his keys and his locks. Order had to be maintained. The rules were simple:

1. Obey.
   Do what you were taught. Do it right. Do it quick.
2. Do not speak to strangers.
   They are not your family, not your father, mother, brothers, and not your uncles who were given the title because they are as good as family.
3. There are no second chances.
   Do what you were taught. Do it right. Do it quick.

Of course children would be tested. How else could anyone discover their strength? The harder the test, the greater the honour to be won. He understood that, unlike those inside children with their whining and crying over every little thing. He pictured them coming forward— running madly, switching uncontrollably, endlessly weeping loud and open-mouthed. What would happen then? But it wouldn't, for he was in charge. The Overseer. Maintaining control. Ensuring that everyone behaved.

He couldn't get past the kitchen, where Sharon rested, unaware of her surroundings. But at the door, he could call her name, "Sharon," the snivelling outsider who spoke to strangers, telling tales out of turn. What right did she have to do that?

"Sharon, Sharon," he said softly, for she could close her eyes but not her ears. "What kind of mother are you? Always too tired. What kind of wife? All the burden is on your husband. He works while you are a waste of space. Filling cupboards with rags and scraps, spending his money. Wasting time and money in therapy, imagining things. You're lucky he hasn't left you. How long do you think that's going to last? Then you'll have nowhere to go and nobody will want you."

CHAPTER SEVEN

*E*very nation has made a pattern of the stars, learning their positions to guide a person travelling, telling tales about the constellations to help memory along. The same group of stars outlined an emperor's chariot in old China, a plough in Britain, a bear among the North American tribes.

In ancient Rome, the story was told like this. There was a huntress, a woman named Callisto. An attendant of the goddess of the hunt, Callisto was a virgin, a necessary condition to be among the goddess's favourites. Unfortunately the king of the gods, Jupiter, desired Callisto, even if she didn't desire him. To gain her trust, he disguised himself as the goddess. When he opened his arms and pulled her into a hug, Callisto was pleased to be noticed until she couldn't extract herself. Only then did she discover who had hold of her, as he reverted to his true shape and raped her.

Some months afterward, seeing Callisto bathe in a creek—pregnant and ruined—the goddess had no sympathy. As punishment, she turned Callisto into a bear, who soon gave birth to a son, Arcas. When the boy was old enough to hunt, he came across a bear in the woods. Not knowing it was his mother, he raised his arm to throw a spear at it. But the king of the gods, believing himself more merciful than the goddess, intervened. He turned Arcas into a bear cub and then put mother and son in the sky as constellations so they might be together always, calling them Ursa Major and Ursa Minor.

At the tip of little bear's tail, the North Star shone over Crookshank's Lane. A couple of cats howled and hissed, fighting in a yard. On the sidewalk, a redhead in jeans and a sweater was pulling a wagon home from Eleanor's house, while inside that head—imperceptible to any passerby—a conversation took place. *What's going on in that house? Forget it, none of our business. If it's not our business, what is? The mummy cut Cathy's sister. Bad mummy. No, hon, you don't understand. The sister was gone and her mom was saving the baby. We should've done something before, then maybe there wouldn't be a funeral. Don't go off like that. You're thinking of our crap, getting triggered. I am not.*

As they argued, one of them came forward. She slipped out as she always did when the situation required it, pausing only a moment to get her bearings, gripping the handle of the wagon, her feet on the ground, the cool air on her face. Her head tilted back, she could spot the Big Dipper even in this pallid night sky polluted by circling beams of light from the great towers by the lake. She wished to know how stars were made, where they began, where they would end. She liked looking at the stars, at their distance and indifferent shining. She had no given name. But she called herself Callisto, after the girl who became the bear in the sky. And so she walked back to the house on Ontario Street, doing what she had always done, waiting out the darkness.

At last the day was ending. She glanced in at Josh, who was in his room, texting his friends or playing a game on his phone. He was back in his PJ bottoms and the T-shirt he'd decorated at last Mayfest when Cathy had been helping at the tie-dye stall. After he'd tripped over the bucket of blue dye, it had taken him months to work up the nerve to ask her if she'd like to come over to study. Down the hall his sisters were sleeping, both of them in the lower bunk, arms wrapped around each other, stuffed animals guarding the head and foot of the bed. They'd hung a blanket from the upper bunk to shield them. Above their room, in his third floor office, Dan was sitting between stacks of newspapers on his desk.

He looked up as she stood in the doorway, his dark eyes searching her face. More than anything right now, he wanted sex. Let's forget everything and just hump sex. Afterward holding her close sex. But it had been a while since they'd had any sort of sex, even if that was really her standing in the doorway now—and he thought it was not.

They'd come out to him as multiple a year ago. On a mild winter day, the streets dry, Dan had taken the morning off work to come with Sharon to her therapist's office in the basement of a house on Hope Street. There was a separate entrance to the basement, which did its best not to look or smell like one. The walls were painted a robin's egg blue, decorated with cheerful posters. The carpet was thick, and full-spectrum bulbs in floor lamps with glass shades imitated daylight. The dehumidifier hummed in the background and water trickled over stones in a table fountain. The therapist sat in a leather recliner, wearing furry slippers, the only sign that this was the basement of her home. Sometimes Brigitte leaned the recliner back, her pudgy slippered feet propped on the footrest. But not that session. She sat forward, attentive, a hand on each arm of the chair.

Dan sat at one end of the couch and his wife at the other, heart beating so fast they—Sharon and all—thought they'd pass out until Callisto came forward. The therapist knew they'd switched. She glanced over as her client sat up straighter, hands stilled.

"So what's the big secret?" Dan asked. He wore a suit as he'd be going from the session to the office.

"No secret," Brigitte replied. "I felt that a joint session would be helpful at this stage. I can explain the situation and answer any questions you might have."

"And the situation is?" Dan had a leg crossed over the other, one foot moving up and down. His foot moved like that when he was nervous or angry. It was the possibility that he was angry that had sent the heart knocking against the ribs.

"I'd like to ask you first about your perception. How would you describe things at home?"

"Honestly? I don't know if therapy is helping or making things worse. We hit a bad patch after Emmie was born and four years later it hasn't improved. If anything Sharon seems more withdrawn now than when she started."

"That must be difficult for you."

"She's online talking to her chat friends all the time. If I say anything to her, I feel like I'm interrupting her real life. I just want my wife back." He looked toward the other end of the couch. "Or maybe you're leaving. Is that why I'm here?"

"Leaving where?" Callisto asked.

"Me." His voice choked.

"Certainly not," Callisto said firmly. "What gave you that idea?"

He addressed his answer to the therapist. "When I get into bed she moves over like she can't stand me near her. I thought—I thought she hated me. I was going to fight for joint custody. I was already thinking of all that."

Brigitte spoke gently. "This will be not nearly so bad."

But inside Sharon was thinking, *it will, it will,* and the heart started knocking again, trying to leap from the body rather than witness her husband's revulsion when he discovered the truth.

"One step at a time," Brigitte said, as if she could hear those thoughts. "Dan, have you ever noticed your wife being different?" Brigitte picked up her pen and clipboard to make notes.

"Different how?"

"A sudden change in mood that seemed to come from nowhere. Or doing something that struck you as out of character?"

"Isn't that a woman's prerogative?"

Brigitte didn't laugh. She just waited, letting the silence do its work.

"Sometimes," Dan said, "especially before we had kids, she'd get scared at night. Like a little kid, you know, making those noises. I didn't mind. I'd pat her back until she went to sleep. Was that wrong?"

Brigitte smiled at him. "That was right. Patting her back is such a small thing and yet so significant because you showed her a gentleness she had never known." She had a warm smile, like an apple doll or a kitchen witch. Callisto watched the smile, wondering how the muscles of the face would feel around such an expression.

"Okay then." Dan leaned back, relieved.

His relief was somewhat premature in Callisto's estimation. People often reacted quickly to the word or gesture of a moment, without considering that something else might follow that could cast a rather different light on it.

"You know that she was abused."

"Yes," he said. "Her father molested her and her mother was critical." Sharon had told him the same thing she'd told Eleanor, just that much—a piece of the truth. It explained the nightmares and the flinching when she and Dan first made love. It was enough to stop them from visiting her family; enough to keep their children safe.

"When a child experiences excessive trauma," Brigitte continued, "the mind can split into pieces and each part becomes a separate person. Imagine it as if these people were locked in different rooms. On the outside at least Sharon could grow up and learn normal functioning. But those others are still there, suffering, reliving the trauma over and over because they don't know any different life exists. They don't even realize it's possible. What used to be called multiple personalities is now referred to as dissociative identity disorder, also sometimes as DDNOS, dissociative disorder not otherwise specified. We don't need to bother about the technical differences."

"But she has post-partum depression. She had it after Josh was born, too." He turned to his wife. "Hon, maybe you should see your doctor for a prescription."

Callisto looked away, her hands clasped in her lap. It was as she'd thought—he'd never understand.

"People like your wife are often misdiagnosed," Brigitte explained patiently. "You see a depressed new mom, and you assume PPD. But in your wife's case, hormones weren't the cause. She has DID, though I don't like the term 'disorder.' It would be more accurate to say that it's an adaptation to early childhood trauma."

They could hear the therapist's cat howling like a beagle upstairs. Brigitte had said that when he made this sound he was lonely. Dan looked around, willing to be distracted by a cat leaping into his lap, but it was locked out and there was nothing for his hands to do but intertwine over a knee. He glanced over at his wife's expressionless face. "What kind of trauma?" he asked.

It was up to Callisto to reveal now the extent and nature of what they'd hidden from him—she was the only one who could say the words. As she spoke, her voice slightly hoarse as it always was, the others inside waited for Dan to see that they were tainted, disgusting, repellent and loathsome.

"That happened to you?" He looked from his wife to the therapist, who was nodding.

"Unfortunately it isn't as rare as people think. I've had a number of DID clients over the years. Many of them experienced this."

"Good God." His foot jiggled more, hands clenched over his knee, jawline hardening.

"You sound angry," Brigitte said.

"Of course I'm angry!"

Callisto held back the lils from bursting out. *Don't be mad. I'll be good. Promise. Promise. Promise.* These tears on her face did not belong to her. She was keeping the mind clear. But she could not stop herself from shrinking away when Dan moved closer, trying to take her hand, to stroke her hair.

"This is what I mean," he appealed to the therapist. "It's like I'm the enemy."

"But you are not angry with your wife," Brigitte said.

"No, of course not."

"However, your anger is frightening because terrible things used to happen to her when people were angry. This is what we call a trigger."

"But I'd never hurt Sharon," Dan said, forgetting that it was not Sharon who wept in terror.

"I believe that. The purpose of this session is simply to provide you with information." Brigitte's voice was calm, soothing. Water trickled over the stones in the serenity fountain. She turned to Callisto. "How are you doing?"

With an effort Callisto blinked away the tears, regained her voice. "I'm all right," she said. The price for staying forward would be paid later. In exhaustion. Pain in the body. Shaking. But only in private.

"I want to help," Dan said, looking at Callisto as if he would wish to know her. And for a moment, for a foolish moment, his wife believed him—they, the ones close to the front who were listening, thought it might be all right.

"All of them together are a team, a system. That is who your wife is," Brigitte said.

"Sharon." He uncrossed his legs, leaning on one elbow.

"Sharon is one of them. You could say she's the default."

"The real one?" he asked. As expected.

And who was Callisto? Not real. Not good. Deserving of no life. Did her name appear on a birth certificate, a driver's license, a credit card? Nowhere but the sky. On earth nameless. Bearing what must be borne. The fountain bubbled, the dehumidifier sucked in air. Nothing crashed or broke apart as Callisto breathed. This was her job today. The therapist had said that when this question came, they were simply to breathe. It would take time for Dan to understand.

"They're all real. Your sense of self is just that, a sense, a feeling that you express as 'I.' There is no little man in your head pulling strings. Even scientists can't explain consciousness. People who are multiple have a different feeling, neither more nor less real than yours. Their feeling is 'we,' a family of selves."

"I see," Dan said, crossing his legs again, the foot going up and down, keeping time to the beat of his private thoughts. His pants leg lifted slightly, showing an argyle sock, green and black. "So how do I get Sharon back? What. What did I say?"

He couldn't possibly hear the uproar that these words

had caused inside. Callisto was sitting as before, back straight, hands in her lap. But multitudes were in her eyes, glaring through them at Dan, then turning away from him, retreating, moving further inside. *Away away away.* Unwanted. Despised.

If Sharon was who he wished, then Sharon he would have. "No. Wait," Brigitte had said, watching them. But Callisto was done. She went inside and with the others pushed Sharon out. It was the work of a moment, eyes lowered to hide the change. And then Sharon cleared her throat, hands waving as she spoke, blinking nervously, but it signified nothing to Callisto, deep inside.

And here she was again. Callisto had come to look at the stars, she'd come because it was her job to take over when the others were overwrought. Whether she liked it or not was irrelevant. Yet people made pictures out of stars and this man was now looking at her anxiously. He wore jeans and a plaid shirt; it was always jeans at home and a suit for work. In his closet everything had a place.

"Everything go all right tonight?" He checked his wife's face—not Sharon's, he knew that. But he wasn't sure if he should guess which one she was. If he guessed wrong, would she hate him? More than sex, he wanted his wife, all of her, not to hate him. "You were gone longer than I expected."

"Eleanor had a party for the people bringing food." The head hurt but it would do no good to take pills for a switching headache. "And then the food had to be brought over to Debra's house."

"On your way to bed?" He was taking scissors out of his desk organizer. Beside it was a photo of his family in a digital frame and a rock with a fossil embedded in it. His desk had been the door to the dining room, a solid slab of wood so heavy it had torn out the hinges. The paint had been stripped, the pine sanded and varnished, and now resting on two filing cabinets it made a fine working surface to the side of his computer station. There was a map of the ancient world above his desk, another filing cabinet against one wall, a bookcase filled with books organized by subject: history, economics, evolution, rocks. The window faced west, blinds halfway up, streetlights shining through bare trees and icicles that hung from the eaves. "I'll be at this a while." He was collecting news stories that could be used for fundraising campaigns. He often said that nothing opened a donor's wallet like fear.

"I'm not tired. Perhaps I could help."

"You sure?" He looked pleased when she nodded. There was an empty plate on his desk and the room still smelled of roast chicken. "I want to cut out and file the articles I need so I can toss the rest."

"I could do that."

"All right. I've starred the ones I want. Here's your pile."

She picked up a newspaper, scanning the headlines. VIOLENCE SURGES IN KANDAHAR; "GRANDPA" FROM THE MUNSTERS DIES; BILL GATES PLEDGES 600 MILLION DOLLARS TO STAMP OUT TUBERCULOSIS; STAMPEDE IN THE PHILIPPINES; PLANETS DISCOVERED OUTSIDE THE SOLAR SYSTEM. She wished to read it all, wrapping herself in the fabric of the universe so that no one could say that she was not real without denying reality itself. "Only one of the articles is marked," she said.

"Good. Less to file. From now on I'm getting everything online. It's easier just to download." She was left-handed, he was right-handed, and as he passed the scissors to her, their hands met, shyly, provisionally. "I made a pot of decaf," he said. "I could get you a cup. Freshly ground beans. How would you like it?"

She didn't know, but she said, "Sweet." If he was taking the trouble to ask, then she wouldn't have it the way Sharon did. "Milk and sugar."

When he returned, they sat side by side, the space between them narrow and warm, conscious space, first date space. She tried the coffee. Bitter and sweet, a stronger flavour than tea.

"How are Rick and Debra doing?" he asked.

"In what respect?"

He looked at her sharply, having assumed that she would say that they were doing okay, as well as could be expected, holding up. A reply that wouldn't make him think.

"Physically? Mentally?" he clarified.

"They won't die." She picked up another newspaper and, locating the mark, began to cut out an article. Then as he waited for more, she added, "They won't go insane."

"No, not Rick or Debra. They define sane and rational. If anyone can get through this it would be them. I don't know what I'd do," he said. "Maybe get drunk and stay drunk."

"No," she said. "I would not allow it."

"I believe that." He swivelled his chair toward her, his eyes on her profile, the thin freckled nose, pointy chin, and she turned, too, a flash of storm in her eyes, the green of a sky while winds picked up, slower below, faster above, cloud twisting.

"It was cold," she said.

"What was?"

"The house."

"Maybe Heather was too warm. You were." Then he hesitated, considering that it wasn't this wife who had been pregnant. "I think it was with Josh," he rushed on. "Weren't you?"

Ignoring the question, she pushed ahead doggedly. "This evening Cathy wore summer clothes. They allowed it in a cold house in winter. Don't you think that's odd?"

"Well that's my mother's influence. She's always scolding you to put another sweater on the kids." He smiled at her. With his perfect teeth, made perfect by diligence, he smiled, and with his dark eyes, made perfect by God, he tried to coax the storm out of her gaze as if he didn't realize that she never spoke without a purpose. As if she should be persuaded by his charm. As if she knew nothing of value when she needed to understand and she could not afford to be distracted from it by warm eyes on hers, by fingers covering hers.

"I should check e-mail," she said.

"Okay. I'll finish up here." His smile disappeared. He got the code. He had said something wrong though he didn't know what. She would be up late; she would talk online to other people whose conversation she preferred; he would go to bed alone.

Downstairs she took the laptop from the dining room into the kitchen, setting it up on the blue table. She plugged headphones into the computer, and selected a classical music station. Outside the glass doors, the wind chimes pinged. The birch tree shone white and spare as she clicked on mIRC and signed in.

Welcome to multiples-chat, a supportive chat room for people who have DID or DDNOS. Visit our homepage at www.multiplesweb.com.

    *S&ALL has joined multiples-chat

    S&All› Hello everyone

    Panther› hi s&all

    Janet› callisto! ltns i'm so glad to see you

    S&All› How did you know it was me?

    Janet› you're the only one of you who says hello with a capital H

    Janet› how're things?

Janet lived on the Atlantic coast, where she raised goats, painted, and fostered children. Panther was a nurse in the southwest, mother of four, married to a math teacher. None of them had met in person, but here while the house quietly breathed, there was no need to hide who they were. If Callisto had a word for the warmth in her chest, it would have been friendship. If she ever smiled, she would have then, for in the virtual reality of bursting electrons, she existed, she was known, she had been missed.

$\mathcal{T}$he memorial service for Heather was held on the Saturday after she was cremated. Neighbours who had worn black to flirt with darkness when they were young now dressed darkly to honour death, converging from the direction of Christie Pits and from Amy's Animal Clinic, some coming up from the library or down from the railroad tracks. The service was being held in the gym of the Freedom Boys and Girls Club at Colborne Street and Ontario, a block from the public school, two blocks from the therapist's house and her thickly carpeted, dehumidified basement. In the east the moon was coming out from behind a cloud, a hair short of full, waxing 99 percent gibbous and in the west the sun was falling below snow-covered railroad tracks.

The boys and girls club had been built around 1960, at the same time as the arena, another square brick building that faced it across the street. There was a mulberry bush in front of the arena, and in summer families stopped to pick its berries while walking to the library or Christie Pits. Last year the rink had been refurbished, courtesy of a corporate sponsorship deal arranged by Heather's father. He'd been working on a similar deal for the boys and girls club. Inside the gym, people were settling into the rows of folding chairs, holding black-bordered programs, draping their coats over laps or on the backs of chairs. At the front of the gym there was a podium with a microphone and on the floor nearby an enormous vase overflowed with tropical flowers. Set on window ledges, smaller vases of flowers released their perfume, mingling with the smell of wet boots.

At the back of the gym, trying to be unobtrusive, Ingrid sat between Amy and Eleanor, whose husband, Bram, was next to her. Judy was in the daycare, helping to keep the younger kids busy with some of the staff who had volunteered their time during the service. Dan and his wife, hands folded in her lap, face sombre, were sitting in the middle of the gym. In the same row were their next-door neighbours, Tony Agostino and his son, so broad in the chest, his jacket strained across it. Tony murmured hello, Dan nodded. Josh had found himself a seat right behind his girlfriend, who sat in the front row with her sad parents and the officiating minister, who was of some indeterminate denomination vaguely related to Buddhism, but without the accoutrements. No saffron robe for him, he was wearing a dark suit. Even the owner of the candy-coloured house, slump-shouldered and middle-aged, was indistinguishable from any man at a funeral. This was the essence of Seaton Grove: the authors of fringe festivals had made babies and suited up, too busy to meditate anymore. And yet all through the gym people were invoking light in their own way, with prayer or a reaching stillness, asking peace to surround the bent heads of their sorrowing neighbours in the front row.

Dan checked his watch. The service was supposed to start at seven. It was 7:04. "It's late," he said.

"Do you have something else you have to do?" his wife asked. She held the program in her left hand. She was wearing a black dress, not particularly eye-catching. But there was that left-hand thing. Sharon was right-handed. And so Dan tried to look without looking like he was checking things off a list: the wife he knew best, soft-toned; the wife with moss green eyes who put chocolate chips in cereal; the one who didn't waste words and liked to fix things; and this one—husky voiced, left-handed. The list of his wives, God help him.

"I'd like to get through this and get home." He tapped the program against the palm of his hand. "I don't like funerals."

"Memorial service," she corrected.

"I don't like those either. But I should be here, so I am."

At one time she would have asked him why, but she had learned that there were customs and habits that people relied upon in the same way that animals reduced strife by grooming each other. Take Dan's lists. After he beat Josh at Stratego and gloated unmercifully, he'd retreat to his office to revise his to-do lists, colour-coded and indexed. Then he would emerge, cleansed of his competitiveness, until the next game of Stratego. And yet he would try again, making his lists, domesticating himself. Her father, who took pride in beating his children, would consider anything less a show of weakness. But she had seen the tension in Dan's neck and

shoulders as he sat at his desk, making a list. A man's goodness was not dependent on the quality of his heart. Every
heart was a writhing pit of need and want. His goodness
revealed itself in his choice of action.

"At least they could start on time," he said, looking at his
watch again. She never wore one. Watches went wild on her
wrist, running past the time or stopping altogether. It didn't
matter anymore. She had a cellphone.

She yawned as a squeal from the microphone sent
someone to check the sound system.

"You tired?"

Callisto nodded. Too much had been going on inside. "I
haven't been sleeping."

"I'll put the girls to bed," he offered. "You can have
some downtime."

All around them people were talking quietly. *How's the
baby? Doing well. I heard she can come home next week. Debra visits
her every day. You have to touch babies or they die. What about the
baby's father? Who is he? Nobody knows. They think some street
kid. He might try to get some money out of them. Don't worry, they'll
take care of it. The baby is better off with them. That's obvious.* The
neighbours' murmurs surged and died away as Rick Edwards
took the podium.

He wore a suit, white shirt, dark tie, his golden beard
covering the faint acne scars on his cheeks. He was impec-
cable, shoes polished, hair neatly trimmed, a father who had
failed his child, doing his best to hold his grief in check.
Patting his pocket, he quietly said, "Uh oh, my glasses," the
microphone picking up his voice. Debra opened her purse,

fished out his reading glasses and reached out to hand them to him. Though the purse appeared to be alligator, it had to be imitation. Around here people did not wear animals, except for cows.

"Dear neighbours," Rick began, looking down through his glasses at his notes, then over them at all those assembled for the sake of his wayward daughter, or more, for the sake of her abandoned parents. "Your support for myself, my wife and Cathy is everything I'd expect of Seaton Grove, though I'm sorry that it has to be proven under these circumstances. I hope to God that nobody here ever has to go through what we have in the last week. But with the help of our family and community we will go on.

"We are here to commemorate a life that was all too short. Heather was born sixteen years ago. My first little girl, the apple of my eye. Like any father I hoped for great things from my child. But let's speak plainly because only plain speaking will prevent such a tragedy from happening again. Heather's bright future darkened as she became a troubled child and then a teen at risk. That's the term the psychiatrist used—'at risk.' If only I had known what the risk was. When my daughter came home pregnant, I thought we'd reached the bottom. The worst had happened . . ." His voice broke. Neighbours wept, stifling sobs in tissues.

"Because of my wife's courage, we have another baby in our family," Rick said. "Life goes on. We can't bring Heather back. We can only learn from this and draw strength from each other. That's why I would like to start the Committee for Youth to provide programming and guidance for teens."

He paused, waiting for this to sink in. Neighbours nodded, whispered, wiped their eyes, a few tentatively clapped. Rick held up a hand, staying their response. "My friends, terrible things happen here in Seaton Grove, too. And if a single family can be saved because of my daughter's death . . ." The clapping began again, uncertainly; nobody was sure if it was appropriate. But more joined in, then everyone was clapping, the friends and neighbours who had come from the streets all around making a thunder of their hands to ward off despair.

Callisto's eyes remained dry as she considered the nature of fathers and what they required of their children: beauty, cleverness, stamina. It was warm in the gym. She folded her program into a fan, thinking over Rick's words, neither adding to nor subtracting from them. What he had said: he hoped for great things from Heather. What he had not said: he wished great things for her. His black sheep.

"I couldn't do that." Dan spoke into her ear, so she could hear above the clapping. "Not under these circumstances."

"Do what?" She fanned herself.

"Be able to think of anybody but myself and my kids. If one of ours . . ." He paused, looking at her. He knew the subtlety of words, he was a writer of pleas that drew money out of pockets, and he had said "ours," his and hers, the left-handed wife. "I wouldn't be starting any committees, I can tell you that."

Lost in thought or perhaps in a battle with emotion, Rick gripped the podium, eyes on his notes. After a moment he removed his reading glasses and put them in his breast pocket, waiting for the applause to die down. In the first row, Cathy's hands were flat on her knees until she noticed her father looking at her. Then she clapped loudly, slowly, punctiliously. "My other daughter would like to say a few words to you this evening," he said, moving away from the microphone, but staying near the podium.

All the mothers and the fathers, row upon row in their mourning clothes, sat silently, expectantly, while the living child stood to face them. Darkness behind her and darkness in front, her father a frame as she unfolded a piece of paper and flattened it out, her face pale, her hair shining. "Thank you all for coming tonight. If only my sister . . ." she began, then blinked hard, her shoulders hunching. Everyone was watching. Waiting. Her father took a step closer, ready to take over. "I can speak," she said, her voice unexpectedly strong. She was looking at Josh, who'd moved into her seat to be as close to her as he could, his hand raised, thumb up. She continued, ignoring the written speech, ignoring the congregation, talking just to Josh, colour rising in her face as she spoke. "My sister was an amazing artist. She was supposed to go to an art college next year. She was smart, too. A lot of people didn't realize that but she was smart enough to graduate a year early even though she missed a lot of school. She was working on a project when she died. I saw it in the art room at school. It was a sculpture in plaster. She told me that it was a bird woman because if you can fly, you'll always be free. She did the wings, but she never got to the face. I think it was going to be hers. I guess she didn't really believe that she could fly. But if you want to know . . ." She paused as her father's hand landed on her shoulder. He must have squeezed, and she turned her eyes to his.

What he said, nobody else could hear because he put a hand over the microphone. Then he pointed to the paper. Tapped it. Her shoulders slumped.

Looking down at the speech, she began to read tonelessly: "Thank you all for coming tonight. If only my sister could have appreciated how much people cared about her, she might still be with us. But my hope is that the Committee for Youth will prevent other youth from making the same mistakes as my sister. Here is the sign-up sheet." She lifted it, her eyes still lowered, refusing to look at the congregation, no matter how hard her father squeezed her shoulder. "Please leave your e-mail address. If you don't have one, my father will arrange for his assistant to call you. Again, thanks for being here. Please stay for coffee and cake after. Now I'd like to call on Albert Smythe who has kindly offered to lead the service."

Rick stepped down while all eyes were on Mr. Smythe, all except Callisto's. She was watching her son climb over Cathy's chair to return to his own, the way he leaned forward as Cathy sat down, huddled between her parents. Her father spoke to her again; her mother in dark glasses was opening her alligator bag, extracting a pill bottle, removing a pill and depositing it in her daughter's hand. A group of teenagers was filing to the front. They wore black T-shirts with FREEDOM BOYS AND GIRLS CLUB CHOIR in gold letters on them. Mr. Smythe picked up a guitar, plugged into the amp behind the podium, and they began to sing "Candle in the Wind" with the special lyrics written for the occasion.

Goodbye Heather Rose
May you ever live in our hearts
Though we never knew you as we should . . .

When the song finished, Mr. Smythe asked everyone to read aloud the prayer on the program.

The neighbourhood's voice rose, the voice of the village that had existed for a hundred and fifty years, and the voice of the trees before that, of the ice moving back, scraping the earth to leave a ridge for hunters and traders who walked the trail for ten thousand years, of the railroad, of standard time as the city came and leaped over the ridge. It was the voice of light born and reborn in a gym where earlier in the day the last basketball banged against a backboard and was put away, and flowers set in vases to honour death: "May all beings have happiness and the causes of happiness. May all be free from sorrow and the causes of sorrow. May those who are frightened cease to be frightened, may the powerless find power and may people think of befriending one another . . ."

CHAPTER NINE

*T*hree weeks after the memorial service, Sharon woke up in the dark. For a minute she wasn't sure where she was. She closed her eyes, opened them again. There was the TV stand with the TV on it. The pile of cushions on a chair. A pot of yellow mums on the dresser, which matched the flowers in the scroll painting with Chinese calligraphy. She turned to look at the clock: 7:08—was that morning or evening? No sound of water running in the shower. She reached over to turn on the bedside lamp. Beside the clock was a Thermos, a plate of chocolate chip cookies and a note.

> Supper done, Josh in charge of kids. Had to run out
> for some things. Enjoy.
>
> > love,
> > Dan.

She smelled pizza, which meant it was Thursday. Today. She hoped it was today and not some other Thursday. She hadn't lost time, had she? Oh God, she hoped not. She poured coffee from the Thermos. Hot, black, bitter. Drink the coffee. Bite into a cookie. Let time settle around her. Yesterday she volunteered in Emmie's kindergarten class. They made spring flowers out of tissue paper. She had therapy today. She was tired, that was all, her mind on dial-up, images loading ever so slowly.

This morning: the soothing print of water lilies on the wall in Brigitte's office. Sitting in a plush armchair, kitty-corner to the couch, she was facing Brigitte in the recliner with her feet up, furry slippers keeping her feet warm while Sharon talked. She was explaining why the things she remembered just couldn't be true. If Brigitte ever met her parents, she would never believe it. They were good people; everybody said so. Successful, well-spoken, friendly. One of her brothers was a surgeon, the other a dentist; her sister had gone into law like their father. Sharon was the only one who wasn't a success, so didn't that prove it was just her problem?

They had a great legacy: the family name was a variation of Julius, as in Caesar. Her father had told her about the old legends; he'd taught her to dance. When she was little, she'd stood on his feet and he'd danced her around the living room. He listened to Gregorian chants. Her mother collected antique glass and took classes in ballroom dancing. She had taught Sharon to cook, for goodness' sake, swearing by *The New Kate Aitken Cook Book*. Advice to brides: throw Hubbard squash down the steps to break open the rind. Her mother had given Sharon her own copy and had written on the title page: "From Mummy with love." Did that sound like someone who'd lock her kid in the basement?

She stopped talking, waiting for Brigitte to realize that she didn't belong in therapy. She was wasting her time with things dreamed up for some crazy reason. Boredom. Or a need for attention. She needed pills to make it stop, but Brigitte said there were no pills for DID, only for symptoms of trauma like depression or anxiety. If Sharon wished, she would refer her to a psychiatrist. Sharon did not wish. She had taken pills prescribed by her family doctor after Josh was born. When she'd stopped taking them, her appetite and her sex drive had reappeared, and she was able to have two more children. Sharon brushed the basement carpet with her feet, watching the colour change from gold to beige.

Brigitte snapped her recliner forward, the footrest moving into the base. "Where are you now?" she asked.

"I can see her. My mother. It's like she's standing in front of me."

Brigitte leaned forward. Her cheeks were round, her white hair in a bun on the top of her head, her eyes round and bright, a snowy owl's eyes. "What do you see?"

"How she looked when I was little, around Emmie's age. Maybe five? My mother was attractive. Kind of a girl-next-door only grown-up. She got breast implants that year."

Her mother's hair was in a flip, her makeup perfect. She was wearing a turquoise gown, dressed up for the law firm's spring dance. She had elbow length white gloves with lots of buttons. Sharon liked to count them: twenty-one tiny pearl buttons. Her mother was so beautiful, standing there in the doorway to the basement, smelling of Chanel No. 5. She didn't have carrot hair, but browny-red like wood. Auburn. That was what she called it.

"It doesn't make any sense. Why would the basement door be locked?" Sharon said. "I remember being in my nightgown. There's a smell of ginger-ale and something . . ." Her nose wrinkled. "How could that be?"

"What's the last thing you remember before that?"

"Coming home from school the day before a long weekend, and ringing the doorbell." A spindly tree in the front yard, buds on the branches. A bungalow in a row of bungalows. Their front door had rippled glass in it. "I'd had an accident. My tights were wet. Then I'm in my nightgown and I don't understand why I'm coming up the basement steps."

The door had opened and her mother had been standing in the doorway, dressed for the company dance. She'd said, *I have three other children, but you're the one who always makes the mess. It's time you learned to think of other people.* The door had closed. She'd heard her mother bolt the lock. It had been so dark. A darkness you never get in the city.

The dehumidifier clicked as the motor went on. Mould and mildew were forbidden here. So was perfume because Brigitte was allergic to it. There was only a new carpet smell, and behind it the smallest hint of cat pee. When Sharon looked up, she saw sorrow in Brigitte's eyes. Why? It wasn't that bad. Really it wasn't.

"I'd like to ask you something," Brigitte said. "How did you end up in the basement?"

There was a roar inside and after that nothing until a few minutes ago, when Sharon opened her eyes in her own bedroom and turned on the bedside lamp. Another image slowly uploaded, walking the kids home from school. Giving her youngest a piggyback ride. (That wasn't her, but one of the others. A fact that she shunted aside like a mangled boxcar, uncoupling it, moving it to the railroad siding, leaving the main track free and clear for the rest of the freight train.) The point was that somehow the day had passed. Ouch. The coffee scalded the roof of her mouth. She should have waited until it cooled a bit. Emmie's high voice was floating up the stairs, Josh answering in an angry undertone. Sharon put the mug back on the bedside table, swung her feet over the side of the bed, got herself out the bedroom door.

"Leave Mom alone. I'll do it."

"No! I want to show Mommy!"

"She didn't sleep last night." Josh had his sister by the arm, halfway up the staircase. "Don't bug her."

"What's going on?" Sharon asked. Her son's face was worried. He shouldn't be worrying about her. She was the mom.

"I'm sorry," he said, following as Emmie bolted past him to the top of the stairs, sticking out her tongue. "I tried to keep her downstairs." He was barefoot. He always had hot feet.

"Thank you, hon. I'm fine," Sharon said, patting the shoulder of her sockless boy.

"You sure, Mom?"

"Of course I'm sure." She watched his face. It was all there in the eyes, the brows, the corners of the mouth. His chin had been the tiniest bit squared with worry, now soothed by her mom voice, the sock-finder, the shirt-ironer. "Go on," she said. As he headed back to his room, she turned to her youngest. "Now you." Water trickled from red hair onto Sharon's hand. "What's going on?"

"My hair is pink," Emmie said proudly. There were drops of paint on her cheeks and on the stairs.

"Emmie! This is not okay. Not at all. If you can't use paints responsibly, you won't have paints. Now I have to clean up this mess and I'm tired of cleaning up after you. I should just get rid of the paint that's what I should do."

"Even the blue? I didn't use any blue." A tremulous voice. Her mom was a giant. "Mama?"

Heedless of her daughter walking behind her, Sharon stomped down the stairs and along the hallway toward the bathroom, where the paint was stored under the sink. At Josh's room, she paused in the doorway.

He was back to the real world, slumped in the desk chair, computer on, cellphone under his thumbs. There was a smell in the room, a bit of rank sock and a bit of mouldering sandwich. "Did you unpack your lunch bag? Josh? Josh! I am talking to you." He shrugged, his eyes on his phone. Giants were boring. Annoying. If you ignored them, sooner or later they went away.

Stalking past his room, Sharon saw the bathroom door slightly ajar. She pushed it open all the way with a bang against the wall, startling Nina. She was standing beside the sink, her hair as orange as only hair doused with tempera paints can be. "We were playing hair salon," she said loudly, turning to her mom. But one index finger was hooked over the other, all of her fear locked into them.

Emmie slipped a cold hand into her mother's. "Not the blue paint," she said. "Don't throw out the blue, Mama."

Her children were scared. She was making them scared. Sharon's outrage collapsed and she sat on the side of the tub. "You'll have to have a bath." The girls looked at each other—no yelling, no consequences?

"Yes, yes," Emmie said.

"Mom?" Nina asked. The flame of fear was doused. Her eyes gleamed. "After could I have some gummies?"

"No way!" Sharon said.

While the bath was running and the girls were in the tub, she got the mop from downstairs, a WetJet that her mother-in-law insisted was the best. As Sharon pushed it along the second floor hallway, weightless and swishless and requiring her to buy the disposable pads, which she always forgot, her mind idled around mops and floors, thinking to itself, the phone is going to ring. Bet you it's her.

A minute later, Josh was calling, "Mom!"

She took the phone from him and, cradling it between her ear and shoulder, she turned off the water in the bathroom. The African violets were blooming purple and pink in the south window. "Hi," she said.

"Hi Sharon." It was her mother-in-law. "We have dinner on Sunday."

"Yes. Of course."

"Who is it, Mommy?" Nina asked.

Sharon covered the mouthpiece with her hand. "Nai-Nai. I'll be done in a minute."

"Is anyone else coming?" Mimi asked.

"The usual."

"Sunday is just for family," her mother-in-law said.

"And friends," Sharon replied. Lately Cathy had been joining them for Sunday dinner.

"Nice friends."

"Cathy's nice."

"Her family is no good. You know what happened to them."

"Mimi, it isn't their fault. Her sister was depressed."

"Mental illness runs in families. No good. You have to guide your son."

"Okay, see you Sunday. I've got to go. The girls are having a bath."

Sharon never argued with her mother-in-law. She put the phone down on the counter between the two sinks and knelt beside the tub. Orange hair was shampooed and rinsed, then the pink. Nina came out first, Sharon holding out the big blue towel. Wrap and hug. Then she snuggled her younger daughter, who shivered in her towel while Nina made faces in the mirror, flaring her nostrils, wiggling her ears. "Can you do this, Mom? Can you? Try, Mommy."

Dan came home around nine with a new office chair, a two-drawer filing cabinet to hold the company bills, and a surprise from Amy's Animal Clinic. In the dining room, Sharon was knitting while the girls made a city out of milk cartons. The hoodie she was knitting started out simply enough: largish needles, cast on thirty-seven for her niece's narrow chest, knit one, pearl one for a while to make the ribbed edge of the sweater. A soft yarn, her niece's favourite colours, mix of blue, green. Click, click, click. The sound of peace, hands in their quick and familiar motions. A tight ball of yarn, unravelling as a long and lanky string, ravelling up into a solid piece of colour and shape and beauty. Lots of things start out simply. She looked up as Dan came in, carrying something wrapped in a towel. The surprise mewed, and Dan smiled at the childish expression on his wife's face as a dark nose poked out. Her hand, their hand, gently stroked the kitten. Inside, the lils were saying *wow wow wow. can we call him franky? don't be scared, franky.*

On Sunday Dan's parents arrived at exactly six o'clock. Mimi made sure of that. Her Chinese name was Xiao Mei, Little Plum Blossom, but she had been Mimi for fifty years and there was nothing blossom-like in her five feet of muscular intensity. She'd immigrated on her own, arriving in a strange country where she didn't know the language, not even within the Chinese community, which spoke a different dialect. She'd met Jake, married him, and then she had made her husband the man he'd been, convincing him to go into business for himself, six days a week selling odds and ends and cigars to the reporters who worked near his shop at the *Evening Telegram*. They'd moved out to the suburbs, where her children had had a big backyard and a swimming pool. When Eleanor grew up, she'd moved back to the old neighbourhood as if all that hard work had meant nothing, and then managed to persuade Dan to move there, too. It was an insult to Mimi's intentions and here was another: she had made Jake, but the universe had remade him. His mind was declining, he was frail and he smiled lovingly at his grandchildren with no notion that he'd ever cared whether his son got 90 or 99 percent, and he spouted nonsense. Things like, "So if God is everything, do you poop God in the toilet? I think yes."

Sharon was in the dining room, running Nina's new jeans under the sewing machine to take them in. She'd intended to tidy up, change her clothes, do something with her hair, but she was still in jeans, a tank-top and a hoodie that she could zip and unzip as the others inside came closer and pulled away, making her hot and cold.

"Nai-Nai!" the girls were yelling as they ran down the stairs to get the door. "Zaidey!"

Mimi appeared in the doorway. "If you put things away," she said, "you could eat in the dining room instead of the kitchen. Still using my old table?" Mimi asked this as if she wasn't there every Sunday to see that they did. "You need some lipstick by the way."

"Hi Mimi," Sharon said, getting up and coming over to her mother-in-law, bending down to kiss her cheek, which was still soft. Mimi didn't have any old lady bristles. She wouldn't allow it. "We set up the folding table for the kids. It'll be more comfortable that way."

"How many kids?" Mimi asked. Her hair was short, not yet completely grey even though she was seventy, her glasses square, her jacket red, her wool slacks navy.

"Oh, I guess, let's see now. Five?"

"The girl is here?"

"Her name is Cathy."

She was up in Josh's room with him. He was playing the guitar, singing to her. When Sharon checked on them, pushing the door that they'd left open just a crack, they jerked apart, their eyes glazed, cheeks hot.

"I told you. Weak brains you don't want in the family. You have to guide your son. Make sure he has good friends."

"Uh huh." Sharon didn't bother to point out that the kids were only fourteen—a long way from getting married. She followed her mother-in-law to the kitchen as Mimi continued her lecture. Dan was coming more slowly, supporting his father by the arm. Nina had hold of her zaidey's other hand, her face solemn with the responsibility of getting him to his chair. After he sat down, he patted her head and gave her a candy, not because he still knew that children like candy, but generously sharing his own secret stash, his wife having banned sugar from his diet.

"Okay. Girls. I check your feet," Mimi said.

"Me first!" Nina sat on one of the chairs, sticking out her feet. Her grandmother squatted in front of her, balancing easily on her heels as she pulled off Nina's shoes and lacy socks, feeling her feet.

"Excellent feet," she pronounced, and Nina smiled. "My grandmother's feet were bound and my father had to carry her when we were running away from the war. But you have strong feet. Never depend on anyone to carry you."

"Me! Me!" Emmie said. Her curly hair was done up in six small ponytails all around her head.

"Let me see. Excellent feet. You wash every day? Good girl. Now you get cakes," Mimi said, giving them a bag of Chinese buns. "Where's Eleanor? She's late."

"It's not late. Girls—set the tables. That's your job, remember?"

"Ten after six. It's late."

"I'm sure she'll be here any minute. Josh!" Sharon called up the stairs as the bell rang. "See? Just stay there. I'll get the door."

While the younger girls set the kitchen table and the folding table, Sharon ushered in her sister-in-law's family. Bram lowered himself gingerly into the chair with the ObusForme tied onto it. Eleanor ran her hand through her big brother's hair in greeting, just the way he hated it and had ever since they were kids. Judy showed Nai-Nai her brand new running shoes, and made kissy noises at Josh and Cathy when they came into the kitchen. Ignoring his guest for the moment, Mimi checked out her grandson, scolded him for going barefoot, and slipped some money into his pocket.

"Thanks for finding my keychain, Mrs. Lewis," Cathy said. "My flash drive was on it. I'd have died if I lost it." She looked like a different child than the one who'd spoken at the memorial, her face no longer wan, her posture confident. But she was still jittery, easily startled, and Sharon didn't want her mother-in-law making comments.

"I doubt that. Get the folding chairs, Josh."

"I want to see if supper's any good first." He stuck a spoon into one of the pots.

"Listen to your mother. You have lucky ears but this isn't China," Mimi said sharply. She turned to his girlfriend, but Sharon was already settling her at the kids' table, the little girls fighting over who got to sit next to her.

Finally everyone was seated, the adults at the blue table, the kids at the folding table, made presentable by a floor-length tablecloth. Outside in the yard, darkness had not yet descended and evening light touched the floor, making it shine under their feet as Sharon took the chair closest to the kids, facing the outside. Dan sat opposite, undisturbed by having his back to a door, having no thought of anyone coming through it unasked. He'd just showered, and his hair stood on end as it dried. He wore jeans, of course, as he was at home, and a cotton shirt, perfectly pressed, smelling of fabric softener. This was what he loved about his wife: that she made his life smell good, that she brought his people into the house.

Dan's parents were on one side, his sister and her husband on the other. Bram shifted in his seat, trying to make himself comfortable with the ObusForme. He liked wiring. You started at one end and you traced the wire wherever it went, no matter how torturous the path, until its end. If it wasn't up to code you pulled it out and replaced it. People were dismayed when he gave them the bad news. Illegal patching through knob and tube. Faked grounding. Even worse—aluminum. Hidden behind the walls, a waiting fire. So he never showed that it excited him to remove the thin crackling wire from its twisted path and construct something strong and sound, a clear and logical network for electricity to safely travel, its power channelled, harnessed. In his private imaginings it was a wild horse and he was the horse whisperer.

Dinner was meatless as Mimi was doing battle with the universe. Organic vegetables, beans, tofu, rice and Chinese herbs were going to fix her husband's brain. Only warm foods, nothing cold because he had too much yin, the dark dank feminine principle. In a more superstitious time, she might have suspected a fox spirit of sucking out his male vitality. She might have prayed to the goddess of mercy.

"Do you have enough room there, Dad?" Dan asked.

"Everything's good," Jake said, eating slowly. He was nearly eighty, his belly gone, his hair wispy and white, his eyes watery, the colour faded.

"Your back out again, Bram?" Mimi asked as if he threw his back out every week.

"Yeah. Again." Bram came from a small town back east, where his family owned McMurray's Diner. The town was built beside a marsh, which gave off a sour air that hovered over everything, and all the regulars at the diner ate with sour faces as if they could never get rid of the smell. Men in his hometown spent their wages on nice cars, they didn't fix up houses. Bram had grown up being teased and beaten by his brothers to cure him of being fey. Compared to them, his in-laws were harmless, and he was usually good-natured about these family dinners. But tonight his back hurt, and he hadn't been able to play handball with Dan that weekend. His face soured as if he was breathing the marshy air of his hometown. "I think this is the worst time. Don't say anything, Eleanor."

"Like for instance that you had to carry the old air conditioner yourself?" They preferred fighting with each other to anyone else, making up as vigorously except when his back was out. "It's been sitting in the garage for years. I told you I'd hire someone."

"Eleanor, with you—something new?" Mimi asked. "Maybe you go back to school?" Eleanor stared back at her mother. Bram grimaced. Even with the ObusForme he couldn't sit long.

"Look Mimi," Bram said. "Let it go. It's been twenty years since she quit school. And Sharon went to a lot of trouble to make this f—" (his wife's elbow) "fantastic vegetarian meal. So if you don't mind, I'd like to just eat it and go lie down."

"Hmmph." Mimi's eyes moved past her intractable son-in-law toward the kids' table. They were chattering, digging into mac and cheese, Judy having rice. She had given up on making kissing noises, and instead was asking Cathy about makeup. Sharon glanced over her shoulder at the girls, who were raptly attentive, as, with an imaginary brush, Cathy demonstrated the correct way to apply powder. She looked back at her mother-in-law, certain that Mimi was about to say something she shouldn't.

"Mental illness—" Mimi began

"How's the tofu teriyaki?" Sharon asked.

"You bought it, didn't you?"

"Yes. But it's just the same as if I marinated it in teriyaki sauce. All the vegetables are organic and I didn't use canned beans in the salad." Mimi believed that metal was toxic for Jake.

"You should make the sauce yourself. How do you know what's in it?"

"I can take the package out of the garbage and show you."

"No, don't bother." She dumped his teriyaki into her bowl, and served him bean salad over rice instead. She approved of rice, heaping bowls of it. "You aren't having any rice, Eleanor?" she asked.

"I'm on a diet."

"Even the best wife can't make miracles out of a pantry without rice. What kind of rice cooker is that?" she asked, staring at the microwave rice cooker on the counter. "It's so small."

"I got it for them. It's just the right size," Eleanor said. She turned toward her husband, arguing with him in a whisper. He replied in a testy undertone. Their eyes locked. Even with his bad back, they would manage to make up later. There were ways. Through the wall they could hear the teenage son next door playing the saxophone.

Mimi peered over at the kids, pushing up her square glasses to see better. "The girls look very nice today. You, too, Judy. Even with running shoes, you have a nice sweater. Your Auntie Sharon picked a good colour and a good style to make for you. Put the hood back so everyone can see your face." Judy screwed up her nose, but obeyed. She took after her father, wiry, unmusical, allergic to wheat. "There is nothing wrong with looking nice," Mimi went on. "Josh's friend knows how to dress. Very dainty. Did someone make your sweater, Cathy?"

"No, Mrs. Lewis." A polite tone, a polite smile. "My mother bought it." The sweater was pale pink, with a knit collar and three glitzy buttons. Her jeans had the same buttons on the fly and the pockets. "She buys all my clothes. My closet is stuffed."

"Lucky girl."

"I hate my clothes. I wanted Heather's, but they got rid of everything."

Looking over her shoulder, Sharon saw Cathy stiffen. The little girls were pinching each other. *Mommy! She hurt me! Mommy, she started it!* And then Judy, whose interest in makeup was new and unsure, having spent a good chunk of her childhood learning how to use her father's tools, waved her hand in front of her face and drawled, "Who cut the cheese?"

Their grandpa was sniffing the air. "I farted," he said, and added with wonder, "It was a silent one, but it stinks more than the noisy ones." Everyone stopped talking. He looked surprised by that and pleased. "Someone else's farts always smell worse than your own," he said, since they were interested. "Why is that?"

"Zaidey!" Judy said.

"God makes all the farts. Why should anybody's stink worse?"

"Some people's don't stink at all," Cathy mumbled.

"My wife's do," Jake beamed. "I love you. And you. And you. And you." He pointed to each of his grandchildren, to Cathy, to his children and their spouses, to the floor, to the glass doors, to the tofu that his wife had disdained. He moved his gaze and blessed his wife with an impish smile. "And you most of all. Even your loud farts. Why shouldn't I? God brought you to me. All the way from China." He smiled at Cathy. "You only had to come from around the corner." For a moment Mimi suspected he hadn't lost any marbles at all and in her gratitude left well enough alone.

After dishes were cleared, the kids decided to arm-wrestle.

Emmie watched while Nina took on Judy, and Josh wrestled Cathy, whose blonde hair fell over her face, the part no longer ruler straight. Her back was bowed as she leaned into her arm, other hand pressed against the table, trying not to slip on the tablecloth. She put her all into it, for one contest was all contests, and Josh was equally in earnest, his hand clasping hers, bare feet flat on the floor. When he won she swore, and Sharon nearly laughed to hear the expletive burst from those perfectly glossed lips. Cathy called for a rematch, but Josh just laughed at her.

The sun had set and the sliding glass doors were a mirror now, reflecting her family, the one she had married into and made. At the sink, her mother-in-law was singing a popular song from her childhood: *wo yao hui jia, Shanghai is scary, I want to go home, Mama*. The kitten crept out of his hiding place between the fridge and the washing machine to slurp his supper. The kitchen smelled of soy sauce, vinegar, cinnamon and baking apples, lemony dish soap, and all of it, each separate smell, even the sulphuric odour that had emanated from Jake, was the smell of love. And if it wouldn't have seemed absurd, Sharon might have cried, because, inside, there was such longing to have had a family like this.

INSIDE

"Forget it, Ally."
　　"Why?"
　　"You know why."

"I'm not scary." She stamped her foot.

"Lils aren't allowed out." Alec had her by the arm, pulling her back.

"Oh come on," Lyssa said. "Nobody has to know. Let her have some ice cream. She won't talk."

"I won't," Ally said. "Promise!"

Her teddy bear wanted ice cream. Two kinds. With chocolate sauce on it. And marshmallows. And sprinkles. And cherries. But no nuts. Oh, and caramel sauce. And cookie pieces. And M&M's. And gummies. And Nerds.

Cathy was putting two huge scoops on her cone. Joshy said she couldn't eat it all and she was saying you bet, just watch and she made her mouth big, taking big bites. Ally liked that girl. The daughters ate their ice cream slow. Jake sneaked some when Mimi wasn't looking and she said, Jake! Everyone sat together at the blue table. The little girls on laps and big kids squished in. Danny licked his ice cream fast like a cat. He made Ally laugh and the laugh comed out of the mouth and Sharon went to wash a dish in the sink.

"Later," Alec said. "When there's no one around."

"Hey," Lyssa said. "Don't look so sad. You've got Echo and the other lils and all of us. Singletons don't have anybody. They're all alone inside."

They pushed her away and she slid down to the playroom. Some of the lils were playing in a tent, and others with the castle and someone was swinging but Echo was sitting on the teeter-totter, waiting for her. A wall was pink, a wall was blue, a wall was yellow and a wall was green. If she wanted paints, she could have paints, and with her fingers polka dot the walls and nobody would get mad because it was inside and it was their room. "I don't want to play," she said. But she did. With real playdough squished in her fingers. She could make a turtle. She could make a hat. She could put the hat on the turtle. Outside.

"You don't like me anymore," Echo said.

"I do so." She got on the teeter-totter.

"Why are you mad?"

"I'm not." She made the teeter-totter bump hard.

She liked to go everywhere with Echo. Except sometimes. If she was let outside with her outside people that she loved. She'd do that. Nina, Emmie, Joshy, Danny, Jake and Mimi. Her peoples. But she wasn't let. She wasn't supposed to be alive.

CHAPTER

ELEVEN

*M*agee's Family Restaurant, established 1931, had previously been the lunchroom for women workers at the Ford Motor Company on Hammond Street, where they'd eaten opposite the showroom with its potted trees and chandeliers and the latest Model Ts. Later the building had been taken over by Planters' Peanuts. On the main floor, newsmen from the *Evening Telegram* had eaten lunch at Magee's and bought cigars from Jake. Now where his shop had been, smartphones were sold. Debra Dawson's pediatric practice was on the second floor, Dan's office on the fifth. But the exterior of the building was the same, with its great arched windows and oxidized copper, built when machines and factories were made beautiful to celebrate the glories of industry.

"Do you think Dad misses the store?" Eleanor asked. It was the second Tuesday of the month, breakfast club at Magee's, and she'd got her sister-in-law to agree to come by running with her first.

"Maybe," Lyssa said. "I bet a part of him still remembers."

She'd dressed in leggings and leg warmers to run, an under-shirt, sweater, sweatband, clothes she'd dug out of drawers that held nothing pretty. She yanked off the sweatband, pushed back her hair. "Let's get a seat. I'm starving."

Four tables were pushed together for the breakfast club. Some of the women were dressed for the office, others in moms' going-out attire: makeup, earrings, the sexy top (so called because it actually fit and had no stains on it). The menu used to be on paper placemats, but was now in a book of laminated sheets with a red and gold cover. The walls were still covered with autographed pictures of famous hockey players and actors in cheap frames.

"Who's next?" Harold Magee was asking, a gnomish man with a knobby nose and a fringe of grey hair. Only the lower part of his mouth moved when he spoke. He always took the orders himself for breakfast club.

Lyssa plunked herself in the chair that Ana—in a blue sari today—pulled out for her. In her sari and heavy gold jewellery, thick hair in a long braid, her smile modest, Ana looked deceptively traditional. But she was a chemist, and her best friend was Laura Anderson because she loved Ana's baby. Taking the empty chair that was opposite Lyssa's and beside Debra Dawson, Eleanor sat down to study the "Healthy Choices" section of the menu.

Debra was wearing more makeup than usual, but she was managing to keep up with her routine. Her suit was fitted at the waist. On its lapel, she had a silver and gold pin, the silver hand-beaten so nobody could mistake it for base metal. She never missed breakfast club with the moms, not even after her daughter's death. That was the kind of person she was. Everyone said so. She lived here in Seaton Grove even though she could afford a bigger house just south of the original village.

Lyssa picked up a bun from the breadbasket, spreading it thickly with butter, ignoring the chat all around her.

I can't decide what to have. What are you having? A cheese omelette, egg whites only. How's your mom doing? Better thanks. Did you hear that someone bought those two boarded-up cottages near the school? It's about time they were torn down. Where are you putting your kids this summer? I'm not sure about the others, but Rupert will go back to the boys and girls club. He's used to it.

This last was Sofia speaking, the homeschooling mom. Her youngest kid was autistic. She wore the coolest retro cat's eye glasses. That was what Lyssa would get if she wore glasses. She liked Sofia's jacket, too. It was black with green lining and flared sleeves with green silk-covered buttons along a slit at the cuff.

"Your jacket is cool. Where'd you get it?" she asked as her eggs and fries arrived.

"Chinatown. You aren't going to eat that, are you?"

"Why not?" Lyssa dipped a fry in the yolk.

"It's loaded with cholesterol."

"Is it?" Like she fucking cared. Eleanor had ordered fruit salad and was digging through it for something that didn't taste like cardboard.

"You'll give yourself a heart attack. You have to start thinking of these things when you get to a certain age." Sofia appealed to Debra. "You're a doctor. Talk to her. She's killing herself." The chatter stopped. The women looked at each other or down at their plates or anywhere that wasn't Sofia, who gasped, "Oh. I am so sorry."

"It's all right," Debra said graciously.

Coffee cups clattered, forks clinked on plates. Nobody knew how to get over the hump of awkwardness, and so they said nothing until Eleanor finally asked, "How's the baby?"

"Doing well." Debra's lips were imprinted on the rim of her coffee cup; she was wearing lipstick too dark for her fair skin. "The nurse will stay until I can finalize arrangements for my practice and then I'll take a mat leave." Debra smiled and the other women smiled back gratefully as they slid into quiet talk, murmuring about their own children, how a cough in the kids' rooms woke them instantly and they'd sit up until they heard steady breathing again, how they'd secretly walk behind their children their first time going to school alone, how bicycles terrified them, and cars. Now it was Debra's turn for silence, staining the rim of the coffee cup as she drank. The west wind sheared through the parking lot, picking up loose bags and paper, ramming the branches of trees and the sky, clearing off the clouds.

Eleanor reached to pick a french fry off Lyssa's plate. "Did you tell Debra about the sweater?"

"What?"

"The sweater." As Lyssa continued to look blank, Eleanor added, "The green sweater. That you made for Heather."

"Really," Debra said, no exclamation mark in her voice, only civility. A lady, even a lady doctor, was always polite.

"She worked on it a long time. It's beautiful. Different."
Eleanor picked up another french fry.

"Is that so?" Debra probably hadn't had a french fry in
years. Maybe never.

"She worked a pattern of flowers and leaves just by
changing the stitches."

"I'm sure somebody would appreciate that. I've got a
bag for Goodwill and I could add the sweater."

"That really wasn't . . ." Eleanor's face reddened, but she
kicked her sister-in-law under the table, warning her to stay
out of this. "I thought maybe Cathy would like to have it."

"Of course I should repay you for the materials." Debra
touched a napkin to her lips. "How much was it?"

"The angora wool? A hundred I think," Eleanor replied.

"Fine. I was planning to head up to Goodwill after work.
Let's see." She tapped her BlackBerry. "My first patient isn't
until nine thirty. I could come over right now. Never put off
until tomorrow what you can do today."

While she went to the cash register to pay, Lyssa leaned
forward to hiss at Eleanor. "I don't want any money for it!"

"Don't be an idiot," Eleanor whispered back. "It's not
like it was ever worn. At least get your materials cost."

Lyssa didn't want anything to do with it, but okay. Whatever. She took a twenty out of her pocket and left it on
the table. She liked the high wind and wanted to walk, but
Debra insisted on driving them home in her Lexus hybrid.
Naturally she found a parking spot right across from the
house with the peaked roof like a witch's hat and vines
growing up the front.

"So this is the famous dining room," Debra said. The window faced south, an arm's length from the house next door. The dining room was crammed from end to end, a mishmash of things. No pictures on the wall. Lyssa would have liked pictures. That was the problem with being out in the world. You started wanting to make it yours.

"Famous how?" she asked, scratching an itchy bump on her shoulder. She was standing barefoot on a chair, working her way through the oak cabinet from the top shelf down. Sharon might know where everything was, but she wasn't close and Lyssa had no idea how to find the toad-sucking sweater. She wanted to go back inside, but nobody else was coming.

"Cathy's always going on about your house. She's fascinated by the mess in here." Debra sat on the edge of a chair as if she'd catch some germs if she leaned back, one leg crossed over the other, elegant in dark stockings and ankle boots. Her skirt was short and it didn't look dumb on her. How lucky was that? "My daughter thinks it's wonderful to have a dining room that is never used for eating." Debra was multi-tasking, replying to her e-mail and text messages.

"I'm sure if Cathy's interested, Sharon could teach her to knit." Eleanor bent to pick up another bag from the floor, looking for a place to put it, then plopped it on the table beside the sewing machine.

Debra glanced up from her e-mail. "I wish I had time for a hobby. It's hard enough to keep up with medical journals.

I expect that it'll be better when I'm on leave from the practice and I'm just a mom for a while. It must be nice having nothing to do. I only took a couple of months off with each of my daughters. I had to have a nanny . . ." Under her makeup, Debra's forehead wrinkled. "I took Heather to a top psychiatrist. Last night I found her pills stuffed into a crack along her windowsill." The storm of words suddenly stopped as she stared at Eleanor, an ordinary mom in velveteen sweats the colour of plums, straight dark hair cut to chin length, conscious of her double chin, uncomfortable with those eyes boring into her. "Where was I?"

"You're looking forward to some time at home." Eleanor pulled down her sweatshirt so that when she bent forward to pick up something, no skin would show, no rolls of fat.

"We were talking about renovating after our last tenant left. At least the kitchen. Then you can be picky about who rents from you." Debra opened her leather bag, eyes lowered as she dug through its many compartments for her chequebook. She looked up again, gazing at Eleanor with incredulity. "How did you ever convince me?"

Lyssa looked harder for the sweater now. Inside a box, she found several skeins of sparkly yarn, a jar of peculiar buttons.

"It was just supposed to be temporary. Until Ingrid and Amy were able to buy." Eleanor busied herself moving the sewing machine to clear a space on the table. It was a forty-year-old Kenmore, all metal and heavy enough to make a *thunk* on the sideboard as she put it down, covering up the clink of something that fell unremarked from Debra's bag.

"Why do people feel they have to mind everyone else's

business?" Debra asked. Her civility was fraying here in close quarters.

"Hey," Lyssa said. "I found it."

"Terrific." Snapping her bag shut, Debra put her cheque-book on the table, opened it, and filled out a cheque, writing with a swift efficient hand. "Here you are." Her shoulder turned slightly to shut out Eleanor, the busybody mom and her hundred tasteless knick-knacks.

"Thanks." Lyssa folded the cheque, stuck it in the money jar, shoved it out of sight.

"Not at all. I should be thanking you for taking care of my daughter. We'll have to have you over soon. I'll call."

"Sure, okay," Lyssa said.

"Brilliant." Debra slung her bag over her shoulder, and turned on her heel.

After locking the door behind her, Lyssa returned to the dining room. She had a few choice words to say about Debra, but nothing came out, for the money jar stood empty on the table, the contents upended into the space her sister-in-law had cleared. The dollars sat there in a pile, quivering, wanting to be more than they were. Payment for some baby outfits. For a quilt. Bookkeeping cheques in a neat pile. "What do you think you're doing?" she asked.

"If you cleaned up in here, you'd have a real dining room," Eleanor said.

"Like I care."

"It's a pigsty." Eleanor might be unsuccessful, she was certainly fat, but she was not messy and her mortgage was paid off and if she couldn't say that to Debra, she could make her sister-in-law feel as bad as she did. "This cheque is five months old."

"Bite me." But the words didn't come out with the right kind of zip.

"Why didn't you deposit these? There's about two thousand dollars right here."

"I don't know. I'll get around to it." Now would be a good time for someone else to come forward, but she couldn't feel anyone nearby. They were busy or they didn't care, and she was shut out.

"When the cheques are stale-dated? Let's see how much you've got in cash—don't interrupt, I'll lose my count." Eleanor's lips moved. *Forty-five, fifty-five, seventy-five, eighty.* When she was done she wrote something down on a piece of paper. "How much have you paid for yarn and fabric?"

"I don't know," Lyssa said. The pile of money was making her sick. It was too small a pile. That was the point. Too small because she was a dirty, lazy . . .

"You need someone to straighten you out."

"And you think you're the boss of everybody. You're just like your mom."

Eleanor glared. "I'm nothing like her. If I were, you know what I'd say?"

"What?" Lyssa asked though she knew, having found the words online in numerous languages.

Eleanor was peering at her as if she'd finally seen through her sister-in-law's nice front to the trash behind it. She stood up quickly. "Oh, crap. You look awful. Are you sick?" She put out her hand to touch Lyssa's forehead.

"No!" Lyssa jerked away. On the table there was a crumpled twenty and a ten sticking out, a five folded in half and some bills she couldn't identify alongside the piece of paper with its figures that she couldn't read because her eyes were blurring.

Eleanor shoved the money back into the jar, putting it away in the oak cabinet where it had been stashed. "You've got to lie down. Can you make it upstairs?"

Lyssa shook her head. "Couch." She had to get herself together to pick up Emmie from school. She'd promised Emmie a piggyback on the way home. She could make it to the couch without puking if she just kept her mouth shut. It was a short hobble to the living room with Dan's leather chair in a corner, the re-covered wing chair beside it, a vase on the coffee table, the flowery couch. Lyssa flopped down and stared at the ceiling while Eleanor disappeared into the kitchen. A whistle, the kettle boiling.

"Ginger tea. Sit up," Eleanor said, handing a mug to Lyssa.

"Thanks." Gingery steam curled up from the cup. She blew on it and drank. Her stomach settled, her palms no longer clammy.

Sitting beside her, Eleanor cupped her mug, eyes lowered, her voice contrite. "If I hadn't stuck my nose in . . . Every time I see Debra or any of them, I think it's my fault."

"Shut up. Listen," Lyssa paused, gathering information. "If it wasn't a gun it would have been something else and the baby might have died, too. That's what Debra said herself."

"She did?"

"Yup. She was just being a pighead." She tried to grin.

"I guess Debra's entitled for a while."

Above Hammond Street, a train whistled like an echo to the kettle. If Lyssa had a camera, she would walk along the train tracks looking for every lovely thing she could see through the viewfinder. Nesting birds, wildflowers in spring, geese returning north. And her feet would run across clouds to the northern lights where she'd dance with the solar wind. But she didn't have a camera nor anything except a body that was, for the moment, hers.

"Hey, Ellie, we should go to Hammond House soon. How long has it been since you went dancing?"

"I'll go dancing if you come shooting with me and Ingrid." The light had come back into Eleanor's eyes, dimples flashing in her plump cheeks.

"You've got to be kidding. After what happened?"

"Yes, because of that," Eleanor said. "Ingrid's a good friend. I want to show some faith in her."

As Eleanor spoke, Lyssa could feel Alec move in behind her. *So now you show up,* she said inside. *It took a while,* he said; *I don't know why, it just did. Oh sure,* she said, wanting to stay mad. But on the outside Eleanor was talking about taking her shopping for new clothes, and on the inside Alec stayed close even though he rolled his eyes.

In the dining room, a thin grey rectangle lay on the floor, unnoticed beneath the table.

CHAPTER

TWELVE

*T*he set-up of the Garrison Shooting Club hadn't changed in sixty years. There were wooden dividers, gun rests, metal poles with paper targets—bull's eyes only, no human figures. One of these days the club, down at heel, would have to close, much to the satisfaction of most of Seaton Grove. But that day hadn't yet come. In the meantime the average age of membership was seventy-two, having come down from seventy-seven by the influx of some strays who had ended up in the vicinity, now indulged and cherished by the club, even women like Ingrid, whose sexual orientation was a matter of indifference to these odd old men who stubbornly clung to their club. The only compromise with modernity was a loudspeaker to amplify the whispery voice of the shooter in charge.

"Hello Ingrid," he said. "Brought your friends?" Vernon was eighty-eight. When he was young, he'd been thin-shouldered and homely. Now he was an old man like other old men, only better, because he still drove his car to the shooting club every day. And it was a good car, reliable, comfortable, without those plastic bits that always broke off in cheaper cars.

"Yes, Vernon. They're my guests."

"Fine, fine," he said, checking that everyone had earplugs as Ingrid unpacked the duffle bag. The shooting club was named for Garrison Creek, which had run south, emptying into the lake near the fort on its shore. Two hundred years ago under the general's orders, the soldiers had chopped down the forest to build the first road up over the ridge. The deforested land had been divided into estates, and the gentlemen of the estates had formed the club. "Nice gun you got there."

"It's accurate," she shouted back. Vernon turned off his hearing aids when he was at the club.

"Yup, that Remington Nylon is a good rifle." Happy to see new people, he handed them each a paper target, black background with white circles in the centre, a lighter background with dark circles on the outside.

Ingrid picked up three metal poles, each of them topped by a square of corrugated cardboard wedged into a notch. While she taped the targets to the cardboard, her friends looked around. Three of the stalls were occupied. There were two old men standing to shoot. One of them had a palsy that made his gun shake while he reloaded it, but not while he was shooting. The owner of the candy-coloured house sat on a stool, his rifle on the gun rest. He was a newcomer to the shooting range, apparently looking for another hobby, for the time being finished with decorating his house. Taking off sunglasses now that they were indoors, Eleanor's sister-in-law noted the exits on either side before casting a glance at the club members.

"You want to go first?" Eleanor asked.

"Naw. Your idea. You go ahead," Alec said. There were eight stalls with gun rests and stools for those who wanted to sit while shooting. Twenty-five yards from each stall was a metal stand that held the target poles.

Vernon was picking up the phone receiver, his voice coming through the loudspeakers as he called, "Shooters, unlatch your guns and move back from the shooting area."

The two old men and the owner of the candy-coloured house waited while Vernon walked up and down with a good firm step, being the man in charge as he checked the range and made sure that all the guns were disabled. Any shots in a wall or ceiling meant immediate dismissal from the club. When it was all clear, he told the men to fetch their targets and the women to put up theirs. Then Vernon walked through again, even though anyone could see that all the shooters were at their stalls. But there was a way to do things, and walking through was one of them.

"Commence shooting," he announced.

Ingrid loaded the rifle for Eleanor, showing her how to keep her finger away from the trigger, look through the sight and pull when she was ready. Once she was set up, Ingrid moved to the next stall, holding her handgun with both hands, long fingers wrapped around it as she looked carefully at the target. Shoot. Kick. Pistol veering up. Shoot, kick. She had a Beretta M9. A good gun if you had big enough hands for it. Hers weren't as steady as they ought to be while she fired. Alec wondered if it was the same gun that Heather had used, and, if it was, whether he could hold it any steadier. At one time, he'd have been sure of that. Now he looked at the gun, picturing a girl with awkwardly small hands, a barrel pressed into her ear. Did the baby hear the shot? Heather had taken no chances with turning herself into a vegetable, using the wall and pillows to support her back, head and arm, making sure she had the gun angled right. That was what he'd heard.

So it wasn't any spur-of-the-moment thing. She'd taken her time. She'd planned it all out. And while she was planning, all she'd have needed was one person to stand between her and the deep shit. Someone to say it don't gotta be game over, kiddo. But she didn't have that one. There couldn't have been because she took herself out and meant to take her baby with her. Those were his thoughts as he stood silently, watching his sister-in-law struggle with the rifle while the sun shone through dusty windows.

When Vernon called, "Stop shooting," Ingrid disabled the guns, then picked up the targets.

"That's not bad," she said to Eleanor. "You got 2.97."

"Out of ten?" Eleanor laughed, her dimples flashing. "And that's not bad?"

"It isn't. You need a three to pass hunter safety, so you're almost there."

Eleanor looked pleased.

"Better than mine today," Ingrid added generously, shaking her head over her target.

"Commence shooting," Vernon called.

Alec balanced the rifle in his hands, butt touching his shoulder. It had been a lot of years since he'd held a gun like this, but his hands remembered, his eyes, too. He leaned his cheek against the stock and looked through the sight, setting the crosshairs on the centre of the target. He breathed in slowly, and when he breathed out, he squeezed the trigger. It wasn't hard or loud. Just a *pfft* and the bullet shot out at the target. He took his time, concentrating on each shot. Nothing else existed but the sight and the target and holding the rifle steady. He ran out of ammo just as Vernon called for everyone to open their guns and he snapped the rifle apart. The shooters stood away from the stalls until Vernon announced that it was clear.

When Alec came back with his target, his sister-in-law said, "I didn't know you could do that," looking at him half bemused, half admiring. The bullet holes were all in the black area, many right in the centre.

"And you never go to a shooting range?" Ingrid asked.

"Never."

"This is tremendous." She was counting the shots, doing some figuring on a piece of paper. "Look at this," she said. "You see all the holes here and here?"

"Yeah."

"You got a 9.69. That's really good."

"Naw."

"Yes it is."

Shit. Alec didn't know what to say.

"We should go hunting. The meat is healthier for your kids. How did you learn to shoot like that?"

"My uncle." His one person, though he was a drunk.

"Which uncle?" Eleanor asked as Ingrid repacked the duffle bag.

"My father's brother. They hated each other."

Uncle Frank was a shame to the family, a criminologist who'd given up on his thriving career. His wife had walked out on him and taken his kids. A survivalist, he drank and had one hell of a temper. Being sent to Uncle Frank's was a punishment to make a kid appreciate home because you had to work till you got blisters and there were no amenities like electricity or indoor plumbing. As per custom, Uncle Frank beat the shit out of his niece on the first night. But when he passed out drunk, Alec beat the shit out of him. Alec was eight. He took a board and smashed Uncle Frank all over. Good thing he wasn't bigger or he might have done serious damage. Alec figured when his uncle woke up he'd get killed. So he hid out in the woods in back of the house for two days. The third day Alec was so hungry, he came sneaking back and the asshole was waiting. Only Uncle Frank didn't touch him. He had a gun. He said that he was going to teach Alec to shoot because if you want to kill someone, beating them up just means they are going to come back for you. Alec said, *Are you sure you wanna do that cuz you might not wake up one morning.* And Uncle Frank said, *Jesus F. Christ, shut your smart mouth and listen good. You are the first one in this family that is worth a fucking nickel. You show me how hard you can work and I'll let you stay for the whole summer.* And Alec said, *Oh yeah? Just so you can get drunk and beat me up again?* Uncle Frank said that he wouldn't drink while they worked the farm. They shook on it. And Uncle Frank kept his word. Six days a week he was sober. On Sundays he drank and Alec hid out in the woods, taking food and water and a poncho in case it rained. It was a good summer. He slept on the porch. He swam in the lake. There were water lilies.

They were walking back along Hammond Street, past the car mechanic, which in a former time had been a coal depot selling egg coal, pea coal, stove coal, nut coal and buckwheat coal. The sun was strong, the wind cool. It was the spring equinox, day balanced evenly with night, the earth momentarily neither leaning toward the sun nor away from it, like the shooting club balanced precariously between existence and non-existence. On the other side of the road, cars were turning into the parking lot of Best Foods on the right and Magee's on the left, the arched windows and copper trim of the old Ford factory shining in the sun. Next to it, the walls of the underpass were painted with sunflowers and the Ford logo.

"I wish I wasn't so busy," Ingrid said. "I'd like to come back to the shooting range. I didn't want to keep the gun that . . . you know . . . so I traded in my Makarov for a Beretta. It's bigger, and I'm not comfortable with it yet."

"Did the cops hassle you about the gun?" Alec asked.

"Not really. They gave it right back after questioning me. It wasn't needed for evidence and I wasn't the one who broke any laws, whatever Debra thinks about it. I thought the old lock on the gun cabinet would do. But it turns out you could slide it open with a credit card."

"Is that how Heather broke in?" Eleanor asked.

"That's what everyone assumes." Ingrid's eyes were dark grey, a clouded sky. "I don't think it was Heather." Delivery trucks and cars drove by. She studied the houses, some dilapidated and others renovated, for it was the nature of time in Seaton Grove to jump ahead and twist back.

"She could have got one of those street kids she hung out with to do it," Eleanor said, and it was only natural she should, for people have worried about strangers ever since their lives depended on being part of a tribe.

"What's the difference?" Ingrid said. "At the end of the day, she used my gun. A sixteen-year-old girl used it and I'll never be able to forget that. I saved a little money on a cheap lock. I've got a new one now. But I should have realized . . ."

As she paused, Eleanor made encouraging sounds and Alec said, "We're cheaper than therapy."

"Okay, it's like this." Ingrid stopped walking, forcing them to stop with her. "Some nights I'm at the observatory and I get home at five or six in the morning. Then when I'm not, my hours are turned around and I work upstairs in the office until I can get to sleep. Heather's bedroom was on the other side of that wall. There were a lot of nights I heard her up, moving things around, and her mother coming in and shouting at her. I couldn't hear words, just the sound of their voices, her mother upset. And Heather speaking very fast or sometimes laughing. At first I thought maybe she was on drugs."

"That would explain some things," Eleanor said.

"No, that's not it. I talked to her and her sister several times and I know what someone on drugs is like. She didn't seem depressed either."

"You can't always tell."

"No, but I had the distinct impression that she was an angry kid, which is also something I know about. I was an angry kid, too. They came over . . ." She hesitated again. "The girls came over to see the guns. I thought their parents knew, but when I mentioned it to Rick that evening, he was pretty choked about it. I heard him talking to her the night she died. Her mother too. And she was quiet. If they'd just had more time."

"I wish I'd talked to her when I had the chance," Alec said. "Maybe it would've made a difference."

"Everybody who knew her is asking themselves if they could have done something to prevent Heather's death," Eleanor said. "But 'ifs' don't get you anywhere. You do what's in your nature to. I'm nosey and you keep things to yourself." Eleanor dug into her sister-in-law's side with her elbow as they waited for the green light. "You can't change that. Like my bubbie used to say—if she had balls she'd be my grandfather."

"You've got more balls than a lot of guys," Alec said. "Most people are assholes." And he meant it, though she laughed, unabashedly shaking with it, cheeks dimpled, eyes nearly shut.

"But not us," she said.

"Of course not us," Ingrid echoed, finally laughing, too.

Their laughter was contagious, even to him, Ingrid swinging her duffle bag and Eleanor in her plus-sized velour and matching scarf. Alec's mirrored sunglasses reflected the street light as it changed, red turning off and green turning on. Behind him Sharon knew that she hadn't remembered the summer with Uncle Frank. She hadn't remembered ever handling a gun. But she could still feel the steadiness of Alec's hands on the rifle and it rattled her. She was appalled; she was proud.

CHAPTER THIRTEEN

*A*fter his mother and father both died in a train derailment, Rick Edwards was raised by his grandparents. His grandfather had been a police officer, his grandmother a piano teacher who had squirrelled away everything she earned so that her grandson could go to college and graduate school. That was their story, one of hard work and achievement, which Rick had recounted to his own children many times. (In fact it was his grandmother's inheritance that had paid for his education, but that was beside the point.) His whole life had been about instilling values—it was why he'd done a Ph.D. in business ethics. The reason he'd founded the Learn About the World program. And now the Committee for Youth. His first marriage had been with a woman who taught English every summer as a volunteer in third world countries. One year she just didn't come back. It was a simple divorce—no kids—and he met Debra Dawson in the simplest way, through friends. When they looked at each other, it was love at first sight, for they saw the mirror image of themselves, male and female, blonde beard and blonde hair, his eyes a paler blue, her eyes darker blue, like water and wet stone.

Debra had wanted a son, but not enough to keep trying after their second daughter was born. There were compensations. A son is a son till he takes a wife, a daughter is a daughter all of her life. Debra had never considered that it might be short or what she might do about that. Her father had been the last doctor to stop doing house calls, her mother had been among the first people to be diagnosed with chronic fatigue syndrome. Debra could have had a fellowship in surgery, but she chose pediatric medicine instead. She had tried the neighbourhood book club and moms' nights and was bored, but stuck with the breakfast club because it was right below her office. She didn't want people to think she was a snob, even though she was, but she didn't mind that people thought she was the boss of her house because she was bossy.

Rick and Debra had invited Dan and Sharon and a few other people for drinks and dessert on the last Saturday of March. The living room was full but not crowded with Rick's cousin Mitch and his wife, Yvonne; Dan and Sharon; the chair of Rick's department, Harry Cooper; and the doctors that shared Debra's practice. Dr. Nash had come on his own. Dr. Kim had brought her boyfriend, who was a judge in a northern township and visited her on weekends.

After everyone had arrived, Rick clinked a spoon against his glass. "Thank you all for coming," he said. "Everyone here has gone beyond the call of duty and I could think of no better way to express our appreciation than to bring you together. A death in the family lets you know who your friends are. And although Debra and I couldn't have hoped for a more supportive community, there are some people who really stepped up. If there's one thing I've learned lately, it's that one shouldn't take anything for granted. So it's my hope that you'll get to know each other a bit better tonight and enjoy the simple pleasures we have on offer."

"Can I give anyone a slice of this delicious-looking cake?" Debra asked.

Sharon had brought a complicated dessert that involved numerous ingredients and liqueur in the chocolate sauce. The house was warm and she took off the sweater she'd thrown over her dress. "Just a drink for me," Sharon said, uncertain if she could balance both a glass and a plate, even the small ones stacked beside the desserts.

"I'll have some," Harry said. His hair was grey, his beard white, and he was still tanned from his vacation down south. It wouldn't be long until he retired, and there was a good chance that Rick would take over as chair when he did.

"Rick, I have to tell you about the new patient I had last week," Mitch said. He didn't look like his cousin, for he was taller, broader, darker, running to fat since he didn't get the workout he had when he was younger, swearing to cut back on office hours so he'd have time for the gym, but he was a psychiatrist and there was a waiting list of people who needed him. "I about jumped out of my chair, he reminded me so much of Grandpa Amos."

His third wife, Yvonne, wearing ropes of gold chain, refilled his glass with red wine. Her surface was lacquered with sprays and patted with powders, her blouse a stiff satin, her skirt an overturned bowl. Her children were all teenagers, diagnosed with ADHD and various other letters, for which prescriptions had been provided. She herself had a fabulous prescription, which didn't prohibit drinking and didn't make her fat. In fact quite the opposite. She had no appetite.

"No way." Rick held out his glass. He was looking dapper, genial.

"He was a police officer, too," Mitch said, taking a plate of cake from Debra. "Retired. He had the same kind of presence as Grandpa. You'd never guess he was ninety-one. You know what he's seeing me for? Sex addiction."

Dr. Nash, bald except for a fringe around his ears, said, "Is there such a thing?"

Rick laughed. "Grandpa was a big man like Mitch here. He had his own way of dealing with criminals and they respected him for it. Seaton Grove was his turf and I'd hazard a guess that after he died, crime jumped by ten percent. He was at the Christie Pits riot."

"Really. My father was too," Dan said, and offered Sharon a taste of his cake.

"When the girls were small, Rick used to tell them that if they didn't behave, Grandpa Amos would make them," Debra said. Her cheeks and nose were rosy as if she wasn't used to drinking. "It worked better than a wooden spoon. Rick?" Her husband was clucking his tongue against the roof of his mouth. It was a small sound, hardly audible, but enough to make her put down her wine glass, a flash of heat spreading from her cheeks to her forehead and chin.

"There were ten thousand people going berserk all

around Christie Pits," he continued, "and just a few police officers. But they imposed the law and there's never been anything like it since."

Debra turned away from the men, busying herself with the ice bucket, which was on one of the little tables that had marvellously slid out of concealed places in the living room. "Ice?" she asked the women.

"No, I'm good." Yvonne shook the gin in her glass.

Dr. Kim (Ruth, Sharon reminded herself, who somehow looked ultra-feminine in jeans) said, "For me please. How's the baby sleeping?"

"Very well. About four hours between feedings at night."

"Still, that must be tiring," Sharon said.

"I hope so. It ought to be. Cathy's the one getting up. She needs to know how much work a baby is." Debra put a hand to her throat, stroking her neck, calming herself until she was in control again. "Let's call it an inoculation. Don't you think it should be in the high school curriculum?"

The women gravitated toward one end of the living room, talking about children, the heels of their shoes leaving tracks in the cream carpet. Debra supplied details: the baby could coo vowels like "ohhh" and "ahhhh." And sometimes she actually said "goo-goo ga-ga." On her tummy she could lift her head or turn it to the side. She preferred the right side. She smiled but not if she was tickled. These were the things that Debra said, always referring to her as "the baby," never "my granddaughter."

They were standing near the bay window at the front of the house and through the sheer curtains Sharon could see the motion detectors turn on, lighting up the yard and the tree with last year's nest in it. So when the bell rang, it was Debra, closest to the door, who went to answer it, her voice easily heard even by the men, distracted from their laughter. "Yes?"

"I've got our notice here." That was Ingrid with her slight western accent. She might have heard the party from the house next door. The living room walls were back to back. The two semis shared a single chimney.

The sound of an envelope ripped open, a paper unfolded. "Two months."

"Yes—according to the lease."

"You have some nerve staying at all." Debra's back was reflected in the hall mirror, her fair hair in a French knot, her neck rigid, tension riding down her back, arching it.

"We have to find another place." The voice strained, apologetic.

Yvonne pressed in close to Sharon, the grains of face powder that had settled in the lines above her lip visible as she whispered, "Debra was amazing after Heather died. The way she took charge. But now that Rick's doing better, she's gone downhill."

"Really," Sharon muttered, taking a step back but there was nowhere to go other than the window seat. She sat and Yvonne bent toward her.

"Mitch says she's having a delayed reaction. He called it something else. I forget what. You know that jargon." Yvonne smiled, showing her gums, then covered her mouth with her hand because her husband didn't think gums were attractive.

"Well, I shouldn't say this, but Debra's coming apart at the seams." Yvonne took a swallow of the gin and tonic. "So if she says something, don't take it personally, okay?"

"Okay." In her mind's eye Sharon saw a jacket with sleeves basted and stapled into shoulders, which were thickly padded. Now why would she think of that? A style that was going out when Heather was born. It must be a metaphor, a symbol of her hostess's state of mind. That was probably what Dr. Mitch would say.

"My husband is on the board of Families Against Guns," Debra was saying. "There is a reason that organization was established. You should have been charged."

"What for? I didn't do anything."

"Aren't there laws about leaving guns lying around?"

"It wasn't lying around. I keep . . ."

"You keep away from my kids. Any kids, that's what."

A pause. Then Ingrid's voice, a bit muffled. "You've got my notice."

"Don't turn your back on me." Debra shut the door and in a moment she reappeared in the living room, throwing the envelope and letter on a table, picking up her plate, smiling tightly.

"The baby was six pounds, three ounces at birth," she said. "But she's in the fiftieth percentile for weight now." She wasn't wearing a jacket, just a V-neck dress, and her neck looked stringy when she turned her head to one side. "That dessert was fabulous. What is it?"

"Three-layer cherry cake. I thought Cathy would like it," Sharon said. "Could I bring her a slice?"

"She's upstairs. Studying." Debra frowned.

"I'll just run up." As she moved to put her glass down, Debra put a hand on her arm. The fingernails were rounded, manicured, faintly coloured.

"Don't bother."

"Pardon?" Out of the corner of her eye, she caught Yvonne mouthing "see" and Sharon steeled herself for unpleasantness.

But Debra let go of her arm and said, "We had an intercom put in. You do enough for her already. I'll call her down. I want you to see the baby."

Cathy came down with the baby in her arms. The baby's face had rounded, her chubby hands waved, her gummy smile was vague and indiscriminate. The women clustered around her, touching the baby's hands with a finger, cooing over her, imitating her: *ooooh, ahhhhh, you're a sweet little girl, yes you are, you smell so good.* The baby's eyes were unfocused, her gaze not following theirs but open, large, taking in the light around objects as much as the objects themselves, for she was still closer to the source of life than the material world.

"This is Madeline," Debra said, taking the baby with ease, holding her in the crook of her arm.

Cathy was dressed to look sweet, too, in pink and white like her niece, lacking only the frilly cap. Sharon smiled at her, but she didn't smile back.

"Can I go now?" Cathy asked, glancing from one parent to the other.

"Wait until your mother's ready," Rick said.

Cathy's hair was mussed as if she'd been sleeping, but her eyes were alert, darting around the room, taking everything in though she stood quite still. There was nothing civil in her smirk. She took a pack of gum from her pocket, unwrapped a wedge and popped it in her mouth. The men were laughing at Mitch's story of a female patient who had a fear of leprechauns. The women were mesmerized in the baby's smile. Cathy chewed her gum loudly, open-mouthed, cracking it, snapping bubbles.

"Catherine." Her father looked over his shoulder at her. "That's rude and I don't appreciate it," he said in a tone that made Sharon start though it wasn't loud. "Get rid of the gum." Cathy spit it into her hand, cupping the chewed-up wad as she straightened up.

If that tone could be patented and sold to parents of teens everywhere, it would make the owner of it rich. A smile plastered itself onto Sharon's face.

"I will have something to say to you later. Now. Kitchen. March." Rick pointed and his daughter marched.

Sharon did what she always did when she was uncomfortable: found something to clean. Picking up discarded plates and a couple of glasses, Sharon followed. In the kitchen Cathy opened the cupboard under the sink and tossed her gum in the trash. Then the girl put her hands on the edge of the sink, her forearms trembling as she stood facing the window.

"What's the matter?" Sharon asked. The kitchen gleamed, it smelled of chlorine cleanser. A pair of yellow rubber gloves were draped over the faucet. Size, small. As Sharon put the dishes in the sink, Cathy stepped back and crossed her arms, hiding her hands, gathering herself in.

"It's just, like . . ." Her voice trailed off, her arms still shaking, though she had them pressed against her chest. "You know." Eyes looking up and to one side as if in the air above Sharon's left shoulder there were words to mollify an adult, some feeble explanation to catch on the hook of her thoughts and reel in, for adults were stupid enough to believe anything was a fish. The shaking stopped. "I've got cramps," she said. "I want to lie down, but I have to wait so I can take the baby when they're done."

"It's all right. You can go. I don't mind bringing her up. I love holding babies."

Cathy hesitated, her blue eyes flicking left and right. "They won't want you upstairs."

"Why not?"

She shrugged. "It's a mess?" The trembling had begun again.

"Is it that bad?" Sharon asked, meaning the mess, as nothing else occurred to her, though if she'd been listening inside something might. For example she could have asked how the gun got into Cathy's house. Or what she was afraid of. Or even why chewing gum could be an act of bravery. But denying the existence of everyone inside was an old habit for Sharon, listening a new one. And so she didn't ask anything more.

"Uh huh," Cathy said

"It can't be worse than my dining room." Sharon watched her son's girlfriend, puzzled. What could be upsetting her so badly? Teenagers! Obnoxious, oblivious, yet pale and sensitive as cave fish.

"It's not fit to be seen." Cathy sounded so much like her mother that Sharon laughed. She was sorry she did because Cathy slipped away, first behind shuttered eyes, and then out to the hallway, where she sat on a stair. She kicked off her shoes. Her socks were white with pink hearts, a hole in the toe, and she picked at it, stretching it, her head bent so that her hair hung down on either side of her face, a golden shade, waiting for her father to say that she could go.

INSIDE

It was the voice that brought the Overseer running up the stairs. The tone was unmistakable. Riveted, he moved as close as he could get to the Outside so he could see who spoke in that way, but people were standing all around Sharon. The voice had been male—to which of those men did it belong? He watched, listening until he heard it again. There—the man who spoke with such authority wasn't tall, but held himself as if he were. People called him Rick; he was the centre of their attention. When he clucked his tongue, his wife blushed. He pointed and his child trembled. He didn't raise his voice; he didn't call notice to them in public. That was the way to do it.

The father used to say that the Mafia and other gangs were sheep in wolves' clothing. They waved their guns around where anyone could see and if they got caught and went to jail, they thought it was something to be proud of, dancing around for the sheep in their wolves' clothes. A man who was master of himself was the master of others and didn't need to do more than look at someone to show his power.

The Overseer had not mewled and puked when the father had beat him. He had counted the stripes in the wallpaper. It was a contest. The father said he would make the child scream. The child counted until the father's arm grew tired. That was how he'd proven his worth, and because of it, the father had taken care not to cut his back with the belt so there would be no scars. Afterward, his father would say, *You're my favourite. I know I can depend on you.*

It had been so long since he'd heard his father's voice. All this time, the Overseer had done his duty, trying to keep the others inside from telling his family's business to strangers. He was stronger than they were. He was bigger. He alone had kept them in line after they'd blocked their family's phone numbers. But he hadn't been able to get them to return home, to see, again, their own flesh and blood. For all his efforts, they spoke to the therapist. One by one they moved farther away from him, until he was the only one who stood between order and chaos.

Worst of all was the Housekeeper, who had banished him to the basement.

"Let me out!" he shouted at the doorway to the kitchen.

"I'm right here. All you have to do is come in," the Housekeeper said.

Not through there. Never. He turned to the left, then the right, trying to move down the hallway past the kitchen, but the Housekeeper was quicker, blocking his way. Nothing made sense. Insiders had become outsiders, the weak took charge, a voice of authority had called him closer, and it was not his father's. But he wouldn't give in. Though his eyes leaked in the burning light that came from the kitchen, he stayed and he pushed.

CHAPTER FOURTEEN

"Who's here now?" the therapist asked. Brigitte was allowed to ask, the only one who was. They had tested her. Sworn at her. Sat silent. Arrived early; arrived late. And no punishment had ensued. If only she could have been their mom! A longing surged forward, with a wish to suck on a thumb. One of the child alters. She was pulled back inside, the wish, the thought dismissed. Impossible. Forbidden.

"I am." Callisto looked around the basement office. It had been over a year since she'd been out in therapy, not since the session with Dan. The carpet was thicker than she remembered. The walls were still turquoise, posters in bright colours except for Monet's water lilies. A hint of lavender, which the therapist put in her vacuum cleaner bag. It was supposed to be calming but Callisto had her doubts about its efficacy. Shells had been added to the serenity fountain. There was now an aquarium with many coloured fish. "That's new."

"I wanted something alive, but a basement is not suitable for plants." Brigitte was leaning back in the recliner, her slippered feet up on the footrest, her white hair in a bun, wearing an embroidered vest and balloon pants. When Callisto had first come forward, she'd thought that Brigitte's kind face must hide cruelty. She had discovered instead that it hid a sharp intellect.

"It's Callisto here. We have a concern about our son's girlfriend." Callisto paused to order the thoughts coming at her from all directions inside. "We believe something is not as it appears."

"How so?"

"Her mother did a Caesarean in the moments after Heather died. We realize that Debra is a doctor but even so that's unfeeling. Heather was always cold—that was why we knitted her the sweater—yet her house was cold when we visited unexpectedly. Cathy was dressed in light clothes, not what she wears when she goes to school, but clothes that show her skin. Also she changes. We don't wish to say she switched. But she changes. And Sharon will not listen. She says Cathy is being a teenager."

The therapist was nodding, making notes. "Go on."

"It's more than mood. Her face, her words, her manners change. She is frightened of her father. At first it seemed like the mother was in charge. She has a sharp tongue, but even she backed down when he looked at her. And another odd thing: she said that threatening the children with words was better than a wooden spoon. A spoon is used for cooking or perhaps she meant a spoon used for beating. Why would she think of this? Why would she say this as if it's something to laugh about? Also this: she told us that she'd sent her daughter to a top psychiatrist. We found out it was the father's cousin."

"He or she might have been the best available."

"He. Perhaps. Or perhaps if their daughter said anything they didn't want her to, the cousin would tell her she was imagining things or lying."

"Did that happen to you?" Brigitte asked, her owl eyes alert.

"Yes."

"Do you think you might be projecting? This is a gruesome tragedy and close to home. It would be understandable for you to be triggered and for your own history to get entangled with the present reality."

"We considered this and it's why we have waited and watched. We don't know what is going on but all of these things together—they feel wrong. And to the Overseer they feel right."

"I see." And Brigitte did.

The change was abrupt. They often closed their eyes when they switched in therapy. Not because they needed to, but for privacy, or while they spoke inside. But on hearing his name, the Overseer had pushed hard. When the Housekeeper had suddenly moved out of his way, he'd been flung forward.

"Who are you?" The voice was harsh, head thrown back, shoulders squared, hands on knees, eyes narrowed and cold, the eyes of war.

"I'm Brigitte. And you are?"

"The Overseer." Without moving, he took in everything that was here. Things with no names, their functions unknown to him. And an unfamiliar smell. From inside came a word: lavender. He did not need that word. He did not need the others' knowledge. This was the world of the weak.

"I've heard the others speak of you. I'm the therapist," Brigitte said calmly. "Do you know what that is?"

He gave the barest nod as he studied her. Watching intently. Listening intently. Wishing for the only world that he knew, where all that mattered took place. His home. Why had the Housekeeper let him out here? "You're the one they speak to. I don't know why."

"It provides relief of pain, anger, fear. Is there something you'd like to tell me? All of you are welcome to speak here."

"They should not interfere in a house of power," the Overseer said urgently. The others listened to this therapist, and she must tell them. "Wolves belong to wolves, not sheep. They should forget Cathy's family. They should tell her not to come to their house anymore, for wolves may eat sheep."

"You sound worried. Do you think they could get in trouble?"

He thought that her face would not be so calm if she could see the danger. "They must stop therapy." He raised his voice so that the loudness of it could penetrate where the meaning of words did not. "Things must be restored to the way they were. They do not obey."

"Rules are important to you," the woman said as if she understood at last.

For a moment he hoped that she would return the others to their proper place inside, return all of them to where they belonged. "Yes." On the outside he was contained, on the inside a furnace. He shifted for a brief moment, allowing his strength to show. She did not flinch or look away.

"I don't know all of your family's rules," she said. "But I do know about families who have those kinds of rules. It's difficult to grow up in such a family."

"It's an honour," he said. "One they have forgotten. People die for less."

"You worry that they might get hurt."

He shook his head no, protesting, for he could not care about the fate of weaklings.

"I would like to ask you something if I may. Would that be all right with you?"

He considered her request. The old woman was respectful and not entirely stupid. "Yes," he said.

"Would you want your children to go through what you did?" she asked.

"No." The word came forth quickly, and once spoken, couldn't be retracted. An image rose before him: a knife, large, sharp, the point on a belly. Then his father's shadow on the floor, and the hiss of a thousand whispering wings.

There were scattered feathers amid pieces of broken glass catching the light. A voice. The father said, *You shall come to me.* And the child walked, naked, across the broken glass.

Father said, *Sit here with me.* The child's feet stuck out over the edge of the couch as they sat side by side, the father a giant, cheeks bristled with what he called a five o'clock shadow. The child wished for his cheeks to have this shadow, too. The wallpaper was striped. The child knew how many stripes there were. He could count all the way to a hundred.

Father said, *The first rule is obey. You're my favourite. I know I can depend on you to do your duty.* At this, his hand rested on the child's head. For a moment, wanted. Beloved. Then the hand withdrew. *The second rule is never talk about our business to strangers. If you do I will know and the punishment will be what you deserve. Remember that there are no second chances. A child is always the father's. Nature is red in tooth and claw. We are wolves.*

The Overseer returned his gaze to this room. Everything was wrong. The objects, the smell. The wrongness tore at him, ripped at him with claws. This was not the place they were meant to be. "The child belongs to the father. We should not interfere with Cathy's family."

"And yours?" Brigitte asked.

"In Sharon's house the children belong to their father. To the sheep."

"They belong to you, too. This life is yours."

He shook his head. If he could not go home, he was nothing. He should be nothing. A spectre haunting a basement. He had been allowed to emerge so that, at last, he'd learn there was no hope for him.

"You have your own house now and you make the rules in it. Look around and see for yourself if what I'm saying is right." But even as she spoke, he was turning back inside, leaving her words in his wake.

"Hi." The voice was high, the face rounder.

"Who's here now?" the lady asked. She didn't sound like bad peoples. She had lots of fishies. They was all shiny colours.

"Ally." One time the lady let her hold the cat. The cat was fat, too. He was soft. She wished the lady would let the cat in.

She wished the lady was her real mommy. "I got Echo with me. He hurts. Can you fix him?"

"Could Echo talk to me?"

Ally tried, but she couldn't get Echo out. "No. He won't come."

"Could Echo talk to you and you tell me what he says?"

"Uh huh."

"Good. Can you tell me where he hurts?"

"Uh uh." Ally couldn't say more. It was starting to hurt her too. It hurt a lot.

"Can you show me?"

She pointed to the feet. Tears ran down her face. "It hurts," she whispered.

"I'm sorry it hurts." The lady's face looked sad. Ally wanted to reach up and touch the face, make it not sad anymore. "Can you tell me how the feet got hurt?"

"Cut," Ally whispered. "All cut. Ugly feet."

The therapist got up out of her chair, slowly so as not to scare them, watching Ally. She sat very still, watching back. *The lady is nice, the lady is nice,* she said to herself and Echo. The therapist kneeled in front of them. A nice fat lady. She looked funny kneeling on the floor. "May I see the feet?"

Ally reached down, pulling off the shoes and the socks. "See?" she asked, lifting the feet so the bottoms showed.

"Can you tell me how they were hurt?"

"Walkin' on glass," Ally said. "The daddy made us."

"He was a bad father," the lady said. Ally breathed out. Daddy was bad. He was.

"And he was friends with bad peoples," Ally said, looking

down at her feet and up at the lady under her eyelids so the lady wouldn't see her eyes in case that made her mad. Children wasn't supposed to look.

"Nobody is allowed to hurt children here," the lady said. Her voice was mad. Was it mad at Ally? Maybe she should run away. But the feet didn't work good. "I don't allow it," the lady said, softer. Ally looked up. She looked through the lady's eyes and inside her head, cuz if there was mad and bad in there she would know. But there was a lady inside the lady, and she was looking through the eyes at Ally and her face was even nicer than the outside face showed, and for sure she would never be friends with bad peoples.

Their eyes closed and opened. Blink blink. She went in but nobody wanted to come out. Eyes closed. Everybody arguing. *You go, no you go. Uh Uh. Not me no. Somebody gotta get out and take us home. Let's push out Sharon!* The eyes opened.

Sharon sat quite still, her eyes on the therapist's print of water lilies at dusk. Upstairs the cat mewed in loud round *ow's*, wanting to be with his person. Or maybe eat the fish in her aquarium. That was the instinct for life, so strong that most people would endure almost any pain to get a little more of it. Did animals ever know that they could end their own pain? Or did they, too, wait it out because they loved their children more?

"I don't understand how Heather could do it," she said. "We were talking about baby clothes and the high chair and next thing you know, she shot herself."

"It does sound like there is more to the situation than meets the eye when you consider everything they said."

"They! There is no 'they'!" Sharon snapped.

"I see that denial is rearing its head, again," Brigitte said. "So can you tell me why your feet hurt so badly when there isn't a mark on them?"

"I'm a bored, crazy housewife imagining crap that nobody could believe." Sharon pulled on her socks. Why ever did she buy yellow socks with duckies on them? She put on her sneakers, tying the laces clumsily with hands that were cold and sweaty.

"This is hard work, Sharon. I'm not surprised that you'd want some distance from it. And that's all right as long as it's temporary." Brigitte eyed the clock. "We're about out of time, but we'll talk more about this next week. If anything comes up, remember you can call."

"Fine." Sharon unsnapped her bag with such venom that everything fell out in a heap and she blushed as she gathered it up, writing a cheque for the session, thinking that therapy really was a waste of time and money. No wonder she felt queasy, shelling out a fortune for nothing. It was all ridiculous, fantastical, revolting nonsense with no foundation whatsoever. Except that the soles of her feet still hurt. There was that.

Welcome to multiples-chat, a supportive chat room for people who have DID or DDNOS. Visit our homepage at www.multiplesweb.com.

　*S&All has joined multiples-chat

　*S&All is now known as Sharon

　Sharon› hi everyone

　Janet› hi sharon how's it going

Sharon› i hate therapy

Sharon› i mean what they said in the session today i can't believe it about me, my parents

Janet› (((((sharon))))

The washing machine was spinning, 1200 rotations per minute, the floor under her feet trembling. The first load was done and in the laundry basket. One of Dan's shirts lay on the ironing board, the collar pressed. It must be the endless laundry and ironing that had spurred her imagination. Cathy switching? What an idea!

Sharon› and then they get going on my son's girlfriend

Sharon› i mean really, they even think they might have seen her switch can you believe that? isn't it ludicrous?

Janet› no but it's serious

Sharon› it's one thing to say things to my therapist, i mean does it really matter what i make up? but when it goes beyond that

Janet› what if they're right and she's in trouble?

Janet› sharon—you are the mom

Janet› don't be one of those that close their eyes

Janet› trust the inside, they've been watching your whole life

Janet› watch with them, you'll know

Sharon› and then what?

CHAPTER FIFTEEN

*F*our kinds of popsicles somehow ended up in the grocery cart on Saturday. There was a list, Dan put it on the fridge, but Sharon didn't take it. Best Foods was right across the road from Magee's. Walking up and down the aisles, Sharon realized that she was nearly out of shampoo, you can't ever have too much toilet paper or tampons, stir fry would be good for supper, maybe a turkey for tomorrow, there was a sale on potted plants. And suddenly the store had become, not the usual eight aisles, baking items in number seven, meat at the back, eggs and cheese across from the ice cream freezers, but an entrancing mystery of stuff. Even the ceiling. Balloons! Wow! A Dora balloon and a Spider-Man balloon. She looked up sideways, eyelids shielding her childish glance while, on the inside, Alec was right behind her, ready to move out if she needed help. So many treats! A table of bunnies, chickies, and chocolate. Boxes and boxes and boxes of chocolate. Humungous chocolate eggs. A basket with a bunny. It had a button so she pressed it and the bunny sang a song. That was funny! Oh look at the teeny chickie all fuzzy and yellow.

It was so little even littler than her hand and she could put it in her pocket but no you aren't allowed you have to put it in the cart and pay for it. A lady said, "Excuse me." She had a little boy sitting up in her grocery cart. The boy had a ice cream cone.

A mischievous grin appeared on her face, her gait slightly pigeon toed as she pushed the grocery cart. Nobody knowed that a kid was out cuz she was big! Hahahahaha. She pushed the cart some more, leaning on it and sliding. Fairies can fly. What do they do when it rains? Maybe they have fairy umbrellas. Ohhhhh. Pretty flowers over there. Smelly ones. They made her sneeze. And right next to the flowers was the freezers. Look at ALL the popsicles. There must be a gazillion kinds. Banana for her and grape for Echo. Why was a chocolate one called a Fudgesicle? She put a box in the cart. Everybody liked chocolate. And Creamsicles, next time she'd eat the orange outside first and the vanilla last. Echo was missing everything. He was scared of Easter stuff so he was hiding.

At the checkout the lady said, "How are you today?" and she said, "Fine." That's what you're supposed to say. Then she gave the lady lots of money from the wallet and the lady gave her some money, too. She pushed the cart to the car and she put the groceries in the car and she pushed the cart to the cart place. She could do lots of stuff. But in the car she waited for a big because lils was not ever ever allowed to drive. It was a rule. It was number infinity. That's how big a rule it was. Uh oh. She had the chickie in her pocket. Uh oh. Maybe they was in trouble. Maybe they was going to jail.

Sun flashed through the dust on the windshield. It needed washing. In the spot beside her, a mom juggled her keys, a toddler, the sliding door of a minivan. Sharon looked at the toy in her hand. It was unbelievable. She'd just lifted a ninety-nine-cent toy. If anybody saw her . . . She put the key in the ignition, opened the window to toss the damning ball of yellow fluff, then paused. A train was moving along the railroad tracks behind the parking lot. It came from the direction of her hometown, bringing goods from west to east. In her grandfather's day, the trains had supplied parts to the Ford factory at the corner. But now good coffee was served there, and the train carried products made in China, like this tiny toy, which she would never have received as a kid, considered undeserving of even that. She took the key out of the ignition and a dollar from her wallet, and walked back through the parking lot.

When she got home, Dan and Josh were in the living room playing Stratego while in the kitchen Emmie and Cathy— who'd been invited for brunch—were waving their hands in the air, fingernails painted in an assortment of colours. Polish and polish remover, nail hardener and cotton balls were spread across the table. Blowing on her nails, Cathy sat in Sharon's chair, facing the backyard. Her eyelashes and eyebrows had been subjected to mascara and pencil, her lips shimmering as she blew. Tips for spring: wear bold lipstick with soft eye makeup, or bold eyes with natural lips. The magazine was on the table.

"Where's Nina?"

"Upstairs," Cathy said, looking at Emmie and shaking her head because Emmie was giggling. "She's sleeping."

"Isn't she feeling well? I'd better check on her."

In the girls' room, Sharon climbed up the ladder to the upper bunk where her daughter was under a hump of blankets, nothing sticking out but the ends of her black hair because she liked to sleep with her head covered, in a cave of warmth. Still, it wasn't like Nina to nap. Maybe she was coming down with something. Sharon reached out to gently pat her daughter's back, her other hand pulling the blanket down a bit so she could check Nina's forehead for fever.

Just as her mother lifted the blanket, Nina popped out from behind the closet door. "April Fool's!"

"Nina! You scared me." Sharon laughed, throwing aside the blanket. Under it were pillows, stuffies and Emmie's Chinese dolly arranged so that just the dark hair showed.

"Did you really get tricked, Mommy? Did you really believe it?"

"I did," Sharon said, climbing down and putting an arm around her daughter, kissing her definitely cool forehead.

"It worked, it worked," Nina yelled, pulling away, running down the stairs to the kitchen.

"I helped." Cathy grinned.

"It was my dolly!" Emmie said.

Nina was in overalls, Emmie with half a dozen hairclips pinning back her curls. A stranger might not even know they were sisters, they looked so different, Nina all chocolate and mochaccino, Emmie a freckled rose. Not like Cathy's family, all cut from the same gold cloth. When she was four and Heather six, they used to wear ridiculous matching dresses, the nanny complaining to Sharon about the nuisance of washing and ironing. And the ribbons in their hair! Cathy would lose hers in the sand and more than once Sharon dug it out while Cathy was playing in the sandbox with Josh. Her sister, with the same hair and eyes and chin and hands, would scold her for acting like a boy until Cathy jumped into the sandbox on top of the sand cakes beautifully decorated with twigs carefully selected for leafiness and height, pebbles arranged just so. "My beeuteeful cake. You ruined it! Clumsy oat!" Heather would cry. That was what sisters did. What would one sister not do to another? For the other? Sharon thought of her own sister, how each of them had begged the other, how she had been the one to leave her sister behind.

The first summer she was back from university, Sharon had slept in the bedroom they had always shared. There was no art on the wall, no posters or mementos, just their childhood locked in with the white and gold French provincial furniture that had held her clothes and her books and her schoolwork. They'd never been allowed to put anything on the walls, though an empty birdcage made of red wire still hung from the ceiling. Shelves held a dictionary, a book of quotations, and a thesaurus. There was a globe on her sister's desk, on hers a radio. When she was little she'd sometimes plug in earphones and listen to the radio at night just to know there was a world outside her head. The window faced the back-yard where a skinny maple tree grew, not much more than the sapling it had been when they'd moved into the house, not big enough to climb. Every backyard had one maple tree in it. Every front lawn had a garden with tulips. The lots were big enough so that nobody could hear their neighbours.

One night, she woke up and saw her sister lying on her side, eyes open. Pauline was five years younger yet fuller in the chest, her breasts round. Sharon could legally drink but she was the one who'd be asked for ID, not Pauline who plucked her eyebrows, shaved her bikini line to make a neat triangle. She sneezed in a genteel and musical *choo.* Her nails never broke.

"Paulie?"

"Yes?"

"How long have I been back?"

"A month," her sister said as if it was a normal question, as if it was one that Sharon had asked before and she had asked Sharon, a question between sisters losing a battle with sneaky time, which hid and then jumped out at them.

"I thought it was longer."

Pauline smiled. It was her nighttime smile, sweet, young. "I missed you."

"I missed you, too, sweetie. But I need to leave. When school starts, I'm not coming back again."

Pauline sat up. "No!"

"Shh. You'll wake Dad."

"Please. Don't go. Can't you go to school here?" In her cotton nightgown, she looked smaller, shoulders hunched as she hugged her knees, face bare of makeup. Sharon knew the curve of her sister's cheeks, the long lashes when her eyes were closed. Sometimes at night she used to watch her sister sleep in moonlight, keeping guard, though she didn't know from what.

"Don't worry. I'm not going yet, Paulie."

When the summer ended and she was packing for school, Sharon asked her sister to come with her and stay for a while. But Pauline wouldn't, she couldn't, for she was the good daughter and her parents would never give their permission. She was just starting high school. *Come for a visit,* Sharon said. *If you stay I'll register you for school. I'll get another job. I'll support you. Or come later,* Sharon said. *When you're eighteen you can do anything you want. They won't let me,* Pauline said. *Don't go. Please don't go. You can't go. If you go I'll never speak to you again. That I promise you.* She kept her promise.

And here was another good daughter, touching her thumbnail to her upper lip, pronouncing her nails done. "It's Emmie's turn to help with the pancakes. Nina and Cathy, you can get back to your knitting if you want." Sharon left the sliding doors open, a breeze bringing in the smell of rain-drenched earth as she put away the groceries, setting a small aloe vera on the windowsill above the sink. Franky the kitten, accustomed to the family now, was lapping water while Nina stood on a stool, reaching for popsicles in the freezer. "Not now. You can have one for dessert."

"Awwwwwwww, Mommmmm."

Sharon put all the ingredients on the blue table along with measuring cups, measuring spoons and a mixing bowl. Emmie kneeled on a chair while Sharon handed her a cup and said, "Fill that up with flour, honey." Cathy's head was bent, her lips puffed out as she concentrated on the yarn. "That scarf will look nice when you're done. Josh will love it."

Nina was using small plastic needles and Cathy larger bamboo ones, both of them laboriously digging the point into a knot, wrapping yarn, pulling. Emmie slowly measured more flour, oat bran, baking soda and baking powder. Sharon added vanilla. Emmie cracked eggs. A breeze tinkled the wind chimes on the back deck. Franky chased a stray piece of yarn.

"Is this good, Mom?" Nina held up her knitting.

"Excellent." She put a hand on her daughter's shoulder. Nina had a plan. She was going to knit a scarf for each of her teddy bears. One in each colour of the rainbow. "How's Madeline?" she asked Cathy.

"Linny's over her cold." The older girl rubbed her nose. "I think I'm getting it. You know what Heather wanted to call her?" The girls shook their heads. What? What? Tell us. Cathy rolled her eyes. "Amethyst. Isn't that so precious?"

"It's pretty," Emmie said. "Ammmmmthissss."

"Not Amthis, Amthist!" Nina said. "Don't you know anything?"

Emmie stuck out her tongue, reaching for Nina's knitting with her floury hands. Green eyes blazed, dark eyes flashed, Nina was shouting *Mom!* while her mom put an arm across Emmie's chest, blocking her from leaning forward, threatening no maple syrup or worse—they'd have to go to their room and make up. They glared at each other as they settled back down in their chairs. There was flour on Emmie's freckled nose. Nina's nose, a smaller version of her Chinese grandma's, was flaring. Cathy kept knitting, head bent, not looking up.

"Madeline was my grandma's name," she said as if there had been no interruption. "I guess it's okay. But it's too long. Linny is better for a baby."

She moved the needle with the full row to her left hand, shifting the empty needle to her right, the skein of blue wool on the table. Not dollar-store yarn. Sharon believed in using good wool, even for kids who were learning. It was cobalt blue, like beautiful china, like the kitchen tiles, and soft in the hands. It was the feeling in her hands that she loved about knitting, needles moving faster than the eyes could follow, wrap and lift, wrap and lift, counting stitches, the rhythmic click clack, knit eight from back stitch holder, knit sixteen from front stitch holder, increase four evenly across. That was the hood of the hoodie she'd made for her niece.

"I like that. It makes me think of the Madeline books that I read to Emmie," Sharon said. "That Madeline is an orphan, too, and she's got spunk."

"My grandma had chronic fatigue." Cathy examined her knitting. "S! I dropped a stitch."

"Let me have a look."

"I'm sorry, Mrs. Lewis. I ruined it. I'm so clumsy. I can't do anything."

"Mom will fix it," Nina said. "She always fixes mine."

Cathy shook her bit of scarf as if the hole was a chasm. "How?"

"Please," Sharon said. "I've dropped a million stitches." She pulled a crochet hook from the knitting bag. "You see this ladder right here? Just hook it with this and then slip your needle through. There you got it! Now wrap the yarn and it's just a regular stitch."

Cathy looked at it critically. "You can still tell."

"Okay. I want to show you something." It didn't take long to run upstairs and come back down wearing the old cashmere sweater and carrying a jacket, which she dropped onto an empty chair next to Cathy. "Ta-da! This is my first sweater. I made it for Dan and he wore it, believe it or not, until it shrunk."

"But it's awful!"

"You know what's worse? I wore it to Eleanor's house and everyone saw me in it."

"Seriously?"

"Yes." Sharon smiled. "Thank goodness your mother didn't. Can you imagine what she'd have thought?"

"What, Mommy?" Emmie asked.

"That it was butt ugly!" Nina crowed.

"She said butt!"

Now the little girls were laughing uproariously, so hard they started to hiccup, their fight forgotten. Cathy laughed with them, everybody laughing so hard, even Sharon, that it wasn't until Cathy put her hands over her face that they realized her tears weren't laughing tears anymore. Nina peered at her inquisitively, then said, "She's crying, Mom." Emmie picked up the kitten, but her mom motioned her away before she could shove him at Cathy. An arm around the weeping girl's shoulders, Sharon made soft sounds, Shhh it's okay it's okay, shhh, just as she did with her girls on a night of bad dreams. Nina and Emmie stood close, arms around each other.

"I can't even hang on to a stick," Cathy wailed.

"A stick?"

"The stupid flash drive. They took it."

"You can get another," Sharon said. "I'll get you one."

"No you can't." Cathy cried harder. She cried so she could hardly breathe and it was a while until she could speak. "It was my sister's," she gasped between sobs. "Now it's gone."

"I'm so sorry," Sharon said.

Cathy was rocking in her chair, hands over her face, multicoloured fingertips spread wide to hide as much as she could. As the sobs subsided, she wiped her eyes, leaving trails of mascara on the back of her hands. Her head was still bent, hair covering her face. "It doesn't matter. My mom's got it." She lifted a thumbnail to her teeth.

"No, no, no," Sharon said, pulling Cathy's hand gently down. "Not with that great new polish on it. Your nails are getting so nice now. Did you stop biting them?"

"Uh huh," Cathy said through the curtain of her hair.

"My nails always split," Sharon said. "My mother never had any hope of me."

"I could do your nails. They wouldn't split."

"That would be nice," Sharon said. She stood up and went to the glass doors, sliding them shut. On the other side of the wall, the grandma next door, who still waxed her kitchen floor, was revving up her ancient floor polisher. "You haven't seen the other thing I brought down to show you. I found it yesterday at Value Village." It was the jacket she'd seen in her mind—she must have seen it some other time when she was at the store and forgotten. For here it was, exactly the same, with the bad stitching at the shoulders and the staples as if someone had tried to alter it and, failing, had just stapled it back together. It was only two dollars and so for a lark she'd bought it. An eighties silk jacket with vertical black stripes overlaying a pastel plaid, nipped at the waist and long, like a riding jacket, but who would ride a horse wearing silk? "I've got no idea what to do with this. I'd never wear it."

"But it's fantastic," Cathy said, hoarse from crying. "It is so retro, it's sick."

"That good?" Sharon laughed. "Let's make it over for you, then."

"What for? If I take it home, they'll put it in the bag for Goodwill."

Sharon might have left it at that, for you have to respect other parents' rules if you want to get along with your neighbours. But words were said inside, urgently, insistently and she was listening. "I have an idea. There's lots of space in my basement closet. How about if I help you fix the jacket and we keep it there?"

"Okay." Cathy smiled. She had a lot of smiles. The polite girl next door. The savage grin. The smirk. And this new one, hopeful. Had Sharon really never seen her smile this way before?

"Good. You girls need to clean up for lunch. Cathy, can you take them upstairs and help them?" As Cathy got up to follow the younger kids, she stopped, turned and put her arms around Sharon, hugging her quickly, releasing her as soon as Sharon hugged back. Then she ran up the stairs after the girls while Sharon called, "Faces and hands everybody. With soap!"

Plugging in the griddle, Sharon listened to the clatter of feet overhead. She had real maple syrup—none of that sugar water dyed brown for her family. Pipes rattled upstairs as water flushed down, flowing into larger pipes laid underground a hundred years ago when Seaton Grove's bylaws stipulated that no whole sheep or hogs or geese were allowed to run free in the streets on pain of a ten-cent fine. Before that the roots of a forest intertwined and Garrison Creek flowed between ferns. Now pipes connected the houses on either side, across the street, around the corner, their sewage led far away. That was how civilized people handled shit: pipe it; bury it. And they sacrificed the creeks, the streams, the living waters in order to do it, their land dry and quiet except for the sound of sprinklers.

Later Sharon took the silk jacket to the dining room to unstitch and unstaple it while Franky, black except for the white tip of his tail and two of his paws, stalked a dust bunny in the corner. Asking Cathy to stay still, Sharon pulled sleeves over her arms, pinning shoulders and cuffs, explaining that it was the fabric that mattered. No matter how misused or misshapen, it could be made again into something lovely.

"Mama! Mama!"

"I'm here."

Emmie was sitting up in the lower bunk, her older sister still asleep. "I saw Heather. Her hair fell off."

"It was just a dream, kiddo." Alec had come running when he heard his child scream, no memory of how he'd got to the girls' room. He was in the kitchen, talking online. Then he was on the second floor. Nothing was out of place, nobody else there. His breathing slowed, eyes still scanning to be sure.

There was a doll on the floor. Before bed the girls had been playing, "Get the baby out," re-enacting the Caesarean that had been done on Heather's body. Brigitte had said that was a healthy way to process the tragedy, but she didn't hear these kids scream at night.

"Everything's okay," Alec said. "I'll sit here. Go back to sleep."

Emmie rolled over in her nest of stuffed animals, clutching Lambie, eyes fluttering open occasionally to make sure that her nighttime mommy was still sitting in one of the plastic chairs, legs stretched out. She still refused to eat lamb chops, though she'd eaten roast beef for dinner and asked for seconds, not realizing it was cow as Josh had been threatened with dire consequences if he told her. Grounding, loss of allowance, garbage duty.

The moon was full. Somebody inside had noticed it and knew the calendar, that Easter was coming and Good Friday. Holidays were always hard for them. There had been no refuge on days when school was out and adults home from work. Now the lils were hiding inside as if the walls of the house were penetrable, terror on its way through their skin. Alec got up to check doors and windows, make sure everything was locked. After he sat down again, he heard the sound of footsteps in the hallway, then the click of a light switch, the bathroom door closing. A train was squealing along the railroad tracks, starting and stopping. Warning whistles. A heavy load. The toilet flushed, rattle of pipes, door creaking. Bare feet slapped slapped on the wood floor, which squeaked just past the stairwell. Josh stood in the doorway, his shadow long and narrow in the girls' dancing fairies night light. His hair stood on end like his dad's. T-shirt and SpongeBob PJ bottoms, ancient and threadbare.

"What are you doing, Mom?"

"Shhh. Emmie was having bad dreams. Why are you still up?"

"I heard you when I went to the bathroom." Josh sat down in the other small chair, his legs stretched out alongside his mom's. He was a kid who took his sweet time figuring things out for himself, keeping it to himself until long after the fact. When he was five, Dan had given him "medicine" for nightmares. A year later Josh had said that he knew the medicine was just molasses but it was funny that it worked anyway. Alec glanced over at the bunk beds. Emmie hadn't stirred, not even at the sound of her brother's voice, which, if she'd been the slightest bit alert would have had her up and jumping on him.

Alec's stomach was rumbling. "I didn't eat any supper. I'm going to fix a snack."

"Can I have something, too?" Josh asked. If it was his daytime mom, she'd have directed him back to bed. And he'd have gone, sullenly, more or less obediently. But everything was different in the night. He might talk, his mom might say yes. Food tasted better.

"I'm thinking cocoa and sandwiches. You want to help?"

Alec made cocoa the way he'd learned from Uncle Frank. Half milk, half water, chocolate syrup, a glob of honey. Uncle Frank used to heat it in a coffee tin over a fire. They'd drink cocoa and watch meteor showers while Uncle Frank showed him the constellations. Ursa Major pointed down to the North Star, the tail end of Ursa Minor. Big bear and little bear, Callisto and Arcas.

Condensed milk made better cocoa, but there wasn't any in the pantry, and Alec had to search way at the back to retrieve the syrup. Offering no advice and no instruction, he put the bread out on the board, telling Josh to slice it while he rummaged in the fridge for cold meat, mustard, pickles. The microwave hummed. *Beep beep beep.* The cocoa was ready.

"This is good, Mom," Josh said. The bread was uneven and so was the meat. Slathers of mustard. Wedges of pickle. Standing at the counter, they chewed on their sandwiches. Slugged down cocoa.

"So what's up?" Alec was trying not to look at the masking tape holding back his son's ears, his gaze on the aloe and the ivy on the windowsill. Franky had appeared out of nowhere and was rubbing his head on Alec's foot, clearly unaware that Alec didn't go for small animals. Or perhaps it was. Cats were like that. Alec shoved the kitten aside with his foot, as gently as the little bugger deserved.

Josh took another bite, talking with his mouth full. "Cathy's parents are sending her to a shrink."

"Who?" The kitten was mewing pitifully, kneading Alec's toes. He got a can of cat food from the cupboard, opened it, and dropped the food in the kitten's dish, all the while wondering if the kid was being sent to see her father's cousin and what he'd put her on.

"I don't know. She doesn't really want to go, but I told her you talk to someone and it's okay. It is, isn't it?"

"Yeah. Sure. If you got someone you can trust."

"Like you used to have headaches all the time and you don't anymore."

"True." He didn't know that Josh had noticed. He wondered what else Josh had noticed. Someone should ask the therapist if this was bad. If seeing their suffering could hurt their son.

"Mom, why don't we ever see your parents?"

"Whoa . . ." Out of left field and he hadn't seen it coming.

He made himself pick up his sandwich, take a bite, chew and swallow. "What brought that up?"

"Just thinking about it."

"What you been thinking?"

But Josh wouldn't hand over his thoughts that easy. "Why don't we see them?" he asked again, waiting for his nighttime mom to answer his nighttime questions.

"They came here once. That was enough. Do you remember?"

"Just that you didn't feel well so I got to watch a lot of TV. I thought it was fun and then I got bored. And . . ."

"And what?" On the inside folks were sharing information, passing the pieces of their memories back and forth, running through the visit in their head. Josh was three years old. Had they left him alone for an hour they didn't remember? Had the father touched him. The mother. If so, if so . . .

"Your mom got me a big banana split when you were sleeping. She told me not to tell. I really wanted her to come back again and make me another one. She said that Dad should get you real jewellery. She had a shiny bracelet."

Alec exhaled. "Nice lady."

"How come, Mom? Is it because she didn't think Dad was good enough? Is that why we don't see them?"

"It's late. You should get back to bed."

"Oh, right." Josh was looking at him with adolescent scorn. With hurt. Being treated as if he was stupid or as if he couldn't be trusted with the truth. Was that how they'd raised him? To be unworthy of truth? This kid who carried an air of dignity around him, even when he forgot deodorant.

Alec put his plate in the sink. "Let's go outside." The nights were mild and spring had come though the birch tree was still bare. "If we're going to talk about this, then I need to get some air."

He slid open the glass doors, stepped outside on the deck, his son beside him, both of them in bare feet. Next door laundry was flapping in the wind. As he walked across the deck, lights went on, bright enough to read by. Alec would prefer not to have motion detectors. You could see better in the dark without lights blinding you to the shadows. He liked the cold wood of the deck under his feet, the crinkling grass, the square of mud that would be their garden, then the parking pad that made a bouncing surface for basketball, the hoop screwed into the side of the shed. "You want to know the real reason?"

"Yes." It smelled of gas back here. They should get the car checked.

"That banana split was a trick. That's how people get kids to trust them. One step at a time." He picked up the basketball, threw it through the hoop. Passed it to Josh.

"So?" Josh threw the ball, his arm extending above his shoulder, elegant, confident. The ball fell neatly through the hoop.

"Nice shot. Josh, my parents look fine from the outside."

"Uh huh," Josh said, aiming again. You wouldn't know from his voice that this conversation mattered, but the tips of his ears were red.

"People can put on a good act. Lots of people respected my parents. But the fact is that they were abusers."

"Like they hit you?"

"That. And other stuff. There was no way we were going to let them get to our kids." The *we* was a slip. But it could mean him and Dan. Nobody ever picked up on that kind of thing. "Your dad is a good guy. I've watched him in action. But given where I come from, I don't even trust him a hundred percent. You can't take anything at face value, not even your girlfriend or her folks. You don't know what's going on behind closed doors."

"But Mom, we talk all the time. Like real talking. Deep stuff."

"So you feel like you really know Cathy and everything about her?"

Josh nodded.

"And she never said anything about herself that you wouldn't expect." Alec dribbled the ball, jumped, made the shot. Dribbled again. Josh got the ball away from him.

Josh grinned. "I told her that you and Aunt Eleanor went to the shooting range. She thought that was cool and she asked me if you'd take her. That surprised me! Would you, Mom? Teach me?"

"You really want to?" He spoke casually, not wanting to expose his own astonishment: that he had anything of value to give this boy, that his son was eager for it. And so he became distracted from the matter at hand. The girl, her problems, her peculiarities, her family's were all forgotten as Alec threw the ball through the hoop nailed to the shed, glancing sideways at Josh.

"Seriously," Josh said.

"Okay, we'll see." They might even go hunting, him and his son. Camp overnight, get up before dawn. If it was clear, they'd look at the stars. He'd need to buy a rifle, but first he'd have to get a license for possession of a firearm and another for transporting it. "I'll talk to Dad about it."

They played for a while. Counted points, Josh relishing his twenty to his mom's six. Seven. Eight. Alec was on a roll, but Josh got the ball away from him. "You going to throw or just hang onto that?"

"Mom?" He was standing there, hugging the ball. "Did they, you know, sexually abuse you?"

Alec paused, but there was no other answer. "Yeah," he said.

Josh threw the ball wide. It slammed into the shed. "I wish I was there. To help you."

"It's my job to stand up for you, Josh. Not the other way around."

"Not always, Mom. Not anymore."

Alec looked at his son, a boy still and more than a boy, moving toward the wall of his mother's protection, asking the bricks to open up and allow him to pass through. Not yet. Not yet. But soon. In the darkness, everything looked larger, merging with its own shadow. His son's smooth cheek was roughened, his shoulder broadening in an outline of the honourable man he was becoming while the moon flew over the roof from east to west, the earth turning under their feet.

Dan had had a hard day. His newest client, a referral from Rick, was Families Against Guns. The phone campaign, which had kicked off its fundraising, had brought in an adequate number of pledges, if not what he'd hoped, but the mail-out that followed had been screwed up. The printer claimed that they'd printed the list as received. The vendor of the list claimed that all the duplicates had been eliminated at their end. He'd spent the afternoon in a stuffy mailroom at the printer's, sorting through hundreds of envelopes with two employees who then left early for the Easter weekend. But even after all his efforts, the mailing wasn't ready to go out. In dense holiday traffic, he'd driven home along the highway, kicking himself for dealing with a company in the suburbs. Finally the turn-off to Crookshank's Lane and down to the railway bridge. All he'd wanted was a hot shower, a good supper and then a good book. But it was Thursday. After therapy, Sharon always had to nap. On the table were a pizza box, dirty napkins and glasses half full of pop going flat. Josh had stacked the plates in the dishwasher and he'd done it all wrong.

After chomping down a slice of cold pizza, Dan had inspected his wife's money jar, removing the cheques for deposit, and got back into his car. At the ATM he'd got a call from Rick on his cell, wanting to know whether the mailing had gone out. There were a lot of fundraisers to choose from, Rick had said, but he'd believed in Dan, and had recommended his company to other charities. Rick's voice was clipped, each syllable enunciated with cold correctness. He'd been too hasty, counting on friendship, he'd said. This charity was important to him and he'd thought it was just as important to his friend, but aside from any personal feelings, his professional reputation was on the line. Perhaps it would have been wiser to have seen presentations from other fund-raisers before making a decision. But what was done was done. For the time being.

When he'd got home again, Sharon was awake. Dan had retreated to his office and gone to bed alone as per usual while his wife talked to other people on the computer. But even the blessing of sleep was taken from him this night as sometime after midnight he was rudely woken up by the sound of a drawer being unstuck, then rummaged. "What is it?" he asked, sitting up.

"I'm looking for the application I printed off. I put it in here."

"What application?" Dan said. His wife was looking through the drawer in the dressing table.

"For a firearms license."

"What are you talking about guns for?"

"Josh wants me to take him shooting. Ingrid's invited me to go hunting. I could take him along. What do you think?"

Dan turned on the bedside lamp. "I think it's asinine." The mailing would be delayed until some unspecified date after the long weekend. When it finally did go out, the mailing would cost the client extra even though Dan had spent hours negotiating on their behalf. And now he was up in the middle of the night with his wife, this wife, wanting to take his son hunting. Nobody had even asked about his day. His awful, crappy, worrisome day. His eyes fell on the target taped to his wall. Something he would never put there, nor would the Sharon he knew. He hated it. For no reason at all he hated it and he wanted to tear it down, and he hated the unreasonableness rising in his chest.

When printers screwed up and your client blamed it on you, didn't you have the right to expect your own wife to be in your own room? A man had to have some small order in this world. Stack the dishes the right way. Set his alarm for seven a.m. and shower for fifteen minutes. Go to bed at eleven p.m. and watch the news. Turn out the light. Have bills paid and cheques deposited. He shouldn't be only hoping that the person who comes into his bed is someone he knows. Not this stranger, inexplicably taller, jaw thrust forward.

"Would you take that down? I don't want to open my eyes and be staring at a target," Dan asked in as reasonable a tone as he could muster while his nostrils widened to take in more oxygen, expanding his lungs sufficient for the hoarse half-whisper, half-shout of parents fighting at night. He walked over to the wall where his wife was leaning, an arm resting against the target, covering it protectively.

"That's mine," Alec said.

"You don't tape things to the wall like a kid." Dan tapped the wall, dark eyes narrowed. If that hand got any closer Alec was going to knock it down. "Especially not that."

"What the hell do you mean?"

Dan was on a roll, and he went with it, like a train at top speed, and he was not the conductor, not even a passenger. He was standing on top of the train, riding it. "How does it look if my wife has a gun when my client is Families Against

Guns? I just met with Rick yesterday." Assuring him that the mailing would be out today though he already knew about the screw-up and Rick's pale blue eyes were looking at him skeptically. Dan was not nearly as persuasive as the business professor who had talked a stingy real estate developer into sponsoring a renovation of the arena. "Not to mention the man's grief about his daughter's suicide. With a gun!"

"You hunt with a rifle," Alec said, "not a handgun." He was tired. Therapy had been rough. He was so damn tired, keeping everything in. Dan better move. He was not going to step away from him. "Fuck Rick," he said. "This is not his house."

The train was heading for a tunnel. Dan could feel it coming, the darkness, the coldness, and he couldn't stop himself. "This is my house. I work hard for my family. And I've tried to be supportive. Not that you appreciate it. I've never complained about the amount of money, time and space taken up with knitting and sewing. And when you do have a small job, you don't even bother to deposit your pay. If I hadn't gone and done that tonight, there would have been stale-dated cheques. But I guess it never occurs to you that someone else besides me could bring in some money. You don't give a shit, do you?"

"Got other things on my plate." Alec couldn't waste words because he was busy clamping down on the inside, not letting anything show. Not letting anything be said. Not letting a freak show unroll before this man. Inside had to stay inside: folks crying because they were bad; the husband was mad; they didn't make money for him. "Whatever. It's yours."

He ripped the target off the wall, and thrust it at Dan. Alec had to get away from here, talk to people who got who he was, who they were. "I'm going downstairs." He could feel Dan behind him, following him, too close. One more step and Alec wouldn't be held to account. He turned around. "Will you lay off? I gave you the fucking target. What more do you want?"

"You're going to talk to those special people. Too bad I'm not special. I guess I'm just the moneybags. I come home and I never know who is going to be here. Or what you're going to do. Or even who you might run off with."

"That's what you think of us?" So it finally came out. This was the husband's real opinion of them. Alec didn't know whether to stay out or run inside and put his arm around Lyssa, who was weeping in shame. Sharon— nowhere to be found.

"You're always on the computer," Dan said. "You don't want to talk to me. One day you're one thing, another you're something else. I don't know what you want. How can I be the man you want if I don't know what that is?" Dan sat down in the chair near his wife's dressing table. "Why would you stay with me?"

"Shit." His wife sat on the end of the bed, facing him, astounded. "You want us?"

"Don't you know?" Last summer when they'd put in a new a/c unit upstairs, he was surprised by his wife's unaccustomed helpfulness. *How come you're so handy all of a sudden?* he'd asked. The answer sat before him. Dan raised his eyes to meet his wife's, the green of malachite.

"The thing is, I can't be her," Alec said. "I'm not her."

"I know." Dan looked sad. Maybe he thought it was better to have her some of the time than none of the time. But couldn't he like the rest of them a little?

In the dimness of a room he hadn't made with its puffy fluffy velvetiness, Alec didn't try to sound like Sharon. "I'm not goin' anywhere. None of us is."

Dan couldn't speak because if he did he might weep. So he just nodded and they sat knee to knee, his pajamas, his wife's jeans. The target was on the floor. Dan picked it up, clearing his throat. "I think there's a frame in the office somewhere," he said. "It might fit."

And so in the middle of the night, they looked through the office for a frame. They found two, one on the closet shelf, one in a filing cabinet under *F*. Simply constructed with dark wood, the second frame fit. And when the target was behind glass, they propped it up on the dressing table so the kids wouldn't be awakened by the pounding of a nail. Dan went back to bed and Alec joined him, though he couldn't fall asleep. He lay on his back, steadfastly shoulder to shoulder with his husband as Dan slipped into slumber.

CHAPTER SEVENTEEN

*F*or Easter and Passover, Sharon had put flowers, chocolate and matzo on the table, as well as glazed carrots, potatoes, a roast, tofu and a mixed green salad with bok choy, but no rice. The leaf was in the blue table to make room for Ingrid and Amy, while the kids crowded around the folding table. The spring bouquet that Amy had brought was on the counter in the vase that Josh had made out of a jar for Mother's Day when he was ten.

Ingrid had insisted on contributing to the meal, and had delivered the venison, which Sharon had cooked. Compliments were exchanged for the cooking, for the meat, Dan thanking Ingrid while looking down the table at Sharon and smiling happily. His house smelled just right: gravy, baking, flowers. He wore the log cabin sweater she'd knit for him, she wore her shift dress and the jade heart he'd given her for their first anniversary. It was the only jewellery she'd ever wanted though he thought she deserved more. Everyone was dressed up. Even Bram wore a jacket, though not a tie. He dug into the roast venison and potatoes with good spirit.

"Where's the rice?" Mimi asked. As her husband had gained a little weight, she was willing to put a sliver of roast beside the prescribed vegetarian fare on his plate, but it wasn't a meal without rice. She was sitting in her usual place beside him on Sharon's left, opposite her daughter and her daughter's husband, the other guests seated at the end near Dan.

"I thought potatoes would be a nice change," Sharon said. There was nothing to be gained in arguing with a force of nature. Better to be a reed, bending with the gale force wind, letting the rains wash over. For example: the dining room was still a mess, and though Sharon couldn't shake the feeling that she'd lost something in there, she didn't react to her mother-in-law's clucks and tsks. Nor did she take offence when Mimi saw the table set for five kids. Mimi had plenty to say about that and Sharon let her say it all again. Josh was too young for a girlfriend. They didn't match. He was dark and she was blonde. (Sharon didn't interrupt to point out that she was ginger and Dan dark, or that Eleanor was big and her husband slender.) Mimi went on and on: the tangerine looks gold on the outside but is rotten inside. She didn't come from good stock; her sister had committed suicide. If the wind blows from an empty cave it's not without a reason. The girl should be at home with her parents. Holidays were for families. Only at the end, when her mother-in-law's arguments were exhausted, Sharon had said that Cathy's family wasn't in a holiday mood so wasn't it nice that they were letting her spend the evening here?

"The five grains are more precious than jade or pearls

and number one is rice." On the word "rice," Mimi clapped her hands together.

"For the first peoples who settled in the Great Lakes region, wild rice is a sacred food," Ingrid said.

"Smart people." Mimi shook her head at Sharon who was offering Jake a choice of drinks. He had to have wine to warm his blood. Didn't she remember? He was overflowing with yin, a superfluity of dark and wet and cold, altogether too much of the female principle. And who did they have as guests? Women and girls.

"Mom, did you see the target up in Dan and Sharon's room?" Eleanor asked. She smiled innocently, waggling her eyebrows at her husband, grinning into his dinner. At last—nothing about going back to school! "It's hanging next to the scroll painting. You know, the one with the classical poem brush painted on it?"

"What target?" Mimi asked. Sharon glanced at Dan, happily occupied in pouring gravy over his potatoes. He shrugged and ploughed into his food. He'd played handball with his brother-in-law and won two out of three games this morning.

"We went to the shooting range," Eleanor answered, all the more enthusiastically because it would annoy her mother. Finally a family dinner with entertainment.

"Shooting what?"

"Bullets. I didn't do badly for the first time," Eleanor said. "But Sharon was amazing."

"Next time will you take me?" Cathy asked.

"I don't think your parents would like it," Sharon murmured.

"A Nobel Prize is amazing," Mimi said. "Not grown women playing cowboys. What do you achieve from shooting a gun?"

"When I held a rifle for the first time I realized that I wasn't afraid. As a woman I felt secure. Equal," Ingrid replied, taking Mimi seriously, not realizing that this was a family conversation and so had nothing to do with the words being said but with other matters entirely, things far under the surface, swimming like fish in the pure yin of the ocean depths.

"So." Mimi pushed up her glasses. "When I marry Jake, I tell him, don't think you are Confucius. You get dumplings, not an obedient wife. I left China. I can leave you too."

Happily eating matzo with margarine, Jake was unaware that he had left his wife or of the effort she exerted to get him back. He wondered aloud if matzo wouldn't go better with fried chicken fat, wiggling his little finger inside his hairy ear and then, to make conversation with Ingrid, he said, "So you're a lesbian?"

Eleanor rolled her eyes at Bram, who diligently ate his salad, even the bok choy, used to all this by now. He was slender but his cholesterol was high. The greens were supposed to lower it.

"Yes I am and part Native too." Ingrid smiled, the relief of securing a new place to live making her as friendly with the world as an old man with a dubious brain.

Jake leaned forward to peer at her. "It must be a very small part."

"Maybe so. But it counts."

"Huh. Jews and Indians are the same."

"How, Zaidey?" Judy asked from the kids' table. Josh elbowed her, mouthing, *Shut up, tool.* Don't get Zaidey going. Especially in front of company. His own company, Cathy, was acting a little too much like one of the family, kidding around with his pesky sisters. The girls were in their holiday finery, too. Lacy socks, shiny shoes, Nina in a jean jumper and Emmie in a flowery frock. Their cousin was not in a dress. Her mother couldn't make her. She had on her blue-green knit hoodie and the pants with the secret pockets. She concentrated on Josh as he demonstrated the disappearing-coin trick, sure that this time she'd figure it out. A glass, a coin, a towel. Plink, the coin fell into the glass. But look! It's vanished. And here it is under your nose. Cathy was trying to grab the towel from him.

"Don't you have a *shvitz*?" Jake asked Ingrid. He was in a jacket and a tie that Mimi had chosen and knotted for him and which he was loosening. "I used to go to a *shvitz* with my father every week."

"He means a sweat," Dan explained.

"Yes, a sweat. It was on Hammond Street near the shooting range. You could hear the bang bang while you sat on the bench. Then they closed it after the riot."

"What riot?" Ingrid asked.

"In Christie Pits," Amy said, her grey eyes softly meeting her partner's. They were both wearing nice pants and shirts, Amy with a vest over hers. "It was in the 1930s. Jews and Italians fighting with the Swastika Club."

Sharon got up and went to the sink, refilling the pitcher of water. Wars made headlines. Race riots. But rarely the crimes against humanity that were enacted inside a tax-payer's house.

"My great-grandfather was at Christie Pits," Cathy said. Her hair was mussed, the part zigzagging as she ran her hand through it. She wore a white dress of fragile cotton and over it the silk jacket with its big shoulders and bold stripes over the pastel plaid. "He bashed heads. Did you see that, Mr. Lewis? My father says the police kept order."

"I was only six, but I was there. And no offence to your papa but the police did *bobkes*."

"What do you mean?" she asked. "They had horses and guns. My parents say that my great-grandfather was one scary dude."

"I didn't see any guns. Nobody got shot and nobody died." His voice was kind as if he'd realized who she was and who her sister was, but she didn't look upset, only confused. "Listen to me, *maideleh*. The night before, the Pit Gang painted a swastika on the clubhouse in Christie Pits. And during the softball game they held up a white blanket with a swastika painted on it. When they yelled 'Heil Hitler,' people got mad. Boys fought. They came at each other with bats, pipes, broom handles, pool cues. It was a lot of excitement. Then they got tired and went home. The mayor was the smart one; he didn't love us Jews but he banned the swastika anyway. In those days we weren't considered white. Now—a miracle. We're white!"

"But you could always hide being Jewish," Ingrid said. "People of colour can't hide."

"Ahh," Jake said, warming to the argument, almost like his old self. "My father changed his name from Zalkind to

Lewis before he left England. So on paper he was like anyone else. But in person? No. So this is the question. If people don't like you because you're not like them, what? You should have a war with them or make yourself the same?" He turned his mild eyes on Ingrid. "Like you, *bubbeleh*. You want to be in a cupboard?"

"Closet," Ingrid laughed. "No. But when I receive hate mail, for a minute or so I wonder."

"Live and let live. It's written on the pub. That's why I bought the house on Hammond Street." Jake pushed away his plate, smiling at Sharon.

There were things that were suitable for dinner conversation and things that were not. Racism, yes. Gay rights, yes. Parents who split their children's brains, no. People with DID didn't come out at presidential inaugurations. They assimilated, they blended in.

"After that the *shvitz* was closed. Indians have a *shvitz*, don't they?" Jake asked.

"Not a steam bath. A sweat lodge. It's not for cleaning the body but for clearing physical or mental distress."

"Now we have psychiatrists," Mimi said, determinedly looking past her daughter-in-law to the children's table. "Are you seeing a good doctor?" she asked Cathy.

The girl looked back at the old woman. "A hell of one," she replied with a wicked smirk.

"Dessert is in the living room," Sharon jumped in, kicking her sister-in-law under the table. Eleanor caught her eye. Sharon tilted her head toward the kids' table. It was enough: they understood each other.

Eleanor pushed her chair back and stood up. "There's lots of cake and chocolate, kids. Don't eat it all before I get there! Judy, you can have anything but the lemon cake. It's got wheat flour in it. We'll bring the plates." Eleanor took them down from the cupboard, handing them to her mother, then fished the small forks from the cutlery drawer.

"Great supper, Mom. Thanks," Josh said, the other kids echoing him. *Thank you, Mama.* Dan extracted himself from behind the table, and came around to put an arm around her. *Thanks, Aunt Sharon. Thanks, Mrs. Lewis.*

While the others moved to the living room, Ingrid stepped outside for a smoke and Sharon put the kettle on for tea. Even from the kitchen she could hear her younger children showing off for Mimi, bringing her their homemade books and crafts. Judy was saying, "Everyone has germs. Even rich people who don't pick their noses. Watch me, Nai-Nai. I can do a headstand." Sharon put eight scoops of coffee in the filter, turned on the coffee maker, then began on the dishes. Dan would load the dessert plates later, but she enjoyed washing by hand, the soapiness and warmth of the water, the faint smell of cigarette smoke coming in from the yard. She hummed to herself a tune that she didn't recognize. Franky had come out of some hiding place to chase a crumpled napkin. Now he lay on his back, tearing it with his claws, amber eyes ecstatic.

"Do you have candy, Zaidey?" That was Emmie's high voice. Then a rumbling reply. He'd wait until Mimi was out of the room, then slip a candy into his grandchild's hand. In the meantime she whined, "Do I have to wait for Mommy?

It's too yummy, Daddy." This was what mattered. Candies. Dessert. Fruit plate, gluten-free gingerbread cookies to dip in coconut mousse, lemon cake, chocolate farm animals and a chocolate barn.

No matter what the others inside thought, Sharon hadn't forgotten what was said during therapy. But this was the gift she gave her children: a life of pleasantries and pettiness; a mother who did not scream or howl from the roof, but stood at the sink, washing dishes, rinsing them, placing them in the dish rack.

"Can I have a glass of water, please?" Cathy asked as she came into the kitchen. Franky mewed and went back to shredding the napkin.

"Sure, let me just get this first." Sharon picked up a napkin to wipe a bit of chocolate from the corner of Cathy's mouth. The chocolate was persistent and rather than dig at the soft skin, she flipped up the handle of the faucet, dipping the napkin in water. They stood close, Sharon bending a little, Cathy lifting her chin as Sharon held it, fingers supporting the delicate underside, thumb near an ear and the earrings dangling from it, no longer hidden by hair. "New earrings," Sharon said as she dabbed. "A different look for you. I like it." Black and white checked button studs in the lower hole, chains in the higher. When did her parents allow a second piercing? "There. All done. That jacket's nice on you." Sharon fetched down a glass, ice, lemon, water.

"Thanks." Cathy took the glass, just holding it. "I don't think Josh's grandmother likes me."

"Sure she does," Sharon lied.

"What if she finds out I'm seeing a psychiatrist?"

Sharon paused, considering not the answer but the question, for Mimi had already asked and heard the answer to it. Yet here was Cathy, looking troubled, wanting advice as if time had been rewound to some earlier point in the evening. "That shouldn't bother her," Sharon said, going along.

"It's embarrassing," Cathy said.

"Mimi knows I see a therapist."

"Not a shrink though. Not like you're sick. And he's a jerk." Cathy watched for Sharon's reaction, but she just nodded. "Heather's gone and she's still messing up my life. If I . . ." Cathy turned as the sliding glass doors opened.

"Can I help?" Ingrid asked, coming in from her smoke, unaware that she'd interrupted anything. "I could dry."

"Great. Here." Sharon tossed her a tea towel while Cathy slowly drank her water, looking over the rim of her glass, holding onto her excuse to remain in the kitchen.

Ingrid launched into the story of their apartment hunt and the places they'd seen, one of them with a cockroach in plain sight, another supposedly two bedroom but one of the rooms was the size of a closet, and the rent! Then they'd found the perfect place, the lower unit of a duplex with a yard for the dogs to run around. Sharon nodded, listening over the din of voices in her head as she set pots and cups on a tray. After she carried the tray to the living room, she came back to the kitchen for more napkins.

Cathy was standing next to Ingrid. "What are you doing here?" she was saying.

"The same as you, I think."

"I hope you're moving far away." The girl's hair fell over eyes that had darkened to a stormy blue. Her hands were in her pockets, and she was rocking on her heels.

"I'm not going to tell. You don't have to worry."

"Why?"

"There's no reason," Ingrid said in a quiet tone meant to quiet Cathy's. "Would it make any difference?"

"Nope." The girl's voice was sharp-edged, like her eyes. Sharon had seen exactly that look and heard exactly that voice before. Cathy arm-wrestling with Josh, swearing out of incongruously pink lips when she lost. Chewing gum, snapping it with a smirk.

"Tell what?" Sharon asked.

"Nothing," Ingrid said, and began to chatter about packing and moving and wasn't it a pain, though the new place was still in the neighbourhood and right near the dog park.

But Sharon was looking at her son's girlfriend. Just a few minutes ago, those same eyes, excited, suspicious, a hand running through that blonde hair messing it up. In between, the polite girl smile. Please and thank you. Vagueness. Catching up on what she'd missed because she hadn't been there. This child, her son's girlfriend, had switched. Now what was she supposed to do?

Sharon went to the bathroom on the second floor and sat on the toilet seat next to the blooming African violets, her head in her hands, still holding the bundle of napkins. For a moment, she felt dizzy, a flood of memories threatening to engulf her.

"Get back!" the punishers yelled. They ran, pushing people down the stairs, pushing people up the stairs, it didn't matter where, as long as it was far from Sharon. They ran up to the attic, they fled down to the sub-basement. There they huddled, keeping their memories away from Sharon: day one, day two, day five hundred, day five thousand of the things that had made them like that girl.

Alone in the middle of the house, a couple of kids hid under the teeter-totter in the playroom.

"Let's go up to the attic," Echo whispered.

"We have to go downstairs," Ally said.

"I don't want to hide in the boot closet. It's dark."

"Not so dark."

"The punishers say there's a monster in the kitchen."

"There isn't," Ally said.

"How do you know?" he asked.

"I looked," she said, even though the knothole was too small to see very much. "Okay?"

Echo nodded, trying not to cry.

"Come on." She grabbed his hand and led him out of the playroom.

They snuck along the hallway, all the rooms on either side empty and quiet as if there were only the two of them in the whole house, waiting for something scary to swoop down on them. At the staircase they paused, listening. Not a sound. Ally and Echo crept down the stairs and along the short hall to the end where the boot closet was. And there stood a punisher.

"Get back," he yelled, starting to move toward them.

"This way," Ally said, and Echo followed her, though he cried, *I can't, No, Wait, We're not allowed* as she made a dash for the kitchen, slowing her steps just a bit as she rounded the corner, waiting until Echo caught up. At the doorway to the kitchen they held hands, peeking in, ready to bolt if the punishers were right, if there really was a monster.

"I've been waiting for you," the Housekeeper said. Her arms moved fast, like she had a thousand arms, the light in the kitchen so bright it made Ally blink. There were windows and through them she could see the field she'd imagined and, yes, there was a creek and near the house a tree where someone could have a tree house. "Do your feet still hurt, Echo?" the Housekeeper asked.

"Uh huh," Echo said.

"Come," she said.

Echo went into the kitchen and when she opened her arms, he climbed onto her lap. It wasn't fair. Ally was always first, Echo behind. But she came after him, and the Housekeeper's lap was big enough for both of them. The Housekeeper's arms went around Ally and Echo. Her hands touched the soles of Echo's feet.

"How's that?" the Housekeeper asked him after a while.

"Lots better." He wiggled his toes.

"Good," she said.

Then she kissed the top of Ally's head and, for the first time ever, Ally felt what it was like to be a good girl. After a million years of sitting there, she sighed. "Cathy's in trouble," she said. "I don't want her to die."

"Neither do I." Another million years went by, Ally sitting on the Housekeeper's lap. Maybe it was just a minute. Light, warm. "You can help her."

"Not me," Ally said. She was too little.

"Yes, you."

The windows were open and maybe she could smell grass or flowers but she wasn't going anywhere. She was staying in the kitchen with Echo and the Housekeeper, and she wasn't going to tell anybody about it ever. Just her and Echo here in the kitchen. But the Housekeeper was standing up, slowly, and Ally slid off her lap like she was sliding down a slide. The Housekeeper took her by the hand and Echo by his and walked them to the door.

CHAPTER EIGHTEEN

*W*hen Sharon left the bathroom, she came down the stairs, smiling her company smile and carrying the napkins. She still had no idea what to do. Could she talk to Dan? What would she say—she had no proof, just the evidence of her eyes, and she didn't want another fight with him. She always said any child in her house was her child, but that was about making milkshakes and knitting. Not this.

The living room was fragrant from the pot of purple hyacinths on the window ledge, the daffodils beside the spider plant on the bookcase. The younger kids had already demolished the chocolate animals and a good chunk of the lemon cake was gone. Josh was still deciding what to have. He was sharing the ottoman with Cathy, his father sprawled on the rug between his older daughter and his niece. They were blowing bubbles into milk with their straws, seeing how high they could go without overflowing their glasses. Bram was down in the basement, checking out a fuse that kept blowing. She envied him. Anything to get a few minutes away from the chatter and noise.

"What else did Uncle Dan do?" Judy asked. Tired after a sleepover, she was momentarily diverted from pinching her cousin.

"Let's see. He hated wearing clothes," Eleanor said, ignoring her brother's pointed look. She never took him as seriously as he took himself. Emmie was sitting on her lap, feeding her bites of cake. "Your daddy used to strip off and run into the wading pool naked and someone had to hold him down to get a swimsuit on him. Boy could he scream."

"And you enjoyed it!" Dan accused his sister.

"I sure did." Her plump arms were around her niece, her top cut low, her arms bare, stretchy pants hugging bottom and hips. In the morning she had fought with Bram, and then they had made up luxuriously before Judy got home. "Remember, Dad?"

"Naked is nice," Jake said absently as his son-in-law came back from the basement.

"Fixed." Bram tossed the old fuse onto the bookcase. He'd left his jacket in the basement, his sleeves were rolled up. He had muscular arms. "Who's naked?" he asked his wife, his thin face breaking into a smile in recollection of their morning.

Emmie was holding her fork, forgotten cake falling onto the plate, face agog with wonder, looking at her daddy who went naked! Outside!

"Oh and there was this kid who used to pick on Dan in grade three until I beat her up," Eleanor added.

"Not the way I remember it!" Dan protested. "She was picking on you. I tripped her and you sat on her, Ellie. You were as big as me in grade one but you weren't as smart."

"Are they always like this?" Cathy asked.

"My family's nuts. Do you want to go upstairs?" Josh said.

"Not yet. I'm still eating." She toyed with her cake as if to prove it, listening, watching.

Sharon handed around the extra napkins, setting up the collapsible TV trays so her in-laws didn't have to balance plates on their knees. While Amy exclaimed over the trays, which she hadn't seen since her childhood, Sharon perched on the arm of the couch, holding her mug of coffee. Franky was on Amy's lap, purring as Ingrid scratched between his ears, leaning into her partner.

"The TV trays were in my parents' garage," Dan said, "along with the kitchen table. Completely forgotten until Sharon found them."

Sharon had told him they were practical because she couldn't bring herself to say retro was cool: it had been so unlike her, that thought in her head, now eerily quiet.

"She has good taste." Mimi shook her head and frowned as if it was unbelievable given her indifference to Mimi's opinion on other matters, such as Josh's girlfriend.

"Oh?" Sharon couldn't think of anything else to say, not even thank you. Bram looked over at her in mock astonishment. A compliment from their mother-in-law!

"The table is worth money. Turquoise you can find, but blue is rare," Mimi said. "And that one came with the extra leaf and chrome crown on the chairs. Very rare. The trays hand-painted. I took good care of them. See how colours are still vivid? Young people don't take care of things. They think a money tree grows in the backyard."

"*A woman of valour is better than rubies,*" Jake said. "It's in the Bible. Mmmm. Sharon, this is good cake, *bubbeleh.*"

"Since when do you read the Bible?" Dan asked.

"Since never. Every Friday my father said it to my mother. *She sees that her merchandise is good and her lamp never goes out at night.*" Jake smiled at his wife, pleased that he'd managed to locate this magnificent nugget of memory for her, while she, better than jewels, took away his plate. Too much sugar!

Sharon was watching her son and his girlfriend, now eating cake with gusto, bumping her hip against his to push him over and give her more room, till he finally slid off the ottoman altogether, laughing. When they finished, they excused themselves, or rather Josh said, "Excuse me," as he burped into his hand and grinned at his girlfriend. He didn't have to know that the polite Cathy was gone, replaced by someone else who thought burping was funny. Instinct told him. He had lived with his mother for fourteen years. "Can I be excused?"

"Keep your door open," Sharon said automatically.

Later when Rick picked up Cathy, insisting that he come to get her and not put anyone out, Sharon watched him as he stood at the door, chatting with Dan, waiting for the kids to say their goodbyes. They didn't talk about Families Against Guns or the mailing that was supposed to go out and hadn't yet. It was all about war, economy, sports—things on a grand scale, things that involved teams, companies, countries. Rick's hair was starting to grey. Because it was blonde, the grey wasn't immediately noticeable. As he spoke, she watched his lips form words, his tongue scarcely visible as it moved behind his teeth. When he smiled only his upper teeth showed. The lines in his face were evenly distributed, except for one deeper gash between his brows. His right nostril was slightly more elongated than his left. He didn't gesticulate, he didn't point. He stood with his hands in his pockets, fingers tapping when the conversation lagged. He called upstairs, "Cathy! We need to get going." His fingers were blunt at the tips. His wedding band was octagonal. His Adam's apple appeared and retreated between his beard and his collar. That was all the skin that showed, everything else under the good leather of shoes and jacket, the twill of his trousers. His wallet was in his back pocket. He kept a lock of Heather's hair in it, which he showed Dan now, golden hair in a plastic casing. Then the light over the stairs went on, and his other daughter walked down. The silk jacket left upstairs, her dress floated around her, steps inaudible on the runner. Rick cleared his throat. He took her coat from the stand and held it out for her. Sharon watched, wishing she could see inside his head, hoping that all she would see was a sad and aging dad. As he turned to say thanks and goodbye, his eyes were impenetrable and he shivered slightly. Perhaps it was caused by the north wind blowing in as he opened the door.

After everyone was gone, Dan put the folding table back in the basement and stacked the dessert dishes and cups in the dishwasher. Sharon wiped the table and counters, swept the floor. They both pulled the ends of the blue table away from the leaf and rotated it below, pushing the table back together. It was nearly eleven when they headed up the stairs, brushed their teeth, got into their pajamas, picking up the remote as they settled into bed. The moon was waning, but still fat in the sky as it rose above the alley behind their house.

The news (short for bad news) had its usual quota of disaster: car bombs and flooding, mad cow disease, a mountain lion that attacked a little boy, aid projects to Afghanistan suspended because it had become too dangerous. Dan was sitting up in bed, his back supported by a pile of velvety cushions, Sharon cross-legged in front of him. She swept her hair forward to expose her neck, turning her head as he worked on one side then the other, massaging the knots of muscle, his hands strong from playing handball. "Nice merchandise," he said. She slapped his knee. On her night table was *The Kite Runner*. If she couldn't sleep, she'd finish it tonight.

They discussed the bubble in the kitchen ceiling and calling the plasterer, which was on the list, but she had forgotten. Tomorrow for sure. They talked about Jake's balance and whether he was shakier. The success of putting out "man's strength" deodorant for Josh. Having the "talk" with him—soon. The window was open to let in the smell of spring. The wind was blowing from the north, chasing away clouds. It would be clear tomorrow.

And Sharon's head, unusually quiet, wasn't entirely so, for all the while a small voice whispered, *You are the mommy and he is the daddy. Tell him.* It was worse than the tinnitus she'd had during an ear infection because the buzzing and ringing of tinnitus couldn't speak through her own mouth and she was getting worried that this unceasing little voice might. So at last she spoke, not from bravery and not from conviction, but out of fear of embarrassment. "I noticed something tonight," she said.

"Oh yeah?"

"I saw Cathy switch," she said tentatively.

"Switch what?" He picked up the remote and was flicking the channels as if there might be better news on another one.

"Switch. Someone else came forward." Okay fine—she was the mom. Any child in her house was her child. *Shh already.* "Like me."

"How can you tell?"

"The way her face changes. And her voice."

"Come on, Sharon. Everybody has moods."

"Moods don't change like that. What do I look like?" She hated talking like this, as if she was admitting it. "You've seen me."

"I know." He put the remote on the nightstand, measuring his words so he wouldn't say the wrong thing. "But Cathy?"

"I've seen her a lot more than you have. And I know what I'm seeing, Dan."

"Shit," he said.

"Yes. Exactly."

"So she's had stuff happen to her."

She was listening to his mind work, his voice slow as he put the pieces together. "Yes. And likely by someone who was alone with her a lot when she was little. Probably a relative."

"Shit. Are you sure you saw her switch?"

Sharon turned to look at him. He'd shaved before coming to bed because he was in the mood. But he'd left his watch on his wrist because he knew she wasn't. These were the signs of their life together, the language of their marriage. People who shared a language ought to understand it, but his eyes, dark as the dark ale he favoured, were doubtful.

"This isn't fun for me," she said. "Do you think I'd bring this up if I wasn't?"

"Then we should talk to her parents."

"What if they're the abusers?" This was the impossible point. Their own neighbours. The people who had got funding for the arena and started the Committee for Youth. But if one in a hundred kids were multiple, as Brigitte said, then there was one in every grade in the junior school; there were two in every grade in high school. And they all had parents, aunts, uncles, grandparents who had made them so. They were all someone's neighbours.

"Not Rick," Dan said.

"You can't tell from the outside," she said.

"It's hard to believe." Then, adding quickly because he didn't want to start another fight, "Which doesn't mean I don't." His eyes searched hers as if he, too, had the ability to see the many peeking out at him through the green of moss and bracken, of water, of jade. "Just that it's hard to imagine Rick . . . I've known him a long time. I've worked with him. He's sent clients my way."

"It might be someone else. Maybe it all happened when she was little and it's been over for years. But you can't rule out Rick or Debra or that she might still be at risk."

"Debra?" That was even harder for Dan to conceive. All you had to do was look at any Mother's Day card.

"I'm just saying," Sharon slid past the question. "Talking to her parents could make life harder for her. I don't know what to do. You can't call someplace and report a kid switching. I'm sure you have to witness the abuse or at least see a bruise or something."

"In that case," he rolled over. "There's nothing for us to do right now. Let's get to sleep."

When the light was off and Dan was curled around her back, his arm over her, Sharon said, "Maybe it's my fault that Josh likes her. He sees someone familiar in her."

"Well, aside from the obvious, you're nothing like her."

"How do you mean?" Sharon propped herself up on an elbow.

Hands behind his head, Dan gazed at the ceiling. "When you switch you look different and you sound different and you can do different things," he said hesitantly, "but even so there is something that is the same. Like all of you are protective of kids. I don't know much about Cathy but she strikes me as a girl who doesn't take in stray kittens. She's more of an achiever." In the faint streetlight filtered by the curtains, Dan was yawning, rubbing his hand over his face. "Josh likes her because she's a hot chick and she isn't boring. That's the only thing you have in common."

"I'm hot? Still?"

"Yes." He closed his eyes.

The moon hung in the east, shining on the back of curtains the colour of russet apples. She'd sewn those curtains in the dining room where a meal hadn't been eaten since they'd moved in. But many things had been made there: all the cushion covers, costumes for Halloween and school plays, tiny outfits for Heather's baby, a sweater for her, given to Goodwill instead. The kids' knitting was in a basket on top of the sideboard. The work of women's hands, but she was not a woman of valour, her merchandise of little value. She watched her husband as sleep descended. He was wrong, she thought. Other boys might have been confused when Cathy switched. They might have thought her too moody. Not her son.

Dan's eyes opened. "I'm here with you," he said, rolling onto his side. One of his arms lay across her pillow, and his hand caressed the crown of her head. They fell asleep, curled together.

*O*n the month after Easter, the locust trees bloomed, infusing the neighbourhood with their honey scent. The leaves of maple trees came out, reddish bronze in the sun, then the lilacs in bursts of purple and white. The sky was a lucid blue, unmarred by smog. Sharon watched her son's girlfriend, waiting for an opportunity to talk, unsure of what to do or say. Meanwhile she baked a gluten-free cake for her niece's birthday party. The bubble in the kitchen ceiling was peeled away, the injured surface plastered and painted. Cathy finished the scarf she'd been knitting and Josh wore it while playing hockey at the arena. Cathy studied with him, she watched movies with his family, she cleared the table without being asked. She was unremarkable, good-girl classic, note-worthy only for her bland constancy. Even Josh was puzzled, wondering why she didn't want to arm-wrestle anymore, why she was squeamish about horror movies.

In the middle of May, Sharon woke up before the alarm clock went off, thinking it was the sun that had awakened her. She pulled her pillow over her head, half-waking Dan, who rolled over, punching his own pillow and settling back to sleep. She had an urge to search the dining room. It needled her. It itched her like an unscratchable itch in her nipple or deep inside her ear. It felt like something grey. A bland colour, the colour of lampposts, and cold, like brushed aluminum appliances that showed every smudge. She rolled to one side, turned over again. Sighing, she flung back her side of the comforter and got up.

Taking the broom from the pantry, she figured she might as well get the threads and dust bunnies out from under the dining room table, though Franky wouldn't thank her for it. As she swept, he jumped in and out of the dustpan, batting a dust bunny, trying to stand on his hind legs as it floated. Then he caught another on his claw and as he shook it, something hard skittered across the room, hitting the oak cabinet. He chased it. Squatting on her heels, Sharon pushed the kitty away from his prize and picked it up. A grey flash drive. She was sure it didn't belong to anyone in this house, but a normal, sane person would first ask her husband and son if it was theirs, so she went upstairs to do so. The pipes squealed. Dan was having his shower.

It was her day at the animal clinic, which shared the block on Crookshank's Lane with a dry cleaner, Berliner's Hardware and the Korean pharmacy, ivy growing up the bricks topped by a grey canopy that still had SAMUEL GOODCHILD DRUGGIST and BROMO SELTZER FOR HEADACHES printed on it. The maple tree out front had been planted when the streetcar lines were laid down a hundred and seventeen years earlier, ending at the railroad tracks. Back then the trains passed at street level, and Grossman's Surgical Supply, on the other side of the tracks, had gotten its start supplying prosthetic feet and legs to unfortunate pedestrians. Now there was an overpass for the train, and the maple tree shaded a homeless man who slept in the deep entrance of the Korean pharmacy.

The veterinary clinic had a large glass storefront, a reception area with chairs on three sides where an assortment of people sat. Carriers were on the floor and inside them pets shed fur, peeing in their anxiety. The receptionist's counter was to the rear on the left. Sharon sat beside shelves stocked with vet-recommended pet food: diets for fat cats and elderly dogs, for male cats with crystals in their urinary tract, dogs that were diabetic, desultory kittens, runty puppies. A weight-sensitive switch under the doormat triggered the first few notes of "Old MacDonald Had a Farm" whenever someone came in or out, which was every five minutes on a Saturday. The office was behind the reception area, a small room about the size of the bathroom that was directly opposite. When Sharon absolutely had to use the toilet, she closed the office door so the smell wouldn't penetrate and dashed across the hall, eyes averted from the surgery. Behind it were the kennels and the keening animals incarcerated there. Even in the office, she could hear dogs and cats and the occasional guinea pig voicing their unhappiness while she entered invoices and payments, receipts and inventory.

"I've got a puppy for you," Amy said. Her lab coat had paw marks on the chest where one of her favourite patients, a Great Dane, had greeted her with enthusiasm. Standing at a filing cabinet, she pulled out a drawer, removing a file to check a patient's previous test results. Her practice still wasn't fully computerized.

"We don't need a puppy," Sharon said, ignoring the inside ruckus of *we do, we do.* She'd been arguing with Dan about getting their cat fixed. Males spray, he'd said. She knew he was right and that she'd have to give in eventually. But she just couldn't stand the thought of Franky in the vet's back room, waking up from surgery, scared, hurting, with things done to him that he couldn't remember. Cheque number 517. Sunnycare Rehab, where Amy's brother was installed. Account: shareholder's loan. When money changes hands, there are no secrets from the bookkeeper.

"I didn't say you need one—but I have one." Amy's head was bent over the file, the sun burnishing her hair red like the new maple leaves, making her cousin to Sharon but only when she stood in the light from the window.

"We just got a kitten."

"Oh, it'll be a couple of weeks yet." Replacing the file, Amy took out another, leaning with her elbow on the filing cabinet as she perused it. "The puppies are still with their mom. She's a yellow Lab. When she was in heat a neighbourhood dog broke through the fence and the owner doesn't want the puppies. One of them has your name on it, Sharon. She's the smallest but very alert. I don't think she's going to grow up small. She's got big paws and big ears."

From inside, *yes yes yes yes yes.* "We'll see," Sharon said. "For now I'll just get on with the bookkeeping, shall I?" It was an odd word for something that had no relationship to books or keeping them anymore, but Sharon still remembered the heft of specially lined paper bound in heavy ledgers.

Her mother had kept the books, and so the privacy, of the family business. There were two sets: one was for the law firm downtown; the other was for other things, and locked away in a fireproof cabinet. She'd taught Sharon to keep accounts. Debit cash three hundred dollars. Credit revenue. The numbers had to balance. The adding machine was old and heavy and as the paper tape unfurled from it, numbers blue and red cancelled each other out, amounting to zero. If they didn't, Sharon had to check every page, looking for the error or her mother would have something to say about it. She worked in pen. That was mandatory. When she made a mistake, she crossed out the number, using a ruler to keep the line straight, and wrote the correct amount above. Film, cameraman's fee, straps. She didn't remember the purpose and she wasn't allowed to ask. Credit cash, debit expenses. There were many numbers crossed out, sometimes towers of them one above the other, and her mother's mouth would tighten at her daughter's ineptitude. Sharon began to write in pencil, then overwrite it in pen, carefully erasing the pencil, blowing the shavings into her cupped hand, disposing of them in the garden where eraser shavings blended with mulch.

Her cellphone rang. "Hi Josh. What's going on? Uh huh. Uh huh. No problem," she said. "Can I talk to Dad?" When Dan picked up, she said, "There's a pan of lasagna in the freezer. Go ahead. I'm not hungry. Yes, I will. I'm sure I won't be long."

She missed her mother. That was what the others inside didn't understand. She remembered going to Flo's Kitchen for lunch, just the two of them, her mother in a halter top, long flowered skirt and canvas espadrilles laced up her calves. Sharon wore a short plaid jumper with a ruffled blouse under it. She had a hand on her mum's bare arm, feeling the softness of the underskin as they were led to a table. Sharon ordered a milkshake, a hamburger well done. Her mother had steak and salad. They shared a plate of fries, Mum dipping hers in mayonnaise. It broke Sharon's heart to stay away.

"Problem?" Amy asked.

"Cathy needs help with babysitting," Sharon said. "I'll pop over as soon as I'm finished here."

"Just another month next door for us," Amy said. "Ingrid can't wait to move, but I'm glad we have some overlap with the new place. It gives us time to clean and get set up."

"So it's working out?" Just a few more cheques to enter. Number 525. Payer: Sadowsky Realtors. Amount: $1731. Account: rent. Taxes: category 1.

Amy nodded. "We painted and put a better lock on the basement door. Ingrid is OCD about the gun cabinet now."

"I'm not surprised."

"And then with Cathy, well it didn't help."

"What with Cathy?" Sharon looked up quickly then back at the computer.

"You know we caught Cathy sneaking into the house again and trying to get into the gun cabinet."

"Uh huh," Sharon muttered concomitantly as if this wasn't news to her. "When was that exactly?"

"Right before Ingrid went to the shooting range with you."

The target from that day had gone up on her wall in March. It was now nearly Mother's Day. "That long ago," she said.

"Ingrid didn't tell you?" Amy asked.

"Not right then."

"I guess she was too upset. I heard a noise and went downstairs, thinking the dogs needed to be let out. It was pretty funny really. I was calling the dogs and walked in on Cathy looking at me blankly, bold as you please, with a credit card in her hand. Probably her mom's. I was ready to call the police and charge her, but Ingrid said to forget it. No harm done and she's been through enough. I thought, And she's the good one! Her parents have their hands full still. So of course I said that Ingrid had to tell you."

"Of course," Sharon said.

Amy put her hands on her hips. "I know that look, Sharon. She didn't tell you, did she? Typical. Well now you know."

"Yes, I do." But she didn't really. Two and two wasn't giving her four, but three and a third or some other odd number like the square root of negative five. She turned off the computer. "I'm all done for today."

"I'll write you a cheque."

"Thanks," she said.

The receptionist was coming from the surgery as Sharon left the office, and they nearly collided. Behind her Sharon could see the sinks, scales large and small, operating tables, on one a dog anaesthetized, the other vet scaling his teeth.

There was a smell of wet dog around the receptionist. Sharon said, "See you," and rushed out. "Old MacDonald" chimed, and the clinic door closed behind her.

Sharon turned onto Seaton Street, the wind chasing clouds above her head. Cathy had called, asking Josh if his mom would please please come over because the baby wouldn't stop crying and her parents were away and she didn't know what to do. Sharon walked past the yard of the candy-coloured house, where the fountain was running, the boy peeing into the garden of tulips, the lamppost in the corner hidden within lush ivy, its leafy arms stretched along the hydro wires. She turned left onto Lumley. Down the street was the school and the ramshackle cottage, which had been called Mammy Brown's in a less informed time, and was boarded over, still unworthy of a heritage plaque. Sharon looked up at the sky and the roofs of her neighbourhood: pink, green, grey, brown, two-toned. Her own house had black shingles, curled by age, and lately Dan had been talking to roofers. Cathy's house had the highest grade of architectural shingles, a textured look meant to imitate slate. Sharon rang the bell.

"Oh, Mrs. Lewis!" Cathy opened the door, her face panicked. Barefoot, jeans rolled up, she was wearing a white blouse discoloured in a couple of places, smelling faintly of deodorant. There was mail on the hall table, bills addressed to Rick Edwards, a flowery envelope from a women's shelter for Dr. D. Dawson, a magazine renewal for Heather Edwards. "She won't stop!"

"Let's go see," Sharon said, leaving her bag on the hall table.

The den smelled of air freshener, which took away most of the baby poop odour. Cathy's textbooks and binders were on the couch, the TV on. Scattered everywhere: diapers, bottles, baby toys in bright colours, soft, expensive, intended to stimulate a brain already over-stimulated by the myriad sounds and sights outside a darkling womb. The baby's face was red and scrunched, mouth round as she wailed from her infant seat on the rug.

"What's wrong?" Cathy asked, her own face scrunched up. "I fed her, I burped her, I changed her. She won't stop."

"Eh eh eh," hiccup, "Eh eh eh eh." Such was the baby's commentary from her infant seat on the rug.

"I know, I know," Sharon said, kneeling. Soothing the baby with her voice, she unbuckled the harness, moving a hand under the soft curve of the baby's skull as she lifted her out of the infant seat. Sharon's breasts were slightly sore as if she could make milk on demand. "Linny might need to burp again."

"Is that all?"

The crying was less intense as she lifted Madeline. That powdery baby smell—Sharon had missed it more than she'd realized. Her arms still remembered how to hold a baby, her hands the right way to cup the head as she put the baby against her shoulder, patting her.

Cathy turned off the TV. "Did Linny burp?"

"Not yet." Sharon moved the baby to her lap, holding Madeline face down while she rubbed the baby's back. Then a pat. Rub, rub, pat. The little back tensed. Released. Ahh, there it was. Sharon turned Linny over, smiling while the tiny mouth found her fist. Tongue like a kitten's darting in and out. A rosebud mouth sucking strong. Eyes blue-grey, the true colour unknown as yet. A baldy still.

"I thought she was having some kind of attack," Cathy said, squatting, examining the baby for signs of the terrible ordeal they'd just been through. The baby was fine; it was Cathy who was shaky.

"I think she could probably have some more formula. Can you get the bottle?"

The den was quiet now that the baby had stopped crying. Sharon held the bottle, warm from the microwave, and cooed, "aren't you a cutie" and "aren't you a good girl" as the baby nursed. There was a new family portrait on the wall. In it Debra held the baby, Rick's arm was around Debra, Cathy standing beside him with her all-purpose smile. The four of them were shot close within the frame of the photograph, little foreground and no background as if nothing and nobody mattered outside their tight grouping, casting out all memory of what might be missing.

"She's still hungry I guess," Cathy said, sitting cross-legged on the floor beside them. "They decided that I should take care of her every day after school and on weekends. It's my punishment for having a sister that got pregnant."

"Is it a bad one?" Sharon asked.

"No—not that bad."

When she'd had enough, the baby pushed at the bottle and thrust out the nipple with lips and tongue. Another great burp emerged as her back was patted. Then Sharon held the baby upright, feet touching the floor. How wonderful to be vertical! Baby had a name, Madeline, she had a pet name, Linny, and she had reconciled herself to existence, her eyes no longer on the light around things but on things themselves, focused, bright, meeting Sharon's gaze. She turned her head to find her young auntie. A smile as she saw Cathy who smiled back lovingly, gently bouncing the baby's fist on her palm, letting her grab a finger. It occurred to Sharon that what was intended as punishment instead was providing solace for both these children.

"Thanks for coming over. Sorry I was a moron," Cathy said.

"Not at all. I've had three kids. You should have seen me with my first. It isn't true that you know how to breast-feed automatically or that the baby does. I thought my nipple would fall off before I figured it out."

"But you're . . ."

"I know. Flat." Sharon glanced at Cathy. She wasn't exactly enormous either, but she was just fourteen. Still. "Size has nothing to do with how much milk you have. I had lots. I could have fed twins. It was just learning to get it out."

"I don't think I would breastfeed. Bottles are more convenient."

"Not necessarily. Your breasts are always there."

Cathy tickled the baby under her chin. The baby giggled. "Mrs. Lewis, does sex hurt?"

She asked in honest ignorance though her insiders would know the answer to that and their answer would be, *Yes.*

Always. Sharon needed to choose her words carefully and, as the mother of a son, her hands were suddenly moist. "Is this something you're thinking about?"

"Just wondering."

"Even if someone's had a lot of sex, it can hurt if you feel pressured or nervous," Sharon said. "But when you're grown up and feel comfortable and happy with your partner, it's really nice." They sat close, mother and maiden, who was no maiden technically speaking, but a girl whose loneliness passed through her body into Sharon's, where it slipped into a spot that was just its shape. And there was no more wavering, no more thinking she was crazy or imagining things. Sharon leaned toward Cathy, for she was a finder and she'd found these children. In the cleft of her broken heart was a resting place for them. She said as she would to her own daughters, "Like when you're, oh I don't know, twenty-five?"

"Sure, Mrs. Lewis," Cathy said so virtuously that Sharon burst out laughing. And when the girl asked what she was laughing about, Sharon hugged Cathy with reckless abandon, feeling the girl's stiffness melt, cuddling into her shoulder like Emmie or Nina. It lasted no more than half a minute. Then Cathy grabbed hold of herself and her maturity, and sat up straight. The baby was blinking and yawning.

"I think Linny is ready to go down," Sharon said. "Where's her crib?"

"Upstairs." Cathy stood up, getting her backpack from the couch and slinging it over a shoulder out of habit. Even when her parents were out, she wouldn't leave her stuff lying just anywhere. "Coming?"

The staircase was steep and narrow, the handrail of oak, the baluster wrought iron with graceful curves between the posts. On the wall was a gallery of small paintings that matched the rise of the stairs, each of different water creatures: dolphins, seahorses, tropical fish in bright colours. Surely they didn't lead to anything monstrous, Sharon thought, forgetting that humans routinely surpassed the monsters of their imaginations. On the forbidden second floor, she stopped behind Cathy, looking down the hallway. At the far end was a small window of frosted glass. There was only one door, halfway down, which opened into an office.

"Mrs. Lewis?" Cathy called.

Following her, Sharon stepped into the office, which led at either end into bedrooms that had no other way in or out but through the office. The crib was in Heather's room, which was sparsely furnished with the necessaries, cramped by crib and change table. The curtains were made of eyelet cotton, as were the bumper pads and the quilt, the bed covered with a chenille spread, all of it white. The only colour was on the crib itself, the headboard painted with the cow jumping over the moon and the footboard with the cat playing the fiddle for the dish and the spoon. "My sister did that," Cathy said. "Wasn't she good?"

"Yes, very. The detail." Not just a cat, a dish and a spoon, but a willow pattern plate, a carved wooden spoon, a calico cat with strokable fur. "That must have taken her a long time."

"It was the only thing my parents let her paint. I expected her to mess it up on purpose. But she didn't. She worked so hard. I don't understand, Mrs. Lewis." Cathy pulled the latch, lowering the side of the crib. "How could she make this so beautiful and then kill herself?" Her eyes were pained, angry. "And Linny—Heather didn't know Mom could get her out."

"I don't have an answer, honey. I wonder about that, myself." Sharon laid the baby down on her back. The window faced the alley and the garages that lined it, the tiring sun staining clouds red. "The room is so bare. Did your parents give away everything?"

"Uh huh, but there wasn't much." Cathy held on to her backpack protectively. "They stripped her room the last time she ran away. The nanny sleeps there." She pointed to Heather's bed. There were no posters or photographs, no bookshelves. Daisy wallpaper that would have irked a kid who gelled her hair straight up. In the alley a motorcycle was revving. "I used to keep Heather's portfolio on my key chain. But Mom took that too and probably threw it out."

"On your key chain?"

"It was a flash drive."

"Not a grey one."

"Yes, it was small. Just a gigabyte."

"I wonder." And on the inside Sharon could see through another's eyes: Debra searching her bag, fishing for her chequebook. A clinking sound, so slight as to seem imaginary, except to someone who noticed every tiny change. "I found something in the dining room. It couldn't be this, could it?"

"OMG, is it?" Cathy snatched the stick out of Sharon's hand, turning it over greedily. An ordinary flash drive, a cheap brand, it could be any of the kids.' "Let's check. I just need to get the password."

They went through the door to the office. One wall was lined with cabinets, tables against the other walls, four computers, cables running between them, a flat tablet hooked into the laptop. It was a working room with many doors and door jambs stuck under to keep them open so that everything could be seen from here: the hall, the bedrooms, even a tiny bathroom with a shower stall and lockable medicine cabinet. Cathy's room was peach and white, with sheer curtains over the blinds, a swag valence, and ruffled bedspread.

"Emmie would love your room," Sharon said.

"She can have it." Cathy frowned. "The password isn't here. I should have changed it to something I could remember, but numbers and letters are safer." She searched all the pockets of her backpack, then ransacked drawers. There was a lace doily on top of the dresser, a crystal atomizer with gold tassels on the doily, also a lacquer enamel makeup tray. The makeup was pristine, since everything Cathy actually used was in her backpack. There were framed awards on the wall, for dancing, for figure skating, for academic excellence. A hutch of shelves on her desk held a collection of porcelain and wood music boxes. This room was larger than her sister's, or seemed so without the baby furniture. It faced the front of the house and the second floor balcony, though nothing could be seen through the blinds. Cathy lifted the bedspread, her backpack slumping on the peach carpet as she looked under the bed. Kneeling, she paused as if thinking. Or listening. "I forgot. It's in the music box."

"This one?" Sharon tipped up the roof of an alpine chalet. Nothing. Then she lifted the lid of a wooden music box with a painted cat on the lid. Inside was a folded piece of paper with a string of letters and numbers.

Cathy took the paper from her and shut the music box. "That's it. Let's use my laptop." Cathy led Sharon into the office.

Pushing her hair back, Cathy sat down at one of the tables. In a couple of minutes, her laptop was booted up, the flash drive plugged into a USB port. She leaned forward, elbows on the table, face close to the screen as if she could jump into it and be with her sister again.

There were portraits of kids. Dozens of them. Toddlers. Kids in a park. Street kids. Twins in a jogging stroller. Many of a boy with cloudy eyes and a little girl who'd lost her front teeth and resembled him. Like the crib paintings, they were drawn with painstaking detail, the texture of hair, the wrinkle of clothes, the hue of skin and the softness of it, the set of a mouth, the twist of posture. She must have erased and redrawn her lines again and again to get that realism. Why would a girl so preoccupied with the crackling vividness of children want to prevent the birth of her own? There were several portraits of Cathy: stormy eyes; the lips about to swear; the girl next door smile; others. Heather had known her sister in all her forms.

"She was talented," Sharon said.

"That's why I took art. I told my parents I was supposed to have a drawing tablet for class. It plugs into the computer or you can use it on its own, then you back it up on a stick and delete."

Sharon nodded. Sketchbooks were awkward. A flash drive could be hidden in a sock drawer, a pocket, a tampon purse.

"My parents wouldn't let her get anything. So I told them I needed it for school."

"What's that?" Sharon asked, stopping Cathy as she was about to click next. The image on the screen wasn't like any of the others, depicting Wonder Woman in wild colours throwing her lasso, hair streaming purple and green like the stained glass in the front door, breasts about to pop out of her bodice.

"That's mine. But art is over. I should delete it."

"Leave it." Gently pushing Cathy's hand aside before she pulled out the flash drive, Sharon wondered why she'd never noticed the callus on the girl's middle finger. It came from pressing hard, the faint charcoal marks on her fingertips from smudging paper. Sharon had made assumptions: the other sister was the artist; the other sister was the bad girl. "I like it."

"Why?" A sardonic smile: Cathy had switched. This was the kid who arm-wrestled, the one who snapped bubble gum in her father's face. Eyes of a newborn, more grey than blue—a newborn left in a dumpster. As the girl doodled on the tablet with a stylus, lines appeared on the screen, hinting at the picture that might emerge. She was the artist, not Cathy, Sharon thought.

"I like what you did because it's interesting. Different."

Pause. Staring at Sharon. "Tomorrow's Mother's Day."

"Yes it is," Sharon said.

"I got a card for the mother," she said, dragging out "i" and "the," taunting. The fake "i," the missing "my." Offering the truth, fairly sure it wouldn't be heard by the dumb old mom standing before her. Flat-chested, skinny, long hair rust red. Hardly a wonder woman. "Of course, Heather isn't here to get one."

"Do you miss her?"

"She was an idiot."

"You can still miss an idiot. I miss my sister."

"Did she off herself too?"

"No. She wouldn't leave the family. And I did. But then I was the black sheep like Heather."

The girl snorted. "That's what you think. Heather always came back. Except this time. That's what pisses them off more than anything."

Sharon looked at the computer screen again. Wonder Woman could make anyone tell the truth with that golden lasso, but she'd been displaced by snaky lines that hadn't yet made their shape plain. "I wish Heather could have talked to someone."

"What for? So they could give her a bunch of pills to zone her out again?"

"I took pills," Sharon said. "I got off them and it wasn't fun. Your sister must have gone through hell. But I found a therapist to talk to who didn't tell anybody what I said. If I hadn't, I don't know what I might have done. That's why I would never tell anyone what someone told me." It was Sharon's turn to rudely stare, willing her thoughts into this child's brain: she could be told; she would believe. "I know you stole the gun. Why?"

The girl sat motionless, then lowered her eyes as if talking inside, making a decision about something. "I showed the gun to Heather. I said, if she needed it. So she'd know where it was. Not to hurt herself. For protection, that's all. Now she's gone and," the girl glared, daring Sharon to be shocked, outraged, "I hate her!"

"I understand that," Sharon said. "My sister and I needed protection, too. What do you need protection from?"

Her eyes were on the girl's, offering a promise. She was the mom, a garden wall surrounding all children who came into her house. But this was not her house and Cathy was blinking rapidly as if an eyelash had got into her eyes and she was rubbing them to hide her confusion. She picked up everything from the floor, shoving it into her backpack. She yawned. There were shadows under her eyes. "Thanks for coming, Mrs. Lewis. I've got to finish my homework and clean up before my parents get home."

She stood to walk her boyfriend's mother out, politely dismissing her. But in the hallway, when Sharon retrieved her bag from the table, she opened it to take out a pen and a scrap of paper, writing on the back of a Best Foods receipt. "Here's my cell number. Put it in your backpack, okay? Just call if you need me."

At home after the kids were in bed, Sharon baked and cooked until two a.m., thinking that the truth stank. She made roast chicken with carrots and potatoes. She made cheesecake, chocolate chip cookies, and wheat-free banana muffins. While the food was in the oven, she mopped the floor, she cleaned out the fridge, she didn't think about Mother's Day. The trick was to keep moving. You can run across hot coals if you move quickly enough. It has to do with the properties of thermal conductivity and the fact that human feet are mostly water. Human thought, however, is not. So at last, exhausted, she stood still and let someone else take over.

INSIDE

Ally was in the kitchen with Echo. Since that first time, they'd often come to the kitchen to sit on the Housekeeper's lap, if she wasn't busy, or to play quietly in a corner if she was taking care of Sharon, as she was now. Sharon sat with her eyes closed while the Housekeeper talked, trying to get through to her. Ally thought if she gave Sharon a good pinch, she'd open her eyes, but the Housekeeper wouldn't let her. Sharon had to open her eyes her own self. Ally thought a pinch would be better.

"I like music boxes," Ally said to Echo. Through the window, she could see Lyssa and Alec hanging out by the creek. Maybe she'd go to the creek sometime. "Cathy has lots."

"She closed the cat one fast. She made a funny face," Echo said. He was drawing on the kitchen floor with chalk, faces and circles within circles. "I seed what was in the box."

She turned from the window. "What?"

"Lots of sticks."

"What kinda sticks?"

"The kind you put in a puter. Different coloured ones."

"Like the one with the drawings in it?"

"Uh huh. But they had numbers on them. One, two, three like that. And writing on them."

"Show me," she said.

B-A-C-K-U-P, he wrote in big crooked letters. "What's that, Ally?"

She turned to the Housekeeper to ask but the Housekeeper shook her head, too busy to answer, and Ally looked out the window again at the tree and the field and the creek. She pulled a chair to the window, climbed on the chair and watched for a while. It was just a field, not too scary. There weren't any cows mooing in it, and the window was just a little bit above the ground. She stood on her tiptoes to see better, and then moved back on her heels. Tiptoes and heels, tiptoes and heels while she thought, and then she jumped.

It didn't hurt when she fell onto the grass. She stood up and nobody stopped her as she ran across the grass to the creek. There she squatted on the bank. She liked the sound that frogs made, *creek, creek, creek*. That was why the little river was called a creek. Lyssa was talking to Alec about boring stuff.

She interrupted them. "What is backup?"

"That's what Sharon does after she finishes bookkeeping," Lyssa said. "Sharon puts a flash drive in the USB port and she backs it up."

"What for?"

"She makes a copy of her work and she puts it on the stick in case something happens to the computer. Why do you want to know?"

"Because." Maybe she'd stick out her tongue and run away. She would have, for sure, if Lyssa hadn't come over and sat down beside her.

"Hey," Lyssa said. "We've got Mayfest at the end of the month. Is there anything you want me to get?"

"Like what?"

"Like, oh I dunno, say a teddy bear?"

On the outside Callisto was getting ready to go to their sister-in-law's house, looking for an umbrella because the forecast said rain, but the inside was alight there by the creek. Ally and Lyssa sat side by side, one small and one bigger, knowing what they knew together, and knowing what they knew separately.

*I*t was Mother's Day and the women were in Eleanor's house, putting together gift baskets for the refugee centre across from Christie Pits. "Hand me a soap. Green," Mimi ordered her daughter-in-law. Tied to every handle was a paper heart. Three finished baskets were in a row on the floor. "Why did you leave this for the last minute? This isn't work for today. You should have done it a week ago."

"One green soap." Callisto passed it to Mimi, wondering how Sharon survived this family. At the round table mounded high with items for the baskets, she sat across from her mother-in-law, who, not content with Chinese proverbs, was now righteously reciting English ones. *A stitch in time saves nine. Don't put off until tomorrow what you can do today. A bird in the hand is worth two in the bush.* Eleanor had flown the coop, gone to get more supplies, leaving Callisto alone with her mother-in-law and the knick-knacks displayed on shelves, on top of the stereo and in the bay window: one hundred and four figurines and crystal animals.

"Hand me a loofah," Mimi ordered as if her arms were too short to reach the pile in the middle of the table and filling her basket was more important than anything else.

"One loofah." Callisto handed it over. Silently, sullenly, she put soap, shampoo, deodorant, moisturizer, bubble bath, shower gel, a loofah, peppermint foot liniment, and a box of six chocolates into a basket, then wrapped ribbon around the handle, cutting the end and tucking it under. How did Sharon stand this day after day?

"When is Josh coming to help?" Mimi asked.

"After Dan gets home."

"Handball again," Mimi sniffed. Her hair was newly cut and she wore her good wool jacket, her navy trousers, a silk blouse. On the lapel of her jacket was a brooch, an enamel chrysanthemum. She was not afraid to wear heels, bringing her height to a royal five foot two. It was Mother's Day and so she had dressed up even just to fill baskets for refugees. "Josh can come with the girls now." Judy was playing with her cousins at their house. "They'll play here."

"He has to study for a test," Callisto said.

"With that girl?"

"Yes." The ribbon unwound. Why didn't it stay tucked in, like her mother-in-law's did? Callisto yanked it off and tried again.

"You should tell him no girlfriend. She isn't good for him. How many times do I tell you?"

"I didn't count," Callisto said.

"Like this is better." Mimi grabbed the ribbon.

"I don't care." Callisto grabbed the ribbon back. She was

irritable though she had no right to be, for it was her job to keep the mind clear.

Mimi reached for the ribbon again. "Let me show you the right way."

"No!" she snapped. "I don't want your help. It is none of your business who my son likes." Her mind was not clear. It was a storm, a green hurricane in her eyes.

"I am his nai-nai. I should have a say."

"If a person is free, he makes his own choice."

"He should listen to his mother and his mother should listen to his grandmother. Look what you're wearing. Not even lipstick."

Lipstick? Why were they talking about lipstick? If Callisto was concentrating, she would have seen the fish underwater, the words beneath the words. But she was tired of filling baskets and listening to her mother-in-law bicker and so, like an outsider, not Sharon but herself if she had been the outsider, she said, "Who cares?"

"I tell you how good you look with a little lipstick."

Callisto stood up and walked with dignity to the row of baskets, adding hers. Now there were four. "Excuse me," she said as she squeezed behind her mother-in-law to get to her chair, only the breathlessness of her voice betraying the storm that had not yet died.

"So polite." There was an edge to Mimi's voice. What more did she wish? "My mother-in-law used to say enemies are polite."

"I am not your enemy." Callisto returned to her seat, taking another basket. She deposited soap. Bubble bath.

Shower gel. Perhaps this was why Sharon performed menial tasks, to avoid such conversations.

"You're shouting." Mimi pulled a lace handkerchief from her breast pocket, wiping her eyes.

"Pardon me." She had lost her temper, but it was now regained, her apology as soft as could be.

"In China a woman goes to her husband's family. Before the wedding, everyone is very polite," Mimi said as her daughter-in-law unfurled tissue paper with a snap. "Afterward, mother-in-law can do anything she wants, and daughter-in-law is still polite." Her voice was flat as if she too knew how to keep the mind clear, hands clasped on the table, gripping the lace hanky. "After I got married, we lived with Jake's parents until we could buy a house. I did everything for my mother-in-law. She yelled at me from morning till night, and I accepted it."

"Why?" Callisto asked. Her husband's eyes were the same colour as his mother's. With the new cut her hair was now entirely grey. She had horizontal lines at the corners of her eyes and vertical lines below them, curving over her cheekbones.

"That's how a mother-in-law treats her son's wife. She didn't speak much English and I didn't either, so she shouted in her own language. After a while, I started to understand some words. Then one day, I realized what she was shouting. 'Why don't you talk to me?' All day long she was saying, 'Even a Chinese shiksa must know how to talk. Am I deaf? Am I stupid? What already?'" Mimi's hands trembled, then stopped by force of her will. She reached for her bag, put the handkerchief inside. Her feet barely reached the floor. "After that, we argue all the time. I want to do it my way and she wants me to do it her way. I loved her like my own mother. Even more. She was the one who told me I was pregnant with Eleanor. I said no, I can't be. I can't have more children. The doctors said so." Mimi cleared her throat. "I wanted to be just like her with my son's wife. But no matter what I do, all the time you keep me like this." She stretched out her arm, hand up, head turned away. Then she faced Callisto with unshielded eyes showing the unguarded truth of her existence in them. "Jake isn't Jake anymore. My daughter is busy. You don't need me." There was no self-pity in her voice, only the statement of fact. She had crossed an ocean alone; she was still crossing it. And when death came, she would face it as a fact to be reckoned with and her reckoning would be fierce.

"You're needed," Callisto said. "We need you."

"Today you argue with me." Mimi rose from her chair and came around the table. "First time." Her mother-in-law put her hands on Callisto's shoulders, kissing her forehead. It was the first kiss of Callisto's life, old lips pressed to her forehead where the third eye could see visions, a feathery kiss, dry. "I'm seventy, but . . ." Mimi pinched the hem of her jacket, bringing the folds together. "Then and now is like this for me. Here I was Xiao Mei. Here I was Mimi. It isn't long ago."

"Yes," Callisto said. So time played tricks on singletons, too. When someone aged, the skin wrinkled and creased, features coarsened, dark skin lightened and light skin darkened until even racial origins were obscured by old age.

And yet inside the eyes, time folded into a lightning bolt. "I understand."

"Next time I bring you goldfish. For good luck. And I bring a nice colour of lipstick. You try it," Mimi said.

Callisto laughed, surprising herself with the sound of it as the key turned in the front door and Eleanor entered with two shopping bags and more help. She'd dragged home her daughter, who'd been trying on makeup with her cousins. Her face was red where she'd scrubbed it off. As the younger kids would just be in the way, they were staying home with Josh, but Cathy was here, too, willing to lend a hand. Her right, since her left was bandaged. Ingrid came in behind them.

Mimi stared at Cathy's bandage. "One hand. You won't be much help."

"It's fine," Eleanor said. "Come on in."

They ranged in age from eleven to seventy, and the only one of them who didn't count weeks was Mimi, as even Eleanor's daughter had started her period. Two had known the pain of childbirth (three if Callisto, who was inside during the labour, were to be included); two had known rape; three had made love (four if counting Callisto, who had never been forward for it); two were virgins, and one of those—Ingrid—only in the most technical sense.

They sat around the table, hands busy as they made conversation. Mrs. Brown's cottage was slated to be torn down this summer. What a shame, it being a landmark. Cathy thought someone should petition the city. Who would be eliminated on *Survival of the Fittest*? Mimi made tea and found ready-to-bake Chinese buns in the freezer. Fifteen minutes later the oven timer dinged and she took them out.

"The buns are good. What's in them?" Ingrid said.

"Red bean paste and sesame. Did you call your mother today?" Mimi asked.

"I wish I could." Ingrid separated a couple of sheets of tissue paper from the bundle. "My mother died when I was ten."

"Nai-Nai's mother died when she was a kid, too," Judy said. She was wearing her usual basketball shirt and baggy pants. But her silver sports glasses had a slash of pink on the side, and in her underwear was a sanitary pad.

"What was she like?" Ingrid asked.

Mimi poured herself more tea. "She was very strict because she wanted me to marry well. She combed my hair until I cried. And she wrote poems. Like this: 'Your impudent lips, your fingers like a snail's trail on my skin.'" Mimi stopped reciting. "There's more, not for little girls."

"Nai-Nai! I'm almost as tall as you are. Did you look like her?"

"No, she was beautiful, like the movie star Ruan." Mimi drank her tea, wishing it was something stronger. "My father had two wives, an older one and Mama. She wrote love poems to him. When First Wife found them, she burned them. No use to complain. First Wife can do whatever she wants, Second Wife nothing. After that my mother gave up poetry. She smoked opium and didn't care what I did. Then the war made her alive again for a while." Mimi checked her

basket. Everything but chocolate. She reached for a box.
"What happened to your mama, Ingrid?"

"She died in a car accident." Ingrid pushed back her
chair and carried her basket to the row on the floor. "I was
raised by my grandmother after that."

"I never met my grandmother," Cathy said. There was
no part in her hair today. Someone had brushed it back from
her forehead, put it up in a ponytail; she couldn't have done
it with her hurt hand.

Mimi took the empty plates to the sink, rinsing them
and putting them in the dishwasher, speaking with her back
to the table. "I never expected to have a daughter. You're
my *baobei*."

Eleanor made her way around the counter that separated
the kitchen from the dining area, and put an arm around her
mother's shoulder. "Let's have some wine," she said. "I've
got three-quarters of a bottle in the fridge and it's going to
go bad."

"If it's white, I'll have some. I wouldn't want to spill red
wine on my clothes. It stains," Cathy said, sounding so much
like herself that someone could assume she was if she hadn't
just asked for wine.

"Me, too, Mom. Now that I'm a woman and everything."

"No! What are you girls thinking?" Eleanor glanced
over her shoulder. "Judy, you can fix that basket. You've put
two soaps in there and no shampoo. I'll get you and Cathy
some Coke." Soon the wine bottle, pop bottle and glasses
were on the table, surrounded by tissue paper and green
apple shower gel.

"What's a *baobei*?" Cathy asked.

"Treasure," Callisto explained, though she, herself, had never been anyone's treasure or even anyone's trash—just no one's at all. "Your sister didn't have a mother's day," she said. "I'm sorry."

"Whatever." The girl poured a little wine into her cup. She was favouring the bandaged hand, keeping it in her lap. From inside, Sharon was trying to reach through to say no, to get hold of the cup. But Callisto refused to switch. For an instant too small to measure, she turned around inside and said, *Stop*. Drinking wine is not the worst that could be done.

"How was that hand hurt?" Callisto asked.

"Burned," Cathy—or whoever she now was—replied. "Stove. My mother thinks there probably won't be a scar."

"I see." Such pain could be punishment or distraction or relief from what could not be said. Callisto drank her white wine. It wasn't white, but a translucent gold, and slightly sweet though labelled dry, which did not mean dry, but without sweetness. This was how people used words to mean other than what they were, creating enclaves of secret language.

"Nothing hurts like childbirth," Eleanor said. "They say you forget but I didn't. That's why I only had one."

"How much does it hurt?" Cathy asked, eager to learn the degrees of pain, as if there was something that could wipe out all else.

"There is worse," Mimi said.

"Like what? Name one thing, Mom."

"Watching someone you love lose their mind."

"Dad hasn't lost his mind," Eleanor said. "He's just different."

"I was talking about my mother. I never told anyone this, not even Jake." Mimi looked wistfully at her empty wine glass, wondering if she could ask her daughter to open another bottle. "Every day I'd come home from school, worried that I would find her dead."

"Like my sister. You think about the ways," Cathy said.

Mimi nodded. "She often told me she would kill herself. But she died in the war like many others. I was afraid I would pass her illness on to my children. When you quit school, Eleanor, I thought it was the beginning."

"I'm not sick, Mom."

"Just bossy!" Judy said, Eleanor slapping her hand as she tried to sneak it toward the wine.

"My mother died in a car crash because she'd been drinking, but even now no one in my family admits that she was an alcoholic," Ingrid said.

"My mother was neither ill nor drunk." Callisto paused, but there was no inner protest. The wine, which didn't affect her, had lulled the others. "She punished me by having a pet bird destroyed. Did you know that darkness is not black?" After the budgie died, she had watched colours float in the night, humming to herself until her voice was hoarse. In the morning her mind was clear, all feeling banished. She had cleaned herself up, removing what had been left inside, found the nightgown, and put it on. Then Sharon had tumbled forward to walk up the basement stairs.

"She let you have a pet?" Cathy asked.

"To teach me a lesson." Callisto looked at the girl, but her eyes were shielded so that no one could tell whether she found this inconceivable or not. "That is my mother. I don't have to honour her for donating an ovum. It's nothing sacred. Frogs do the same. But she gave birth to me and that can't be changed."

"If a minor can be emancipated, so can an adult." Ingrid's eyes were the grey of a deep, cold lake with horned snakes below and thunderbirds above. "I'll adopt you."

"And be my mother?" From inside there were hoots and shouts. Callisto smiled. So this was how smiling felt.

"But Mrs. Lewis isn't a baby," Cathy said.

"That doesn't matter. Amy was adopted by her foster parents and changed her name to theirs when she was twenty-five."

"May I call you Mommy?" Callisto asked, making her face as serious as usual, smiling only when everyone laughed.

While they filled more baskets, Ingrid told jokes: *Bear bells are a good warning device, the trick is getting them on the bear.* And: *Lint is an effective fire starter, just take it out of your belly button before lighting the match.* And: *The pilot told the hunters that their game was too heavy for the plane, but they insisted that they'd taken three elks on a bush plane before; so up they went and down they came and when they got out of the wreckage, the hunters said, damn, this looks like the place we crashed last time.*

Cathy told Judy that she didn't have to turn into a suck just because she got her period. *There was only a little bit of pink on her new glasses,* Judy protested, but the older girl teased: *that's how it starts.*

Mimi said: *In China there are ancient paintings of Nuwa, the Chinese snake goddess who created human beings and grants women children.* And, *You have to use more detergent in the dishwasher.*

Callisto, pouring the detergent, said, "I do not! In ancient China there were no dishwashers."

Slightly tipsy, they loaded up Eleanor's minivan. The baskets looked festive, beribboned, starry tissue paper mounded over fruity oils and gels. They waved to Ingrid, the only one with a driver's license who was entirely sober, as she backed the car out of the driveway and onto the street, then headed toward the refugee centre. Up and down the road tree branches shook, bending toward the park as the east wind brought the smell of rain.

*I*t was past midday when Callisto got home, expecting to relieve Josh of his babysitting duties. But nobody greeted her as she walked upstairs, the house sleepily humming and creaking from first to second to third floor. She stopped on the landing. On her right was the office, the laptop on top of a filing cabinet, the maple tree outside the window shining bronze. To the left was the bedroom, Dan napping, a book fallen to one side. A framed target on the wall, a scroll painting of chrysanthemums with a Tang dynasty poem. Two nightstands, a prizewinning novel on one, the *Economist* on the other. A pine wardrobe, dressing table, bed with extra foam to make the surface soft, floor-length velvet curtains held back with a velvet sash. Nothing here was hers. As a cloud passed over the sun, its light softened. The windows were up, the scent of lilacs on the cross-breeze. Dan was lying on his back, hands behind his head, cupping it. There was a guitar on the chair. His eyes opened.

"Hi hon." He yawned, rubbing his face, sitting up. "The kids were using me as a jungle gym. It was more exercise than the handball. Did you get it all done?"

"Yes," Callisto said. "Where are they?"

He smiled. "I gave Josh some money and told him to take them to Christie Pits. How was my mother?"

"Interesting." He laughed. "Where did the guitar come from?" she asked.

Dan's knees were drawn up, his elbows on knees, chin on hands. He was a bit taller than she was, a bit broader. Enough to comfortably hold his wife if he was allowed. "It's my old guitar. I got it out of the basement to jam with Josh. I found some sheet music too. I still like those eighties songs. We can do some Tears for Fears and some Foreigner. We tried it out before he left. Not bad."

"You sang? Outside the shower?"

"Ha, ha. Yes. I can change too, by the way."

"Don't change too much." Callisto sat on the bed, looking at him. This at least she must be allowed. His eyes were as dark as charcoal, fringed with dark lashes, his short hair sticking up. She wished to touch the hair, to know if it was bristly.

"I should do some work. I'm just feeling too lazy," he said. "I've got to keep my strength up for Sunday dinner with my family. What are we having?"

She considered his question and she considered another. Was the kiss on her forehead the only one she would ever receive? Surely this much she was allowed. She leaned forward, her lips touching Dan's, warm lips, neither dry nor wet. His lips pressed into hers and her lips wished to part.

Inside there was fear, little ones weeping. *No burning, no hitting,* someone cried. And someone answering, *It's just Dan. He won't hurt us.* But their terror was not assuaged.

234

Anyone else would have pulled away, unable to bear it. That was why there had been so little sex for a while. But her lips parted and his tongue touched hers. This much she allowed herself, putting her hands on his head to feel the softness of a brush cut. On TV she had seen people speak of positions, variations, boredom. She had known all the variations before she was eight and wished to experience none. But surely this was possible, to touch her husband's face, discovering the roughness of a shadow beard, the cartilage of his ears, the tender folds of skin along it. Turning his head, she touched the ears with her lips, then with her tongue, a sharp taste, roughness here, smoothness there, a low growl in his throat. This much yes. And perhaps his throat, the hollow of it, the pulse. Just that.

Inside there was fear, the little ones paralyzed.

His smells: shower gel, shaving gel, deodorant, lemon, tea tree oil, smoky, he'd sneaked a cigarette, chocolaty lips even though he'd brushed his teeth. He always brushed his teeth for two minutes and washed his face, but miraculously he'd missed a speck of chocolate on his lower lip.

His hands were on her shirt and beneath it her breasts wished to feel his palms. Her nipples were hardening, her breath coming faster, feeling the cloth and his hands and wanting only his hands. He reached under her shirt, cupping her breasts, skin on skin, the nipples harder, larger as the palms caressed. He pulled the shirt over her head and she allowed it.

Her own hands reached back as if they knew what was required, unhooking a bra, floating it down her arms and off the bed while he unbuttoned his shirt, shrugging it off, reaching for his pants. Her hands unzipped her slacks, pushing them down with the underwear in one motion. She perched on her side of the bed, gazing at her husband so that she could know him in his skin, this man who was hers though she had never seen him naked. Others of them, of course, but not her. Not until now. He waited, looking while she looked, and she wondered what he was seeing as she noticed his collarbone, his nipples, small and hard in the aureoles surrounded by hair, the line of hair down the centre of his chest, his belly with a puckering at the belly button, the thickness of hair around his pubic bone. His feet were long and narrow, legs thick in the calves, his knees square, one knee dimpled. A round birthmark. The hair on his arms and legs was fine and dark. There was a bare place on his right thigh. She would like to stroke it. He was erect.

Little ones watched. *It's not so big,* someone said. *Just regular. Cuz we are big now.*

She stroked his leg. He kissed her shoulder, he lifted her left arm, licking the underside, and her skin was electric. Her hands ached with it. She stretched out her right arm and he kissed the fingers, his lips softly mouthing each one.

Inside, the little ones said, *It's just Dan. This is boring.* Turning their backs, they ran to their playroom.

She was propped against the many pillows as he licked the inside of her other arm, and along her side, and in the crease of her thigh, and the outside of her thigh. She ached, light shooting up through her feet as she arched, wanting him to hurry while he lingered along the inside of her legs, first one then the other. He was kissing her belly and there was no more question of what was allowed only of what she wished. His tongue found what she wished and the heat was hotter than her temper, flames along her arms and her legs and her belly. She did not scream, but she moaned and just when the heat was unbearable, he was inside her, legs wrapped around his back, rocking together, legs tightening as he moaned.

And then she said, "Again."

This time he held her close, his fingers finding their way between her legs and inside. She moaned with the heat and she said, "Again."

Afterward she lay back and the room seemed very far away until the fluttering inside calmed, the wetness evaporating. When she went to pee, she smelled the bitterness of sperm, the musk of herself. She put her hand down, raised it, inhaled. An adult odour, a woman's smell. And through her, the others felt what it was to have made love for the first time.

"I got you something for Mother's Day," Dan said as she got back into bed.

"A present for us?" In the soft light of the bedroom, in the thrumming of a house without children in it, she could be excused for saying "us" instead of "I."

"It's beside the laptop. I thought you'd see it when you got home."

"I came in here," she said.

"Well, it's time to get rid of that dinosaur in the kitchen that you put CDs on. I downloaded some classical music onto the iPod. That's why it's not in the box. But it's new. Why are you looking at me like that?"

"I didn't expect anything." She was the one who listened to classical music at night. The others inside preferred rock or country or pop. A gift for her. It was astonishing: he'd seen her, he'd known her as if she had every right to exist out here. And so she dared to lie with her head on his shoulder, his arms around her. One more thing: to fall into sleep, her breath slowing with his as if there was only one breath.

The slam of a door woke them up, and they scrambled into their clothes as she discovered how suddenly and wonderfully the mind could clear when children were calling up the stairs to their naked parents.

Welcome to multiples-chat, a supportive chat room for people who have DID or DDNOS. Visit our homepage at www.multiplesweb.com.

*S&ALL has joined multiples-chat

S&All› hihihihi

S&All› im heer now ally

Mother's Day was over, the moon just past full illuminating the backyard brighter than lamplight. A fat raccoon followed by her babies, having fed well on city leavings, waddled across the deck, looking for a comfortable place to use as a latrine. Perhaps right here in front of the glass doors, where she could admire her reflection.

Janet› hey how are you doing kiddo?

S&All› u no wat?

Janet› what

S&All› we git a kitty and him be blak and soft

There was a plate of cookies beside the laptop. And coffee. She wouldn't drink coffee, it didn't taste nice. The cookie was good. She nibbled around the chocolate chips, saving the best for last.

Janet› wow wow do u givd him a nam?
S&All› franky i like smelllin him he smeld gud
S&All› him tiklin my nos
Janet› hehehe

"Mommy . . ." Nina was in the kitchen, a dark-eyed elf in pajamas, tilting her head as her mother turned to look at her with a rounded face and a smile like her little sister's, puffy-cheeked, a tangle of hair falling over her face.

Uh oh. Uh oh. A daughter was here. Ally looked down, watching from under lowered lids. The daughter watched too. Nina could ride a bike and skate and wash her own hair and paint it. She could add numbers and minus them. She was good. A weird little inside girl was not supposed to be out with the son or daughters. Franky meowed. Long squeaky meow.

"Meow!" Ally imitated the kitten. The daughter laughed. It made sparkles like the lights in a faraway sky. "He smells good," she said, offering Franky.

Nina took him and held him to her face, nuzzling the soft fur. "I wish he was my present. You're lucky."

"Uh huh." She smiled fast. *Bye-bye. You are a good girl. A big is coming!* And the daughter smiled back, squinting as the light switch flipped on.

"Nina, why are you up?" Callisto's voice was different, the usual hoarseness stripped away with her clothes this afternoon. It was now slightly deeper than Sharon's, and creamy. She studied her daughter's face, looking for fear, for edginess, but there was only a curious smile, fading. "You should be asleep. You'll be tired tomorrow."

"I forgot this." Nina held out a notebook. "You have to sign my homework."

Depositing the kitten beside the laptop, Callisto fetched a pen from the junk drawer. On the open page, next to the word *playing,* written out five times, she scrawled the body's initials, SAL. Sharon Alyssa Lewis.

"Why did you write with your left hand?" Nina asked.

"I like to sometimes."

"I'm going to try it. Can you go upstairs with me, Mommy? I think there's maybe spiders."

Through the glass doors, opened to let in the spring breeze, Callisto could see Dan's car, the birch tree, the shed with the basketball net nailed to it, the iron and glass patio table, all in wondrous shades and shapes of black, now familiar, not long ago strange. Callisto held out her hand to her daughter, who had grown in her body and been born without her knowledge. Her daughter took it, walking confidently back to bed with no fear of darkness as long as her mothers walked with her like the thousand-armed goddess of mercy, left-handed and right-handed.

CHAPTER

TWENTY-TWO

*M*ayfest was always held in Christie Pits on the last weekend of May. Standing where the glue factory had been, now Hope Market, you could hear the barkers' cries: *Hit the bull's eye and win a dinner at Magee's—only five tickets* and *Dunk the principal—fifteen tickets.* In the bowl of the park there were booths. Hand-crafted jewellery of silver, beads, tiger's eye, papier mâché, silk jackets, silk bags, leather bags, quilted bags, crafts made of wood, art made of metal, toys used and new, books by local authors: a children's poet, two novelists, including Bonnie Yoon, and a historian on hand to sign. And food: pizza, ice cream, home-baked treats of every kind, Cajun corn on the cob, hot dogs, burgers, every kind of drink that could rot your teeth. There was an inflated castle, an inflated basketball court, and inflated rock climbing with a chute to slide down. Information booths: the boys and girls club, street safety with a real police car to climb inside, insurance advice from a man well-practised in latching onto uninterested passersby, the Committee for Youth display, Amy's booth on Caring for Your Pet with rabbits, a guinea pig, and a lizard. The silent-auction table organized by Sofia. Their next-door neighbour was bidding.

"There's your afghan, Mom!" Nina said. "Maybe Mrs. Agostino wants it for her porch chair. It'd keep her warm." She was holding her mom's hand as her brother scanned the hillside for his friends. He was heading toward the tae kwon do demonstration on the crest of the hill in the basketball court (in winter the ice rink). Just outside the fence was the clubhouse that had sported a swastika on the roof when their zaidey was a boy. It was Mayfest and though there was a haze in the air and rain in the forecast, nothing could dampen their joy.

"Come on, Nina. Let's beat Dad!" Her mom ran down the hill, laughing as Dan followed, jogging with Emmie on his shoulders, who slapped his head, shouting, *Faster, faster.*

At the bottom of the hill, Lyssa collapsed onto the grass, but she didn't stay there long. The castle needed exploring and the girls were pulling her up by the hands to line up and buy tickets, looking for people they knew, calling to their friends. She took a turn with them at dunking the principal and missed, got them roasted corn, looked for her sister-in-law but couldn't find her, clapped as Nina tried to do a cartwheel. *Way to go! Awesome!* Emmie was sitting in the police car, chatting with the officers. They stood next to a poster of the Christie Pits riot: blurry men in white shirts, several women in long dresses, colour unknown, balls of light reflecting off the camera's flash. The names of police officers who'd been called to quell the riot were listed alphabetically. Lyssa read through them all in case there was a mistake.

"There's no Amos Edwards," she said to Dan.

"Rick's grandfather? Huh. I wonder why."

"Maybe he wasn't there. Maybe he wasn't even a cop." Lyssa was looking up the hill to where Cathy was pushing the stroller along the path toward her parents' booth. "Can I leave the kids with you?"

"Sure." Dan lifted his camera and snapped a shot of the stilt walkers. Then he followed his wife's glance. "You're going to try to talk to her again?"

"Yup."

"And get upset again? You've done your best. There's nothing more you can do."

"Ha! Watch me," Lyssa said, waving as she jogged backward, nearly bumping into a woman handing over a credit card at the next table.

The Committee for Youth information booth consisted of a table, an easel with a sign on it, a backboard with blown up photographs and big, bold terrifying statistics: every year a million people committed suicide around the world, more than died in wars; the most common method was firearms; annually eight out of every hundred thousand teens died this way. Pamphlets were printed with the logo that Dan had designed, CFY coming out of cupped hands in embossed gold, and in smaller black letters below, IN MEMORY OF HEATHER EDWARDS. People were crowding around the table, reading pamphlets, signing up for the e-mail list, giving donations by cheque, by credit card, taking their receipts from Rick. He marked the amount on the large drawing of a thermometer, mercury rising ever higher. Standing to one side, Lyssa leaned against a cotton-wood tree, waiting.

Debra wore her white doctor's coat, a stethoscope around her neck. "It's your turn," she was saying to a child who was getting impatient, putting the earpieces into the girl's ears, the drum against her chest.

"I hear it!" The kid was about six, chubby, rapt as Debra explained how the sounds were produced when different heart valves closed against the reverse flow of blood.

Rick kept rubbing his chin as if to rub away the grey of his beard. "It took you long enough," he said, pointing at his watch as Cathy reached the booth, putting the stroller with the sleeping baby in it behind the table.

"Sorry, Dad." She wore white shorts and a polka-dot shirt gathered under the bust, bangs newly cut across her forehead, a light fringe of gold.

"Hey, can I borrow Cathy?" Lyssa asked. "I need her opinion."

"Just a moment." Debra put down her stethoscope, ignoring the kids' *awws* and *When's my turn?* She came around the table, standing close to Lyssa beneath the cottonwood tree. She wore a new, ambery perfume. "Cathy hasn't been herself lately. She even threatened to call children's services. Where would she get an idea like that?" She peered at Lyssa suspiciously. Her lipstick was red, her face pale.

"Wow." There were shouts from inside and Lyssa crossed her arms, balancing on one foot, pressing the other into the trunk of the tree. She wasn't going to run. The others had tried and failed. It was her turn now.

"After Heather died the police had to look over the scene." Debra made quotation marks around "scene" with her fingers. "You can't imagine how it feels to have strangers come into your house and walk around as if they own it." She came in close. Her perfume was thick, her pale eyelashes dotted with mascara. "Nobody will ever do that to me again."

"No kidding," Lyssa said, running through possible answers faster than she'd have guessed possible, throwing each useless one aside until, Bingo, there it was. Just what she needed. "I know what you mean—awful," she said.

"Pardon?" Suspicion faded to puzzlement.

"I called social services when I was nine."

"No! Why?" Debra asked.

"I was upset so I called. The social worker asked what I was doing out of school."

On a winter's day in grade four, with no warning, Lyssa had been pushed forward. She'd had no idea of what had been happening on the outside. All she knew was that Sharon was gone and she was lying on the ground in the school-yard, surrounded by a circle of kids pointing, elbowing each other, shrieking with laughter and shouting *butt-head, stinky-butt, fart-face*. Her coat had been open, her panties around her ankles. The kids had been holding projects, the solar system, a tepee made of paper and Popsicle sticks, the girls' knees red between their socks and skirts. The Plasticine model of a volcano on a sheet of cardboard had been put on the snow near one of the boys, who was empty-handed and laughing the hardest. He must have been the one who'd pulled her panties down. She'd kicked off the panties, got to her feet and, holding up her dress, peed on his volcano. As the teacher on duty had moved toward her, she'd run, intending to make the most of this unexpected gift of time. With nobody home, she could look up the phone number in the front of the white pages. Not that she would say any of this to Debra except for the end result.

"What did you tell the social worker?" Debra asked.

"Oh, I tried to say something was going on at home, but all they did was talk to my parents and tell them I was skipping school. Naturally I was punished."

Her parents had ordered her to stay in her room for a week, so sure of themselves they hadn't even locked her in. But the ice rink was at the end of the road. There was a fence and a field and then the railroad tracks. Every day after her parents left for work, she'd gone there to skate, using up Sharon's allowance to rent skates and buy cups of cocoa. The old man in the snack bar had put marshmallows in it. He'd looked over his glasses, unsmiling, and he hadn't asked Lyssa how come she wasn't in school. He'd just given her free marshmallows, had said that the french fries were on special, half price, and had taken her money. The man had had grey hair in a ponytail, he'd worn wire-rimmed glasses and a big greasy apron. He'd sat on a stool and read newspapers. He'd never even said, *I've done something for you so now you do something for me.* It was this kindness that had kept her from walking in front of a car. On the ice she'd fallen and she'd got up. Falling on ice had hurt less than her other bruises. The snow had been white, the sky had been white. Nothing stained. Nothing stank.

"While I was skipping school, I learned to skate," Lyssa told Debra. "If I was a boy they'd have sent me away to military school."

Debra nodded sympathetically. "We need to get away and make a new start. Usually we just go up to the cottage on weekends, but this year we're planning to spend the whole summer up there. We can put our house up for sale and stay at the cottage until we locate something permanent. Given that it's winterized, there's no rush."

"So far?"

"It would be a long commute for Rick, but doable."

"When?" Lyssa glanced over at Cathy, who was standing near the stroller. She was close enough to hear the conversation between Lyssa and her mom, though she looked as if she wasn't paying any attention, staring past them, a bored expression on her face.

"As soon as Cathy's exams are over," Debra said.

This was it then. They were running out of time. "Hey, Cathy," Lyssa said. "I want to pick out something new at the clothing boutique. I'm done with this beige look. Totally done. But I don't know what would look good on me. Come with me and tell me what you think."

"Can I, Mom?" Cathy asked. She spoke like any kid eager to get out of babysitting for a while. Her fingernails were bitten to the quick, the rims red and sore. On the palm of her left hand was a dime-shaped scar, which looked nothing like a stovetop burn, but a lot like the wrong end of a cigarette.

"Don't be too long," Debra replied. She smiled pleasantly, like any mom giving in.

As Lyssa pushed her way through the lines of people waiting to get books signed, Bonnie Yoon waved and she waved back. She guided Cathy past the inflatable castle and the cotton candy booth where Dan would soon be getting pink for Emmie and blue for Nina, both bags containing the same spun sugar mixed with dye. She stopped at the table of teddy bears and remained long enough to pay for one in a kilt and put it in the backpack. Then she was off again, past the wooden toys and past the beaded purses, past the metal art and past the mugs and T-shirts, stopping finally at the clothing boutique that was out of sight of the Committee for Youth. There were racks of clothes of mixed styles and sizes. Lyssa stood before them, wondering what to do next.

"Try this. Very nice with your hair," the Chinese saleswoman said, holding out a jacket. "It fit nice. You have good figure."

"Me?" Lyssa rolled her eyes at Cathy. "Sure I'll try it. Why not?" She took the jacket from the saleswoman and shrugged it on.

Laura Anderson was in front of the mirror, trying on a jacket that was the exact shade of her blue pumps, pointy-toed and stiletto heeled, miraculously not sinking into the grass. "I need something longer to cover my hips, but that jacket works for you," she said.

"What do you think?" Lyssa asked.

Cathy was gazing at her critically. "You look like somebody's mother," she said. "Here." She pulled a jacket off a hanger. Faux leather with a diagonal zipper and a ruffled border at the waist. "Try these." Faded jeans, back pockets embroidered, low on the hips. "And these." She picked up some bangles from the table, and eyed the display of earrings.

Lyssa pulled on the jeans over her shorts, then glanced at the mirror. "They fit," she said, hopping on one foot and leaning on Cathy as she removed the jeans. "I'm trusting you." She nudged the girl.

"The jacket is pretty on you," she said shyly, looking down.

"I'll take these and also," Lyssa pointed to the display of punky earrings, "those silver ones. No, not that, I want the anchors. These are for you," she said to Cathy. "And the skulls. Yup, that's all. No, wait." It had taken her a moment to realize that Cathy had switched to someone whose voice and face were slightly familiar.

The girl's hand was hovering over a tray of hair claws, drawn by the coloured crystals. Then she snatched it away as if she wasn't allowed.

"Can I try that?" Lyssa asked the saleswoman, picking up a hair claw shaped like a butterfly and decorated with white and blue crystals. She bunched the girl's hair, twisted and clipped it up, revealing the long neck. "It goes with your eyes. Turn around. You can see it if you hold up this mirror."

The girl smiled tentatively, then shook her head, looking up at Lyssa through her lashes. "It's too pretty," she said.

And in those few words, Lyssa understood that here was a flirty girl, one of those dirty girls not allowed shiny things that show the lovely colour of the eyes. "Hey, didn't you help me pick out this great jacket and the jeans?" Lyssa asked. "If that's okay for me, then it must be for you since I've done everything you could do and more."

"Daddy likes pink on girls." The girl glanced up quickly then away, eyes on her feet. She wore silver flip-flops. Her toenails were painted pink. "I heard what you said to Mom about calling social services, but we can't do that," she whispered. "I'm not allowed to talk to strangers."

Lyssa could say kiss my ass. She knew how to say it in numerous languages. In Turkish it was lick my ass. But instead she said, "I've always wanted pretty things. I'm not a stranger. Talk to me."

"I don't know what to say."

"What do you think about your sister's baby growing up like her?"

"It's not so bad."

"She killed herself. Isn't that bad enough?"

The girl shook her head, then unclipped the hair claw, letting her hair fall around her face. Sometime when this kid was middle-aged, she might wander into a therapist's office. God had more patience than Lyssa.

"By the end of next month you'll be gone. You've got till then. That's your chance. Just think of that," Lyssa said. And she bought the hair claw.

Pushing through lines and wending her way between displays, Lyssa led the girl back toward the Caring for Your Pet booth, where Ingrid had joined Amy, bringing lunch. It smelled good, roast corn and burgers. Over on the grass, their next-door neighbour Nico Agostino was playing the saxophone, the case open, people throwing in coins. He would soon graduate from high school and his father was opening his wallet to give a donation to the Committee for

Youth. Rick turned the receipt book to a fresh page. This was Mayfest; who among them was the snake in the garden?

Debra put her stethoscope in the ears of a little boy, next in the line of kids wanting to tap each other's knees and hear their own hearts. Heavy clouds covered the sun. "Did you get what you needed?"

"Yup. I nearly bought a jacket that was awful. But this girl saved me. She has a good eye. Thanks," she said to Cathy but it was her mother who smiled back.

"At the cottage I'll be able to spend more time with her," Debra said. "We've been in a state of shock and let things go in a way we shouldn't have. She used to be such a good girl." At the word *good,* the girl tilted her head coyly, glancing at her parents from under her lashes. "She was just like Madeline as a baby. Madeline hardly cries at all, even at night. I've checked on her in the crib and she's just lying there with her eyes open."

Tony Agostino took his receipt and there was a momentary break in the crowd, nobody looking at pamphlets, no one signing up.

Frowning, Rick looked at the sky. "Is that a raindrop?" He lifted his palm. Seagulls were squalling. "We've got to load the car in a hurry. Pack these up, Cathy." Umbrellas were coming out, newspapers held over heads, the guinea pig chirping as a cloth was dropped over its cage.

"See you!" Lyssa called, waving one last time. In the western heaven water and ice collided. Lightning flashed as she went to collect her family.

*B*y the Friday after Mayfest, warm rain had turned to cold rain as the north wind gathered speed. Lyssa was looking through the closet for something to wear with her new jeans. That shirt might do, she thought, or that one. After trying on each combination, she gazed at herself in the mirror and shook her head. What about the lacy camisole she'd seen underneath the cotton tops in the dresser? Nina and Emmie were asleep, Cathy and Josh in his room, studying for exams, Dan working in the office.

"Can I have some money?" Josh called from the bottom of the staircase.

"Sure," Lyssa called back. She went to the dressing table, opened the purse that was on it, and took out the wallet as Josh came into the bedroom.

"What do you need money for?" Dan asked, emerging from the office.

"Snacks. There's nothing to eat," Josh said. The fridge was full, but he couldn't study on a cheese sandwich or carrot sticks. "And I want to get a movie for later." When

Dan raised his eyebrows, Josh added, "It's not a school night."

"Great. Bring back donuts, too," Lyssa said, giving Josh some money. "I like the lemon jelly."

After Josh left, Dan stayed in the bedroom, watching Lyssa with a smile while she dug the camisole out of the dresser drawer and changed into it. She studied herself in the mirror. Possible. Tucked in or out? Definitely out.

"What do you think?" she asked.

"Nice," he said.

"I should ask Cathy." She didn't have any jewellery to wear with it except for the jade heart. What about makeup— would the guys inside put up with it?

"My opinion not good enough?" he teased.

"It's a chance to talk to her alone," she said. "Josh will be a while. He has to go farther for the donuts."

"You don't give up, do you?"

"Nope." She started down the stairs.

"Maybe I can help this time," he said and followed her.

Stopping, she turned her head to look at him dubiously. "I don't know."

"I haven't tried, yet. What if she sees that both of Josh's parents are willing to believe her?"

"Okay," she said, and, together they continued down the stairs and along the hallway to Josh's room.

Cathy was sitting at his desk, a tablet plugged into the computer, moving a stylus on its surface. She lifted the pen and leaned to touch the monitor as she studied the image, so absorbed she didn't notice her boyfriend's parents walk in.

Dan swore under his breath when he saw the computer screen. It was one thing to know such things existed, another to see it in colour and in his house. Lyssa thought: *Not this, I can't do it, I need to get out of here.*

Cathy turned, pointing the grey e-pen at her. From where she stood, Lyssa could read the URL: www.angelsoftranquility. com. The little angel on the computer screen was blonde. Her hair was in pigtails. Her nose sunburned. She was naked and mounted by a grimacing rider nearly twice her height and four times her weight. Lyssa made herself stay though she wanted to run out the window and into the sky and along the trail of stars as far as she could get. On the inside some folks were moving lils back, others on alert. Thinkers thinking. Protectors protecting.

Cathy—not Cathy, but someone else in the same body, the same white top and pink skirt, hair in a ponytail, scarred palm, turned toward them, blue-grey eyes of a newborn, edgy voice, sardonic smile. The girl who'd drawn Wonder Woman with stained glass hair said, "Sorry," as she closed the browser. "I gotta go."

"Don't. I saw that. I know what it is," Lyssa said. Inside a furore, a scream that was cut off. Dead silence.

"What do you know?" Her voice was contemptuous. There were only two kinds of grown-ups: those who hurt kids, those who were stupid. And yet she'd let herself get caught. She'd come here to do it.

Dan said, "That was kiddie porn." He sounded appalled, horrified, disgusted, all the things that would drive away the girl with the newborn eyes.

"Shhh," Lyssa hissed. The blink of an eye and Cathy would switch back. Once she was back, she'd know nothing except that she didn't feel very good. People who hurt children counted on that.

"We should call her parents," Dan said.

"No, we shouldn't. And we're not, right?" she said quickly, looking at him, a warning in her eyes. If he started to lecture, they'd get nowhere. "You said you wanted to show Cathy that you'd believe her. First you have to listen."

"Okay," Dan said. "I'm listening."

The girl opened her mouth to tell some lie, anything to deny what they'd just seen. "I . . ."

"Don't." Lyssa interrupted. "You hooked up that art tablet but you weren't drawing. Why?"

"I have no idea what you're talking about," the girl said. But she was looking at Lyssa, not at the floor or the ceiling or blinking to switch.

"Just because I have a nice ass doesn't mean I'm brainless." A protector was trying to get out and push her aside. They were shifting back and forth, closer and further, melding and separating. "You were doing something to the picture. What?"

"Homework." Behind the eyes Lyssa saw a flicker of fear. The girl crossed her arms, daring the grown-ups to figure it out.

"Was that you or Heather? I could tell it was one of you, but you look a lot alike and it was a while ago. Like—when you were maybe five?"

Dan looked stunned, and the fear in the girl's eyes was turning into panic. But she didn't switch though one hand was on her stomach like it was hurting. She grinned. Or something like a grin. She could have been gritting her teeth.

"Fuck you," she muttered.

"I'm not into girls," Lyssa said with a straight face. "Besides, you're jailbait and I'm married."

Jolted, the girl laughed and then for a moment she relaxed, no longer smiling, looking up at the grown-ups with a little bit of hope.

The way to answer that hope was by sharing the truth, and Lyssa was the one to do it. She could ask the questions that nobody but her would think to ask, though she and the others inside weren't supposed to let on what they knew. It was hard enough to talk to the therapist about things they were never supposed to say. If she didn't choke on the words, if she didn't get overcome by nausea, if someone inside didn't haul her back, she could tell this girl that she knew exactly what the picture on the computer screen had been all about. From inside came a howl. *No!* But the girl who drew pictures was a kid in their house. Protect the children. Wasn't that what they lived for? Lyssa moved forward as far as she could go and right behind her she could feel Sharon—the idiot outsider, the *it's nothing,* the *be nice* one—saying, *Talk. Talk your head off. Now! We are the MOM!*

"Are your parents hurting you?" Lyssa asked.

"My parents are wonderful."

"I've got wonderful parents too," Lyssa said. "Everyone likes them." The girl was staring as if she could see inside Lyssa's head and maybe she could. Let her. All she'd find was someone who wasn't running even though Lyssa had to fight every instinct to stay where she was. "But my father liked kids."

Next to her, Dan stood quietly, nodding to show that he was listening, even if it cost him nearly as much to remain silent as it did Lyssa to say more.

"Don't they all," the girl said.

"He had sex with his," Lyssa said, blood drumming in her ears.

Dan put his arm around her, but she shrugged him off, unable to bear any kind of touch right now.

"I did pictures like that, too," Lyssa said. "And movies. And parties. Both my parents sold us."

"But you're married," the girl said, face confused.

"Funny thing," she answered softly. "I thought I'd always be a little whore. Sometimes I still feel like one."

"I'd like to kill them for making you feel like that," Dan said, trying to keep his tone level so as not to frighten anyone. "The people who did that to you are scumbags. But you, hon—you're beautiful."

And though Lyssa would rather have done anything but look at him, she did. This was what she saw in Dan's eyes: anger, worry, love so sure she had to look away, but she let him entwine his fingers through hers.

"You don't think she's gross?" the girl asked.

"Why would I think that?" Dan asked, insulted.

"Because it's disgusting."

"It—and the adults who liked it. Not the kids. Not my wife."

The girl looked down, looked up. Still present but barely holding on. "Heather was too old for the business so she had to do web maintenance."

Dan swore again, and Lyssa pressed his hand, reminding him to stay calm. The question had to be posed even though it was risky because the girl might take off. "Your father, is he still doing you?" Lyssa asked.

The girl nodded. No words. There would have been threats about telling. There would have been demonstrations of consequences.

"They're both in the business?"

The barest nod of the chin. Half the people Lyssa had met in multiples-chat had been done by both parents. It had nothing to do with being gay or straight. Breaking into a child's body was something else entirely. "Does she use you?"

"Not anymore. I'm too big. But she'll go berserk if she knows I'm doing this." Looking from her boyfriend's mom to his dad.

"It's okay," Dan said. "I'm not upset with you."

"Please. I can get some of this done before Josh comes back."

"Some of what?" Lyssa asked.

"I do the web maintenance now. So I'm taking out Heather's face and putting mine in. I don't want anybody looking at my sister like that." She was pleading with them, this tough kid who'd as soon scratch your eyes out as say hello.

"Neither would I," Lyssa said. "I've got a sister, too. But there are so many ways this could get you into worse trouble."

"I don't care. I'm going to fix this. I've got to. It's my fault she shot herself. I stole the gun."

"For protection, not for her to kill herself."

"You still don't get it. If I hadn't, she would have jumped like she planned."

"And the baby would have died, too," Dan said, as if that was the worst thing possible, while his wife was considering the other options.

They had alters that were babies. The abuse started younger than any sane person could imagine. The younger the pricier. And now people could buy real-time on the Internet. It was a three-billion-dollar business.

"If I was pregnant in my parents' house, I'd be thinking that they were going to start training my baby when she was in diapers," Lyssa said. "And that before she started school, they'd be putting her in porn and selling her to men. Before she could write her name, she'd wish she was dead. I'd be thinking nothing was worse than that."

"You see?" the girl said, explaining as if for the first time in her life she wasn't walking among the blind. "Every time Heather got away, like, she'd forget everything. And she'd come home as if it was a great place and she was so bad to even think of leaving it. The same thing happened after she got knocked up. She painted that crappy crib like nothing had ever happened. I had to tell her. What else was I supposed to do? I showed her the website so she could remember. I just wanted her to run away again, that's all. Then she started putting her desk in front of the door every night. My mom would push at the door and make her move it back.

She said it was a fire hazard. They fought and my mom yelled and Heather said as soon as she got some money she was out of there and they'd never see the baby again. Then they had a little talk with her about that idea. Afterward she got so quiet it was scary. That's why I showed her where I hid the gun. I said she could have it. I thought she'd go away and take it with her, you know? And she hugged me. She said, thanks, you're the best. Everything was cool. I figured she'd get her own place and I could go live with her. I was sleeping on the floor in her room and she must've walked over me to get the gun. I didn't even know. So stupid. I didn't hear anything until the shot. So guess what? My sister died and, because of me, they can do whatever they want to her baby. You know?"

"I do. But you can leave. I bet they said you couldn't, but they lied," Lyssa said.

The girl shook her head, incredulous. "How could I?"

"There was a better option for your sister," Dan said. "You can call the police. That was what she should have done."

"That's not what I meant," Lyssa said as the girl shivered.

"Don't, don't. I'll be good." Her voice was high, her eyes fluttering. "Promise." A little one was out. A child alter who'd be thinking that punishment was due for telling: sex, a beating, jail, all the things that had been done or threatened.

"It's okay. Nobody's in trouble." Lyssa turned to Dan. "She's a lil. I can't leave her like that. We need to get an adult out." The kid was hugging her knees, rocking a little bit, trying not to be noticed.

"Did I do something wrong?" he asked.

"Just let me talk to her," Lyssa said, and knelt in front of the desk chair. "I'd like you to do something, sweetie. Can you get a big out?"

The girl shook her head.

"Okay." Lyssa stood up again. Turning to the computer, she put her hand on the mouse. Most lils could read and write phonetically. If you were five for long enough, you'd learn how. But the girl who did the web maintenance might come forward again if Lyssa talked about the Internet. "See here? You can download this chat software free. This is the port address. You click here to get to a chat room for people like us. Take a look."

Welcome to multiples-chat, a supportive chat room for people who have DID or DDNOS. Visit our homepage at www.multiplesweb.com.

    *S&ALL has joined multiples-chat

    Panther› hi s&all how are you

    *S&All is now known as lyssa

    lyssa› i'm just showing a friend how to get to chat

    *Janet is now known as RG

    RG› hey lyssa, good to see ya, tell your friend welcome

"Who's Lyssa?" the girl asked.

Lyssa glanced at Dan. This wasn't the way she'd imagined telling him her name. "Me," she said, and gestured at the monitor. "Those are our friends. They all got away and they're safe now. RG stands for rockgirl. And you're?"

"Call me Ceecee. It stands for cunt." The girl smiled her sharp and bitter smile though the person she was talking to knew all the kinds of names there were and was surprised by none.

In that spare, neat boy's room there were two adults and a girl visible to the average eye, as well as a multitude of children who knew how to split and separate and cope with being whipped, burned, beaten, shocked, terrorized, threatened, mocked, raped in every way by man, woman and animal, for kicks and for profit. They were reaching out through the eyes to the children outside, all the children of the night being used for pleasure and for pain, small hands reaching to small hands, invisible, despairing, scrabbling for hope.

"Hey, Ceecee. Why don't you stay here tonight?"

The smile vanished. "I can't. I have to go home. The baby's there."

They looked at each other, sizing things up. Greeting each other as warriors of the children's war, battle weary, wanting only to rest and knowing they couldn't, not yet, maybe not ever.

Lyssa's heart sank as Ceecee looked away, unable to hold on anymore. The good girl was back, covering up her confusion that her art tablet was plugged into the computer when she'd come here to study, not to draw.

"I should be getting home," Cathy said. She unplugged the tablet and put it back into her bag.

"But Josh will be back soon with snacks and a movie," Lyssa said, hoping for another chance to talk. "It's not that late."

The girl's eyes went flat, opaque, the blue of an eggshell. And just for a moment, someone else came forward to say,

"My parents let me sleep in Heather's room with the baby. I'll take good care of her." Then Cathy was back, blinking. She rubbed her tired eyes. "I've got to call my dad," she said. "It's not safe to walk home in the dark. He said he'd pick me up."

While she took out her cell, Dan pulled Lyssa out into the hallway. "How can we let her go home?" he asked.

"I don't know," she said.

Rick rang the bell twice, not impatient, but cheerful. He was in an expansive mood. Even his hair seemed less grey, maybe touched up to match his good spirits. He said he'd spent the afternoon with architects, who were quoting on an addition to the cottage. You have to keep looking ahead. He'd have a good-sized study, with built-in drawers for his digital cameras. His new camera had twelve megapixels. And there would be an ensuite guest room. It was exciting to design your own home. You could put in secret passageways or a dungeon, he joked, standing with an arm around his daughter. She neither leaned into him nor resisted, like a stick of wood, like petrified wood as hard as stone, waiting for the sun to age and the earth to grow cold.

He didn't seem to notice Dan's stiffness or Lyssa's pained expression, her stomach hurting as he went on talking. After the move, he'd keep a hand in the Committee for Youth. He'd be teaching downtown and if the commute was too onerous, he could rent a small place for weekdays. He was just in the midst of arranging a corporate sponsorship for

the gifted class in Seaton School. The kids needed computers and cameras for multimedia presentations.

He was still going on that way, all of them standing in
the hallway, when Josh unlocked the door and came in. His
backpack was loaded with chips and drinks and the movie,
a big box of donuts in his hands. "You're going, Cathy?" he
asked. "So early?"

"I have to," she said to Josh.

"Early to bed and early to rise, my friend," Rick said. "I'll
see you soon to talk about the fundraising for the Committee
for Youth, Dan."

It was all Lyssa could do not to kick him in the nuts.
Finally he left, and she was able to lock the door. Her stomach
cramped and she dashed up to the bathroom, switching on
the light at the top of the stairs.

CHAPTER TWENTY-FOUR

*T*here were two sinks in the second floor bathroom. Beside one was a Barney toothbrush and a SpongeBob toothbrush, a stack of yoghurt tubs used for rinsing the girls' hair, a brush, Emmie's hair clips with a couple of red hairs stuck in them, Nina's Silly Putty. Beside the other sink, toothpaste with baking soda, deodorant, a magician's biography, a shoelace. On the window ledge, African violets. Talking inside: *we are safe, nobody can get us anymore, we are big, this is our house, with flowers.*

Lyssa stripped, clothes too painful on her skin, and lay naked on the floor of the bathroom, her eyes on the windowsill. As long as she kept her eyes fixed on the flowers, the room wasn't so spinny, and she could get to the toilet again if she needed to.

If only she could get the pictures out of her head. She swore in French and she swore in Chinese but the girl she'd seen on the computer screen kept morphing into her cousin Karen, who also had blonde hair and blue eyes. Karen wasn't a real cousin but that was what they called her, a big girl in grade one. She made good money for her dad, even at the parties. Later she was in a wheelchair, but back then she did everything better.

They worked in the business room, the finished part of the basement, which was furnished like a bedroom with an orange shag carpet, a bed, a night table, and a velvet painting of a clown. At the back, next to the door to the garage, there was a couch to sit on while they waited their turn. The floodlights and camera were set up at the front. There was a table and a big chair for her father. At the top of the stairs, the door to the rest of the house was kept locked.

Lyssa's earliest memory took place in that basement. Lester was working them that day. He had a bushy beard, he smoked brown cigarettes and he smelled of the same after-shave as the father. They were both Aqua Velva men. First the kids drank their medicine mixed with red Kool-Aid. It made them dizzy and queasy, but throwing up wasn't allowed. Across the windows there were bars and blackout curtains, on the walls striped wallpaper. Mummy always put a clean white sheet on the bed, sprinkled with Chanel No. 5 so it smelled nice. There were bunnies on the night table because it was Easter. The straps were on a shelf in the headboard.

Karen went first because she was prettier, Alyssa was second. They always called her by her middle name when she was working, or Ally for short. She wasn't very good and she didn't get a treat hardly ever. She had pigeon-toes. She was supposed to keep her feet turned out while she sat on the couch at the back of the business room, waiting her turn. It was vinyl and in summer the cushion stuck to her. In winter it was cold. If she moved it squeaked. She moved too much. That's why she was always making Daddy mad. He was never in a movie only in a bedroom. He had an important face so he just watched. She could tell he was mad before his face changed. She looked inside his head and it was there. She wished she could have a little chickie. Some people got chickies at Easter. They were soft and yellow. If she got her feet to turn out maybe she could have a chickie, too.

After Karen was finished, Mummy came downstairs with a tray of ginger ale. Stripes in the wallpaper. Squares on the ginger ale glasses. Ally didn't get a drink. Mummy said, "If you are a good girl, you'll get some later." Everybody else got some ginger ale and there was a glass on the table for Daddy and a glass for the cameraman. Lester went to pee. When he came back it was Ally's turn and the couch squeaked when she got up. She looked at Daddy but he wasn't mad. Maybe Ally would be good. Maybe she'd get a big glass of ginger ale and a treat. But there was another idea, too. Of being very bad, so bad nobody could ever be as bad as that. *Shhh* she said in her head. She had to talk in her head without making her lips move because if lips move then somebody could say she was crazy. And crazy kids got sold down the river to bad people.

Lester smiled at her. "Okay, sweetheart. You're next. Let's play school." He put out two chairs for Ally and her next older brother. Ted was nine, skinny like her. He had marks on his back from a hanger. So did their bigger brother, Gary, even though he was not skinny. One of them answered the door without permission to a lady selling makeup in a

pink suitcase and they both got it. Ted was a good runner but
not such a good speller. He wouldn't be very good at playing
school. He was biting his lip. They had to sit with their backs
to Lester and their legs around the chairs, facing the bed and
the picture of the clown holding balloons. Teddy's shoulder
was touching hers. Click. Movie lamps went on. The light
was hot and hurty and she squinted her eyes.

Lester had a long thin stick. He said to Teddy, "Spell
'Antarctica.'"

It was a big word. Ally kept her fingers crossed.

"A-n-a-r-t-i-k-a," Teddy tried.

"Wrong," Lester said and Teddy had to turn around and
face Lester to be hit with the long thin stick. The stick whistled. Then it whacked. His shoulder jerked. She could feel it
every time, jerking against her.

The only words she knew how to spell were "cat" and
"bed" and she couldn't stop her legs from shaking.

"Spell 'cat,'" Lester said.

She nearly peed she was so happy. "C-a-t," she said.

"Good girl," Lester said. He had red hair, too. He liked her.
She was good. "Turn around. Show me how good you can be."

Ted's face was mad. She got such an easy word. But he
didn't have to be mad about it because he got to be assistant
teacher and whack her all over even though she kept saying
"c-a-t" and again, "c-a-t," the stick biting her ribs and her
chest and her legs until something exploded through the
drugs in the Kool-Aid. She kicked and she screamed. Lester
picked her up and threw her onto the bed. The body was
wetting so it wouldn't get torn inside but she wiggled and

yelled while he put the leather straps around her wrists and ankles, biting right through the wart on his hand, only that wasn't her anymore.

"Alyssa! Obey!" The father got up from his chair. When he got up, he knocked glasses off the table. Crash. The mad in his head was very very mad.

So Ally went away inside, as deep as she could go, leaving Lyssa on the bed to scream and try to bite the man again as he turned her over, yanked her head back by the hair. It had to be someone else who cried. Lyssa wanted to kill them. She wanted to throw a bomb on them. Then she'd run so fast nobody would ever catch her. Afterward they played a game, the silly men. That's what her mother called them. The silly men put a brown cigarette in her bottom, the filter end pressed between the cheeks, to see if it smoked when they lit the top. The silly men laughed.

Then everybody else got dressed and went home, except for her because she had to learn her lesson in the darkness. She was cold. Her throat hurt. She heard a distant train whistle and she thought it was an angel coming to save her. She waited for a long time, shivering. *Click.* The door unlocked. It was the angel. She came! The sudden light made her squeeze her eyes shut. When she opened her eyes, she saw that the sheet wasn't white anymore.

Mother was wearing a hairnet over her curlers and a flowered housedress and Lyssa thought of ginger ale glasses with flowers. She was so thirsty. She'd have put up her bum if she could just get a drink. So she said, "Can I have some ginger ale?"

Mother said, "Can you? Yes. May you? No. You didn't earn it." She put her hand down there inside Lyssa and then she pinched her face with wet fingers. "A pig in its own filth. Who is ever going to want a little whore like you? Russell!" She called upstairs, "Russell! Bring down the budgie, will you?"

Dan knocked on the bathroom door. "Hon? Are you okay? You've been in there a while."

"The toilet's blocked."

"Let me in," Dan called through the door. "I'll fix it."

"No. It stinks in here." Lyssa grimaced as another cramp went through her.

"I can deal with stink. Remember when the kids all had the stomach flu at the same time?" He tapped on the door.

"Just a sec." Okay she could breathe again. She just couldn't stand up. "I don't have the flu. You can go to bed."

Her voice sounded fine she thought. But Dan was rattling the knob, twisting it back and forth until the silly little lock gave, pushing the door open. "Pew. It does stink. God, you look awful."

"Gee thanks."

Dan stepped over her, turned on the taps in the bathtub. "Come on. I'll help you in."

"Wait." Somehow she got herself off the floor and on the toilet. Splat. Wipe. Not looking at Dan as she got into the tub, splashing the hot water over her belly. "I flushed three times. I think there's something wrong with the floatie thing." She leaned back, the hot water starting to untangle her knotted belly.

"You can just relax now. I'll deal with this," he said. *Splunch. Splunch. Splunch.* Flush. Toilets were a man's business. Garbage and toilets and taking care of his family.

"Great." Her voice low, eyes on her knobby knees sticking up out of the water. She hated her knees. At least the tub was big and deep, an old claw-footed tub, and when it was full her knees would be covered.

"We need to call social services about Cathy's family. They might have questions you could answer better, but I'll do it if you'd rather."

"You don't have to," she said.

He bent his head to inspect the inside of the tank. "I don't know how I'm going to deal with clients that Rick's associated with." He attacked the toilet with renewed determination. Press, lift. Press, lift. Get the water in the bowl moving down faster than the fresh water coming in. "I wanted to beat the crap out of him. I hated having to be civil. Is that what made you so sick?"

"Partly."

He flushed the toilet, studying the water as it poured in from the tank, the level in the bowl rising, plunger at the ready. "What else?" He turned to look at her.

"That and seeing the picture on the computer."

"It was hard to take," he said.

"I know." Her shame deepened, and she dismissed everything he'd said to her earlier in the evening. If he couldn't take one picture, how could he accept her? Soaping her arms and her chest, her neck, she washed off the night, rubbing hard with a loofah, washing away herself.

"I should be able to do more," he said. Balancing the plunger over one of the sinks, he poured bleach over it, his back to her so all she could see of his frustration was the hunched shoulders, a flushed neck. Then he turned to face her, anguished, holding the plunger as if he intended to make all the shit in the world go down into the bowels of the earth. "I can't do anything about Cathy, and I can't change what happened to you as a kid. But I'm here for you now."

"You don't even know me. Not really. Not *me*," she said, turning her eyes back to her ugly knees. Her mother was right. Who could want someone like her? She could hardly stand to be in her own skin right now.

"You're wrong about that."

"It's okay. It's better if you don't," she said.

Her voice was barely audible, but he heard. "Do you know how many people love you?" he asked. "There's me, the kids, Eleanor, Bram, my parents." He put the plunger in the corner beside the toilet. "Here, let me wash your back."

"I can use the back brush."

"This is better." Taking a clean washcloth from the vanity, he kneeled beside the tub. The washcloth was pale blue with a blue butterfly and satin piping along the edge.

"That's Nina's," she said, so he would know. So that he wouldn't dirty it with her skin.

"You think I don't know you?" He rubbed soap on the washcloth until it foamed up, soft and white. "You're strong," he said. "I can barely keep up with you when you're running.

I feel like an idiot compared to you when we're dancing, but I'm willing to feel like an idiot so I can be with you dancing."

She leaned forward as he washed her back, neither slow nor fast, neither soft nor hard, one hand on her shoulder as if he still liked the feel of her, the other hand moving the washcloth in circles. And he talked. About how much fun it would be dancing at Hammond House. She looked great in jeans and that lacy thing she'd put on. Wasn't she wearing something like that when they first met?

"I had an army surplus jacket. It was cheap."

"I don't think I was paying attention to any jacket when you skated into me. That wasn't Sharon, was it? You were the one skating. And when we had cocoa at Magee's, you took off the jacket," he said. "I noticed that."

Of course he did. That was what she was for. But he kept talking until she told him about the sky above the railroad tracks, and the wildflowers that were tiny and perfect and the rabbit that had surprised her on the path, and how she wished that one day she might see the northern lights. He rinsed her back. He kissed her shoulder as if it was a privilege. He held out a towel as she stepped out of the tub, wrapping it around her. Then she followed him up to bed and she knew that they would make love another day when she said so. He fell asleep holding her hand, and his touch kept her from spinning off into the endless dark matter that fills the universe.

It rained again on Saturday. In the morning, while everyone was downstairs eating breakfast, Alec got the car keys off
the dressing table and the phone from the nightstand. Sitting
on the bed, his elbow knocking into a bunch of cushions, he
looked up the number at the front of the phone book.

A woman's voice answered. "Child abuse hotline. How
can I help you?"

"What do you need to know to get a kid out of her
house?"

A pause. "Can you give me your name?"

"No."

"I see." Another pause. "I'm asking because we sometimes get calls from people with malicious intent, and every
call is investigated."

"Good. This kid needs help."

"What is your relationship with her?"

"Yeah. Okay. She's my son's girlfriend. She just told me
that she's being abused."

"In what way?"

"Sexually. Maybe more."

"Did you see any bruises or other injuries?"

"Her hand has a scar. She said from the stove. I don't know if it's from the abuse. She might've done it herself."

Clicking sounds. The person at the other end of the line on the keyboard. "Who is the perpetrator?"

"Father is still messing with her."

"Can you give me her name and the school she attends?"

"What'll you do?"

"The procedure is that a social worker and a police officer go to the child's school. They'll question her there. If she discloses we can remove her immediately. After that we visit the parents."

"What if she won't say anything?"

"Then we'll still talk to mom and dad. But in all honesty, without disclosure it's unlikely anything more will happen. The perpetrator almost always denies it and the non-offending parent usually supports him."

"Her mom hurt her, too."

"I see." Silence. "Her name and school, please?"

"If you just show up, she'll be scared."

"The social worker and police are trained to talk to abused kids. They realize she's scared."

"Do you know anything about DID?"

"A little." Probably *The Three Faces of Eve* or something like that. Where alters were so obviously different they might as well be wearing signs. Like yeah.

"This girl is multiple. I've seen her switch. It's hard to tell when you don't know what to look for."

"If she tells us that she's being abused, we'll get her to a safe place right away."

"But if she's scared, the one who is forward won't know anything to tell. Are you guys trained for that? The kid'll be in worse trouble unless you can get her out of there. The cops talking to her parents will make them hit the roof. I don't want her getting more hurt. She took a chance on telling me. If we can't help, she'll never trust us again. It'll be game over."

"I'm sorry." The voice was gentler. "I had a case like this recently. I knew the child was being abused but the child was too frightened to disclose. It's frustrating."

"There's a damn baby in that house. The girl is sleeping in the baby's room, trying to protect her, but she's just a kid herself. There's got to be something you can do."

"If there's no physical evidence of abuse and the child doesn't disclose, then we have no authority to do anything more."

"Look here. She was using my son's computer and I caught her looking at a porn site. There was a picture of her sister when she was like five or something. What if I give you the URL?"

"We aren't allowed to look at it. Not even the regular police are allowed. I can give you the phone number of the Child Exploitation Unit."

"Okay. Let me grab a pen." He wrote down the number and said goodbye, pressing the off button. He sat there for a few minutes, holding the phone in his hand, thinking. Then he put it back in its cradle and went out to the car.

Rain gushed from the sky, overflowing gutters, creating

puddles and ponds. Alec drove through storm-darkened streets, splashing pedestrians who stepped back too late and gave him dirty looks. Thunder boomed and street lamps went on. He stopped the car at the condemned cottage that had once belonged to an escaped slave. Across the street crocuses were getting beaten down by rain as he watched Cathy's house. A balcony on the second floor, with a black railing and a door. That would open into Cathy's room. Her mother had office hours on Saturday morning. She would be there now, examining children for illnesses and injuries and insufficient growth. But her father could be at home. The main floor was dark, so he wasn't eating or watching TV in the den. The third floor was dark—he wasn't in their bedroom. The basement light went on.

Alec decided. He'd just sit here in the car and wait for her to come out. Call her over. Lock the car and drive her home. And then what? Her parents would come and get her, with a police officer if need be. Alec sat in the car, hands gripping the steering wheel as the third floor light went on. The top of the house was lit, with its office full of computers hooked together and into the Internet with high speed cables. And there at the bottom of the house, underground, anything could be going on.

So this was it. Same as usual. Nobody could do anything. He stared at the house with hatred. It licked at the edge of his steadiness, a hot tickle in his belly. His steadiness was mere paper. How easily it caught fire, curling black, flaking away. There was plenty of kindling for this fire. It burned high and the heat felt good. *Be real,* people said. *What can you do?* He was supposed to turn around, drive home like he didn't know shit. Except that he did. And he wasn't helpless. That was a fact. His hands were skilled.

His father had made sure of that and his mother made sure his father taught him well and true. *Russell! Bring down the budgie, will you?*

She wore a housedress, pink hairnet over her curlers. When the father came down the stairs with the red wire cage, she sneered at him.

You can't make that child listen at five years old. What next?

Father sucked in his lips and blew out. *I'll take care of it,* he said.

You do that. I'm sure I don't want to wear the pants.

The budgie flapped its wings like it wanted to fly some-where. Banging against the bars. The dad yelled and snapped his belt. *Spread them wider,* he said. Alec's hands were on the bed. Feet on the floor. *Somebody better stop being a smart aleck and start listening to me,* the dad said. *You are going to get rid of that bird, aren't you?*

No, he said. The carpet was rough under his feet. It stank. *No I'm not.*

Whack.

You are going to obey me. Snap.

Snot running down Alec's face. Something trickling down his leg. Blood, pee. One foot coming off the floor, shaking. The dad put the belt back on his trousers. *Betty,* he said, *I need the baby.*

Alec was leaning against the bed, praying to God. Not the baby. Don't hurt the baby. Mom going up the stairs, and coming down again, holding Pauline, who didn't cry even though she was so little. Not even big enough to walk. Dad lifting the knife. The big kitchen knife that Mom used for chopping meat. *No, Daddy! I'll do it. Stop, please, please.*

Alec took the bird out of the cage. It was pecking at his fingers, its wings banging, heart beating so fast you couldn't count the beats. It made a sound—*chhh chhh.* He kept pushing on its neck and it wouldn't die. He got so mad at the birdie for biting his fingers. It was a bad birdie. So he turned it upside down and pulled on the neck like it was a chicken. Twisted. Threw it back in the cage. But he didn't cry. He was no crybaby.

Alec gripped the steering wheel, windshield wipers sweeping from side to side, clearing rain. Ingrid's handgun was more convenient than the rifle. It could be slipped into the back of his pants, under his shirt. Nobody would know it was there as he rang the doorbell, standing on that porch, whistling until the door was opened. One thing he didn't want to do was miss. At point blank range he couldn't. But after the first shot someone would come running and what happened next was unpredictable. He might have to shoot from a distance and he couldn't be certain of his accuracy with the Beretta. He should've tried it that day at the shooting range. No, it would have to be the rifle. He could call and say he needed to borrow it. Ingrid would trust him. He was pretty sure. He could feel it in his hands, the weight of it, the coolness of stock against his cheek. The way it would recoil against his shoulder after he aimed it at the people who hurt children. Surely any god in heaven would forgive him this.

INSIDE

It was darker and colder as if the storm outside had made its way inside. The heart was beating fast, the breath coming quick, making it hard to see, hard to talk, hard to do anything but be swept away. Only deep inside, far away from Alec's rage, was anyone sheltered enough to think.

And here, in the basement, the Overseer was alone except for the children who cowered in the corners, terrified of him. Even the punishers were lost somewhere in the din above, and though he called, nobody came. There was little for him to do from here. He could stand and listen or pace and listen to Alec's wild thoughts filtering down. Would nobody stop him—not even the Housekeeper?

Of course not. It was up to the Overseer to keep order. He had to get forward, and it had to be now, before anyone did something foolish and irreversible. The Housekeeper had said all he had to do was come into the kitchen, as if it were a small thing. Easy. Very well, then.

He climbed the stairs and at the landing, he stopped. What would happen to him in there? The light was already blinding. Eyes closed, he took a step forward. The light hurt more. Another step, feeling for the door. There were rumours about the kitchen. A light so clear, nothing could be hidden. Nothing forgotten. His hand was on the doorknob; he turned it and pushed the door open. Another step and he was through. He opened his eyes, streaming in the blaze of light.

"Let me out," he said. "It's too much for Alec. I should be there instead."

"All right," the Housekeeper said.

To his surprise, she opened the back door and stood aside. But he had no time to wonder about it, moving quickly before she changed her mind. As soon as he stepped over the threshold, the light was extinguished, but darkness was no impediment to him.

He was behind Alec, hearing him mutter, seeing his hands on the steering wheel. This darkness didn't belong to Alec; it was his. It had always been his. He was the one as strong and cold as his father. Let the others live their life: it belonged to them; he would give it to them. The Overseer moved closer to Alec, and closer still, until he, too, felt the nip of the bird's beak and smelled his father's sweat. He drew in the foulness of it, swallowed the hatred, the fear, the eagerness to strike back, the sound of a young voice, *Daddy!* Thin and high. Then he turned around for more—the glass cutting Echo's feet, the yank of Lyssa's hair. They'd all shared that day and that night, each of them taking a piece. Now he would have all of it. He was more than the body; his hands reached for lightning, his head touched the clouds. He was large, he could contain everything. But, still, he screamed and the scream burned through him as something still larger than he took him up.

This then was death. It must be because the pain was gone. He'd thought death would be heavy and cold but it was a strange sort of light that didn't hurt his eyes with its mildness, and he was cradled in a thousand arms.

A voice rose and fell more peaceful than a lullaby, telling him the story of his life from before he was born, and he watched it unfold as he listened. Back and back to the first animals, the first one-celled beings, the hot crust of the earth, the young sun, the stars hugging close, the single point of existence before it split into things. One point, one heart, a heart-beat, and the universe exploded, became multiple, shards of dazzling fragments that rubbed against each other, polishing and cutting, changing the shapes of existence, generation upon generation, bringing him here, held by the Housekeeper. Beloved. Time rolled and unrolled. The light was merry.

"I don't belong here," he said. "I'm like my father."

The Housekeeper smiled. "Take a better look," she said.

He was sitting at the foot of a tree and the names of things were known to him.

A child stood there. "Hi. I'm Ally," she said. In her hand was a small object, which she placed in his. A teddy bear.

"I died," he said.

"Dead things don't talk. And they stink. You don't stink." She tilted her head back so that she could see his height. "You're shiny."

And so he was. His wings were the silver of stars and the ebony of a velvet night, and light shimmered along his arms. "I'm the Overseer," he said.

"That's not a name," the child said to him. "I'll call you Bert."

On the outside the body wept. After a while, a hand moved the gearshift from park to drive. The motor rumbled. They went home.

$\mathcal{T}$he rest of the weekend passed in a fog. Switching was erratic, everyone too exhausted to stay out for long, though someone managed to leave a message on their therapist's voice-mail. Dan called Eleanor and filled her in on Cathy, though, at Sharon's insistence, he didn't mention that Cathy was multiple. He asked Eleanor to come over and help, which she did, and without question. At least for the weekend. But first thing on Monday after taking the younger kids to school, Eleanor returned to her sister-in-law's house to find out exactly what was going on.

They sat in the kitchen, drinking tea. *But why can't you report it?* Eleanor asked. *If Cathy told you, why won't she tell the police? No, this is ridiculous,* she said. *If you won't talk to the police, I will.* When she took out her cellphone, Sharon put a hand over hers, and said, *Wait.* Then she told Eleanor that there was more to the story. She explained what DID was and how it could prevent Cathy from being able to tell what had happened to her—to them.

Eleanor asked Sharon how she knew.

Sharon had a ready answer. She'd say that she'd realized Cathy was multiple because of a movie she'd seen and a TV show about DID. But when Sharon looked at Eleanor sitting there, her best friend for twenty years, her sister-in-law, the first person she'd told about being pregnant, she couldn't lie.

"The reason I know is that I'm multiple, too," Sharon said.

"Why didn't you ever tell me?" Eleanor asked.

"I don't want you thinking I'm crazy. It's not something you say to people."

"To someone else, maybe. But me? I don't think you're crazy, but . . ." She paused, considering while Sharon tensed and switched. "That makes sense of a lot of things. I'd like to know more about it. How many of you are there?"

Her sister-in-law rolled her eyes. "I didn't take a census. Besides, just for your information, that's a rude question."

"Are you Sharon or who?" Eleanor asked.

"That's rude, too," she said, but as Eleanor was also her best friend, she added, "I'll forgive you this time."

A few minutes later, when Brigitte called, Lyssa was still forward and she answered the phone. She stayed out just long enough to book an extra session.

With Brigitte's help on Tuesday, they—Lyssa and the others—decided that instead of rotating rapidly to cope, each of them could take a longer turn forward while the others rested in a healing place inside. At the next appointment, they would discuss what could be done for Cathy. Brigitte suggested that Dan come, and maybe Eleanor as well, to get more input and support. At home that evening,

Dan took up Brigitte's suggestion with enthusiasm. He told Eleanor, and Eleanor told Mimi, and then he said to his wife, *Everyone's coming; now you'll finally see that you're not alone anymore.*

On Thursday morning they were all seated at the meeting table and chairs, which were at the back of Brigitte's office. Dan wore a suit as he'd be heading to the office right after the session. Next to him, nerves taut, Callisto was alert though she'd been up late and up early, taking her turn outside. Eleanor and Mimi sat opposite, Jake on his own at the end of the table, Bram taking the uncomfortable chair at the corner. Brigitte presided at the head, her bun held in place with a jewelled pin, making notes on her clipboard. The basement smelled of lilac this time.

"I'm glad you could all come here today," she said.

"So." Mimi clutched a cavernous purse. It was new and red and matched her shoes.

"What a mess," Eleanor said. "Why didn't you show up this morning? You were supposed to be at my house at seven a.m. and I was dressed and waiting to run."

"The cellphone rang at 4:11," Callisto said. She'd been up most of the night with the laptop in the kitchen, listening to classical music. When the phone rang, she'd picked it up and heard the whisper of a girl's voice.

"I don't know what to do," Cathy had said and then hung up.

So what could Callisto do at 4:12 a.m.? Only wait as she had done many times. Listening to music, she'd hummed as if humming made minutes move and push the sun into the sky. At 5:38 the sun had crossed the horizon, drawing off the smoky dark of night, slowly turning heaven scarlet then white as fog descended.

The house woke up around her. Water rattling the pipes, kids' sleepy voices, footsteps. She had a quick conversation with Dan, who agreed to get everyone ready for school while she walked over to the Edwards'. The streets were quiet, shrouded in fog, sound muffled by it, a truck beep-beeping its warning somewhere, a dog barking hello, his owner nodding as they came out of the mist.

On the locked mailbox beside the door on Lumley was a nameplate: DR. D. DAWSON, PROF. R. EDWARDS AND FAMILY. There were potted flowers on the porch, immense pots with colourful and ornate arrangements that looked real but were made of silk. Rick had told Dan that arrangements were being made to water the yard and remove junk mail. Timers would turn lights on and off. The house had to look lived in, so that it wouldn't be burglarized or vandalized or otherwise lose its value until the Dawson-Edwards disposed of it.

Carrying a tote bag with a book in it on her shoulder, Callisto rang the bell and in a moment she heard the sound of footsteps.

Debra opened the door. "Come in," she said, though she looked surprised.

"Excuse me for coming over so early," Callisto said as she walked in. She'd thought herself incapable of lying, but it turned out to be among her new-found skills, like smiling. "Cathy called about her algebra book. I told her I would bring it before school."

"Thank you," Debra said. The house smelled of air freshener. There was a vase on the marble table, beside it a book with an Oprah's Book Club sticker on it and a bottle of calcium pills. "I don't know what's wrong with her. She's constantly losing things these days. Cathy!"

Boxes were stacked in the hallway, Rick's landscapes leaning against the wall. There was an open camera bag on the coffee table, lenses in it, and the new camera. "Hello, how are you?" he said as he came from the kitchen with newspaper to wrap the photographs.

"Good and you?" The air conditioning was turned up and he wore a long-sleeved shirt that was loose around his wrists. He yawned, the silver fillings in his teeth visible. Debra's hair was a bit damp from her shower. Callisto examined the room coolly, calmly. "Those are unusual picture frames."

"They're made of recycled bicycle chains. Students in the Learn About the World program made them for me. Ingenious. You see the logo welded into the corner?" The LAW was tiny, jumping into focus only when pointed out.

"I wouldn't have noticed that," Callisto said and Rick looked pleased. "You are both busy. Let me take this up to Cathy." She held out the tote bag weighted by a book about the size and shape of a math text.

To her surprise Rick agreed. At the top of the stairs her surprise gave way to consternation. The computers were disconnected, power cords in bags, boxes with Styrofoam ready for packing on the tables. One of the tables was folded. Though the medicine cabinet in the bathroom was still locked, the shower curtain had been taken down. She called to Cathy, looking first in the room that was peachy and frilled, then in Heather's room.

It was just the same as it had been, blank walled, barren except for the painted crib. Cathy was leaning on the rail, looking down at the sleeping baby. Her hair was in a ponytail, she wore camo shorts, a black tank top. "What are you doing here?" she asked sharply. This was not Cathy then, but Ceecee.

"You called and we came," Callisto answered simply. "What's going on? Why is everything being packed? I thought you had a month before you're leaving."

"Before *I* am." Her face carefully blank, she sat on her sister's bed. The mattress had been bleached and flipped, not replaced. "My mother's taking Linny up to the cottage this weekend. The movers are coming on Saturday and she'll drive up behind them. She decided to start her leave early, and Dad's staying here with me until the end of school."

"You'll be alone with him."

"Not like it matters that much. He'll just be wanting entertainment."

"It does matter."

Ceecee shook her head. "I don't care about me. She's going to be alone with Linny. How can I protect her from here?" The blankness cracked, desperation in her eyes; she'd searched for a way out and found only one. "Even when I get up to the cottage, the crib is going to be in their room.

It's too late. There's nothing anyone can do. I was mad at her, but Heather was right. She just didn't finish things."

"Are you thinking of killing yourself?" Callisto asked outright—this was too serious for tact.

"I'm tired of fighting all the time. It's no use anyway."

"No," Callisto said. "You can't let them win. "

"If I can't help Linny, there's no reason to bother with anything." Her voice was heavy as if speaking took more effort than it was worth.

"Giving up this easily? I didn't think you were such a coward," Callisto snapped.

"You think I haven't tried! Who do you think you are?" That was better. Anger instead of helplessness.

"Callisto—that's the name I go by. I'd rather not say what I was called." She smiled in that wry way she'd learned, and sat down beside Ceecee, looking through the bars of the crib at the baby lying on her back, snoring lightly with the onset of a cold. "Don't give up yet. You're still here and we're on your side. We each have an army inside. Someone who is multiple isn't easily overcome."

"I wish . . . I don't know." In the alley behind the house, a moving truck had pulled up. There was a scraping sound on the other side of the wall. Amy and Ingrid were moving out their last things before the new tenants arrived.

"We called the abuse line. Anonymously," Callisto added as the girl's eyes flashed. "They can remove you from here if you say what you know."

"What? The police won't help." She shook her head. "They'll take me away and then nobody can save Linny."

"She'd come with you."

"I know what'll happen. My great-grandfather was a policeman. Even in his eighties he still could do me. He was the first one. Like they said." She gritted her teeth. "It was an honour."

"They lied," Callisto said. She could hear the murmur of her friends' voices next door, but not make out their words, just as on the night Heather died, Ingrid had heard sounds open to interpretation. But what had actually happened? "They lied about your great-grandfather, too."

"How do you mean?"

"Last night when you called I was online. I found two mentions of Edwards men in this neighbourhood during the 1930s. One was Skinny Edwards, a member of the Pit Gang, who ended up in hospital with minor injuries during the riot. The other was an A. Edwards who owned the coal depot on Hammond Street."

"So he wasn't a policeman," Ceecee said wonderingly, then her eyes narrowed. "Are you sure?"

"I am sure that he had nothing to do with quelling the riot."

"Why would they say that?" Her world was tilting and she could either cling to it or jump. She had thought of jumping, but not like this.

"My father used to say that we were descended from Roman legions as if it made him noble. In fact he is a criminal who was never caught." Callisto pressed on. "We can pick you up after school. I promise that you won't be left alone with the police or anyone else. We'll be with you at every step."

"What about my parents?"

"Leave them to us."

"Maybe . . ." Ceecee looked to the side, her hands clenched. Her face was tensing, jaw tight as she switched, and now cold eyes turned to Callisto. "No."

"I see." Callisto shifted, and someone else came forward with equal coldness, steel meeting steel.

The Overseer rose to his feet. "You will come with us as soon as we can arrange it—perhaps tomorrow?" he asked, though he was more used to giving orders than asking questions.

"Rules are rules." The young voice was hard.

"I have discovered new rules."

"A rule that changes is not a rule," the child said.

Her face was severe, but the Overseer was aware of how much trust it took for her to speak at all. "You know now that they told you one lie. How many others are there? Discover the truth for yourself."

"How?" she asked, a child of battle, made to endure, made for severity.

"Tell what you know, or let someone else inside do it." He paused so that she might take his measure. Shoulders square, harsh-voiced, a tangle of red hair. In the body and yet himself. Free. Wanted.

"Cathy! What's keeping you?" Debra's voice called upstairs. And as Cathy came forward, so did Callisto.

Cathy's face showed less confusion than Callisto expected. "I've got to get ready or I'll be late. See you," she said.

"Very soon." Callisto followed her down the stairs.

"Hurry up," Debra scolded. "You need to thank Mrs. Lewis for her kindness and pull yourself together. You have a closet full of clothes. I told you to get rid of those shorts. They're disgusting. You can't wear them to school."

"They're mine," Cathy said. "I bought them at Honest Ed's with my own money."

"My pretty girl has become a hobo." Rick put a hand on the banister, and his daughter stepped back, eyes riveted to the pale hand on the polished dark wood banister. "I'll deal with your attitude later, Cathy. Right now, you need to get to school."

And it was all so ordinary except that it wasn't.

"I checked the website that we found Cathy working on, Angels of Tranquility," Callisto said. "The homepage looks innocuous, even pretty. It has angels floating on a blue background, and all the links are password protected."

"Did you call the Child Exploitation Unit?" Brigitte asked.

They'd discussed it at the last session, the therapist claiming that this time they—Callisto, Alec or whoever was out for this—would be believed. Not everyone inside was persuaded. "Yes, I called, without giving my name. The detective said to bring her to the local station if I could. I promised Cathy we'd help and we have to do it soon, before we lose her trust. Tomorrow if possible."

"From what you've been telling us, porn is big business,"

Eleanor said. "These people have money. They've got resources. They're violent. What if Rick starts thinking she's getting in his way? What if something happened to her?" She pointed at her sister-in-law.

"If he finds out, I wouldn't be the one to pay." Callisto spoke to those inside as much as those around the table. "The perpetrators who get caught are the obvious ones. Rick and Debra know what they're doing. They wouldn't hurt a neighbour and chance being revealed. But they would punish their daughter so thoroughly that she wouldn't think of trying this again."

"You see how it is, Dr. Felber," Jake addressed Brigitte, unwilling to call a doctor, even a psychologist, by her first name. "The Pit Gang fought and they lost. You think they lost because they didn't know how to fight? You think the Italians and Jews won because they fought better? Let me tell you. It isn't rocket science to swing a pipe. Everyone could fight. It's nothing new."

"Dad, this isn't anything to do with Christie Pits," Dan said as patiently as he could.

"*Boychik,* those people are bullies, too." His mouth twisted as if he might spit. "You tell your kids, stand up to bullies. Show them how. Not with this." He smacked his liver-spotted fist into his hand, surprising his son with the sound of it as if he still had his old strength. "With this." His father tapped his forehead. "Don't have a goyisheh *kop*. No offense, Bram." He smiled at his gentile son-in-law.

"None taken," Bram said. Wiring was a quiet job. You only had to say, *Check the breaker.* Or *I'm here, pull.* But you saw unexpected things when you cut out plaster. "I did the wiring at the Edwards' house." Everyone was looking at him. He stopped talking, embarrassed.

"Go on," Brigitte encouraged.

"It had knob and tube and their insurance company gave them sixty days to replace it. Their basement was sound-proofed, but it was set up as a guest room, so I didn't think anything of it." His quiet voice was tinged with regret.

"You're speaking now," Brigitte said. "It isn't too late." She was writing notes on her yellow pad, Mimi looking over her shoulder to make sure she left nothing out. "If you want to do this tomorrow, how would that work?"

"I could pick her up after school when she's home with the baby so I can take them both," Callisto said.

"We still have a car seat in the basement," Dan said. He started making a list on his smartphone.

"I'm concerned about getting Cathy alone," Callisto said. "Debra might leave work early as it's her last day. Then there's Rick. What if he's at home?"

Dan was still tapping with the stylus. 1. Put infant seat in car. 2. Fill up car. 3. Meeting with Rick?

Deleting the question mark, he said, "I was supposed to go over the fundraising campaign for the Committee for Youth tomorrow. I haven't yet cancelled it because I didn't know what to say. How about if I go? It was set for two but I could ask him to meet at four instead."

"Well," Eleanor said, "I could put together a surprise party at Magee's at the same time. A send-off for Debra."

"On such short notice?" Brigitte asked.

"Easy." Eleanor crossed her arms, and eyed her sister-in-law as if she'd read their thoughts. "Just don't turn your house into a refugee centre. Let the kids go to foster care."

Callisto blinked, feeling Sharon surge forward, ready to protest. But it was her father-in-law who said, "Let? There's no letting. Why do you think we all ended up right here around this table? It's not for nothing."

"You have enough room for two more kids in your house," Mimi said, "if you'd only clean it up. The basement used to be an apartment. Now it's full of boxes. Put this on your list, Danny. Your daddy and I will pick up Emmie and then we'll get Judy and Nina from school."

"That would be great, Mom." Dan made a note of it.

"We can't let Cathy down," Callisto said, putting her hand on his.

"We'll get those kids out," he said. "They deserve better."

"Now you're using your head," Jake said. "If there was only God then who would God love?"

Stars are usually born in molecular clouds. But when a giant gas cloud encounters a giant black hole, it is not entirely destroyed. It is ripped, torn, reshaped into a spiral that takes energy from deep in and moves it far out, birthing stars even here in this most dangerous of places. This is what can be seen through scientific instruments: a necklace of brilliance around a darkness darker than night at the heart of our galaxy.

On the fifth floor of the former Ford factory, Rick was waiting in reception, hands clasped behind his back as he studied the framed photographs of the building in its previous glory: the testing track on the roof, cars being painted on this floor, the assembly line on four, repairs on three, and on the second floor, the salesroom where now his wife had her pediatric practice.

"Hello, Rick," Dan said as he came into reception. "Thank you for changing the appointment time."

"It's totally fine, we can go straight from here to Magee's. It was nice of Eleanor to organize that."

"That's my sister. Organized." Wearing his second best suit and the girls' ugly birthday present, which had become, against all odds, his good-luck tie, he guided Rick toward the corner office. One window faced the railroad tracks, the other window looked across the overpass to Best Foods. Bushes trembled in the light breeze.

"Have a seat, please. I've got everything here," Dan said.

The floorboards creaked as they settled in chairs on either side of his desk.

Rick crossed one leg over the other. "I liked what you did for Families Against Guns even though the mailing was late. I hope you can do as well for the Committee for Youth."

Several samples of mailing designs were spread out on the oak surface of Dan's desk: exterior envelope, reply envelope, letter. Dan explained the benefits of a handwritten envelope, though it was more expensive, but Rick was restless, hardly listening.

"It's up to you, though," Dan said, eyes on the letter copy so he didn't have to look at Rick.

"I want to discuss this." Rick flapped the telephone script. "You haven't put anything about Heather's suicide in here."

Dan looked around his desk for something to occupy his hands, thinking of how good it would feel to take a swing at Rick. He picked up his pen. "I thought it would be effective to focus on the programs you want to set up for teens."

"I want people to remember Heather," Rick said.

"Right." Dan took the script from Rick and scribbled on it.

"We're all set," Alec said. In the school playground half a block down, kids were climbing rope ladders and sliding down slides, shouting with after-school freedom, anticipating summer. The diaper bag was in the trunk, the baby buckled into the infant seat, facing the rear of the car, her young auntie in front. His bag was on the back seat.

"I forgot the tablet," she said, turning off her cellphone and placing it in her backpack.

"We'll get you another one." He pressed the button to lock the doors. If she went back in, she might not come out again.

"You're sure that Dad is occupied?"

"He's with Dan. You want to see the text?" He reached into his pocket and took out his cell, flipping it open so she could look. *Rick here go 4 it.*

"What if the baby poops? Cathy's the one who changes diapers."

"I'll do it," Alec said, adding, as Ceecee raised her eyebrows, "Okay, so I'm not Sharon. But I can handle a bit of shit." He turned the key in the ignition.

"The last couple of days, Cathy can hear when I'm out. She thinks we're crazy or lying. I don't know if I can keep her back," Ceecee said

"Hang in there." Alec looked over his shoulder as he pulled away from the house. You had to be watchful here. The sky was grey, the road was grey, and all you'd see was a flash of colour if some kid ran out of the school yard and across the street, expecting a ton of steel to stop on a dime.

Built in the same year as the Ford factory, the police station was A-shaped, stairs leading up to the ornate wooden door, brick arms stretching to right and left. Inside, several uniformed officers sat among the computers behind the counter. A female officer, short sandy hair, the blue collar of her uniform blouse standing above her jacket, was attending to the kettle while her colleagues relaxed, hands loose, teasing her as they waited for tea. Behind the desks was the mailroom, and behind the mailroom were holding cells with green bars.

In a large room on the second floor, a male detective in a brown suit, his hair buzz cut, sat at one of the desks. Several chairs were empty except for notes taped onto them that said COURT or SPRAINED ANKLE. Near the window overlooking the alley, a female detective with long black hair spoke on the phone. She was slender and well dressed, her shoes flat in case she needed to move fast. "Uh huh. Yes. I'll be right down," she said. There was a whiteboard on the wall behind her desk. In black marker were two headings, CHILDREN MISSING and ABDUCTIONS. Nothing was written underneath.

She let the door swing shut behind her as she came into the narrow waiting area, where a red-haired woman and a pretty girl with a baby in a baby carrier stared at the posters on the corkboard. The woman wore pants with many pockets, a messenger bag slung over a shoulder, one thumb hooked through the strap; she was trying to act casual, but her face was strained. The girl chewed on the ends of her hair. She wore sandals, her toes were wriggling as if she couldn't stand still and only the weight of the baby, lolling against her chest, kept her from taking flight.

"I'm Detective Chan." Beside the corkboard was a blown-up photograph of the Christie Pits riot, farther along the wall a smaller photo of the Metro Police West End Hockey Team, a thank-you from the boys and girls club, a calligraphed poem from the wife of a deceased officer. "You must be Mrs. Lewis. And you're Cathy Edwards?"

"Cathy Dawson-Edwards," the girl corrected.

"I have to apologize, Mrs. Lewis. I don't know why you were told to come to the station. We never do interviews with kids here." She thought of joking about the claustrophobic prisoner interrogation rooms they had, but the expression on the girl's face made her think that wasn't a terrific idea. "We have a child-friendly location on the lakeshore. It's a great place to talk. I'll give you the directions, and we can meet there."

Alec took the address from her, then turned to Ceecee. "It's just fifteen more minutes. Maybe twenty."

Her face was sullen as she followed him out. "They tell you one thing and then they tell you another," she grumbled suspiciously. They walked back to the car and Ceecee got into the front seat, slamming the door.

"Seat belt."

"Fine," she said as he leaned over the infant seat, buckling Linny in. "No, wait. Stop."

"What's up?" Alec straightened and she turned around to face him.

"This is crazy. I can't put my parents in jail." She was biting her nails, which were already bitten down to the quick, a drop of blood on the edge of her thumbnail.

"Let's talk about it," he said, keeping his voice level as he opened the door on the driver's side, and got in behind the wheel. So she'd switched. Better now than at the police station. He just had to deal. "You aren't putting them anywhere." His lips were numb and his hands cold on the steering wheel; too many of his own inside folks were scared to death of cops. Tough shit. He wasn't taking her back to that house. No way. "You're just going to say what you've got to say."

"You think they're bad, don't you?"

"Yeah," he said. "I do."

"It's not like you think. They came to all my dance recitals. And they clapped hard." She shook her head. "I love my mom and dad. What kind of person says terrible things about their parents?"

"The kind that has terrible parents."

"But they're not," she insisted.

"Not to you. Because you get to live a normal life while the others of you take the crap. But let me tell you, the worst isn't what is done to you. It's what you see done to others you care about. I couldn't do shit on a stick for my sister Pauline when we were kids, but that didn't stop me from trying. So don't think I'm sitting on my hands now. Somebody's going to jail. Is it gonna be me or are you going to let me do this?" He met her gaze until she looked down, and nodded.

When he checked the rear-view, he saw a nanny pushing a stroller through the parking lot, probably taking a shortcut to the library across the street. As soon as the rear-view was clear, he backed out, turned right to the exit and left onto the street past the library. He was leaving Seaton Grove, heading south toward the lake.

On the floor above Magee's, the odour of onion rings wafted through the vent in Dr. Dawson's examination room. She didn't see her patients in tiny cramped spaces. Her office was big, with several chairs for conversation, and a good-sized examination table. Dolls from around the world sat on a corner shelf, smiling at young patients. On one wall was a gallery of photographs, from babies to adolescents, all of them adorable.

"Do you have any other concerns?" Debra asked as she filled out the camp check-up form for Bonnie Yoon's son. There was an insulated mug on her desk, which she used for coffee from Magee's.

"Eric's still very small for his age," Bonnie said, her son leaning against her, playing with the stethoscope.

"I don't think there's anything to worry about, but I can refer you to an endocrinologist. If he were my child I'd want to rule out everything."

In the waiting room, the chairs were covered in faux leather, and a tickle trunk overflowed with toys. But nobody was playing with them now, regular hours over. The room smelled of perfume and talcum powder and baby pee and a trace of bitter disinfectant.

The door opened and Eleanor walked in. "Hello," she said.

"Can I help you?" the nurse asked. She was new, otherwise she would have recognized Eleanor, whose daughter was a patient of Dr. Nash's. If he hadn't been such a stubborn old goat, he would have retired five years ago, and Eleanor's daughter would now be a patient of Debra's. The thought of it made Eleanor sweat.

"I'm Eleanor Lewis. I called earlier to invite you to the goodbye party." She waved as Bonnie Yoon came into the waiting room, her son sucking on a lollipop.

"Oh yes." The nurse leaned forward conspiratorially. "Everyone's downstairs waiting. That's her last patient. Let's pop in and surprise her."

Debra was sitting at her desk, writing something in a file, and didn't look up as Eleanor walked in. "Where's my next appointment?" she asked.

"Right here," Eleanor said.

"I thought Judy was Dr. Nash's patient. Is something wrong?"

"Only that you're leaving us too soon," the nurse said, following close behind.

"I booked Magee's so everyone can say goodbye," Eleanor said.

"But I still have so much to do. I have to pack up everything here."

"I could help you, after Bram gets home. If you'd like." Eleanor's eyes were on her cellphone as she checked for messages. Maybe it isn't true, she thought. Maybe there is another explanation. She had to think so, at least for the moment, or she would never be able to face Debra.

"I'm sure I can manage." Debra took off her lab coat, and hung it on a hook behind the door. "I hope you'll excuse the way I've acted toward you, Eleanor. Blaming you for Ingrid living next door was unreasonable, but I've been so stressed. This move is long overdue. I can't wait to get to the cottage with my baby and just relax."

"Dr. Nash and Dr. Kim and everyone from the breakfast club are downstairs," Eleanor said. "We should get going."

Perhaps it was all a mistake. A troubled girl, her troubled sister. Teenagers lie all the time. And if Cathy was telling the truth? Eleanor pretended to admire the cabinet of dolls, walking over as if she needed to see them closer, then turning to look at the gallery of photographs on the wall. No one would notice if she snapped some shots with her cell. On Debra's desk was a family portrait and beside it another photograph: inside a silver frame, a man and a boy with a gap-toothed smile and cowlick. The boy was holding a fish. While Debra took a bottle of pills from a drawer and deposited them in her purse, Eleanor took another shot with her phone and slipped it back in her bag.

"Who's that?" she asked.

"Rick's brother and my godson," Debra said. "Isn't it a great picture?"

The child-friendly location was a small wood-frame house overlooking the lake, with a playroom for young children and an interview room for older kids, furnished with an Ikea couch and armchairs, a couple of plants hanging from the ceiling, and a two-way mirror opposite the couch. In front of the couch was a coffee table and on it a pad of paper and pen. Alec put the infant seat on the coffee table and the diaper bag on the floor.

"Any problem finding the house?" Detective Chan asked.

"Directions were good," Alec said, helping Cathy take the baby out of the carrier and buckle her into the infant seat.

"Can I get you something to drink, Cathy? Are you hungry?"

"No thank you, ma'am." The girl settled on the couch, Alec sitting beside her.

"Just call me Kelly. Let me guess," Detective Chan said. "You must be—fifteen?"

"Fourteen."

"Your sister is alert. Her eyes are everywhere. How old is she?"

"She's my niece." This voice was sharper than Cathy's, the face blander than Ceecee's, eyes hooded, carefully avoiding Alec's.

"Oh, are you babysitting?"

A curt nod.

"Where are her parents?"

"One dead, one unknown. That would be the father."

"I see." Rapport building wasn't going too well, even though Detective Chan smiled encouragingly. "What's your favourite subject in school, Cathy?"

Heather would have cursed and kicked if she didn't want to be communicative. Not this kid. She was the good girl. Considerate. A polite smile. Almost Cathy's except that the smile stretched so wide that just a shade more would be a wolfish grin. "Aren't you too busy for this?"

"Not in the least. I know you talked to Mrs. Lewis about something that's bothering you, but I'd like you to tell me in your own words what's going on for you at home."

"Let's see. It's Friday and I'm glad the weekend is coming up." She sat on the edge of the couch, her knees butting the coffee table. "Mrs. Lewis brought me over here. I'm not really sure what all the fuss is about." While the voice spoke nonchalantly, the hand seemed to have a life of its own, picking up the pen. In quick lines: a man holding a camera, a man on a bed, a child on the bed, mouth wide in a scream. A few more lines. Another child.

"Can you tell me who these people are?"

"I wanted to work on the yearbook, but the editor said I'm too young. I'd like to be the editor." The hand moved quickly sideways, drawing arrows, scribbling words, grabbing the page and crumpling it, tossing it in the wastebasket.

Detective Chan picked up the drawing and smoothed it out. "Let's take a break for a few minutes. Can I get you a drink or some chips?" she asked kindly, calmly, not even a cough revealing the bile that rose up in her throat or the wish to kill the men in the drawing. You crossed the t's, you dotted the i's; you put such people away. The girl nodded, and the detective went to the vending machines. She came back with chips and Coke, then went to make a call.

Unseen behind the two-way mirror, she grimaced at the voice on the other end of the line, an expert from the Child Exploitation Unit. "We have people who are specially trained for this. Why do you always think you can handle anything? You're supposed to bring us in immediately." The voice didn't say, *We're probably going to have to start again from scratch.*

"The girl and her family are in my division," Detective Chan said. She didn't add, *You'll insist on a medical exam when we know it's useless. Why put the kid through that?* But she thought it, for this was her territory, and human beings, even when they are doing good, are territorial. So before the officers from the Child Exploitation Unit arrived, she intended to take Mrs. Lewis's statement, staking her claim.

For Debra's going-away party, Harold Magee had arranged the tables in two long rows and had produced a magnificent cake. He was proudly wheeling it in on a trolley, a starched white apron tied around his waist, which was only moderately broad for a man who fancied his own baking. Rick stood next to Debra, his arm around her shoulders, smiling at their friends and neighbours, their colleagues and associates. It was a smaller crowd than at the memorial, only the people who knew them well, or believed they did, rushing here from work or home, arranging babysitters at the last minute, excited by the spontaneity, by the rightness of saying goodbye with food and wine and this cake of many layers, topped with sparklers.

In the din of forks and glasses and bottles and I'll have another slice, Eleanor and Dan stood away from the crowd, near the arched windows. Eleanor muttered under her breath. Dan fiddled with her new cellphone, trying to send an e-mail with an attachment on it.

The other doctors in Debra's practice made impromptu speeches. Someone had even managed to buy a going-away present and have it professionally wrapped with curly ribbon and bows.

"Cathy should be here," Debra said, smiling as she unwrapped the present.

"She's grounded," Rick said.

"We could make an exception."

"We could." He squeezed her shoulder as she took her cellphone out of her bag and dialed.

"That's funny." She held out the phone as if he needed to see. "No answer. Should I pop home?"

"Just call her again in a bit. She's probably changing a diaper."

First the officers from the Child Exploitation Unit arrived and then the social worker. The baby was asleep in the infant seat while they showed the cameras, the microphone, and the two-way mirror to the sullen girl. Her polite smile was gone, hands stuffed in the pockets of her camo shorts. She said she felt sick, and warned them that she might puke on Detective Armstrong's shoes. He was grizzled and jowly, the gentler of the two officers from the unit, a big man who'd been a boxer in college. After a brief consultation with his colleagues, he stayed in the observation room with Detective Chan, watching through the two-way mirror.

Cameras were placed so that everyone was in view as Alec and Cathy sat on the couch, the social worker in one armchair, Detective Ellison in the other. She was shorter than Alec, her face smooth because she didn't frown or smile much, which made her look younger than she was. She wore a T-shirt, jeans and running shoes, loudly cheerful in yellow and purple. Her movements were precise and controlled, her makeup skilled, minimal. She wore no jewellery except for a wedding band and punky studs in her ears. She began with easy questions—*What grade are you in? What's your favourite subject?* But the girl didn't answer or show any reaction until the social worker asked Alec if he'd like to wait next door with the baby. Then the girl stood up so quickly that she bumped the infant seat. Linny started crying and they all had to wait until the baby was fed, her diaper changed, the girl sitting on the couch again.

"I want Mrs. Lewis to stay." Her voice was small, scared.

"We can do it that way. Whatever makes you the most comfortable," the social worker said.

"I'm not going anywhere," Alec said, still beside her, his feet planted square on the floor.

"Just tell us the truth about what you remember, Cathy, as best you can. If you don't know the answer to a question, that's fine," the social worker said. "Don't feel that you need to say something to please us, just say you don't know. I'm here to ensure your welfare and your niece's, so I might have some different questions than Maggie," she referred to Detective Ellison by her first name.

"I thought police officers were all tall and beefy," the girl drawled, the wolfish smile back. "Aren't you, like, kind of small to deal with criminals?"

"I work out." Detective Ellison didn't add that she was also armed. "Do you understand the difference between truth and lies, Cathy?" she asked.

"Well, duh."

"So if I say I'm wearing a tie—is that true?"

"No."

"And do I have anything blue on me?"

"Yes."

"What?" The detective's voice was surprised. It made the girl grin, then frown to wipe it away, for she was there to be a blank screen. Nothing would get out past her.

"Your eyes are blue," she said.

"Right. Good one. Are my shoes purple?"

"Yes. Partly. Also yellow. Should I describe you, too?" She turned to the social worker.

"That won't be necessary," Frances Grafstein said. Small of waist, broad in the hips, she wore a skirt and favoured long earrings, though babies liked to grab them. She thought the child should have been brought to the hospital. She had talked to the police administration about this before. They ought to conduct the interview in the hospital, and then take her for the exam right after. Now there would be another interruption to drive her to a different location while her anxiety was building. "Are there any drugs or drinking in the home?" she asked. Her bangles clinked as she wrote down the question.

"I sneak wine sometimes. Don't tell my parents, okay?"

"Okay."

A fourteen-year-old could run away. A four-month-old couldn't. The baby would have to be her biggest concern today. Like her supervisor said, keep your mind on what you can prevent, not what's been done; you'll feel better. "How do your parents discipline you when you've done something wrong?"

"It's pretty awful." She paused, waiting for a reaction.

When none came, she said, "I get grounded for a week. But you know what?"

"What?"

She smirked. "They don't take away my computer privileges."

"How did your niece come to be living with you?"

The smirk disappeared. "My sister shot herself a couple of weeks before she was due. The police came. Don't you have a record of that?"

"We can get it. But I'd like to hear your version."

"I was asleep when she did it. The shot woke me up, and I saw my mom do an emergency C-section."

The social worker looked at the detective, wordlessly passing the baton. Maggie Ellison stretched and cracked her knuckles. So this was a pissy kid. A smart, pissy kid who was mouthy without using any four letter words or gestures to match. Taking a coin from her pocket, she placed it on the opposite elbow, arm bent so that her fingers brushed the shoulder. Whipping her arm forward, she flipped the coin and caught it in her hand.

"How do you do that?" The words slipped out of the girl before her mouth tightened regretfully.

"Practice. You want to try? No? Suit yourself." Detective Ellison crossed her t's, she dotted her i's—but sometimes she flipped a coin. Sometimes she threw peanuts in the air and caught them in her mouth. Anything to get a kid's mind off her fear: she knew that behind that smartass attitude was terror. "You spoke to Mrs. Lewis about something that's bothering you. Can you tell me about that, Cathy?"

"What's to tell? My parents get on my case, but don't everybody's?"

"We're not talking about everybody's, we're talking about yours. I know this is a hard conversation, Cathy. And believe it or not, I appreciate your being here."

"This is exciting. Aren't you excited?" Her voice had gotten quiet, her eyes glinting as she got a rise out of the cop. Nothing more than a change of position and crossing her legs. But she'd got to her. "Do you dye your hair? Mine is naturally blonde. I think I'd like it black, like Detective Chan's."

"My hair is naturally skunk striped. I've got a streak of white right here if I don't colour it," she said, pointing to her temple. "But let's talk about this." Ellison held up a sheet of paper. Cathy glanced from the paper to the camera that was recording it. "You drew this for Detective Chan this afternoon. And you wrote the name of a URL on it: www.angelsoftranquility.com."

"I made that up. Like it?" There was a small click from one of the cameras, or maybe it was the glass in the window frame shifting an iota. The sound was enough to make Alec start and so did the girl, shifting, not a total switch, but for a moment her eyes pleaded with his.

In the observation room, Detective Armstrong leaned forward, bulky muscles aching with tension. "I know that website," he said, unbuttoning his suit jacket.

Detective Ellison was watching Cathy, but the girl's face was guarded again. "And how about this? I see an arrow pointing to one of the figures and the word *Dad*."

"I guess I was trying to shock you. I can do better though. How about a two-year-old getting fucked? Shocked, yet?"

"I was shocked the first time I saw it online."

The girl's eyes registered surprise, and she glanced at Alec. He was surprised, too. These folks knew more than he'd expected.

"The Internet is a good venue for criminals, but it also provides an opportunity for us to discover what they're doing and catch them. When we do . . ." Ellison allowed a hint of feeling in her voice, "that is an awesome day."

"How can you catch someone?" The girl leaned back as if she could care less, but her fingers were drumming on her knees.

"We look for an item in the photograph or movie to identify the location." The detective's voice was matter-of-fact. Alec wondered how she managed such control without being multiple. "You'd be surprised at the small things that show up when we enlarge the pictures."

The girl looked away and out the window. "Like what? A picture frame?" she asked.

"Sure. Something like that."

Alec had been warned not to say or do anything at all, so he couldn't be construed as leading Cathy. But he reached into his bag, took out the handful of flash drives he'd removed from the music box on Cathy's bookshelf before they'd left, and set them on the coffee table. They were labelled: backup 1, backup 2, and on up to 6.

"Those are mine," Cathy said. Her fingers flexed, clenched, flexed again as she pushed a stick over to the detective. "I . . . I . . ." she stammered, her voice going high. "I . . . I . . ." She repeated the single word over and over, unable to move past it. Surely someone would stop her. "I'm on . . . I'm on . . ." The two words repeated. For a minute. And another. Why wouldn't anyone interrupt? It must be driving them crazy. It was driving her crazy. She looked at her boyfriend's mom, begging for release.

"Can they come home with me?" Alec asked the social worker. "We've got space."

"Yes, if we determine that the home is unsafe for both children," she said, "and if . . ."

But she didn't finish her sentence because the girl's stammering gave way to a burst of speech. "I'm on there. I worked for Daddy's camera." Her voice was squeaky as if a child had come forward. "They're going to kill me," she wept. "They'll kill me for telling."

"We won't let anyone hurt you. It's okay," the detective said. "You've been very brave to speak, Cathy. I want you to know that. You should be proud of yourself for protecting your niece and keeping other kids from being hurt."

The girl looked up, her hair hiding her face. "I worked in the basement," she croaked. "My mom gave me a shot so I wouldn't make a fuss. She gave the other kids shots, too."

"Where does she get the needles and medication?"

"She's a kid doctor."

"I see. And has she or your father done anything inappropriate to you?" Behind the two-way mirror, Detective Armstrong made a note to call the College of Physicians and Surgeons.

"What's inappropriate?" the girl asked in her small high voice.

"Let's say anything that makes you feel uncomfortable," the social worker said, responding instinctively to the child alter before her.

"No. I'm comfortable when they do things." She peeked through her hair. "I like your earrings. They're sparkly."

"What kind of things?" Grafstein asked as gently as possible.

"Like this." She demonstrated with her mouth. "And . . ." She moved her hips.

"Do you know the words for that?" When the girl nodded, Grafstein asked, "Could you write down the words for me, and who does them to you?"

The list was long. After she read it, the social worker said thank you to the girl and then stepped out for a moment to wipe her eyes and call her supervisor. When she'd regained control, she returned to the interview room with the authority to apprehend the children into her care. "We'll ensure that you're at a place of safety," she explained as she sat down across from Cathy again. It was hard to leave home, even a bad home, but she said that Cathy could go to family—grandparents or an auntie would be ideal, someone close, familiar, providing continuity. "Is there a relative you'd like me to call?"

"No!" The girl switched again, glaring at the social worker. They were going to sell her down the river. They were going to pass her back to people further in the darkness, who'd call her out to do what she'd always done, only harder, only worse. "You tricked me." She'd run like her sister and like her sister if anyone stopped her, she would take herself out the one way they couldn't follow.

"It's not a trick. Ms. Grafstein has no idea. Just tell her," Alec said, his voice blunt and hard to get through the girl's panicked shaking. "Nobody knows unless you explain." It was risky to use her name, revealing it when she was mistrusting everyone, but he had to make her hear him. "Ceecee, just tell them."

The shaking abruptly stopped. Nobody spoke as the girl looked first at the detective, then at the social worker. "Ms. Grafstein, do you think that my parents are aliens or something and everyone else is hunky-dory? They're all in it. You see the name Mitch on that sheet of paper? That's my dad's cousin. He's a shrink. He takes care of kids who get upset. Neil—that's my uncle. He handles the money. They've got good friends, too. Like my mom says, everybody does their job and people who do well, do well."

"I see."

"Do you?"

"Yes. And I'm sorry. We can put you with a foster family or you can stay with Mrs. Lewis if that's what you'd prefer. But please understand, I have to ask these questions."

"Okay." Ceecee nodded. Outside the window, rain slanted down on the lake, water meeting water. "I'll answer."

"Do you have any concerns about your niece?"

"They're getting her ready."

"Who and how?"

And so, while her niece slept in the infant seat, Ceecee told everything she knew, even though she still wasn't a 100 percent certain nobody was going to haul her into a locked and soundproof room. She told them about the equipment in the basement, the training that was done up at the cottage and the renovation that would expand it into a bigger facility. She figured they could do whatever they wanted with her, if talking would save her sister's child from it. And only when she was sure, completely sure, that nobody was going to make her pay for the chips and the Coke with her body, did she lean against Mrs. Lewis, gripping the freckled hand as she told the final thing she had to tell.

CHAPTER TWENTY-EIGHT

*T*he last night of Heather's life had started out like all the other nights for the past month. She had pushed her desk in front of the door between her room and the office. Mom had yelled, "Heather Dawson-Edwards, this is a fire hazard, and it is too late in your pregnancy to be moving furniture."

In her own room Cathy sat on the bed, legs crossed, watching her mother smack Heather's door with the flat of her hand. This was how it went every night. Yelling. Bang on the door. More yelling. Then Mom would pick up the phone in the office and call Cousin Mitch. She'd complain about the prescription and ask if he couldn't give Heather something newer, stronger, and Mitch would talk for a while, Mom saying, *Yes, possibly, all right.*

Only this time was different. Heather shouted back, *Don't bother calling anybody. I haven't been taking your pills. I'm leaving with my baby as soon as she's born and I'm never coming back.*

You will not, Mom said. *You aren't responsible enough to be a mother. I'll get custody. That is my baby.*

You'll never get her. I'll jump first, Heather screamed. Mom just stood there with her hand on the door. *I'm done,* she said. *I've had it. Your father can talk to you.* Then she turned around and stalked downstairs.

Cathy thought, *Uh oh.* Uh oh, for she couldn't find another word anywhere. She wanted to shut her door, put earbuds in her ears, and turn up her iPod as loud as it would go, but instead she crept into the office, staying near the door to the bathroom. There was something in there, something she could grab if need be.

Dad didn't run upstairs. He walked slowly and deliberately, his footsteps softened by his leather slippers. When he got to Heather's room, he put his shoulder to her door and pushed, the desk squeaking as it slid across the floor. Then he stood in the doorway to talk to Heather, ignoring his other daughter, knowing he didn't have to worry about her. "What's going on here?" he asked.

Get away. If you don't leave me alone, I'll jump. That was what Heather said, but her voice was getting quieter, too.

You wouldn't dare, he said, but not like he was mad. His voice was quiet and his voice was pleasant and the sound of it made Cathy's skin crawl. *I brought you into this world and you have no right to leave it without my permission,* he said. *Without me you would be a common tramp. You can't even keep your legs together for two minutes outside this house. Look at your belly. It says everything. You like it, don't you? You want it. You know I'm right.*

Heather looked away as her breath came shallow and fast while he banged her with his voice. *Your baby will like it just as much,* he said. *And I'll take care of her, too. Now say good night.*

Good night, she answered dutifully.

Good night, Cathy, he said.

Night, Dad. And she turned as if she was going to bed, but it was Ceecee turning, and as soon as she was certain that he wasn't coming back up the stairs, she was in her sister's room. When Heather looked up, her eyes were empty. Ceecee started talking fast, words tumbling out in a rush until her sister's eyes came to life. She showed Heather where she'd hidden the gun in the box of sanitary pads in the bathroom. If you need it, she said.

Heather hugged her. She said, *You're the best.*

Ceecee got the quilt from her bedroom. It dragged along the floor as she carried it through the office, getting caught on the cables until she freed the stupid ruffles, gathering the quilt into her arms. In Heather's room, she folded it double, laying it on the floor next to the bed, and then went back for her pillow. Sitting on the pillow, hugging her knees, she teased Heather about her horribly pink nightgown and Heather teased her about her spotlessly white PJs. The floor was hard under the quilt and Ceecee was cold. It took a while for her to fall asleep, listening to the rain, imagining the apartment she would share with her sister and the baby. It would be small, all of them together in one bedroom, within arm's reach. Nothing pink. Nothing frilled. They'd get dishes from Value Village. They'd eat no-name mac and cheese. Heather could paint a mural on the wall.

When she heard the shot, she thought she was dreaming. As she got to her feet, deafened by the sound, smelling smoke and thinking, *Fire,* she was sure she was still dreaming. Even when her mother came upstairs, knife ready, as if she'd known, as if she'd been prepared, Ceecee didn't believe this could be real. Her mother pushed her out of the way and Ceecee lost her balance, tripping against the desk, banging her hip. But she saw Mom cut the nightgown and she saw Mom cut the skin and she saw Mom take her sister's baby out of the hole she made.

"I want my sister," she said. The clouds over the lake were breaking up, the sun making a silver path on the water. And on that path she could see her sister, hair in golden spikes, running along the surface of the lake. *I'm sorry, Heather,* she whispered. *I love you.*

She'd been gripping Alec's hand so hard it was numb, but he didn't move it. Not even when he felt his cell vibrate. The social worker was saying that it wasn't Ceecee's fault and that her sister's memory lived on in her baby and all the things that ought to be said even though Ceecee couldn't believe any of it yet. He thought he'd turned the cellphone off. Must have pressed the wrong button. With his free hand, he dug it out of his pocket, hoping there wasn't some mess-up with the kids. He still had to drive Ceecee and Linny to the hospital, where they'd be examined, and then he'd have to boot Sharon out. There was a limit to the mom stuff he could do. Dealing with stirrups attached to an examination table was beyond it.

"Sorry, I need to check this e-mail," he said, after he read the text from Eleanor.

His thumb moved, clicking on the attachment while Ceecee got up and walked to the window. Her hands were on the glass as if she could push through into another world. And perhaps she could, if she went back inside. But the baby was waking up with a yawn, eyes fluttering and opening, looking for her auntie, and her auntie was thinking that she'd draw pictures for Linny because a girl baby ought to know how Wonder Woman worked her lasso of truth. Handing the cell to Detective Ellison, Alec said, "My sister-in-law sent this. She saw these pictures in Dr. Dawson's office."

"I'll be right back," Ellison said. Then she left with the cellphone and walked next door to the observation room.

Behind the two-way mirror, she plugged the phone into a computer and uploaded the pictures while Detective Armstrong watched. "Stop there," he said. He studied the picture of Debra's godson. "Hell. I've been looking for that kid for a year."

Debra unlocked her front door, throwing the keys and her bag on the marble table. "Cathy!" The house was so quiet. The baby must be asleep and Cathy listening to music. If she'd told her once, she'd told her a hundred times: you'll damage your ears. She walked quickly up the stairs, not running, she never ran, but her footsteps seemed to echo as if the house was empty, though that was impossible. Cathy had been grounded for being careless with her school books. If she couldn't be responsible when she went to her friends' houses to study then she couldn't go. Their mothers should not be coming to the house before breakfast on a school day with her math book. So Cathy should be pleased they were going to give her a break, pleased enough to get rid of those awful shorts and that tacky T-shirt. Debra had just picked up a new summer dress for her and she'd look sweet in it.

"Cathy, there's a going-away party at Magee's," she called, walking into the office. All the doors were closed. The doors were never closed. That was a rule. But her daughter had been breaking rules lately.

She shook off the thought, and checked the baby's room first, then Cathy's. Her pulse raced. The bathroom came last. She slowly turned the handle, afraid she'd see a bloody wrist overhanging the edge of the shower stall. But it was empty, the medicine cabinet still locked, thank God. She climbed up to the third floor and her own bedroom— no one. She ran down the stairs, through the living room, the den, the kitchen. Her daughter could be getting a snack or warming up a bottle, magically making no sound. But nobody was there, either, and the door to the basement was still locked. Her fingers touched the steel surface of the counter, range, fridge, as if she could conjure a note. In the hallway mirror her face looked like a stranger's as she snatched up her bag, unsnapping the side compartment, taking out her cellphone.

As soon as he got the call, Rick made a brief thank-you speech on behalf of the whole family and left Magee's. He was careful not to speed on the three-minute drive home. He didn't want to get a ticket. It was at times like these, when you were sure that you couldn't possibly be caught on such a short trip, that you were. He already had points for speeding on his way up to the cottage at three a.m. on a long weekend.

Nobody was on the road and he was making time, absolutely safely, and he was stopped for it. Ridiculous.

But teenagers were mindless. They never realized how their actions affected others. Debra was wild with worry and all it would have taken was a phone call to let them know where she was going. Of course they wouldn't have let her go, which was why she hadn't called. Cathy was supposed to be home, babysitting, and there would have to be consequences for turning off her cellphone. He drove through the alley, stopped the car to open the gate, and parked in the garage. After straightening the garden rake, which had fallen sideways off its hook, he went inside the house. There was an order to things. First call her friends. She wasn't her sister; she wouldn't have run away. That was what he said to his wife. Then she asked, *But who are her friends? I only know the Lewises.* They were searching Cathy's room for an address book when he heard the sirens: he assumed it was a house alarm triggered accidentally.

Cathy was on her way to the hospital for a medical exam while squad cars surrounded the house on Lumley Street. Neighbours looked curiously out of windows, stood on porches, younger children leaving TVs to gawk, older kids texting friends while they watched the street. Someone was recording a video to upload to the Internet. Was that Rick Edwards splayed against a cop car?

The sun was in the west, still high over Christie Pits, refusing to go down until this was over. It reflected off the roof of the car, dazzling Rick's eyes and gilding his beard. He had a pipe in the pocket of his linen blazer. Who gets arrested with a pipe in his pocket? "What is this about?" he said. "Do you know who I am?"

"Mr. Edwards, I'll have to ask you to keep your hands on the car, sir," Detective Armstrong said. Excessive politeness helped Armstrong keep himself in check: a reminder to be correct in every respect, no matter the cost, for correctness now meant a conviction later. When his work was done, he could work off his tension in the exercise room at the station.

Detective Ellison asked Debra to put her hands behind her back.

"She's putting handcuffs on my wife!" Rick said.

"It's all right, Rick. We'll straighten this out," Debra said. Her lips were pale. She wore a light summer suit, a cream-coloured jacket and a matching cream-coloured skirt and she wished her skirt was longer. "I want to see your badge again. Is this some kind of joke?" she asked Ellison.

The street was blocked, the house in a freeze, officers stationed inside to make sure that nothing was touched or removed until the warrant was executed. "Ma'am, get in the car, please." Thinking of the cold cell that awaited, Detective Ellison placed her, with the utmost care, in the back seat. After the shift was over, she would show Armstrong how to throw peanuts in the air and catch them in his mouth. They would drink to this one.

Now the sun gave its blessing and set, sinking into Christie Pits, while on the shore of the city, the lake turned from silver to pink to blue to the black of night and stars hung like jewels in the net of heaven.

CHAPTER TWENTY-NINE

A couple of weeks later Sharon was in the dining room paying bills when her sister-in-law called. "Hi Eleanor," she said, tapping on the keyboard with one hand as she held the phone with the other.

"How's it going?"

"Busy. The fridge is empty again." After the hospital exam, Frances Grafstein and a police officer had escorted Cathy to her house to pick up what she needed, and then the children had gone straight to the Lewises'. It had all happened with surprising ease, for it turned out the foster care system was stretched to the limit. A willing family near the child's school and among her friends was a gift.

"Have you seen the *Gleaner*?" Eleanor asked.

"Not yet. Why?"

"You're on the front page."

"Me?" Sharon's fingers stopped tapping.

"Hang on. I'll read it to you." The rustle of a newspaper being picked up, folded back.

"Wait," Sharon said. "Let me get the paper myself. I'll call you right back."

She put the phone down and went out onto the front porch to fetch the *Gleaner,* reading as she walked back to the dining room.

LOCAL COUPLE CHARGED IN CHILD PORN BUST

A spokesperson from the Child Exploitation Unit reported that eight children are now safe from further abuse after a child pornography investigation that began with the arrests of Dr. Debra Dawson and Professor Richard Edwards, long-time residents of Seaton Grove.

Sharon already knew about the children: one of them was the little boy with the cowlick, Rick and Debra's godson.

"Our intervention was such that the children will no longer be abused," Det. Armstrong said. "I can't state where the children are at present, other than to say that they are safe."

Edwards, 46 years old, and Dawson, 43, are accused of sexual assault and making, possessing and distributing child porn. In an unusual move, the College of Physicians and Surgeons has sent letters to all the families of Dr. Dawson's patients, asking anyone who has any information regarding this case, or any concerns regarding the appropriateness of their children's medical care, to come forward.

Det. Armstrong said the investigation was launched June 9 after a tip from a local source claimed the accused and other people were exchanging pictures and video of children being sexually abused. That same day, police raided a home in Seaton Grove, seizing computers and other electronics. Based on the evidence recovered from these devices, charges were laid against Professor Edwards and Dr. Dawson on June 9. Computers were also removed from their cottage and offices. Yesterday 11 more people were arrested, and face a total of 34 charges. One suspect had 6 million child porn images stored on hard drives and portable media.

Ten of the suspects were men ranging in age from 16 to 63 years old, from all walks of life. Police stated that many of them were relatives or otherwise well known to victims. Some will also be prosecuted for drug and weapons offences. Forensic examination of the computers is continuing, and is expected to lead to further arrests and charges, both locally and internationally. Officers from the Child Exploitation Unit are communicating with their equivalents in other countries. "The children were apprehended within twenty-four hours. Their safety is our priority," Det. Armstrong told reporters at the press conference.

While satisfied that yesterday's arrests have removed some criminals from the global propagation of Internet child porn, police said it's only a foretaste of the busts to come. "These people may think that because they're hiding behind a computer screen, they can't be prosecuted. They couldn't be more wrong," Det. Armstrong said. "We will find them and bring them to justice, not only through the force's Internet expertise, but in the old-fashioned way, with the cooperation and assistance of concerned citizens who come forward with information."

When she reached the dining room, Sharon put the paper down, picked up the phone and dialed Eleanor's number. "Hi. Great report."

"The local source. That's you," Eleanor said.

Sharon smiled. "You're in it, too. The concerned citizen." She would save the *Gleaner* for Cathy, who was collecting news items about the arrests.

"It took all of us," Eleanor said.

CHAPTER
THIRTY

*B*y the end of June, Debra Dawson and Rick Edwards were out on bail, awaiting trial. Her license had been suspended and he was forced to take a leave from the university, their real and their virtual movements circumscribed by a court order that required them to remain far from any children and off the Internet. Sometimes they saw people staring. Sometimes their friends called to offer support.

One block east, in the Lewises' house on Ontario Street, the girls all shared a room, the crib set up next to the futon couch so that Cathy, who slept very little, could reach out and touch the bars. With two teenagers under the same roof, there needed to be some rules. Josh said he was done with dating, but Sharon wanted to make sure that Cathy was clear about that. "If you still have feelings for Josh, we can ask for another placement," she said. The baby was napping, the other kids at day camp.

Cathy had had her hair cut short for summer, and it was bleaching even paler in the sun. She wore a tank top and second-hand overalls that she'd taken in with Sharon's help, a black ribbon around her neck. Hanging from the ribbon were Green Day dog tags: the band's name and a heart-shaped grenade. She was sitting on the futon couch, painting her toenails black. "I hate being a placement," she said.

"I'd rather you were part of the family."

"Me, too," Cathy mumbled. Then added in a louder voice, "Whatever."

"Good." Sharon picked dirty clothes off the floor, throwing them in the hamper. When she was done in here, she'd have to change the newspaper in the kitchen, as she'd given in on the puppy, whom her father-in-law had named Beans to go with Franky. "The basement should be fixed up by the time school starts. It's up to you whether you'd like to share your new room with Linny."

"I want her with me."

"That's settled, then." Sharon began stripping the beds. "You don't think your toes looks bruised with black polish?"

"No." Cathy rolled her eyes. Stay firm, but flexible, the social worker advised. It was obvious that the social worker didn't have teenagers in her house.

Cathy was still sharing the girls' room when school started that fall, as fixing up the basement was delayed by Bram. On Labour Day, he came over in his truck, and walked in with his tool box and a spool of cable. Saying only, *I'm not letting something happen and wishing I'd done this before,* Bram went out again and returned with a ladder and a portable work light. It was a good day for what he intended to begin, warm but not too hot, especially in the basement. Bram picked a wall and knocked a hole in it. There was aluminum wire behind it, some of it blackened and partially melted. When he cut a hole in the ceiling, he saw that, contrary to code, the aluminum wire had been patched through knob and tube connectors. It was a miracle there hadn't been a fire. Bram said, *You've got five kids with you now and I'm not losing any kids in my family to an electrical fire.*

When the wiring was finished and new drywall installed on a weekend of Indian summer, Alec varnished the pedestal he'd found to go with the tabletop in the dining room. It would make a good desk for Cathy's new room. These days, he and the others switched more gracefully, lightly, because they wanted to rather than they had to.

"I need a break," Dan said, coming out with a couple of beers. He'd been supervising the kids, who were painting the basement. "You want one?"

"Sure." Alec took the beer from Dan and sat on the edge of the deck, knees apart. The puppy, half grown, sandy like her Lab mother, crouched at Alec's feet for a pat and scratch, then chased after a squirrel. "How's it going?"

"Cathy uses too much paint." There was a streak of lilac in Dan's hair where he'd run his hand through it. "The table's looking good."

"Thanks."

"You'll have more space in the dining room with the table top out of there. I don't know how you manage. It's so cramped."

Alec shrugged and grinned. "Not me that sews," he said

and Dan laughed, lifting his bottle. In the dappled shadow of the birch tree, which hadn't yet lost its leaves, they drank together while squirrels stashed seeds for the cold days ahead.

They celebrated Dan's forty-third birthday and Linny's first the next February at the skating rink. Her eyes had finally changed colour, settling on hazel. The stroller was her throne, and from it she looked at the snowy wonders and clapped her hands. Pushing the stroller, Lyssa walked along the rubber runners that covered the concrete between the clubhouse and the rink. Eleanor and Bram were already on the ice among the usual assortment of good skaters and people just learning, little kids getting in everyone's way, the old guy with the beer belly who must've been a hockey player the way he speeded around the rink. Just past the rink parents and grandparents watched kids on toboggans dive down the snowy slope and into the pit, clinging to bushes for purchase as they climbed back up, hauling their sleds.

Lyssa's hair had grown longer in the last six months, red coils hanging down her back, though sometimes there was a thought about cutting it all off. In the rink she unzipped her jacket as Dan pretended to fall, making the baby laugh. Linny bounced and crowed while Lyssa pushed her in the stroller around the slouching, lounging boys and girls.

Ceecee, who had joined a hockey team, was using the blade of her skate to surreptitiously slide a puck to Judy. When the rink guard came over to remind her (as if she'd forgot) that pucks and sticks weren't allowed on the ice during recreational skate, she scowled and shoved her hands in the pockets of her leather jacket.

Josh separated from the clump of his friends, the wind blowing his hair off his forehead. "How about a race?" he asked her.

"You're on!" Ceecee grinned wickedly.

Around and around they raced while Emmie and Nina and Judy leaned over the penalty box. Holding Linny, Lyssa cheered Ceecee, and so did Eleanor while Dan and Bram urged Josh on.

"Move, shitheads!" Josh yelled at his friends. He skated with arms wide, Ceecee with elbows in, minimizing air resistance. Josh ground the ice as he came to a stop, hands held high above his head. Ceecee was right behind him, one of her skate laces trailing. "You're getting old," he said.

"It was my laces," Ceecee said. "I'll beat you next time."

Afterward, they all took off their skates in the clubhouse and wiped the blades. Skates slung over their shoulders, they walked to Magee's for cocoa and fries. They sat down and ordered just as if her mother's office wasn't right above the ceiling, as if there wasn't still a sign on the door saying that she was away on leave.

The firm of Johnston and Olivera had a reputation for obtaining acquittals in difficult cases. Among their recent successes was a sexual assault case in which they made the complainant look like a fool and an idiot, if not a bald-faced liar. This was a firm that understood how a spouse might accuse her husband of heinous crimes just because she was pissed or how a child might fall under the spell of malicious influences. The lawyers sympathized, they looked like accountants, they charged a fortune. Debra and Rick hired them. Their relatives were helping out, but even so, without work, they were on a tight budget.

On a spring day that was clear but cool enough to require a jacket, Rick and Debra parked in Seaton Square. They crossed to the library, pressed the button for the automatic doors, and entered. They looked in the children's section, in fiction, and among the computers, but nobody they cared about was there. Then they stepped into the room where the local history collection was housed. Debra was the one who said hello.

"You're not supposed to be here." Callisto put down the calendar of online graduate programs she'd been perusing. Every Saturday she visited the library and the librarian expected her, ready with recommendations of new books. Today Cathy had come along so she could use the local history material for a school project, relying on her foster mom to show her how to find information without a search function. Cathy sat across from Callisto at the library table.

"This is a public place." Debra clutched her purse, moving to stand on one side of Cathy. "I can't guess where my daughter will be."

"Mom..." Cathy looked up from her notes on Mrs. Brown, whose first name was Deborah, like her mother's. Escaped from slavery. Cottage surrounded by farmland. Worked as a washerwoman. Later listed as "nurse" in the city directory.

Rick moved to stand on her other side. He studied his daughter's shorn hair, the piercing in her eyebrow. "How are you, darling?" His voice was gentle and concerned.

"I'm okay."

Her dad looked worn out. So did her mother, who had been without her children on Mother's Day. They stood so close she could smell her mom's perfume, her dad's soap. She could feel the warmth of their bodies as if she was a little girl crawling into their bed and they would never hurt her.

"I can't believe you'll be sixteen soon. And finishing grade ten. I miss you," her dad said. "We both do. It hurts us terribly."

"I didn't want to," she said sadly and her mother put a hand out to touch hers, then pulled away, because it was against the law. What kind of stupid law was that, banning your own mother from touching you?

"It's been hard on all of us," Debra said. Her daughter's eyes were wet.

"It's not too late. You think you've said things and you're stuck with it. But that isn't the case," Rick said in the same gentle voice.

"It's not?"

"You can come home if you explain that you were just sick from the shock of your sister's death."

"I feel sick." She was blinking away her tears, her father watching, holding her in place with the sound of his voice and the hope it gave her.

"Of course. Anyone would understand that. Losing Heather makes me sick, too."

"How do you explain away the child pornography on your computer?" Callisto asked, interrupting the trance of lies so desirable any child might swallow them.

"I don't know how that got there." He spoke to Callisto but his eyes were only for his daughter's, as blue as his own, reflecting him. "Maybe it was Heather. When she ran away, she must have done terrible things."

"Heather." Her face, upturned to his, registered her sister's name and her jaw tightened.

"You know what kids have to do on the street."

"We gave the police a photograph of the girls playing with Josh in the sandbox," Callisto said. "They match the child pornography they found on your computer."

"That simply can't be true. How could you suggest this beautiful girl was involved in anything so dreadful?" Rick couldn't read the expression in his daughter's eyes. They mirrored him; they shut him out. "It's a coincidence. Another blonde five-year-old. Come home to us, Cathy."

As she got to her feet, he held out a hand to take hers, heedless of any court order, ignoring Callisto, who was removing a cellphone from her bag. The past year could be ploughed under the earth, gravel laid over it, and cement. He smiled, murmuring more reassurances while Callisto spoke into the phone, asking for Detective Chan.

And his daughter, who had also learned how to switch gracefully, without his request and without his permission, smacked his hand. "Get away from me," she said, shoving her chair out of the way, rounding the table to stand next to Callisto.

His face darkened. "So this is what you've become?" He looked at her piercing and sneered. "You sound just like Heather."

"Shut up! My sister died for her baby. And she died for me. Nothing else would have made me tell. But I did. And I will. I'll say everything again and you can't stop me. My sister's baby deserves better than what we got."

"Cathy, please," her mother said. "Don't make a scene."

"That's what you care about? Now I get it." Ceecee eyed her mother and her father, the barriers inside going down so that everyone there could see what she saw: a blonde woman greying, a blonde man stooping. Heartless. Gutless. "You're pathetic."

At the sound of voices, the librarian came around the corner. "We have children in the library," she said to Rick and Debra, her voice thick with disgust. "You'll have to leave."

As it transpired, the Dawson-Edwards parents did their child and her foster family a favour that day, for violating the terms of the injunction sped up the termination of their parental rights. Adoption didn't take that long if someone wasn't waiting for a newborn. The home study was done in four weekly sessions, the medical exams and police clearance obtained at the same time, the engine of government revved up to give the file priority.

A year and a month had passed since the drive to the police station. In the backyard of the Lewises' house tomatoes were ripening, nasturtiums around them, the yellow and red flowers good in salad and distasteful to snails. Sparrows chattered at the crows overhead. Franky meowed and clawed at the tree while the much larger Beans, having grown into her paws, barked at the birds, tail wagging. Next door a new family had moved in, the little kids squealing as they climbed in and out of an inflatable wading pool in their yard. Mrs. Brown's cottage had been declared a heritage site, a plaque affixed to the exterior wall.

The weather was perfect, the wind quietly shifting from north to south, promising another heat wave, but not for a day or two. Balloons hung from the birch tree, a homemade banner on the shed said, HAPPY GOTCHA DAY! Dan thought if he was making a list of good days, this one would be right up there. He surveyed his yard, his small and unpredictable domain, which somehow contained whatever it grew. He caught his wife's gaze and smiled. Josh had the camcorder pointed at them, recording the day for posterity. He hadn't had another girlfriend since Cathy, but would soon. He turned the camcorder slowly around the yard, taking in his grandmother, his dad talking to Uncle Bram, Nina pushing her cousin who was balanced on two scooters, his zaidey snoozing in a lawn chair, snorting and waking up as Aunt Eleanor filled a plate for him. Amy was putting fruit salad on a plate to share with Ingrid.

"What is that?" Ingrid asked, eyeing Jake's knishes, dripping with gravy. For this occasion, he was allowed to eat anything he wanted.

"It's good." He'd shrunk a bit more, his hair wispier. "You want a taste?" He lifted his fork, smiling happily as she took a bite. The closing for Ingrid and Amy's new house was at the end of the month. They'd bought close to the park, for the dogs, and close to the shooting range, though there were rumours it would be shutting down soon.

"Beef in pastry. There's also potato," Eleanor said. She went running every morning with her sister-in-law and had (mostly) stopped caring whether it showed on the scale or not. "Very unhealthy. I brought the knishes and the Chinese bean cakes. I can't resist anything in pastry." She glanced at Sharon, whose eyes were on the baby. Linny Amethyst Lewis was toddling up and down the yard with the determined pleasure of a seventeen-month-old who expected the world to get out of her way, and wailed in shock when it didn't. Emmie had finally got over not being the youngest and Linny adoringly gripped her hand. "I love dumplings, noodle kugel. Oh my God, even gefilte fish."

"It's because you have a double heritage, so you get double the appetite," Sharon teased. In the drawer of her nightstand was a pocket camera, on top a stack of magazines, an application for a distance M.Ed. program, and a teddy bear. In the last year Dan had started reading stories to the lils. There had been dancing at Hammond House and camping under the northern lights, a hunting trip, a seminar on using power tools, an evening course on the origin of the universe, many family dinners and the art of knitting, the keeping of books, the paying of bills while eyes changed from moss green to jade, from malachite to willow or to sage.

"Oh sure. Now you," Eleanor said, her eyes shining with mischief. "Nothing shows on you. Skinny as a rake. Still the sister-in-law I've always loved. Quadruple, quintuple, oh however many you are—it doesn't matter, does it?"

"You! I'll get you."

"What?" But Eleanor laughed, too, for they had talked at midnight in all of the seasons, bared their hearts while the stars looked down, and shared many of their true names.

Sliding the glass doors open, Cathy carried out the cake. Her fingernails were blue, like her new mom's, which she had painted and decorated with punky decals on the thumbs. After the final adoption papers came by courier, she had spent hours on the Internet. Poring over recipes and icing patterns, she decided on chocolate cake with a yellow sunflower in the centre and the writing in orange. Her sister's baby, now her youngest sister, would be tasting chocolate for the first time. The basement had become the girls' bower, where—when she was in the right mood—she taught her sisters to dance or apply makeup or arm-wrestle so that a boy wouldn't win unless they chose. One wall was covered with drawings of Wonder Woman, Catwoman, Princess Amethyst of Gemworld. She'd made her own curtains out of a fabric printed with bold geometric shapes. There was a braided rug on the floor. In a dresser drawer, underneath her socks, was a newspaper with the front-page headline SEATON GROVE COUPLE CONVICTED. Every week, she—Cathy, Ceecee, the flirty girl, all of them—spent some time in a therapist's office, setting free all that was supposed to have been locked inside.

"Happy Gotcha Day!" everyone shouted as she came out.

Her mom and dad brought their children close, sweeping her into their arms, too, as soon as she put the cake on the table. Her mom's arms were freckled from the sun, eyes as changeable as her own. She jostled with her brother and her sisters while the grandparents and aunt and uncle and cousin and friends looked on, taking their turns in front of the camera.

After dishes were done, Mimi ordered her granddaughters to take off their shoes and socks so she could check their feet, from youngest to oldest: Linny, Emmie, Nina, Judy and Cathy. Her grandson's feet were already bare and dirty from the yard, but she made him sit down to be examined, too. As Mimi squatted on her heels, forgiving the universe its propensity for viruses, she proclaimed, *Excellent feet.*

There are nine dimensions in total, or perhaps eleven, some too small to perceive, others too strange, too dark. But that is only because they are not yet known. They are wrapped in membranes and when the membranes collide, a universe is born. This is called M-Theory, or the theory of everything. *M* is said to stand for magic, mystery, matrix or mother.

INSIDE

im ally and im showing the punishers how to have a tea party. dont stick your big feets in my face i tells them. we are having inside pretend tea and pretend cookies. yesterday i sneaked them real ice cream. it isnt nice to stick your feets in somebodys nose when you are having a tea party. we is sitting on the grass in the field cuz that is where the healing tents be. there is a bunch of lils looking but them dont come out just peeking. i look back and wave hihihi.

peoples been talking to the housekeeper. sometimes they sits in her lap. bertie says it is supposed to be wrote like this. Housekeeper with a big letter in front. bertie is bigger then punishers be. he is having the tea party too. he holds a little cup in his big hand it looks so funny. i laugh and laugh and laugh. what is funny bertie asks me. i says you be funny. your wings be sticking out i says bertie why dont you put your wings down. you look like you got elephant ears. the lils look out and go uh oh cuz them think bertie be mad. his wings go flip flop and he laughs. the punishers go hicccccccupp when they laugh too hard. i laugh harder than anybody i laugh so hard tears is coming down my eyes and bertie pick me up and put me in his lap and his wings go round me and i hides cuz i dont want nobody see me cry like a cry baby. i says i want a mommy. and he says i will be your mommy. and i says you are silly and i hiccup too. he says i Love you lil ally. oh. oh. you know what? maybe i get wings too. echo! echo! you want to have wings?

ACKNOWLEDGEMENTS

I'm so glad to have this opportunity to express my gratitude and appreciation to everyone involved in bringing *Web of Angels* to life. Dean Cooke, my sterling agent, had unflagging faith in me and this book. His entire team has been courteous, enthusiastic and efficient. Anne Collins, my brilliant and meticulous editor, understood exactly what this book was aiming to achieve, and led me to make it so. My copy editor, Angelika Glover, reviewed the final draft with intelligence and exactness. Kelly Hill designed a magnificent cover—I couldn't have asked for better. My eyes were opened to the dedication and empathy of Toronto police officers during my research. Detective Sergeant Kimberly Scanlan, Child Exploitation Section–Officer in Charge, took the time to explain the procedures and mind-set of those very special officers who, committed to saving children, do the difficult work of catching child predators online. Detective Stacey Davis, of 14 Division Youth and Family Services, gave me insight into the passion and understanding of the local force, graciously showing me around the station. Avi Versanov,

MSW, from the Children's Aid Society of Toronto, professionally and compassionately explained how the Society responds to calls and interviewing children. Ocean Windsong generously answered my questions about teenage boys and showed me the magic trick in *Web of Angels*. My perceptive friend Cas Rhindress read this novel through many drafts and provided a calm and encouraging voice. My husband, Allan, as always my number one fan and supporter, patiently listened to my self-doubts and exuberantly celebrated every triumph. My delightful daughters, Meira and Hadara, kept me in touch with what really matters in life.

And to my friends who are multiple: thank you for walking by my side; the perps lost, you see, for the cycle is broken and none of us is alone anymore.

LILIAN NATTEL was born in Montreal and now lives in Toronto with her husband and two daughters. She is also the author of *The Singing Fire* and *The River Midnight*, a national bestseller and winner of the Martin and Beatrice Fischer Jewish Book Award.